Edward Bean Underhill

Life of James Mursell Phillippo, Missionary in Jamaica

Edward Bean Underhill

Life of James Mursell Phillippo, Missionary in Jamaica

ISBN/EAN: 9783337325114

Printed in Europe, USA, Canada, Australia, Japan

Cover: Foto ©Raphael Reischuk / pixelio.de

More available books at **www.hansebooks.com**

LIFE

OF

JAMES MURSELL PHILLIPPO,

MISSIONARY IN JAMAICA.

EDWARD BEAN UNDERHILL, LL.D.,

HONORARY SECRETARY OF THE BAPTIST MISSIONARY SOCIETY.

LONDON:

YATES & ALEXANDER, 21, CASTLE STREET, HOLBORN.

E. MARLBOROUGH & CO., 51, OLD BAILEY.

MDCCCLXXXI.

LONDON :
YATES AND ALEXANDER, PRINTERS,
LONSDALE BUILDINGS, CHANCERY LANE, W.C.

PREFACE.

On his last visit to this country, Mr. Phillippo brought with him one or two volumes of manuscript, containing a portion of an autobiography, the preparation of which had occupied his leisure moments for many years. He showed it to me, and asked my opinion as to its publication after his decease. On examining it, I found it to contain very full records of the events through which Jamaica, and the Jamaica Mission of the Baptist Missionary Society, had passed during his long life, combined with records of his own personal experience and history. There appeared to be much information too valuable to be lost, and a picture of a true and successful missionary life that might be of advantage as an example to future generations. In reply to my suggestion that he should make arrangements to secure the publication of these papers, he at once urged me to undertake it. His earnest wish I hardly knew how to resist, and the less so as my personal acquaintance with so many of the events recorded, and my warm affection and esteem for him after nearly forty years of friendship, gave me some special advantages in preparing his manuscript for the press.

Two or three months after his decease, I received from his family a large box, containing a mass of papers and documents for which I was scarcely prepared. It consisted of two parts—a series of diaries kept during many of his later years, with almost daily entries of events as they transpired, and his own summary, in the form of an autobiography, more or less complete; the whole accompanied with letters, papers, and extracts (both manuscript and printed) illustrative of the facts he had recorded. On examination, I soon found that it would be impracticable to publish large portions of the materials before me, if only from the number of volumes that would be required to contain them. The incidents of his early years were narrated at great length, while those of a later period were left in the shape of mere annals or extracts from his diaries. It therefore seemed to me that I should best serve his memory, and attain his object, by re-writing the whole, availing myself as much as possible of his own words, condensing and abridging them where I could not, for want of space, quote them *verbatim.* This course being approved by his family, the result is the volume now in the hands of my readers.

My chief object has been to present a picture of the active Christian life of my friend, and I have, therefore, seldom obtruded my own views. On some subjects it would have been in my power to give information beyond that which these pages furnish; but the purpose of the volume is to depict the life of Mr. Phillippo and its connection with the events in which he bore a part. Hence it is but seldom that I have gone beyond Mr. Phillippo's own collections; and, whether the subjects under discussion relate to the political and social condition of the island, or to the history of the Baptist Mission in Jamaica in particular, resort for fuller information must be had to other sources.

The task has been more laborious than I expected; but it has been a great pleasure to retrace events and to renew acquaintance with persons and places familiar to me in years gone by.

It is my pleasant duty to acknowledge the assistance I have received from the members of Mr. Phillippo's family; from my dear friend, the Rev. D. J. East, the tutor of the Calabar Institution; and from the numerous letters of Mr. Phillippo kindly placed at my disposal by the Committee of the Baptist Missionary Society.

EDW. B. UNDERHILL.

DERWENT LODGE, HAMPSTEAD,
April 11th, 1881.

" I would express him simple, grave, sincere,
  In doctrine uncorrupt : in language plain,
  And plain in manner : decent, solemn, chaste,
  And natural in gesture : much impressed
  Himself, as conscious of his awful charge,
  And anxious mainly that the flock he feeds
  May feel it too ; affectionate in look,
  And tender in address, as well becomes
  A messenger of grace to guilty men."

COWPER.

CONTENTS.

LIFE

OF

JAMES MURSELL PHILLIPPO.

CHAPTER I.

EARLY DAYS—1798 TO 1813.

JAMES PHILLIPPO was born in the little market town of
East Dereham, Norfolk, on the 14th October, 1798. East
Dereham contains some 4,000 inhabitants, and is not
altogether undistinguished in English history. The
famous Bonner was rector of the parish before he entered
on his sanguinary career as Bishop of London. More
pleasant associations attach to the memory of the poet
Cowper, who, towards the close of his sorrowful, yet not
altogether unhappy, life, resided here. His earthly remains have their resting-place in the church, and the
monument which marks the spot was erected by his
attached friend Lady Hesketh, the almost forgotten poet
Hayley supplying the epitaph. It was from Mrs. Ann
Bodham, his cousin and a resident in Dereham, that
Cowper received his mother's picture, and from which
sprang one of the finest poems in the English language.
The site of Cowper's residence is now occupied by an
Independent chapel. George Borrow, a native of Dereham,
and a contemporary of Mr. Phillippo, calls their common
birthplace "the pattern of an English country town,"
lying in picturesque fashion, "pretty and quiet," along
the borders of the little stream which gives fertility to
the valley through which it runs.

B

James was the oldest of the four surviving children—three sons and a daughter—of Peter and Sarah Phillippo. His father was a master builder, and part proprietor of an iron foundry in East Dereham. Mrs. Phillippo was the daughter of Mr. Matthias V. Banyard, a respectable tradesman and farmer. It is, however, probable that the Phillippo family were originally emigrants from the Netherlands, driven hither by the persecutions of Alva in 1575 or 1580. Two descendants of the refugees of this name lie buried in St. Saviour's Church, Norwich, one of whom was High Sheriff of Norfolk in 1675.

Very early in his young life James Phillippo exhibited a striking aptitude for the acquisition and retention of knowledge. At four years of age he began to attend, as a day scholar, a boarding-school in the town. He often carried away the palm from his fellows for ready and fluent recitation of the pieces they learnt. His imitative powers were remarkable, and were frequently put to the test for the amusement of his friends. His apt imitation of the preachers whom he heard led his grandfather to remark that some day the boy himself would become a " Methodist parson."

At seven years of age, James was sent as a pupil to a school conducted by the Rev. Samuel Green, the minister of a small Baptist congregation existing in East Dereham. His stay in the school was not long. He reports himself while there as distinguished for little else than disobedience and mischief, which brought upon him merited chastisement. Probably with the hope of better results he was removed to the grammar school at Scarning, a small village, two miles distant from Dereham, of which the rector was the principal. This gentleman was held in high repute as a scholar, and was of High Church proclivities, but was particularly noted for his forbidding manners. Some years before, the celebrated Robert Robin

son, of Cambridge, had been a scholar in the same institution, and among Mr. Phillippo's contemporaries was the
Rev. W. Gathercole, well known in later years for his bitter
attacks on Dissent. Here James seems to have made fair
progress, especially in those studies which require the
exercise of a good memory; but the discipline of the
school was ill-calculated to bring out the finer qualities of
the scholars. The master was very severe in his treatment of defaulters, capricious in the exercise of his powers,
and tyrannical in his bearing. "He was as much feared
by the boys," said Mr. Phillippo years afterwards, "as the
most tyrannical slave-master I have ever known was by
his slaves." Cruel floggings were inflicted without dis-
crimination, and in paroxysms of anger. On one occasion, for no known cause, he began to flog the whole
school, consisting of fifty boys, till, coming to the seniors,
they broke out into rebellion, and in the *mêlée* that ensued
the master was thrown to the floor. Even his own sons
were not exempt from the infliction of his cruel wrath.

In the diary which Mr. Phillippo kept in after-years,
under date of April 10th, 1851, he thus refers to some of
the incidents of this period:—"During snatches of time,
within the last two or three days, I have read Mr. Borrow's
'Lavengro'—a curious production. He was a fellow-
townsman; I knew his father, mother, brother, and himself; as also the High Church rector, and the still more
aristocratic clerk, Philo, and several of the occurrences he
describes—all truthful. Yes! pretty Dereham, how many
recollections of bygone days did George Borrow's narrative
recall! Old Captain Borrow especially stood before me, a
tall, gaunt, gentlemanly old man. How often, when a boy,
have I gazed at the decorations on thy splendid scarlet
uniform! I also knew his gallant corps, drawn mostly
from that pretty town and neighbourhood. I never saw
a finer set of men than were embodied in the East

Anglian or West Norfolk Militia. I was at that time a great favourite of the old clerk, and also of the rector. The clerk taught me to sing, and from the gallery where I sat I often saw Captain Borrow and the author of 'Lavengro' in the family pew, while I had many a stroll with him about the lanes and alleys of the town and in places where

> 'The primrose, ere her time,
> Peeps through the moss that clothes the hawthorn-root.''

At this period of Mr. Phillippo's life, his parents were attached adherents of the Established Church, but from some cause, probably owing to conscientious scruples on the part of the mother, none of the children had been baptized. The rite was now observed. Soon after, James Phillippo was confirmed by Dr. Bathurst, Bishop of Norwich. But at fourteen years of age he had begun to understand the responsibilities under which he lay to God. Convinced of his unfitness, and sensible of the worldliness of his spirit, he steadily refused to go to the Communion. He shrank from an act so solemn, and one that he knew ought to be accompanied by a change of heart and life.

It was when between twelve and thirteen years of age that he left school, and for a short time assisted in his father's business. He then went to reside with his grandfather, for whose occupation he had a stronger predilection. There he was subject to less restraint than at home, and he seems to have availed himself of every opportunity for worldly pleasure. His chosen companions, though of respectable parentage, were irreligious. The pious instructions and example of his mother were lost to him. " Prayer was restrained," he says, " and religious duties were entirely neglected." His habitual resorts were, the tea-garden, the bowling-green, the theatre, the club-feast, and the country wake. The Lord's-day was more or less desecrated by these pursuits, till at length he began

to cherish contempt for the Word of God, and to entertain
ideas of the non-existence of God and of a future life. He
joined his wild companions in disturbing the worship of
a small community of Methodists, and frequently took part
in deriding them as they passed along the streets. His
old teacher, the venerable minister of the Baptist congregation, with his people, shared in this contemptuous dis-
regard of the civilities of life. Nevertheless, "all my reward," he says at a later time, " consisted in disappointment, disquietude, and remorse."

In the midst of this career of worldliness and sin, God
did not leave Himself without witness in the heart of His
wandering child. A visit now and then, on a dark Lord's-
day evening, to the Independent chapel brought him
under the faithful ministry of the Rev. Mr. Carter, of Mat-
tishall. The impression made by his home instruction
was on these occasions revived, and for a little while his
mind would be filled with fearful apprehensions of a judgment to come. A voice as of thunder would summon him
to repent, and, although appetite and passion might resume
their sway, there was left an abiding conviction that sooner
or later he would be constrained to abandon his worldly
life. The struggle with his inclinations was often violent.
"More than once," he says, " I ran from the house of
prayer to the theatre, there to check the rising tide of
conviction." Several striking escapes from death also had
a lasting influence on his mind. Twice he was saved from
drowning ; once he barely escaped with life from a fall
from an upper floor, with the chain of the factory crane,
on a wagon thirty feet below. At another time, returning
from a harvest-home on a very dark night, his horse
stumbled in a narrow lane said to be haunted, and the
terror of an apparition was added to the frightful fall and
the contusions he received. The horse had stumbled
over the clanking chain of a hobbled donkey.

In this state of feeling the desire sprang up in his mind to go to the Baptist chapel. His habits, and the prejudices which had been sedulously fostered against the Baptist community by the master of the grammar school, were opposed to the idea. A visit to this lowly sanctuary was, however, made. As he sat beneath the pulpit, the preacher's words smote him to the heart. He was overwhelmed with shame. Tortured with anger and remorse, he hasted from the chapel, determined, if possible, to stifle his convictions. For several weeks the strife with conscience and with the Spirit of God was severe. In his distress he at length found a friendly counsellor, who led him to the footstool of mercy, and there, as he himself expresses it, "with all my sins about me, and with an earnestness and fluency I can never forget, I supplicated mercy through the blood of Christ as the greatest boon that Heaven could bestow." The prayer was heard. "I felt," he says, "like Christian when he lost his burden at the sight of the Cross; my mind was filled with joy unspeakable. I thought I was in a new world, surrounded by new objects, and possessed of new senses. Everything assumed a different appearance. It was heaven to me to please God, and to be fashioned into His likeness. Old things emphatically passed away; behold, all things became new!" And James Phillippo entered on that life of consecration and devoted service to the Saviour which the ensuing pages will describe.

CHAPTER II.

A YEAR elapsed, during which James Phillippo left his grandfather for other employment at Elsing, a small village five miles from Dereham, before he summoned courage to present himself for membership with the Baptist church. Various obstructions blocked his way. Many of his intimate friends were in fellowship with the Independent congregation, and desired him to unite with them. His theological opinions on some subjects were unformed and immature. His family also threw impediments in his path, not the least of which was the prevalent prejudice arising from the apparent poverty and weakness of the Baptist church. These difficulties led him to a close study of the Holy Scriptures. With the sacred volume open before him he sought on his knees for the light of heaven. The result was a resolve, even though the act might involve obloquy and worldly disadvantage, to give his life publicly to the Saviour, and by baptism to range himself on the Lord's side. The observance of the sacred rite became an emphatic declaration of fealty to his Lord, such as may be fitly expressed in the words of the two tribes and a-half of Israel to Joshua: "All that thou commandest us we will do, and whithersoever thou sendest us we will go" (Joshua i. 16). As in many similar cases, his difficulties fell away with the decisive act, and some members of his family who had endeavoured to prevent it, impressed with the solemnity of the service, were among the first to obtain a blessing from on high, and follow the example of the brother and the son. The administrator of the rite to the youthful disciple was the venerable pastor of the church, who for a short time had been the early instructor of the boy.

The new life in Christ now openly manifested its power. James Phillippo gave himself to the diligent and systematic study of God's Word. For improvement in general knowledge he placed himself at an evening school. Stirrings of desire for usefulness among his fellow-men began to be felt, especially among the far-off nations lying in darkness and in the shadow of death. He read the missionary publications of the African traveller Campbell with avidity, and gave his leisure to the acquisition of such handicrafts as he thought would be useful in a missionary's career. Medicine, brickmaking, house-building, cabinet work, the wheelwright's toil, agriculture, and the manufacture of articles of food and clothing, all attracted in turn his serious and ardent attention. His progress in knowledge, and his natural gifts, soon marked him out for employment as a preacher of the Gospel in the surrounding villages. His first appearance was as the substitute of a friend, suddenly prevented by illness from fulfilling an engagement, in the village through which Mr. Phillippo and his employer's family regularly journeyed on their way to the Lord's-day services at Dereham. He began also to visit the houses of the villagers for religious conversation. His companions in business were invited to listen to the Word of Salvation, and he records with gratitude to God that in not a few instances his ministrations were blessed. A young friend who succeeded him in his situation at Elsing writes in 1817 :—

"My dear Friend,—I have great pleasure in informing you that Mr. T. and Mr. G., the senior apprentices, were baptized on a confession of faith last month. Mr. T. is

very much altered since he came here. He is now, I am
sure, truly pious. He attributed his first religious impressions to your reproofs, advice, and expostulations.
You will regard his conversion as an answer to your
prayers, and take courage. Mr. G., too, attributed his
first impressions to two sermons which you preached when
in Elsing last. May the Lord give you many more souls
to your ministry!"

It was during the serious illness of his employer, on
whom he attended with great assiduity, giving support and
comfort by his prayers and Scriptural expositions, that the
duty of devoting himself entirely to the ministry of the
Gospel was brought distinctly before him. After grateful
reference to his services, "I should be sorry to part with
you," said his master, "and I do not know what I should
do without you; but I can no longer withhold my impression. Have you never thought of the ministry?"
The secret longings of James Phillippo's heart now found
utterance, and he told of the visions of usefulness he had
entertained in some foreign land, where the Gentiles were
ignorant of "the unsearchable riches of Christ." "Have
you never expressed your desire to our pastor?" He had
not; and, as his master had promised to send Mr. Green
to the neighbouring village of New Buckingham, it was
at once arranged that James should be the driver, and
thus obtain an opportunity to communicate to the pastor
his cherished hopes.

Much occurred on the journey to check the utterance of
his wish. Fear of a repulse tied his tongue. Then the
conversation of the pastor with a farmer on whom they
called by the way was discouraging. Instances of failure
of some young aspirants to the ministry were referred to,
while the cost of their education was said to render the
greatest caution necessary. It was, moreover, of the last
importance that none but truly able and godly men should

be encouraged to abandon their worldly pursuits for the solemn and momentous responsibility of the care of souls.* At the house of another, a highly esteemed friend, who was visited on the route, the conversation turned on the qualifications of a true missionary. Not only, it was argued, must there be good capacity, but the temper and conduct in daily life should exhibit a pattern of exalted piety. It was not till the village worship was over, and the journey home nearly accomplished, that with much trembling and hesitation of speech the subject was broached. Contrary to expectation, and in a tone and manner altogether different to that he feared: "Well," said the pastor, "I have sometimes thought that if Providence should cast your lot in some dark country-place in your own land, you might make yourself useful." Phillippo intimated that his wish was to go abroad, in however mean a capacity, to do service for his Lord. "Then," was the immediate reply, "you must read books on the subject;" and various works were at once named, to be lent from the pastor's library.

The die was cast. Business arrangements of considerable advantage had already been set aside for the object in view. Mr. Green, who was about to remove into Huntingdonshire, lost no time in introducing his "son in the Gospel" to that eminent servant of Christ, the Rev. Joseph Kinghorn, of Norwich. "I conveyed this letter in person," writes Mr. Phillippo in his journal, "my late employer lending me a horse for the journey. As some evidence of my anxiety of mind as to the results of the interview with this venerable and learned minister of the

---

* Mr. Phillippo adds in a note: "This venerable minister, being once asked his opinion respecting a young man proposed for the ministry, inquired, 'Is there clay?'—a question usually proposed by purchasers or lessees of farms in Norfolk, without which a farm would be comparatively valueless."

Gospel, from a fear of my not possessing, in his judgment, the requisite qualifications for the work to which I aspired, not unmixed with awe which his presence and manner inspired, I prayed earnestly to God during the whole of the journey, a distance of fourteen or fifteen miles, sometimes dismounting from my horse and retiring for prayer to private places in the fields or along the road. My earnestness amounted to an agony that God would give me favour in the sight of His honoured servant, so that my journey might be successful."

Those still living who can remember the tall form and dignified mien, the suave manners and grave accents, of Joseph Kinghorn, can readily understand the "awe" which a country youth would feel on entering his presence. His kindness and courtesy, however, soon dispelled all fear. A long conversation ensued. The dealings of God with the young aspirant were fully related. The sincerity of his consecration was tested with kindly care, and at length James Phillippo was encouraged to communicate his views and wishes to the Committee of the Baptist Missionary Society, with the assurance that Mr. Kinghorn would sustain the application by a private letter from himself.

Mr. Phillippo forwarded, in a few days, to the Rev. John Dyer, the Secretary of the Society, a long and interesting paper, in which, in much detail, he explained the origin and motives of his application. He states that in taking this step he was acting on the advice of his pastor, the Rev. Samuel Green, and the Rev. Joseph Kinghorn. He relates the Divine process by which he had been brought out of the darkness of a sinful and injurious life into the marvellous light of the Gospel. From the moment that his own eyes were opened he had longed to be an instrument in the hands of God to turn "the heathen from darkness to light, and from the power of Satan unto God." It had been the subject of constant prayer. The prayer of the "man of Macedonia" was ever sounding in his ears—"Come over and help us." To fulfil this desire he had declined advantageous offers in business, and endeavoured, in various ways, to prepare himself for the great task he had in view. Only the hope of leading even one poor pagan to the Saviour's feet could have persuaded him to leave his native shore for a strange land. "The promotion of the glory of God," he says, "in the conversion of the heathen is, I hope, my only aim." He then briefly states his belief in the main doctrines of the Christian faith, and, as he does not seem to have swerved from them during the whole term of his long ministry, the statement may here be inserted.

"I believe in the total depravity of all mankind; in the absolute necessity of a change of heart; in man's inability to accomplish this work; that it is effected by the Holy Spirit, through the use of means; that Christ is the only way of salvation; the necessity of personal holiness. I recognise also two Ordinances: Baptism, administered to adults on a profession of faith in Christ; and the Lord's Supper. I believe in the final salvation of believers, and the final destruction of unbelievers."

His paper is closed with the pious aspiration that wherever his lot may be fixed, whether in Europe, or Asia, or Africa, or America, "I may copy the example of my glorious Lord and Master, and go about doing good."

This document was forwarded to Mr. Dyer in the last month of 1818. A time of prolonged and wearisome waiting ensued. This was probably owing to the many perplexing events which gave great anxiety to the friends of the Society. Writing about this time Mr. Gutteridge says:—"Difficulties increase from Serampore and Calcutta. Colombo is a source of expense almost unwarrantable. Jamaica is stretching out its arms for assistance,

and we possess not the means of help."* Pecuniary
embarrassments threatened the very existence of the
Society, and considerable sums had to be borrowed to
meet the most pressing obligations.   No reply was
given, till the patience both of Mr. Phillippo and of
his friends was well-nigh exhausted.   A portion of
the time was spent in preaching in various towns and
villages in Norfolk.   But as months passed away, and a
short term of remunerative employment could not be
found, a return to business was painfully contemplated.
Negotiations, which were commenced, failed in some
mysterious way, when suddenly the welcome summons
to London arrived.

On the 27th October, 1819, after nine months' wearisome suspense, the Rev. John Dyer, writing from
Reading, invited Mr. Phillippo to meet the Committee, on
the 25th November, at the Baptist Mission Rooms at 15,
Wood Street, Cheapside.   It was not without anxiety that
Mr. Phillippo obeyed the call.   He had had to resist the
importunities of friends who desired to keep him at
home; but their entreaties were easily endured in comparison with the fear that he might fail to approve
himself before a committee (as he says) "of ministers
and highly educated lay gentlemen."   His duty, however,
was now plain, and, with a letter of introduction from Mr.
Kinghorn to the Rev. Joseph Ivimey, we find him, on the
20th November, taking up his abode at the house of his
uncle, the Rev. J. Denham, then minister of the Baptist
congregation in Poplar.

On entering the ante-room of the Mission House, on
the evening of the appointed day, he says, "I found there
a young man, who, after the usual salutations were
exchanged, inquired if I were one of the members of the

---

* Kinghorn's Life, p. 374.

Committee.   Answering in the negative, and adding that I was come to appear before the Committee as a candidate for missionary service, 'What!' said my interrogator, 'are you the young man from Norfolk?'   On my replying yes, he rose from his chair and, grasping my hand, said with great warmth of feeling, 'My name is Burchell; I am come for the same purpose from Gloucestershire; how glad I am to see you.'"   Mutual explanations ensued, and a fellowship was established which lasted to the end of Mr. Burchell's useful and distinguished career.

Mr. Phillippo was the first to face the assembled board, whose inquisition was so much feared.   Mr. Ivimey's hearty welcome, the kindly greetings, the pleased expression on the countenances of other gentlemen present, speedily dispelled the fears of the youthful candidate, and assured him that his apprehensions of an undue severity in the tests to which he was about to be exposed were visionary.   His examination was brief.   His testimonials were explicit and satisfactory, and, after some cheerful advice from Dr. Newman and others as to the studies he should pursue, he rejoined his friend in the ante-room with the joyful tidings of his acceptance.   A similar welcome reception awaited Mr. Burchell, and the two friends retired together, rejoicing that they were " counted worthy " to serve the Lord among the heathen.   Their future course fully sustained the views which at this time seem to have pressed with more than usual force on the minds of the Committee.   In the Report of this year, referring to the character of a true missionary, the Committee say: " To sustain a character so arduous with reputation and success requires a combination of mental qualities not often united in the same individual, superadded to the indispensable qualification of a heart thoroughly devoted to God."*

---

* Periodical Account, 1819, p. 16.

A few days were pleasantly spent in visiting the novel sights of London, in fulfilling some preaching engagements, and in hearing discourses from the lips of leading ministers of the denomination. Among those to whom he listened must be mentioned the Rev. William Gray, pastor of the Baptist church in Chipping Norton. He had been selected by the Committee as the preceptor of the young missionary.

On the 29th November, Mr. Phillippo received a hearty welcome from the students and the family of the excellent man under whose roof his first essays into the regions of theological study were about to be made.

CHAPTER III.

THE STUDENT—1820 TO 1821.

MR. PHILLIPPO found three associates in his student-life at Chipping Norton, afterwards increased to seven, two of whom, like himself, were destined to missionary service. He began his studies in a very hopeful spirit. " Now," he says, " I can look forward with a hope, full of animation, to that day on which, if spared, I shall embark on the great and wide sea to impart to the infatuated slaves of sin and Satan ' the glorious Gospel of the blessed God.' Henceforward let my motto be, Energy, Prudence, Economy, Temperance, Perseverance, with ardent love to God and man."

In an interesting letter, written about a month after his arrival in Chipping Norton, to the Rev. J. Denham, he thus speaks of the feelings with which he girded himself for his task.

" I arrived here the evening after my departure from town. . . . The days and weeks that have passed away since my coming may be numbered among the happiest of my life. . . . There are several dark villages around us, to which we go alternately to break the bread of life. Last Sabbath I preached at Middleton Cheney, a village in Northamptonshire. I felt more comfortable than I expected, and I trust that my one great aim was, and I hope ever will be so, to preach the truth earnestly, faithfully, and simply, that when called away I may leave the pulpit and the world clear of the blood of all men. I

have commenced my studies. I find them difficult, of
course, but I am determined, by grace given me from
above, to surmount them all, in view of the great object
of my heart, to preach among the Gentiles the unsearchable riches of Christ. I do feel, as the holy Pearce says,
' a glowing satisfaction in the thought of spending my life
in something nobler than the locality of this island will
permit.' In order to make full proof of my ministry I
must, I know, be diligent, and make the best use of my
time. I must have method, and, as you have been
similarly circumstanced, I should be glad of your advice
on the subject. Be assured that I will endeavour to act
upon it to the best of my ability."

To his parents he wrote :—

" Providence has fixed my habitation for a time here,
which is nearly two hundred miles remote from the place of
my birth. My thoughts often disentangle themselves from
the pursuits of study, and force themselves to the place
of your loved abode. I am sure you keenly feel the
separation. But you must remember that I am to be
engaged in a glorious cause. Who would not lend a
hand to dispel the darkness of Satan's kingdom, and erect
upon its ruins the Kingdom of God ? This world is not a
place of repose for a faithful soldier of the Cross. I may
be subject to many trials and difficulties that I should not
be exposed to in the common walks of life at home ; but
how animating the thought that the conflict will soon be
over, even at the longest term of service, and, if faithful,
I shall be crowned with glory and honoured with the
commendation of my great Master.

" Oh ! how blessed is the religion of Jesus ! how it
smooths the furrows of care and gilds the dark paths
of life ! Blessed, for ever blessed, be the day when I was
brought to experience its blessed influence on my heart

and life! Give my best love to sister, brothers, and friends."

Mr. Phillippo about this period began to keep a diary, in which he inserted notes of passing events, with such reflections as occurred to him. A few extracts covering the first term of his student-life will exhibit the nature of his employments, and the spirit with which he prosecuted them.

"January 8th, 1820. Rode to Blockley to-day. The weather was intensely cold; but the most to be lamented was my cold and lifeless heart. It is this which mars my comfort, and prevents my holding that communion with my God and Saviour which is so essential to my happiness and usefulness.

"9th, Sabbath-day. Proceeded from Blockley to Campden, accompanied by Mr. J. Smith. How charming were the prospects! I could not but be struck with the romantic scenery, which surpassed in beauty and grandeur all I had ever seen before. Preached from Isa. liii. 3 and 4. I trembled for fear of man, but the Lord stood by me, and strengthened me, so that I proceeded beyond my most sanguine expectations. Bless the Lord, O my soul!

"Preached in the afternoon at Blockley from 8th Rom. 28. Oh! that I could feel more of the importance of the work. Took tea with Mr. and Mrs. J. Smith, and conversed on the privations and hardships of a missionary's life. But 'none of these things move me.'

"Monday, January 10th. Spent the greater part of the day in reading the memoirs of Henry Martyn. Oh! that I possessed the spirit of this holy man; that I felt more for the salvation of the poor heathen! Blessed Jesus, melt this stony, this rocky heart into tenderness and compassion!

"April 8th. Went to a double lecture at Eatington,

Warwickshire. Messrs. Price, of Alcester; Beetham, of Hooknorton; Coles, of Bourton-on-the-Water, and W. Gray preached. Two or three of the students conducted the devotional services. The sermons were excellent and very appropriate. I was particularly interested in the evening sermon, by our tutor, from the words, 'They shall come from the east,' &c. It was both an interesting and a profitable day. May the services be abundantly blessed by the God of all grace!"

"April 10th. Rose at 6 o'clock and walked about the village until 7. Afterwards accompanied three or four of the ministers and students to Edge Hill, celebrated for the memorable battle fought on it. On ascending the summit of a tower dedicated to the memory of the battle, we saw the spot which receptacled four thousand of our fellow-creatures.

"April 19th. One of our missionary students has left to continue his studies at Bradford under the venerable Dr. Steadman. Our number is thus reduced to five, one other having gone to Bristol for home service. Thus our turns of writing sermons and essays for criticism, also sermons to be preached before our tutor and the congregation on week evenings, in addition to those to be prepared for village congregations, are more frequent. Our hands are always full. Religion, I may say, flourishes in this town and in the villages around. Every place in which Divine service is held is filled. Nothing can be more encouraging than the attendance. One of our number, Mr. Mursell,* is one of the most powerful preachers I have ever heard. His addresses are so adapted to the understandings of the poorer people as to produce a powerful effect on them. He bids fair to be a very superior and popular man. These labours among

* The Rev. James Phillippo Mursell, of Leicester.

cottagers are doubtless a very excellent preparation for ministerial work at home and abroad, especially the latter, and make me long to spend my days in some heathen land."

With Mr. Mursell a very intimate friendship was established, which was sealed by an exchange of names, Mr. Mursell adopting the name of Phillippo, and Mr. Phillippo that of Mursell. This friendship was in subsequent years a source of great comfort and strength to Mr Phillippo, and was only interrupted by his death.

Mr. Phillippo's first vacation commenced on the 30th of May. The slow travelling of those days enabled him to enjoy the scenery on his way, of which he speaks with delight. His road first led him to Oxford, where he paid a brief visit to the author's parents, and then, passing on to London, he made a short sojourn with his relative, the Rev. J. Denham. His holidays in Norfolk were spent in visiting friends, in preaching among its numerous towns and villages, and in pursuing, with diligence, the studies on which he had entered. He relates, with amusing detail, the repetition, among a party of villagers, of the examples of the Latin syntax as an illustration of his skill in acquiring a foreign tongue which, as a missionary, he might be called to exercise. Everywhere he kept his great object in view, reading every missionary publication within reach, and taking every opportunity of consulting with those who had a practical knowledge of missionary work. After one such interview with a retired missionary from Ceylon, he says, " Mr. Griffiths gave me encouragement to go forward. I feel more decided than ever to live and die a missionary. It is my purpose to spend the residue of my years in labouring among the 'rough and savage pagans of the wilderness,' rather than occupy the highest position as a minister, in the crowded cities of my own land, if the Lord should see fit to qualify me for this important work by the inward teachings of His Holy Spirit."

On the 1st of August he resumed his studies at Chipping Norton. The following months were fully occupied with them, only varied by an occasional visit to the surrounding villages, or to more distant places, for the purpose of "holding forth the Word of Life."

The vacation, commencing in April, 1821, was chiefly spent at Lymington, Hants, with the family of his intimate friend, Mr. Mursell. A serious illness, increased in danger by exposure on the sea during a dense fog, in which the party nearly perished, laid him aside for several weeks. Kind care and assiduous nursing brought him safely through, after which he returned to Chipping Norton to complete the term of his probationary studies with the Rev. William Gray. His residence with this devoted servant of Christ was a period of unalloyed pleasure. The small number of the students gave the party the aspect of a family. They lived together as brethren and friends, looking for a closer and holier fellowship in the "better land" when their work was done. Under the wise superintendence of their tutor, their abilities were called forth, and an ardent and devout spirit of piety was cherished. At the same time, cheerfulness without undue levity characterised their intercourse, and the generally grave demeanour of the heads of the household did not weigh too oppressively on the abounding spirits of its younger members.

In January, 1822, by the direction of the Secretary of the Mission, Mr. Phillippo left Chipping Norton for Bradford, to complete his preparations for the missionary life under the able tutorship of the Rev. William Steadman, D.D., then President of the Academy at Horton. Introduced by a former fellow-student at Chipping Norton, Mr. E. Crook, he received a cordial welcome from the students, as well as from the venerable Doctor, and immediately set himself, with his usual diligence, to master the studies of the place. His attainments scarcely fitted him for the lessons of the first class in which he was placed. But by early rising and a diligent economy of time, though at some cost of health, he quickly surmounted this difficulty. His imperfect knowledge of Hebrew was principally made up during a visit of six weeks to Richmond, whither he was sent for rest. In the Castle walks, and in the solitude of its deserted chambers, he conned the grammar of the language, and mastered the first chapters of Genesis, so that on his return he was able to rejoin the class on equal terms, receiving the commendations of his tutor for his industry and perseverance.

In common with his fellow-students, he was a frequent preacher in the villages and hamlets around Bradford. Sometimes among the colliers their zeal and patience were sorely tested by the savage conduct and blasphemous language of groups of free-thinkers, infidels, and Papists, with which the district was infested. At other times, odd and laughable incidents would happen from the uncouth *patois* of the people, which the students from the South could not understand, while, on the other hand, their more polished tongue was alike unintelligible to their grimy auditors. Opposition was not confined to the lower orders. At one village the lady of the squire had herself driven one preacher from his stand beneath an overspreading tree on the village green. On the following Sabbath Mr. Phillippo, with one or two friends, undauntedly challenged the same fate. A large crowd assembled to witness the collision; but the lady now sent her bailiffs. Whether awed by the aspect of the people, or conscious of the unworthy nature of their errand, they contented themselves with observing the order of the service, and, after listening for a time to the earnest appeals of the student-

preacher to the consciences of his hearers, they left the
assembly in peace. The " liberty of prophesying " thus
vindicated, eventually led to the formation of a prosperous
Wesleyan community and the erection of a chapel very
near the spot where the first preacher was so roughly
treated.

CHAPTER IV.

In the autumn of the year 1823, Mr. Phillippo received a communication from Mr. Dyer informing him that the Committee had fixed on the Island of Jamaica as the sphere of his labours, which also was the destination of his friends Phillips and Burchell, whose student-life had been passed in Bristol. The East Indies had for the most part occupied his thoughts ; but he cheerfully and gratefully at once submitted to the wishes of the Committee. It was ever a consolation to him to feel, in hours of difficulty and depression, that his lot was not chosen by him but for him. He was assured that God, by the hands of His servants, had placed him where he was. It was clear to his mind that it was his duty there to stay, until Providence, by an equally emphatic missive, directed his removal from it.

The time fixed for his departure was the month of November, and the period of preparation was short. The designation service was fixed for Wednesday, the 23rd September. A very large congregation assembled in Westgate Chapel, Bradford, to assist at the solemn service, the particulars of which were afterwards published in an interesting pamphlet.* It may be well to give in some

---

* Entitled, " Services at the Designation of Mr. James Phillippo as a Missionary to the Island of Jamaica. Bradford, in Yorkshire, September 24th, 1823."

detail the order of the service, and the more so that
in later times the early practice of Baptist churches on
the ordination of a minister to his charge has been laid
aside, probably to the detriment of the pastoral office
itself, by depriving it of that solemnity and gravity which
should mark a pastor's entrance on his responsible work.
The Rev. J. Acworth, M.A., of Leeds, commenced by
reading the Scriptures and offering prayer. The Rev. B.
Godwin, Mr. Phillippo's classical tutor, delivered the
introductory discourse and proposed the questions. The
Rev. I. Mann, M.A., of Shipley, offered the ordination
prayer, accompanied with the laying on of hands. The
Rev. Dr. Steadman addressed the charge to Mr.
Phillippo ; and the Rev. R. Pool, Independent minister of
Kipping, concluded with prayer. Of these venerable men
only Dr. Acworth lingers amongst us, the calm evening
of whose life is brightened by the assured hope of a
glorious immortality in the presence of the Lord, in whose
service he has so long been honourably employed. The
others have left behind them recollections fragrant with
the holy memory of eminent devotedness and success in
the vineyard of their Master and Lord. In introducing
the service, Dr. Acworth said : " We profess not by this
service to convey to Mr. Phillippo any powers, or to
confer on him any qualifications which he does not
already possess ; our object is simply to show our cordial
approbation of him as a person suitably qualified for
this important undertaking, and to unite in commending
him to the blessing and protection of God in fervent
prayer." After this disclaimer of all sacerdotal privilege
or character, the preacher went on to speak of the
missionary enterprise itself. He pointed out how congenial missionary efforts are with the spirit and genius of
Christianity. " Christianity," he said, " is like the vital
air, or the light of heaven, needed by all, and suited to all.

In its invitations it is unlimited, and its promises make no distinction of sex, or age, or station, or country, or colour. Every Christian feeling prompts to exertions of this kind. In our endeavour for the extension of the Kingdom of Christ we are acting in accordance with the plans and purposes of God. We are treading in the steps of the apostolic churches and primitive Christians." Then, turning to the youthful minister, he thus described his character:—"In religion he is no novice; his piety has been for years unquestionable. For some time, he has given up all secular engagements to devote himself entirely to the study of the Scriptures and the acquisition of useful learning; and his progress has been satisfactory. His general conduct has been such as to give us no apprehension for the future. And we all, who have known him, have witnessed the deep interest he has taken in all that relates to the salvation of the heathen, the animation which the subject of missions has always produced, and the sacred ardour which has appeared to glow in his breast without interruption, determining him to live and die in the work of the missionary."

The following were the questions which Mr. Godwin then addressed to Mr. Phillippo, and to which, with considerable fulness of detail, he replied :—

" 1. We shall be glad to hear an account of your conversion to God. 2. Will you give us a brief outline of your views of Divine Truth? 3. Will you state the motives which induce you to engage in the work of a Christian missionary, and your views of this important undertaking ?"

The replies were eminently satisfactory; a few sentences from the answer to the final question will suffice to show the spirit in which Mr. Phillippo was entering on the work of his life.

" My desires for this work arise from the firm and

decided convictions of my judgment, my thoughts having for seven years, in a greater or less degree, been exercised on the subject. Much less am I induced to engage in so arduous an employ, from a vain opinion of my self-sufficiency; for God, who knows my heart, knoweth that at this moment I deeply feel my weakness. I esteem myself 'less than the least of all saints,' and only a babe in all the important qualifications requisite for the work. Had it not been for the persuasion that, more especially to display the exceeding greatness of His power in the accomplishment of the mightiest of His designs, God has often chosen the 'foolish things of the world, and things that are despised,' I had long abandoned the undertaking in despair.

"The work of a missionary, I am aware, is arduous. I am sensible I shall need much wisdom, much faith, much patience, much devotedness to God, and love to precious souls; and, when I reflect on the small proportion of every Christian grace that I possess, I am discouraged. The sacrifices I must make, and the difficulties I must encounter, I have also steadily contemplated; but, implicitly depending on Almighty aid, none of these things move me, neither count I my life dear unto myself, so that I may finish my course with joy, and the ministry which I have received of the Lord Jesus, to testify the Gospel of the grace of God."

Dr. Steadman next entered the pulpit, and, with the following impressive words, the venerable tutor dismissed his scholar to his chosen work :—

"By this time you are probably led to exclaim—Who is sufficient for these things? In reply, let me entreat you to remember that He who appointed the Apostle to his course of service said to him, and that upon a very trying occasion, 'My grace is sufficient for thee.' He says the same to you, and will not fail to make good His declaration. To Him, therefore, let your eyes be directed. If you are ready to faint, look up to Him to encourage you—if your views of His Gospel be confined and un-animating, look to Him to enlarge and invigorate them—if your love to Him wax cold, look to Him to quicken and enflame it—if you are at a stand as to the path you must pursue, look to Him to direct your steps—if obstacles to success seem insurmountable, look to Him for the removal of them—if dangers and death surround you on every hand, look to Him to inspire you with courage superior to them, to enable you to feel safe under His protection, to resign your immortal spirit into His hands, and to triumph in the prospect of the 'crown of righteous-ness laid up for you, and for all those that love His appearing.'"

It was a solemn moment, and the impression of it left an abiding mark on the future life of Mr. Phillippo.

One other necessary preparation had to be made—his marriage. While yet a student at Chipping Norton he had met with the lady who ultimately became his wife. A strong affection ensued, and a few days before his departure he was united to Miss Hannah Selina Cecil at the parish church of her native place. This union was followed by a long and happy life of conjugal blessedness. Mr. Phillippo found in his bride one every way calculated to hold up his hands in his arduous and successful career.

In the following lines from a well-known poem on the life of a missionary, Mr. Phillippo records the feelings with which he entered on his course:—

> "Henceforth, then,
> It matters not if storm or sunshine be
> My earthly lot ; bitter or sweet my cup ;
> I only pray—God fit me for the work ;

God make me holy, and my spirit nerve
For the stern hour of strife.   Let me but know
There is an arm unseen that holds me up,
An eye that kindly watches all my path
Till I my weary pilgrimage have done;
Let me but know I have a Friend that waits
To welcome me to glory;—and I joy
To tread the dark and death-fraught wilderness."

CHAPTER V.

On Wednesday, the 29th of October, Mr. and Mrs. Phillippo sailed from Gravesend in the congenial company of Mr. and Mrs. Phillips. Mr. Phillips had been a fellow-student at Chipping Norton. The name of the vessel was the *Ocean*, bound for Honduras, and was the property of a well-known friend of the Mission, Mr. G. Fife Angus, by whom a free passage was given them to their destination. They found in Captain Whittle a courteous and Christian friend, who, during an imprisonment at Arras, in France, was instrumental in the conversion of the Rev. Thomas Godden, the predecessor of Mr. Phillippo in his work at Spanish Town. Mr. Godden, in early life, had entered the Royal Navy. After several years' service his naval career was brought to an end by the ship to which he belonged falling a prey to a French cruiser. A captivity of eight years followed, in which he met with Captain Whittle, like himself a prisoner of war, and by him Mr. Godden was led to the Saviour. The voyage began unfavourably. The weather was gloomy, the accommodation on board inconvenient. They were also ill-prepared for the gale which sprang up in the night, and detained them for days tossing about in the Downs. Such was the fury of the storm that several vessels were driven from their moorings, among which the large ship bound for Portugal that had on board the celebrated Don Miguel was in great jeopardy for many hours.

With a calmer sea the *Ocean* trimmed her sails, quickly passed down the Channel, and crossed the dreaded Bay of Biscay in fine weather. Madeira was reached without any special incident. The monotony of the voyage was pleasantly varied by converse, and by study and religious exercises, and in recording the impressions which the changing aspects of the sea and sky were calculated to produce. The mind of Mr. Phillippo was from his earliest years peculiarly susceptible of the beauties of nature, and his diaries frequently contain sketches of the scenery through which, in his many journeys, he passed. Thus, in the latitude of the trade-winds, he speaks of the "beauty of repose upon the sea" created by "the unintermitting sunshine." The world of waters, spread out on every side, "was tinted with lines of most delicate colour. Pathways of beryl, emerald, amethyst, and pearl were traced upon the surface of the deep, sometimes stirred by a flood of restless and insufferable lustre poured forth by the orb of day," and he thought of that crystal sea which is ever before the throne of God and the Lamb.

Proceeding Southward, the night watches disclosed a new heaven to his excited gaze. Its calm depths, intensely blue and gloriously bright, revealed innumerable stars unknown to dwellers in Northern latitudes. One night he relates how the constellations seemed to glow with unusual splendour. "Jupiter and Saturn appeared nearly touching each other, shining with a steady lustre in the north-east. In the zenith and in the north the fixed stars were sown so thickly that they seemed to twinkle all at once, and the galaxy gleamed beyond them, as it were the twilight of eternity. It was a spectacle of wonder and beauty, whose silence spoke to the soul in language that may be felt, but not uttered. I forgot everything entirely for the time. The hope of immortality

carried adoring thoughts to the footstool of the throne of
Him who liveth for ever and ever." On such evenings
the friends would linger on deck till a late hour, often
giving relief to their feelings in sacred song, ming-
ling therewith thoughts of home, of the dear ones left
behind, and of the unknown life that awaited them in the
land towards which their eyes were ever turned.

The course of the vessel gave the voyagers a sight of
the varied, but grand and fertile, scenery of the islands of
Guadaloupe, Antigua, and Porto Rico, and on the 18th
December the Blue Mountains of Jamaica were seen on
the horizon. The majestic heights of this magnificent
range were before them, distinct and clear, as though cut
out on the dark blue sky. On the following day they
reached land at Point Morant. They were soon boarded
by negro boatmen, who demanded exorbitant fares to
carry them ashore. With some trouble they at length
landed, and were glad to accept the hospitality of a
Scotch gentleman, a storekeeper of the place. The
readiness of their reception for a moment made them
imagine they were the guests of an hotel-keeper, but
they soon found that, then as now, hotel accommodation
is rarely to be met with in Jamaica. The owner of the
house was absent, but, returning in the evening, he gave
them a warm welcome. Early the following morning,
after a bountiful breakfast, they started for Kingston,
forty miles distant, by boat, laden by their host with fresh
fruit and other necessaries for the long day's voyage
before them. Mr. Phillippo writes:—" The sea was calm,
the land breeze having died away, and the early freshness
of the day was most delightful. We beguiled the
tediousness of the way by singing favourite hymns,
reciting pieces of sacred poetry, but especially by
observations on the novelty, the beauty, and the magnificence of the coast scenery. A flood of glory was shed

over the entire landscape at noon, but towards evening
the spectacle of splendour gradually diminished, the
atmosphere became dense, the brightness of the sunset
faded away, and a blue mist rose from the sea and
enveloped us on every side."   The haze partially concealed from them the long spit of land known as The
Palisades, which closes in the harbour of Kingston.   It
was dark as they rowed by the gibbeted bodies of a
notorious gang of pirates that had lately infested these
seas, but about nine o'clock they safely landed under the
guns of the fort of Port Royal.   "The cheering of the
sailors," says Mr. Phillippo, "the lights from the ship-
ping and the shore, made us, for a moment, think that our
passage from England was a dream."

" On landing we were taken," he continues, " to the house
of a respectable widow of colour, a Mrs. Thomas, a
member of the Baptist church at Kingston.   The house was
soon crowded with coloured people.   We were welcomed
with the liveliest cordiality by our hostess and her pious
friends. Among them was a Mrs. Freeman, a good old black
woman, well known among sailors who visit this port from
England and elsewhere for her generous kindness in
poverty and sickness. On the following morning, the 21st
December, being the Sabbath, we were taken in a boat to
Kingston by two black men, members of the East Queen
Street Church, and conducted to the mission-house, forcing
our way through the dense masses that thronged the market-
place, almost stunned by the loud vociferations of the
traffickers.   We were soon visited by brethren Tinson and
Thomas Knibb and their wives, Mr. and Mrs. Coultart, the
missionaries of the station, being then in England.   At
eleven o'clock we attended the service, Mr. Knibb
preaching in the morning, and Mr. Tinson in the
afternoon, to immense congregations.   Both of them,
by their pale appearance, impressed us unfavourably

with regard to the climate in which we were about to live."

Mr. and Mrs. Phillippo remained in Kingston till Christmas-day was past, when they left the companions of their voyage in charge of the station, which arrangement continued till the arrival of Mr. Coultart in the following April.

CHAPTER VI.

The Christmas carnival over, Mr. Phillippo on the next day paid his first visit to Spanish Town, to which station he had been appointed by the Committee of the Missionary Society, and which he continued to occupy till within two or three years of his departure, at a good old age, to his rest. The ancient name of the place was St. Jago de la Vega. It was at that time the capital of the island, which it continued to be till a few years ago, when the Government offices were removed to Kingston. Mr. Phillippo has left on record the following description of the city in his interesting work on Jamaica :—

"Spanish Town is situated on the banks of the Rio Cobre, nearly at the extremity of a noble plain, bounded by the Cedar Valley Mountains on the N. and N.W., and is six miles distant from the sea at Port Henderson and Passage Fort. A large square occupies the centre of the town, formed by public buildings in the Spanish American style, which are extensive, and display considerable architectural taste. Government House, Including beneath the same roof the Council Chamber, the Court of Chancery, and various other offices, occupies the whole of the west side. It was erected by the colonists at a cost of £50,000. A range of equal extent, called the House of Assembly, but which includes the County Court-house, and the offices of judicial and other functionaries, stands directly opposite. At one end of the northern range is

the Arsenal and Guard-house ; at the other, the offices of
the Island Secretary, connected by a temple that contains
a statue of Lord Rodney, erected in commemoration of
his victory over the French fleet in 1782, and a beautiful
semi-circular colonnade. A range on the south side
contains magnificent rooms for public amusement, and
offices for miscellaneous public purposes. A considerable
portion of the area thus formed contains a garden in
beautiful order, intersected by gravel walks, ornamented
by choice trees, flowers, and shrubs, and protected from
spoliation by elegant palisades. The barracks, the
church, the Wesleyan chapel, and the premises of the
Baptist Missionary Society, in addition to a few beautiful
villas that adorn the suburbs of the town, are the principal
objects of attraction to the stranger. The population is
estimated at about 10,000." *

The mission premises referred to were not the buildings
that awaited his occupation in 1824. On entering
Spanish Town, he found the streets crowded with
Christmas revellers, whose hideous yells and revolting
attitudes, with the rough music of their African ancestry,
deafened the ears of the missionary and his companions
as they almost forced their way to the mission-house. An
unsightly brick wall formed an enclosure (once the
artillery ground) containing a dwelling of two rooms
with a piazza. It was inconvenient and dirty, and the
walls of the dilapidated interior were daubed with lamp-
black as a protection to the eyes of a former occupant.
Miserable as was the outlook, Mr. and Mrs. Phillippo set
to work with characteristic courage, and soon rendered
the place fairly habitable.

These were not the original premises of the mission.

---

* "Jamaica : its Past and Present State," by James M. Phillippo, of
Spanish Town, Jamaica (London : John Snow ; 1843), p. 63.

They had been purchased as a temporary residence on the burning down of the mission-house, by an incendiary hand, on the evening of the 17th July, 1820. The station owed its origin to the labours of the Rev. Thomas Godden, who came to Spanish Town in April, 1819. At first, he was not permitted openly to preach the Gospel; but, having obtained a licence, on the 11th of the following July he preached for the first time from the words, " What think ye of Christ ? "

His congregations were immediately large. The enthusiasm of the people was beyond description. In the early part of the following year a considerable number of persons were baptized, and a church was formed with every token of prosperity. Mr. Godden's labours were, however, soon interrupted by sickness, which was greatly increased by his narrow escape from being burnt in his bed on the night of the fire, and by the early death of his wife. In 1823 he was compelled to return to England, shortly after which he expired at Lawrence Hill, near Bristol, " faithful unto death."

Mr. and Mrs. Phillippo were scarcely settled in their wretched habitation, when the difficulties of the work began to make themselves felt. From a very early period, the planters had shown a most determined hostility to the propagation of the Gospel among their slaves. But the first organised effort to stop the work took place in 1802, when a Mr. Taylor, of the parish of Trelawney, by his influence with the House of Assembly, obtained an " Act to prevent preaching by persons not duly qualified by law," which was at once approved by the Lieutenant-Governor, Nugent.* The Act was disallowed by the home authorities, amidst the bitter remonstrances and indigna-

---

* " History of Jamaica," by W. J. Gardner (London : Stock ; 1873),
P. 348

tion of the planters, but not before several Wesleyan ministers had been silenced. Other similar attempts to repress the Word of God followed, in the teeth of the strongly expressed orders of the English Government to the Governors of Jamaica to veto all such measures. But in 1823 this hostility assumed a form of more than usual virulence. It sprang out of the action taken by Mr. Thomas Fowell Buxton in the House of Commons. In March of that year that eminent man brought forward a resolution declaring that slavery was repugnant to the principles of the British Constitution and of the Christian religion, and that it ought to be gradually abolished throughout the British dominions. It was not adopted, but a resolution of a similar, though less comprehensive, kind was carried by Mr. Canning and commended by him to the consideration of the colonial legislature.

"This mild recommendation was received," says Mr. Phillippo, " with indignation, and finally rejected with contempt and scorn. Ebullitions of feeling against the missionaries of different denominations, but against the Baptist missionaries in particular, were now more violent than ever. They were denounced by the white portion of the populace, by the press, and by the colonial legislature as being in league with the Anti-Slavery Society, by whom the Government was instigated to effect their ruin. They were frequently cited before Committees of the House of Assembly for the most coutemptible of purposes, harassed with warrants for not serving in the militia, circumscribed and impeded by oppressive laws, and treated with all the indignity and virulence which prejudice and mortified tyranny could dictate."

It was in this state of affairs that Mr. Phillippo presented himself to the authorities to ask permission to preach. He laid before them at a court of quarter sessions his credentials from the Society, the recommendations of his brother missionaries, together with the testimony of an excellent Christian gentleman residing in Spanish Town, Major Anderson, of the 91st Regiment. Two of the three magistrates present angrily objected to grant the licence, on the frivolous ground that the signatures on the paper were not accompanied by the seals of the signatories. Notwithstanding the remonstrances of the Chairman, who was the Custos of the parish, the licence was peremptorily refused. To return home to England, baffled in his object, Mr. Phillippo was resolved not to do, even though, as he told the magistrates, he were made to wait seven years for their permission.* The scandalous conduct of the majority of the bench was reflected in the insulting language and demeanour of the attendants in the court.

Four or five months necessarily elapsed, in those days of sailing vessels, before another certificate, having the names and seals of the leading ministers of the denomination, was received from England. It was immediately taken to the Custos, who at once pronounced it satisfactory, and gave Mr. Phillippo leave to preach till the next sessions

---

* It may be well to preserve the following characteristic account of this incident, taken from a colonial paper, under date of July 10, 1824 :—

"At a court of quarter sessions, held in this town on Tuesday, an application was made by the Rev. James Phillippo, a Baptist missionary, for leave to preach in this parish, but the documents he produced, being without a known seal or signature, were considered unsatisfactory, and leave was refused. He was informed that, in the present perilous state of these colonies, it became the duty of the magistrates to be extremely cautious in granting such permissions ; more especially as many of the sectaries in the mother country had declared their avowed intention of effecting our ruin, and had united in becoming publicly and clamorously the justifiers of such a man as Smith, whose seditious practices in Demerara had been proved by the clearest evidence. The papers now produced had several signatures, all, no doubt, sectaries, and, in all probability, ranking among the number of our enemies. Such questionable recommendations could not be

were held. The congregations were large, the people
animated with hope, and the prospects cheering. They
were, however, doomed to disappointment.   Amid the
insults of the clerk of the peace, and the supercilious
sneers of a crowded auditory, Mr. Phillippo presented his
new credentials to the court.   But the document was again
contemptuously rejected.   It was declared to be nothing
better than waste paper, being without the sanction and
seal of the Lord Mayor of London! If the result gave
pleasure to those connected with the planting interest,
the coloured and black people were smitten with grief.
Many wept aloud.   Prayer-meetings and religious services
were set up and multiplied in private houses, until more
months elapsed and the required affidavits were procured.
Meanwhile, further annoyances were in store for the
missionary.   Though seriously ill, he was suddenly
arrested by two young officers of the militia, on a
summons that he had not, according to law, enrolled
himself in the militia.   The president of the court would
not listen to the plea that he was a minister of the Gospel.
He was enrolled and dismissed amid the jeers of the officers
present.   Three months' leave of absence was granted

attended to, nor any but such as came supported by authorised seals
and well-known signatures. We sincerely hope this example will be
followed throughout the island, for there never was a time when more
caution was required from the magistrates. The fears we have for
some time laboured under, from the efforts of the saints and sectaries
in England, seconded by many of our mistaken friends, have induced
us to be much too easy in permitting preachers and teachers of all
descriptions to be introduced among us, greatly to the injury of the
slaves; and it would, perhaps, be a very useful inquiry, in every
parish, to ascertain the reduction in comforts they have experienced by
the fasts imposed upon them, and the moneys they are obliged to
contribute, out of their slender means, towards the support of their
teachers. This is a consideration which, in the end, may prove, perhaps, of as much importance to the welfare of the island as the
suppression even of seditious practices."

him ; but, as the term expired before the arrival of the Lord Mayor's seal, he was again summoned. On this occasion, the marshal of the regiment came to the Lord's-day morning service, and, flourishing the warrant* in the preacher's face, demanded his immediate surrender, or the payment of the fine. The attitude of the congregation seems to have cowed this boisterous and insulting agent of the law, and he retired, threatening the next day either to carry Mr. Phillippo to gaol, or to levy the fine on his goods. Two attempts were made to free Mr. Phillippo from militia duty, and a protection order was at length obtained from the Governor, the Duke of Manchester; but it was not till the court which sat on the 7th January, 1825, when his credentials, attested by Lord Mayor Waithman's signature and seal, were presented, that the licence, which could no longer be refused, was duly granted, to the extreme vexation of his antagonists. " How," says Mr. Phillippo, " shall I describe the scene which followed ! Crowds pressed onward along the streets towards the mission premises, and I was received by the multitude with clamorous congratulations and unbounded expressions of joy. The whole of the morning had been spent

---

* It may be interesting to preserve this curious document. It runs thus :—

" Jamaica. St. Catharine.

" You are hereby authorised to require and levy on the goods and chattels of James Phillippo, private of the Light Infantry Company, the sum of 20s., being due for absence at a muster on the 11th of December, being for the said offence, and for default of goods and chattels whereon a levy can be made, to take his body to the common gaol, there to remain, without bail or mainprize, for the space of twenty-four hours, agreeable to the militia law now in force.

" Given under my hand and seal, this 11th day of December, in the year of our Lord, One thousand eight hundred and twenty-four.

" To Mr. D. Fonseca,   " J. G. JACKSON, Col.
" St. Cath. Regt."

by the church in fasting and prayer, and the day was closed with thanksgiving and praise. On the following Sabbath I commenced my stated labours, after a delay of upwards of twelve months, with audiences that crowded the chapel and the premises around."

The weary months of waiting had not been wasted. Mr. Phillippo had begun the preparations for a new chapel. He had also announced his intention of opening a school, and in the course of a few days after his advertisement appeared he received numerous applications for admission, among which were twenty from Jewish parents, Jews forming a numerous and influential portion of the Jamaica community. A Sabbath-school and a Bible-class were formed. He had also visited the neighbouring towns, preaching wherever the prohibition was either not known 'or not regarded. Nor was he without the discipline of sorrow, arising from the illness of himself and his dear wife, and the trial which befell them in the death of their eldest child. Nevertheless, amidst every discouragement and trial, his faith failed not. He felt that he was " in the Lord's hand, to live or to die as might be His will."

CHAPTER VII.

WITH the opening of the year 1825, Mr. Phillippo was able to devote himself, without fear of any further claim upon him for military duty, to the great object of his life. A despatch from the Colonial Secretary, Earl Bathurst, was received, giving instructions that not only Mr. Phillippo, but all ministers of religion, and all schoolmasters sent out by Christian societies at home, should be held free from militia service and from attendance on juries throughout the colonies. Not that Mr. Phillippo was entirely free from molestation or from many petty annoyances within the reach of the enemies of the Gospel. One day he was informed that the rector of the parish had made an affidavit before the magistrates that he had interfered with his rights and duties as chaplain of the gaol, by visiting a poor man under sentence of death, although it was done at the convict's own request. The excitement of this incident had hardly subsided before Mr. Phillippo was brought before the bench of magistrates for harbouring persons (that is, slaves) on the mission premises before six o'clock in the morning and after sunset in the evening. The occasion was a public baptism on the premises. Soon after he was cited again on a similar charge of baptizing in the river Rio Cobre. Indeed scarcely a month passed without a summons to meet some frivolous complaint of violating law or order.

Towards the close of the year the hostility of the so-called " aristocracy of Jamaica " culminated in the passing of a new slave law by the House of Assembly. It was styled in the original motion : "An Ordinance to prevent the profanation of religious rites, and of false worshipping of God, under pretence of preaching and teaching by illiterate and ill-disposed persons, and the mischief consequent thereupon." It was, in fact, a revival of an old law first enacted in 1816.

"The object of one section," writes Mr. Phillippo, " was said to be to show to the religious, or ' Religio-Politico Missionaries,' that the magistrates had not only power to prevent their prostituting Christianity for the purposes of sedition, and to forewarn their audiences of the serious evils that contumacy and resistance bring upon them, but to prevent the slaves from contributing their own money and other means for religious objects, and the missionaries from receiving it from them under a heavy penalty."

On the motion of Mr. Buxton in the House of Commons this law was vetoed by Mr. Canning, who was then Prime Minister. This exercise of Royal authority was met by the planting interest with an outbreak of wrath and bitterness, and an attempt to pass yet more cruel and oppressive enactments. It was Mr. Canning's wish to give the owners of slaves time to prepare for the inevitable period of emancipation. But, in a violent address of the Assembly to the King, they declared that " it was a false assumption that the slaves were either ill-treated or unhappy. They recapitulated their own sufferings, as planters, in consequence of English wars and war duties ; said they had never taken an oath of allegiance to the English Parliament, and would not submit to the degradation of having their internal affairs regulated by a body whose power in Great Britain was not greater than their own in Jamaica." *   Such lofty language and undisguised threats of rebellion we shall find recurring again and again during the struggle for the destruction of slavery, which had now earnestly begun.

The difficulties of his position did not, however, deter Mr. Phillippo from prosecuting with untiring energy his plans for the erection of a chapel suitable to the wants of the station ; and truly it was greatly needed. " The Word of God was not bound." Crowded audiences wherever he preached evinced the intense desire of the slaves for the knowledge of the consoling truths of the Gospel. On the 6th of November, he writes to his mother-in-law :—" My congregation increases astonishingly. Last Sabbath evening there were more hearers outside than within. The school also prospers beyond my most sanguine expectations. The present number of scholars is 150, forty of whom are children of Jewish parents, and it is not a little surprising that almost all voluntarily attend the Sunday-school, which is now very large and prosperous, and practically superintended by my dear wife. ' Oh, for a heart to praise my God!' My dear wife is at present in good health. We are not only both of us happy in our work, but also in ourselves."

In urging on the Secretary of the Society that he should receive some aid from home towards the erection of the large structure he required to accommodate his growing congregation, he says :—" I conscientiously declare that I never ascend the pulpit but at the risk of my life. I am in a tropical climate, a small place of worship, the pulpit only two feet from the floor, and my head nearly touching the ceiling, a congregation literally packed together, some standing on the pulpit stairs even to the top ; the rays of the sun piercing through the shattered roof, not a breath

* Gardner s History, p. 259.

of air stirring, every avenue to its admission stopped up by the crowds—all this, from which you must be convinced that the heat must be almost insupportable and the disadvantages in other respects incalculable. I assure you I feel it to be so. On going into my chamber after having exerted myself to make all the people hear, I have felt myself so enfeebled by excessive perspiration that I have been hardly able to stand. For two or three days afterwards I have felt the effects. I am sure if the Committee knew all the circumstances, they would never let it be said that the cause at Spanish Town droops, and that Mr. Phillippo is dead, for the sake of a few hundred pounds."

If further reasons were required, they might be found in the constantly increasing number of the members of the church. On Mr. Phillippo's arrival the church consisted of about two hundred and fifty persons, all black people, with the exception of three or four white and brown persons. In the course of the year 1825, he added many more. Thus, on the 1st of May, he records the baptism of sixty candidates,* besides some forty others in an earlier month.

The appeal was not in vain. Considerable sums were received from England; and he tells us, "I was much engaged in collecting funds for the erection of the new chapel. In addition to monthly contributions by the people, I obtained, by personal application to the most respectable inhabitants of the town, upwards of £490 currency, several of them my former opponents."† It is

---

* One of the persons baptized was a well-proportioned, intelligent black man, perfectly blind, who, with all his companions on the slave ship, had been cruelly deprived of sight to prevent their rising in mutiny, on the appearance of some symptoms of resistance during the passage.

† Mr. Phillippo notes that £10 14s. 4d. currency was given by an old Court House antagonist.

gratifying to see that at this early period of his missionary career the Christian, courteous demeanour and strict integrity of Mr. Phillippo had won general respect and esteem, even from many of his adversaries. He soon obtained sufficient means to justify him in proceeding to build, and the memorial-stone of the new chapel was laid on the 13th of November. "Very interesting and impressive services," he says, " were conducted on the occasion by brethren Coultart and Tinson, and listened to with great apparent attention and interest by the very large assemblage on the occasion." The building was planned of large dimensions, of red brick, and estimated to cost £5,400 currency, exclusive of furniture and the enclosure of the premises by a wall and railing. Slaves, under his daily superintendence, were almost entirely employed in its erection, giving the time they could spare from the cultivation of their own provision grounds.

From the commencement of his work in Jamaica, Mr. Phillippo had been impressed with the importance of education as an invaluable instrument in the elevation of the people, and as necessary to prepare them for freedom. He therefore lost no time in laying the foundation of an institution which later on became a very prominent branch of his labours. Some years afterwards he thus records its commencement :—" On or about the 5th of May I established a private school and a Lancastrian school. The one for the education of scholars in the higher departments of elementary knowledge, classical and literary, admitted on regular terms (of payment), which was conducted by myself. The other for the gratuitous instruction of children of the poorer classes, slave and free. On the first public advertisement of my purpose, and for months—I may say years—the press poured out torrents of abuse from day to day, attributing to me the basest motives, and as acting under the influence of a pseudo-philanthropic crew who sought the aggrandisement of themselves by destroying the institutions of the country and jeopardising the lives of the colonists. Some of the most influential inhabitants of the town actually called to remonstrate with me, saying I was about to revolutionise the country by attempting to put the slaves on an equality with white men, rendering them discontented with their condition." One gentleman of high position, finding remonstrances with the husband inefficacious, actually visited Mrs. Phillippo to urge her to stop him in the dangerous course he had resolved to pursue. The school was opened under the charge of a young man whose salary, as well as the cost of the necessary furniture of the school-room, was provided from the receipts of the high school. After a few months the health of the teacher broke down, and for some time both schools were conducted by Mr. Phillippo on the ground floor of his dwelling. This amalgamation of white, coloured, and black, slave and free, in one school gave great offence to the parents of the better classes, and that part of his project failed till he was able to re-establish the institution afresh, with the assistance rendered by the Missionary Committee and the Society of Friends.

The molestation to which Mr. Phillippo had been exposed in Spanish Town did not extend to his efforts to introduce the Gospel into Passage Fort and Old Harbour, villages on the coast, about six miles from the capital. The scenery around Passage Fort is peculiarly lovely. "The sea or harbour," says Mr. Phillippo, "is nearly surrounded with long reaches of land glittering as with emeralds in the golden sun, waving trees and shrubs dropping their branches into the water. The smooth sands of the beach are covered with shells, sparkling with all the hues of the prism. Birds of beautiful plumage skim over the surface of the silver sea, and glance in and out from groves laden with fruits and flowers. The harbour, landlocked by these flowery labyrinths, retains its tranquillity even during the tempests of the summer months. Across the harbour may be seen the town of Kingston and the embrasures of Fort Augustus, and, beyond, the magnificent Blue Mountains, well defined on the clear blue sky." Here Mr. Phillippo had the happiness of baptizing into Christ many converts during his long ministry, and at Old Harbour of directing the building of a large chapel for the use of the increasing numbers that flocked to the services from the country round.* It was accomplished by the loving toil of slaves anxious to provide themselves with a house for the worship of God, working during the bright moonlight nights after their day's tasks were done. Mr. Phillippo's visits to these stations were chiefly made in the evenings of the week.

The last part of the year 1825, with the early months of the following one, was a time of pleasant and encouraging labour in Spanish Town. His enemies were made to be at peace with him. Writing to the Committee under date of September 19, he says :—" All hostility has ceased, and persecution hides its head. My congregation continues overflowing. Nor am I without witnesses of the power and efficacy of sovereign grace. Many, I hope, are earnestly imploring mercy through the blood of Christ. If I recollect rightly, about fifty more are candidates for baptism. One is an elderly lady of colour, in circumstances

---

* At a baptism of thirty-six persons at Old Harbour in the middle of the year, Mr. Phillippo notes particularly the benefit derived by a lame woman at the celebration of the rite. She "went down" into the water on her crutches, which she laid aside at the moment of her immersion. She did not need to resume them on rising from the water, and from that moment recovered the complete and healthy use of her limbs. "She gave," says Mr. Phillippo, "evidence of unusual faith and devotedness to the period of her death, several years after."

of affluence. A little time ago, she was proud and scornful; but now, O delightful spectacle! she is sitting at the feet of Jesus, clothed, and in her right mind. Believe me, with travelling and preaching, the school, the chapel, the church, and a variety of other engagements, I sometimes feel nearly exhausted. Hitherto, however, 'the Lord hath helped me,' and, I hope, 'stood by and strengthened me.' I do not shrink from labour; I trust that I feel an increasing desire to 'work while it is called to-day;' but my kind friends, who have had greater experience of the influence of the climate than I, are constantly telling me that I am doing what is impossible for any man in Jamaica to do long."

Five months later he writes:—

" My school increases beyond my most sanguine expectations. I have now 140 children, thirty of whom are children of Jewish parents who read the New Testament daily. One, of about thirteen or fourteen years of age, is the son of the Rabbi of this town. Several of the number, from the inferior circumstances of their parents, I have taken into the school gratuitously. About thirty of my scholars are advanced considerably beyond the limits of the system in arithmetic; some are in mensuration and fractions. Many learn Latin, Hebrew, geography, and grammar. You know my other duties; and when I inform you that for three months past I have had no one to assist me, and the school to organise, that I am obliged to superintend the building of the chapel and exert myself for subscriptions towards it, I am confident that you will be convinced that I not only require assistance, but will forward it to me as expeditiously as possible. Nor is the prosperity of my school establishment my only encouragement. God has graciously condescended to smile on my ministerial exertions. Since my arrival here, I think no one has had greater reason for gratitude to the

Father of Mercies. Some little time ago, I had the happiness of adding to the church about sixty individuals whose conduct hitherto appears to be 'such as becometh the Gospel of Christ.'"

The assistance for which Mr. Phillippo so earnestly longed reached him on the 7th of June, when Mr. Edward Baylis arrived from England, and at once undertook the management of the school. He also assisted Mr. Phillippo in the ministerial work at Spanish Town and Old Harbour until, in the month of April, 1827, he was removed to a new station at Mount Charles, some thirty-six miles distant. But he continued for some time longer to preach at Old Harbour on alternate Sabbaths.

In the first months of 1825, the bad health of Mrs. Phillippo was the source of great sorrow and anxiety to her husband, occasioned by the perfidy of a trusted servant. The premature confinement brought on endangered for many days the life of his beloved partner, while the loss of the child was the cause of deep disappointment. It was the third child in succession that death had torn from their embrace. One brief extract from Mr. Phillippo's diary will sufficiently disclose the feelings with which he regarded this bitter trial :—" I cannot, will not, dare not repine ! O Thou All-wise and ever-blessed God, my Father and my Friend, assist me rather to rejoice for having spared to me the dearest object of my tenderest, fondest, earthly love. Is not this more than I ought to have expected ? Dear brother and sister Knibb were here, and have been witnesses of the sad, sad scene ; I am truly grateful for their sympathising and friendly aid." He also found support in the warm and affectionate words of his people: " Dear minister, don't grieve so much ; don't you often tell us that it is wrong to sorrow as those without hope, and that we must thank God for all things ? God is too good to us poor sinners. What minister do, if God take missus, and left the child ?"

The weakness entailed on Mrs. Phillippo, and also the pressure on the health of the husband, led them to resort to the salubrious mountain air of the district around Spanish Town, where at Red Hill, St. John's, they found a temporary shelter in a hired house. From this residence they were soon driven by the intolerable multitudes of rats which constantly invaded their rooms at night, and even in the day the house was not entirely free from their inroads. Another cottage was obtained at Garden Hill. Here, on his weekly journeys from Spanish Town, Mr. Phillippo was in the habit of preaching every evening to the large numbers of slaves who came together from the estates of the neighbourhood. A station was ultimately formed in the district as the result of his energetic toil. The health of Mrs. Phillippo received, however, no permanent benefit, so that in the month of March, 1827, her husband was constrained, with feelings of deep grief, to send her to her native land. From this visit she derived the greatest benefit, and re-joined her husband early in the following year, refreshed in body and mind, and able to resume her needed duties in the family and school.

CHAPTER VIII.

On the 18th of February, 1827, Mr. Phillippo's labours in the erection of the new chapel were brought to an end, and he had the happiness on this opening day to see its spacious interior crowded with a deeply interested congregation. He speaks in the warmest terms of the spirit which had animated the people. "The interest," he says, writing on the 7th of August preceding, "the people take in the new chapel is astonishing. The steadiness and zeal with which they adhere to their determination of affording all the pecuniary aid in their power, the cheerfulness with which they bring their offerings, and the universal harmony which prevails among them, cannot fail to animate my zeal and warm my heart. Many free persons of colour both in the church and congregation actually submit to the greatest drudgery, solely that they may present the profits thereof as an offering to the house of God." In a long letter to his beloved tutor, Dr. Steadman, he relates at length the particulars of the opening services. A few extracts will be interesting :—

"The chapel is now finished. It is a substantial and peculiarly neat building, estimated to accommodate from twelve to 1,500 hearers. The site it occupies is excellent. The premises form a large square, or nearly so, enclosed with palisades attached to neat brick pillars, and almost surrounded by public roads. On the west side, commanding a view of three roads, stands the school, on the front of which appears in large printed letters, 'The Lancastrian Institution.' Between, and in front of the chapel and the school, there is an area of about a hundred feet, on which are growing in verdure and beauty orange and other ever-blooming, ever-bearing fruit-trees. The chapel was crowded to excess. Upwards of two thousand persons, with those who could not gain admission, were present on the occasion. Numbers came from Port Royal, many from a distance of thirty or forty miles, and multitudes from Kingston. The road, I am told, from the latter place exhibited the day previous every sign of life and motion. Some were in chaises, some in carts, some in wains drawn by oxen, some on horseback, and not a few on foot, bearing in baskets on their heads their better garments for the morrow.''

"On the morning of the day brother Tinson preached a very appropriate sermon from Isa. lv. 10, 11. In the afternoon one no less suitable and edifying was delivered by brother Flood from Ps. cxxii. 1. The hymns were given out, and the devotional services conducted, by brother William Knibb, brother Baylis, and myself. It was indeed an interesting day! The pleasure it was calculated to create in our minds can scarcely be conceived by those who have never beheld the marked attention, the decent appearance, and the motley aspect of a West Indian congregation. The collection amounted to £84 6s. 8d.''

Notwithstanding the liberality of the slaves, and of many well-wishers in the island, and the still larger contributions from England, about £2,000 remained as a debt, which, for some years, caused Mr. Phillippo great anxiety, and rendered necessary, on his part, much personal sacrifice and self-denial.

This work completed, Mr. Phillippo turned his attention to the dilapidated mission-house, which it was necessary to enlarge and re-model.   To effect this his kind friend, the Custos, the chief magistrate of Spanish Town, lent him the sum required, which was repaid in annual instalments of the value of the rent, till the entire debt was extinguished.   By these means, and with severe economy, he was able to make the house all that could be desired for convenience and comfort.

The labours of Mr. Phillippo in the largely increased sphere opened to him by the erection of his chapel, were speedily followed by many marks of the Divine blessing. The administration of the Ordinance of Baptism was especially attractive to the people, and multitudes would assemble to witness the initiation of their fellow-slaves into the Kingdom of the Redeemer.   One such scene at Spanish Town the grateful pastor has pictured for us in a very vivid manner.   He is writing to Dr. Steadman:—

"What will you say when I inform you that a few weeks ago I was called to administer the ordinance in Spanish Town to eighty-nine more?   Surely you will say, 'The time to favour Zion, yea, the set time, is come.' These were baptized in the Rio Cobre, a celebrated river which rises in the interior of the country, and, after dashing through a wilderness of nature, adding perfection to scenery the most romantic and highly diversified, assumes a milder aspect as it washes the eastern boundaries of the town.

"The morning was far from being favourable.   Torrents of rain had fallen during the night, accompanied by such bursts of thunder and flashes of lightning (scarcely conceivable by those who have never been within the tropics) as made me decide on postponing the administration to a future day.   Several times after the hour of midnight I looked anxiously through the window for a star.   Nothing, however, was discoverable but the appalling gloom and wild confusion of a tempest-driven sky—nothing but what forbade the least hope of relieving the anxious minds of the candidates that morning. Under this impression I again laid me down. Scarcely had I done so when I was aroused and told that the candidates, and hundreds of spectators, were waiting at the river-side.

"It was now five o'clock, and the rain was still falling, though more moderately. Brother Flood and myself immediately hastened to the spot, and, after the usual introduction to this solemn rite, I baptized the number mentioned in the presence of a large and respectable assembly, who witnessed the impressive scene with such a degree of interest as to remain in the most peaceful and, apparently, solemn manner, notwithstanding the falling of the rain and the clouds of exhalation which rose around them.

"The place we selected for the purpose was not only convenient, but magnificent and enchanting in a high degree. In looking around me, at the water's edge, to which we descended by a narrow and precipitous avenue, I found myself encircled by an apparently boundless amphitheatre of wood; trees and shrubs of every diversity of form, tint, and perfume met the eye in every direction. A little above us the river divided itself, without any perceptible cause, into two streams, having between them an island (crowned with lofty trees and rank luxuriance), to which the candidates and others passed over on a rude bridge constructed for the occasion. Directly opposite was a plain (over which, during the periodical inundations, the river sweeps with impetuous fury), where the candidates were arranged, and where booths were erected for their accommodation. Many of the spectators stood in two nearly parallel lines on each side the stream, beneath trees of almost impervious foliage, whose branches formed a beautiful arcade, while the hoarse murmur of the opposite stream as it tumbled over its rocky bed, the beautiful scenery all around us, the distant mountains with their sides shrouded in mist, and occasionally illuminated by the lightning that played on their summit in ten thousand brilliant coruscations, the thunder reverberating from peak to peak, added to the screeches and the liquid melody of the birds, as though hailing the appearance of a tranquil sky, could not fail to inspire the mind with a mixture of delight and awe.

"In such large additions to our churches it may be supposed that we rejoice over them with trembling; although, considering the previous habits of the people, and the few advantages we possess of giving many of them private instruction or exhortation, instances of exclusion are less frequent than might be imagined. This may be accounted for partly from the strictness of our discipline, partly from delay in admitting them into the church. I am not aware that there are more than two individuals out of the 172 recently baptized, but who have been probationers, and led a life becoming the Gospel of Christ for the period of two, three, or four years. Some of them, indeed, had made a profession of religion for even seven years, and, as far as I could learn, had conducted themselves, during that time, with the consistency of real disciples of the Redeemer. The account they gave of their conversion to God was not only satisfactory, but in many cases highly interesting, and evidently proved that the ignorance with which their race is charged arises not from stupidity of intellect, but merely from a lack of mental improvement."

The rapid growth of the various missionary churches throughout the island could not but be observed by the slaveholding interest with somewhat like dismay. Writes one of these gentlemen in the *St. Jago Gazette,* just after the opening of the chapel: " In coming through Spanish Town, a few days ago, I viewed with surprise the magnificent Anabaptist chapel which has arisen like an exhalation in a community of very limited extent and very diminished resources. And my astonishment has been increased by hearing that a building is about to be erected for a Methodist chapel on a similar scale of magnificence, whilst the cathedral of the Bishop looks like an old barn, without accommodation for the inhabitants, and not only without ornament or decoration, but without a decent exterior." He therefore urges that every proprietor of slaves should explain to them that after the 1st day of May they can be prosecuted for giving any money, or other aid, to any Dissenting minister or religious teacher. The deluded people, he says, are simply cheated out of their small means, for the support of establishments intended to overawe Church and State.

The Act referred to was passed in the House of Assembly in the previous month of December,* and was

---

* The clause, the 85th, referred to above, runs as follows :— '

And whereas, under pretence of offerings and contributions, large sums of money and other chattels have been extorted by designing men professing to be teachers of religion, practising on the ignorance and superstition of the negroes in this island, to their great loss and impoverishment : *And whereas* an ample provision is already made, by the public and by private persons, for the religious instruction of the slaves : *Be it enacted by the authority aforesaid,* That, from and after the commencement of this Act, it shall not be lawful for any Dissenting minister, religious teacher, or other person whatsoever to demand or receive any money or other chattel whatsoever from any slave or slaves within this island for affording such slave or slaves religious instruction, by way of offering contributions, or under any other pretence whatsoever ; and, if any person or persons shall, contrary to the true intent and meaning of this Act, offend herein, such person or persons shall, upon conviction before any three justices, forfeit and pay the sum of twenty pounds for each offence, to be recovered in a summary manner, by warrant of distress and sale, under the hands and seals of the said justices, one moiety thereof to be paid to the informer, who is hereby declared a competent witness, and the other moiety to the poor of the parish in which such offence shall be committed, and, in default of pay-

ordered to come into operation on the 1st of May, though it should not have received the sanction of the home Government. Its purpose was to break up the religious organisations which in any way derived their support from the slaves. Mr. Phillippo soon found that he was not to be allowed to pursue his ministry of peace unmolested. On the 11th of June he received intelligence that an information had been filed against him in the police-court for breach of the clause which enacted " that no sectarian minister, or other teacher of religion, is to keep open his place of meeting between sunset and sunrise." The charge was that, on the night previous to the baptism recorded above, Mr. Phillippo had held an illegal meeting. Up to this time it had been the custom of the slaves coming from great distances to assemble during the night, as their only opportunity for prayer before the administration of the ordinance at sunrise. To avoid every cause of complaint, Mr. Phillippo on this occasion had arranged for the omission of the customary service ; but many individuals, wearied with their long journey, had sought rest and shelter within the chapel. The police, on visiting the building, found a few negroes occupying the benches. After some inquiries, they left, threatening the people with the workhouse (the place of penal punishment) and the minister with arrest. On reaching the court-house, in obedience to the summons, Mr. Phillippo found a quorum of magistrates awaiting his presence. After the information, the affidavits of the informer, and the clause of the Slave Law under which the action

---

ment, the said justices are hereby empowered and required to commit such offender or offenders to the common gaol for any space of time not exceeding one calendar month.

Another clause provided that " slaves found guilty of preaching and teaching as Anabaptists, or otherwise, without a permission from their owner and the quarter sessions for the parish, shall be punished by whipping, or by imprisonment in the workhouse to hard labour."

was laid had been read, the following examination ensued :—

The Custos: "You see, sir, that the law expressly prohibits all meetings of slaves after dark."

Mr. Phillippo: "Being unaccustomed to appear before gentlemen of your position, and unacquainted as I am with the forms adhered to on such occasions, I take the liberty of requesting you to tell me whether I may be allowed to question the informant."

This was permitted.

Mr. Phillippo (turning to the informant): "Will you, then, allow me, sir, to ask you whether you saw me in the chapel at the hour you entered it?"

Informant: "My affidavit attests the contrary."

Mr. P.: "Did you hear any singing?"

Informant: "No."

Mr. P.: "Was any one teaching, or preaching, or praying?"

Informant: "No."

Mr. P.: "Was there any confusion in the chapel?"

Informant: "None. Some were sitting, others lying, on the benches; but all were peaceable."

Mr. P.: "What might be the number assembled?"

Informant: "I do not know exactly; but sufficient to make it an unlawful assembly."

Mr. P.: "Was it not your duty, sir, if you knew the assembly to be unlawful, to have immediately dispersed it, or, as I lived at such a short distance, to have availed yourself of the offer of a person to go for me?"

His duty, it was stated, was only to lodge an information with the magistrates.

Mr. Phillippo then explained that he had always taught his hearers to be obedient to the law, that he had discountenanced such assemblages at night and discontinued them; that, expecting a large number of persons

to be present at the baptismal service, he had gathered
many together at six o'clock the previous evening, and
strictly forbade anything to be done that could be con-
strued into a breach of the law; and, on receiving promises
of strict obedience, he had left for his residence for the
night.

Magistrate: "But there was a meeting in the chapel,
and as the chapel was under your control you ought to
have seen that the gates were locked, and that there was
no unlawful proceeding."

Mr. P.: "As, sir, I do not keep the keys of the
chapel, and as it is a well-known custom even in England
to open the doors, both of chapels and churches, on the
evening preceding the Sabbath for the purpose of ventila-
tion, I really do not think that I can be accountable for
the act of a few tired persons from the country resting
themselves in such a public place, to be ready for worship
on the ensuing day.   I will, however, do my best to
prevent any unpleasantness of the kind for the future."

Magistrate : "We certainly shall consider you responsible for what is going on in the chapel, Mr. Phillippo,
and you must beware of acting contrary to law. This is
not the first time that meetings have been held in the
chapel at night."

Mr. P.: " Begging your pardon, sir, for contradicting
you, but it is the first time. I am ready to testify on
oath that for two years past not half-a-dozen persons
have been found on the premises after dark."

Magistrate : "You said, sir, that the people in the
chapel on Saturday night did not meet there by your
desire; was it with your knowledge ? "

Mr. P.: "It was not with my knowledge, as I have
already asserted."

Custos: "As the assembly of the people was not with
your knowledge the magistrates have nothing further to

say to you on the subject, but to admonish you to be more obedient to the laws in future."

Some observations followed on the humiliation to which Mr. Phillippo was subjected by appearing in a police-court, when a gentleman present remarked on the impropriety Mr. Phillippo was guilty of in assembling such a vast crowd of people before sunrise to witness the baptismal rite. To this Mr. Phillippo replied that he did not leave his house for the river-side before the sun had risen, and that he surely could not be responsible for the conduct of people who came from all quarters and at their own desire.

Custos: "But you are wrong, sir, in supposing that you are not responsible for the conduct of the people then assembled; for if your chapel attracts such multitudes of people that a mob is apprehended, it will be our duty, as magistrates, to shut the doors."

Mr. P.: "There was no mob, sir, or the least appearance of one."

Custos: "I hope we shall not see you here again, sir, on a similar business. If we do we must enforce the law with the utmost rigour."

CHAPTER IX.

THE SLAVE CODE—1827.

THE opinion of the home Government on the Slave Code, the operation of which is above exemplified, was not known until the 22nd of September. A remarkable despatch from Mr. Huskisson conveyed the Order in Council disallowing the Act. It was a surprise to the ruling classes of the island authoritatively to learn that the Toleration Act was in force in Jamaica, in common with all other parts of his Majesty's dominions; that the Island Legislature could not imprison, at their will, the ministers of religion, who, to use the language of an island print, were "dismally grunting and groaning, because, forsooth, two of their brotherhood have been confined in gaol for defying and contravening the law of this island." The excitement created was intense. The white inhabitants held meetings in every parish to denounce the conduct of the parent Government, and of Mr. Huskisson, the Colonial Secretary, in particular. The speeches were of the most inflammatory character. In their wild oratory the planters threatened to transfer their allegiance to the United States, or even to assert their independence after the manner of their continental neighbours.

Writing to Mr. Dyer on the 30th of November, Mr. Phillippo says :—" Nothing was more unexpected than the disallowance of the slave law ; nothing could have created greater consternation in the House of Assembly.

Meetings respecting Mr. Huskisson's despatch were called in every parish on the island, and I know not what will be done or said to us, it being supposed that we are the authors of their calamities. One minister in Kingston (not of our denomination, I am happy to say) appeared uninvited at a meeting convened for the express purpose of taking into consideration this act of his Majesty's Government, and declared, to the no small satisfaction of the Assembly, that he and his denomination were as much opposed to the said despatch as they were; that they had never collected more than £40 per annum from slaves; and that they never had anything to do with the disallowed laws but to obey them. In consequence of this declaration, a resolution (to be forwarded to Mr. Huskisson) appeared in the public prints stating that the disallowance of the law was opposed by all the 'sectarian' ministers themselves. It affords me the highest happiness to say that this was no sooner discovered by us than we totally disclaimed them as our sentiments, and declared that we considered ourselves laid under the deepest obligations of gratitude to the British Government for having thus struck off our fetters. I believe a storm in consequence is gathering over us; but we fear it not."

The resolution Mr. Phillippo refers to was the fourth of the series passed at the meeting. It stated that the clauses of the disallowed Act which concerned religion were necessary as a means of defence against " the spurious tenets of the sectarians "—and of preserving " the religion which has been handed down to them from their forefathers, and that it has ever been our most anxious desire to promote by every possible means the moral and religious improvement of the slave population," and immediately subjoins, " yet we are convinced, from our own experience, as well as from the testimony of the

sectarian ministers themselves, that the restrictions
contained in our slave law with respect to Dissenters are
indispensable." The reply to this audacious statement
was signed by all the Baptist ministers in the island, and a
like remonstrance was also published by the Wesleyan missionaries. " We are decidedly of opinion," say the former,
" that the restrictions are not indispensable, that they are
not calculated to promote the welfare of the colony, and
that they are strongly opposed to the equitable and
peaceable doctrines of Christianity, to the liberties of
good and loyal subjects, and to the rights of Christians."

The commotion throughout the island was, however,
only as the outskirts of a storm to the tempest of wrath
which burst from the benches of the House of Assembly.
Calumnies of the vilest kind, expressed in the most virulent
language, were heaped on the heads of the " sectarian
ministers."

The leaders of the anti-slavery party in England, Clarkson, Wilberforce, Macaulay, and others, were assailed by
name, from day to day, in the most malignant language.
This violence certainly could find no justification in the
language or tone of the message in which the Lieutenant-
Governor, Sir John Keane, conveyed the Colonial
Secretary's despatch to the House of Assembly. He
said that his Majesty fully appreciated the valuable improvements contained in portions of the new Slave Code,
and he was convinced that the House would give the
measure a temperate re-consideration. He trusted that
the House would endeavour to avoid, in any new Bill,
those provisions which would act " as a restraint on the
religious liberties to which all his Majesty's subjects,
whatever may be their civil condition, are alike entitled."
He called attention to the calm and measured language
in which Mr. Huskisson had stated that the restrictions
on religious instruction were an invasion of that toleration

which is due to all his Majesty's subjects, that the prohibition of religious meetings between sunset and sunrise would operate as a total denial of the privilege of common worship, and would be felt with peculiar severity by domestic slaves. The despatch further commented on the invidious distinctions established among the various denominations in the island, and objected to the penalties imposed upon persons collecting contributions for religious purposes among the slaves. Such a law was a stigma on the religious teacher, and prevented the slave from obeying a Christian precept. It was finally and distinctly declared to be "the purpose of his Majesty's Government to sanction no colonial law which needlessly infringes on the religious liberty of any class of his Majesty's subjects," and forbade the Governor to assent to any measure containing such restrictions, unless it contained a clause suspending its operation till his Majesty's pleasure could be known.

The reading of the despatch excited the most violent sensation. The House was beside itself with anger, and again and again the most opprobrious language burst forth with respect to it. Nevertheless it was determined to prepare a reply, and a committee was appointed to take it into consideration. It is not possible in any brief compass to epitomise the extraordinary and lengthy document which was adopted by the House of Assembly as an answer to Mr. Huskisson's despatch. It must suffice to cull a few of the more noticeable statements it contains. It was declared to be impossible to discover any sound reason for the course that had been pursued ; his Majesty's Government had lost sight of the fact that the House was legislating, not for free men, but for slaves. Toleration on religious subjects was utterly at variance with the institutions of Jamaica. The preaching and teaching of slaves had been attended with the most pernicious consequences. The "pious motives of the King's

Ministers " are appreciated, but they know nothing of the African character. The slave must not be permitted to injure his health, nor strip himself of clothing, nor barter his tools and food, to support itinerant expounders of the Gospel. The Negro must not be left to be the prey of " the oily and delusive tongue of a self-ordained preacher." Unhallowed men " are known to cajole slaves out of their substance," and even threaten their simple followers with " hell fire and eternal damnation if they are slow and scanty in their contributions." Owners of slaves will never allow a spy to enter their families under the guise of a protector of the slaves ; nor will they allow any public supervision of the punishments it may be necessary to inflict upon them. The use of the whip in the field cannot be abandoned, nor "until Negro women have acquired more of the sense of shame that distinguishes European females" will it be possible to " lay aside punishment by flogging." Masters must continue to retain unchecked the power of imprisoning their slaves and of authorising the gaoler to inflict punishment without trial. This strange document is closed by the statement that they cannot pass a new Bill " without sacrificing their independence and endangering the safety of the island." Only when the Crown withdraws its instruction to the Governor, by which their legislative power is unlawfully limited, will the House of Assembly once more take the Slave Code into their serious consideration.

To obtain proofs of these allegations respecting the practices of the " sectarian preachers," the House of Assembly resolved to summon them from all parts of the island before a committee. The questions put were of the most inquisitorial nature. Mr. Phillippo has preserved a portion of his own examination, and an extract from it will give a fair idea of the puerile as well as inquisitorial character of the inquiry.

"My turn," he says, "at length came, and I was ushered into the presence of these august inquisitors. As the oath to be taken was said to be unconditional, I respectfully declined taking it, assigning as my reason the probability of the evidence being published, and of its involving a disclosure of private affairs. This was resented as a breach of privilege, and I was reminded of the presence of the serjeant-at-arms. I was at length allowed to object to any question not specially relating to the subject under investigation.

"After a few preliminary inquiries as to my name, office, creed, ordination, the difference between Particular and General Baptists, the length of time I had been in the island, &c., I was questioned by the Secretary and others.

"Question: We wish to know how you are supported, whether by your Society in England, or by your congregation here?

"Answer: I have received a regular salary from the Society at home.

"Q.: What may be the amount of your salary per annum?

"A.: I must beg you to excuse my declining to reply to this question for the reason I have already stated

"Q.: Why? The answer would involve nothing that you need care for the world to know.

"A.: Possibly not; but it is not pleasant for everybody to know what one receives and spends.

"Q.: The Wesleyans have been very frank, and have told us that their salaries are proportioned according to circumstances—a single man has so much, and so on in proportion to the number of his children.

"A.: I have before told you that I am a Baptist and not a Wesleyan, and the organisation and practices of these societies differ.

" Q.: Well, sir, do you make any collections among the slaves and others of your congregations ? If so, how often, and to what amount ?

" A.: Yes ; I make collections once a month and oftener, as circumstances may require ; but I cannot tell the amount, as I keep no books.*

" Q.: Who receives these collections ?

" A.: They are usually received by the officers of the church, and are afterwards handed or accounted for to me.

" Q.: You said just now that you received your salary regularly from home.

" A.: I did not say that I received it regularly from home, but that I received a regular salary from home ; that is, I draw for it when I want it, sometimes before and sometimes after it is due.

" Q.: Well, then, what do you appropriate the amount to that you make by collections ?

" A.: I apply it to buying grass for my horse. (Chairman smiling, as I bought the grass from him.)

" Q.: You had better say, perhaps, that you apply it to the incidental expenses of your establishment.

" A.: Yes. Establishment or station, as you please.

" Q.: Be good enough, now, to inform us if you receive any presents or offerings from the slaves and others of your congregation—such as fowls, pigs, goats, provisions, fruits, &c., &c.†

" A.: Presents of fowls, &c. ! I am at a loss to under-

---

* The accounts were kept by the deacons.

† For some time previous to, and during, the inquiry Mr. Phillippo had declined to receive such contributions from his people, because informers had been sent in every direction to discover matter for accusation. The slaves had also been told by their masters that any gifts to their ministers would bring upon them severe punishment.— Letter to Mr. Dyer, December 24th, 1827.

stand the bearing of this question on this investigation. I have before said that the Society to which I belong did not send me out here to be dependent upon the precarious benevolence of a few poor Negro slaves.

"Q.: Shall I say, then, that you do not receive any very great presents. You know there would be nothing wrong in this. It is natural for the people to show their love and gratitude to their minister in this way. I should feel no difficulty in doing so myself if in your situation.

"A.: I do not doubt it.

"Q.: Well, sir, I wait for your reply. You have not answered the question.

"A.: As I do not exactly comprehend the bearing or object of the question, I shall be obliged by your giving it me in writing.

"(I was again called to order.)

"Mr. Capon (one of the Committee), to the President, angrily: 'Really, Mr. Chairman, this person seems to be trifling with us, and we are losing time. The question is plain enough. Ask him if he receives the offerings named from the slaves of his church. Yes or no?' (Haughtily casting a look at the sectarian parson.)

"A.: As you, sir (looking at the questioner), seem so anxious to know if I am in the habit of receiving presents from my congregation, I have no objection to say that I have not received any for some time, except a capon which a good woman brought me the other day.

"(A suppressed titter followed, in which all joined except the questioner himself.)*

"The Secretary, doubtless enjoying the fun, inquired what he should record.

---

* This gentleman had made himself somewhat notorious by the insulting remarks he had, on more than one occasion, addressed to the missionaries and their wives, and by his bitter hostility to missionary work.

"Mr. Capon, looking up to the Chairman, said: 'I should think, sir, that question had better be omitted altogether.'

"Chairman: Yes. You, sir (to Mr. Phillippo, with a smile), are now at liberty to withdraw."

Mr. Phillippo bowed, and withdrew accordingly.

The session of the Assembly closed by the re-enactment of the Slave Law, in all its material features unchanged. But before separating the House of Assembly directed a guard of honour to attend at King's House, and voted a grant of 3,000 guineas for a sword of honour, with the hope that the Lieutenant-Governor would thereby be induced to transmit the Code to the Colonial Office with his recommendation. As may be supposed, Sir John Keane rejected the bribe, and obeyed the instructions he had received by placing his veto on the Bill.

CHAPTER X.

THE busy life of Mr. Phillippo in Spanish Town did not preclude frequent endeavours to diffuse the knowledge of salvation in the neighbouring parishes. For some years Mr. Gibbs, a native Baptist, had preached to a small gathering of people at Jericho, in St. Thomas-in-the-Vale. After his death most of these people joined the congregation in Spanish Town. The chapel in which they met had been destroyed by a planter of the vicinity, but the site, with a large piece of land adjoining, was now offered to Mr. Phillippo. On his first visit he had preached under a tree, on the premises of a Miss Cooper, a free woman of colour, and, finding no better accommodation, he spent the night in her hut. This was represented as being done for seditious purposes, and the rector denounced the missionary at the next meeting of the Vestry as a low, uneducated man, animated by the worst intentions. Even the land could not be surveyed without opposition, and the timber collected for the erection of a new chapel was in open day carted away by the owner of the adjoining estate, and used in the erection of his own house. The Attorney-General was appealed to; but he gave it as his opinion that the cost of seeking redress, and the risk of obtaining it, were too great to be ventured upon. A jury of slave-holders would certainly refuse to convict where the defendant was a slaveholder and the plaintiff a Baptist missionary. A further difficulty sprung up. The owner of the land was a

slave, and by law had no power to give a title to land.
Mr. Phillippo was therefore dispossessed, and compelled
reluctantly to submit to this gross act of injustice.
Coming from the estate, "I was met in the road," says
Mr. Phillippo, "by the noble-looking coloured female
already named, who at that time made no pretension to
religion. She was much excited on hearing the result
of the survey, and exclaimed, ' Minister! have they really
taken away the land? They don't want the Gospel to
come into the parish. But keep heart. Follow me,' and
going on before me with great energy, till we came to a
rising ground beyond her cottage, ' Here,' she said, ' is a
beautiful spot where you can build a chapel, with as much
land as you will want; and let them come and turn you
off if they dare. It is my own freehold.'"

Mr. Phillippo at once accepted the generous gift, and
arranged with the donor to celebrate Divine service on
her premises till suitable accommodation could be provided. Not long after, he had the pleasure of receiving
her into the church, and for many years she sustained,
undismayed by persecution, the character of a genuine
Christian.

About this time, Mr. Phillippo was urged to carry the
Gospel into Vere, which was represented to be in a more
deplorable condition than any other parish, both as to the
ignorance of the people and the depraved and irreligious
character of the overseers and white inhabitants. The
departure, however, of Mr. Baylis for Mount Charles
threw the school again on Mr. Phillippo's care, and he
was compelled to cease from the efforts which he had
begun.

The arrival of Mr. Taylor in the following year enabled
Mr. Phillippo to give Old Harbour into his charge, and to
make better provision for the spiritual need of this large
district. Mr. Taylor had come to Jamaica in connection

with the Church Missionary Society, but, changing his
views, he relinquished that connection, and was baptized
by Mr. Phillippo. It was not without the most persistent
hostility, and much persecution of the poor slaves, that
the Gospel at last obtained a footing in Vere. In the
issue, the labours of Mr. Phillippo and his willing
coadjutor were crowned with large success.

The return of Mrs. Phillippo early in 1828, much
benefited by her voyage home, and the engagement of a
young man of the name of Andrews, whose discharge from
the army Mr. Phillippo purchased, gave a new impetus
to the schools in Spanish Town. The general aspect of
the congregation was also the source of great joy. Writing
to Mr. Dyer on the 5th of May, he says: " Mr. Andrews
affords me valuable assistance in almost everything
connected with the duties of my station. The schools,
both Sabbath and weekly, are in a very thriving condition, the Sabbath-school especially. It contains now
about one hundred and twenty children and twenty
adults. The station in all its departments continues to
wear a very smiling aspect. I might have said, appearances are more pleasing than at any former time. Our
chapel on a Sabbath afternoon is often crowded. The
congregation, being principally composed of young and
interesting persons, really exhibits, on a Lord's-day, a
very pleasing spectacle. But, above all, I have the
most gratifying evidence that I do not 'labour in
vain, nor spend my strength for nought.' On the first
Sabbath in June, I expect to baptize about sixty persons,
many of whom are very interesting characters indeed.
Among them is Mr. Andrews, two more white persons,
and about a dozen respectable individuals of colour. I
have every reason to believe that the sacred leaven is still
operating in the hearts of many of my congregation.
What a cause for zeal and thankfulness ! "

From a letter to a friend in Oxford, later in the year, is extracted the following fuller account of his schools. He was an ardent advocate of education for the Negro, and struggled through many difficulties and much opposition to maintain them in an efficient state.

"There are two schools in connection with this station, a Sabbath and a weekly one. The former has been in operation four years and a-half; the latter since July, 1825. The object of their establishment was to afford moral and religious instruction gratuitously, and on the most liberal principles, to slave children and those of the indigent free, both black and of colour. The Sabbath-school is entirely a gratuitous institution, but, owing to a total destitution of resources, children are admitted into the other on terms suitable to the circumstances of their parents, or corresponding with the benevolence or the pecuniary abilities of their owners. Thus, of the eighty children this school now contains, forty-two are admitted free, about twenty at the small sum of £1 4s. each per annum, and the remainder at the rate of from £2 8s. to £4 16s. per ditto, making the whole receipt per annum, as nearly as can be calculated, deducting for bad debts, about £70 sterling.

"The Sabbath-school contains 201 children and twenty-four efficient teachers. Of the latter, exclusive of the superintendent and patron, five are whites. Both these schools are conducted principally on the Lancasterian plan. It might be said that they were conducted on a plan which embraced the excellences of both the popular systems, as the person to whom their management is more especially entrusted, having previously superintended one in the army on the National plan, considers that by such a union he has improved the discipline of the school, and in some degree facilitated the progress of the scholars.

"Owing to the great proficiency of the children generally, the uniform consistency of the discipline maintained, the excellent qualifications of my assistant, together with my own and Mrs. Phillippo's constant oversight, residing beneath the same roof, these schools are now highly interesting and prosperous. The instruction of negro children is no longer an experiment; their capacity to receive it is proved beyond a doubt. Difficulties, too, have vanished, prejudices are subsiding, and sufficient fruit has been collected to warrant the most sanguine hopes of an approaching rich and abundant harvest."

The expenses attendant on these institutions, and his family requirements, often pressed heavily on his resources. But Mr. Phillippo was ever ready to endure straits, if need be, for the cause on which his heart was set. To a friend he writes, on the 29th of May:—"I can conscientiously declare that every fragment of my incomings, over and above what has been expended for the necessaries and conveniences of life, has been appropriated to the blessed cause to which I have consecrated my life. I was peculiarly struck, soon after entering Bradford Academy, with the singular disinterestedness of its venerated president, Dr. Steadman, in his great Master's cause. I earnestly pray that his example, in this respect as well as in others, may be imitated by me to the latest period of my life. If I know anything of my own heart I feel a greater interest than ever in the prosperity of the Redeemer's Kingdom. The cause here is very near my heart, and my attachment to Spanish Town, the immediate sphere of my labour, is far greater than I should feel for any other under heaven. I earnestly hope that I shall at last be numbered with those who will be accounted faithful."

The pecuniary difficulties of the position were much enhanced by the growing opposition of the planters. In the same letter he says: "The community here is more hostile than ever to our receiving contributions from slaves, and men are positively lying in wait to ascertain whether we do so or not. Our characters are traduced on this account more grossly than ever in the public print."

Nevertheless, the Word of God was not bound. Writing on the 4th of August, Mr. Phillippo says : " My prospects of usefulness are wider and better than at any former period. The field for exertion is extending on the right hand and on the left. Multitudes are anxiously inquiring after the pearl of great price, and multitudes, I trust, have found it. A few Sabbaths ago I baptized sixty-seven individuals on a public profession of their faith in the Lord Jesus. Two of them were whites, twenty were respectable persons of colour, and the rest blacks. I never recollect having spent a happier day. Not fewer, I should imagine, than one thousand six hundred persons witnessed the solemn spectacle, and, with the exception of a little confusion before the gates were thrown open, scarcely a word was uttered during the whole ceremony. Many were in tears. About four hundred and fifty were present at the ordinance of the Lord's Supper—six whites, myself excepted, the rest of every diversity of colour. Our congregation is oftentimes as large as the chapel will admit of, and additions to it are constantly making. In these few last Sabbaths not a seat has been unoccupied ; many, indeed, have been obliged to sit on the window-seats and on the staircases."

Again, in November, he writes :—" Having preached three times yesterday, and occupied two hours in each service, I feel very tired. Had it been otherwise, I should have sent you an account of a baptizing at Old Harbour on the Sabbath before last. I administered that ordinance to ninety-five persons in the presence of, I suppose, a thousand spectators, and then preached out of doors, on a chair, soon after, to a congregation of the same number. On the following morning Mr. Taylor accompanied me to another parish, about sixteen miles from Old Harbour and twenty-seven from Spanish Town, where we have succeeded in forming a new station, not likely to be of any expense to the Society."

Towards the close of the year an incident happened which became the source of much distress to Mr. and Mrs. Phillippo, and of misapprehension of their motives of action. Owing to the legal difficulties in the way of the immediate manumission of a slave,* and the imperfect acquaintance of Mr. Phillippo with the law, his name appeared in the Almanack of the year as the registered proprietor of certain slaves. The circumstances of the case will be clearly understood from the following letter, addressed by Mrs. Phillippo to the Rev. John Dyer, but it gave occasion to the unfounded charge that Mr. Phillippo was a dealer in slaves, and, though a minister of the Gospel, a man who did not scruple to hold in degrading bondage his fellow-men. Even some of his missionary brethren too readily entertained the reproach, and for a little while he lay under suspicions which only his integrity, together with a true knowledge of the facts, ultimately dispelled. Mrs. Phillippo thus explains the affair:—

"To the Rev. John Dyer.

"I must beg you to excuse the liberty I take in addressing you. My object is to endeavour to repel the serious accusation made against my dear husband, as the charge more immediately refers to my own conduct, not

---

* One condition imposed by the law of Jamaica on manumission was that if a slave obtained his freedom by purchase, or by the gift of his master, a security bond must be lodged with the churchwarden of the parish for an annuity of £5, contingent on his ever becoming a pauper. The bond could be given by any free person of any class or colour. —Barclay's "West Indies," p. 274.

to his. He, I can assure you, never had the least to do whatever with the purchase of slaves. The case is simply this. Mr. Coultart had a woman he had hired for some time as a servant, who having proved an excellent and trustworthy woman, her owner gave two of her children their freedom, and I believe had given her also reason to expect her own manumission on the same account. Before that, however, was done the owner died, and the poor woman and her family were immediately for sale. She had a paper given her to find a purchaser by a certain time, which if she did not, herself and family were to be put up at public auction and sold to the highest bidder. The poor creature, from the dread of being separated, perhaps for ever, from her husband, her children, and the ordinances of God's house (for she was a pious woman and a member of Mr. Coultart's church), and being sold to a cruel master or one who would turn her into the field, to which labour she had never been accustomed, was, as may easily be conceived, much distressed ; she implored Mr. Coultart, with tears running down her cheeks, to purchase her, or to get some one of his acquaintance to do it for her. Mr. Coultart was then about leaving the island, and therefore could not do anything himself for her ; but, being no longer able to resist her unremitting and moving importunities, he begged me, if I possibly could, to get some kind person in Spanish Town to purchase her and her family. On hearing the above I felt exceedingly for the poor creature, and began to think if something could not be done. Had I been a person of property I felt as though I would most cheerfully have laid the money down for her ; but I had not the means. At length, after much thought, a plan occurred to me. I felt convinced that it might be done, and in such a way too as to ensure her entire manumission and that of her whole family in a short time. My plan succeeded. The money at which she and her family were valued was kindly advanced by a few members of the church, on the very easy condition that I should pay it them at the rate of three dollars a week until it was entirely paid—a sum which I had been obliged to pay to the owners of the two servants I then had—and then they should be manumitted. Thus you will perceive I have done no more than hire this family, and yet at the same time I have had what I consider the *honour*, and what I really felt to be a gratification, of freeing this whole family and all their posterity from perpetual bondage. For I can assure you that, according to my original purpose, they are, and have been for some time, as Mr. Coultart can testify, duly and properly manumitted. I have had to do with only one more instance of the kind. This was the case of a poor old Negro woman who lived with Mr. Godden two or three years, and who has been our washerwoman from the time of our arrival. As kind and good a creature, I believe, as ever lived, she worked for us for less than half the regular wages, and never would be prevailed on by me to take more, often replying, when I said, 'Rosina, I am afraid you will hurt yourself,' 'Neber mind, missa ; I know you can't afford for pay much, and you gib up all for de good of me poor Negro, and me ought not to mind work a little for de good Word.' She was Mr. Godden's faithful attendant in all his sickness, and I really believe would almost lay down her life for myself and Mr. Phillippo. She has attended us and watched over us with all the solicitude of the fondest and most indulgent parent, and has even wept and rejoiced over us as occasion seemed to dictate. This dear old creature, sixty years of age, who does not stir out of the yard for weeks for fear of being seized and carried to gaol for her master's debts (where, probably, she might have remained until she pined away and died), was at last seized in our yard by the sheriff's officer and cast into that dismal dungeon. I, of course, felt distressed on her account, as I knew her poor worn-out frame could not long endure such confinement; but while I was deliberating on what to do a black man, a member of our church, who, with his wife, had formerly been a slave, but who now is worth considerable property, came and said if I would be answerable for Rosina's appearance on the day of sale—for it was afterwards determined upon that she should be sold—he would go and be bound for her. I was, of course, thankful for such a proposal, and she was accordingly let out of gaol the next day. This good man, moreover, came to me soon after, and said, ' Me know missa no able to buy Rosina, and him be very sorry for him to be sold away; myself will buy him for him own good, if missa will keep part of de money him give Rosina every week for washing till him pay him again, and him manumission papers shall be made out and missa shall have no more trouble.' It was impossible to have rejected such a proposal. This man purchased her the next day for £10 currency. In less than twelve months, in the manner before mentioned, she paid the purchase-money, and has ever since been receiving for herself the whole of her earnings, when before she had to pay ten shillings per week to her master. This, sir, is the utmost I have ever had to do with purchasing of slaves, and surely, as it must appear from this that my sole desire has been to deliver them from bondage, I shall not be charged for a moment as an aider and abettor of slavery.

" I am, my dear Sir,

" Very truly yours,

" H. S. PHILLIPPO."

When the case became known in England several friends in Reading, Kingston, Oxford, and other places remitted money for the redemption of others from slavery, and not a few individuals were rescued from a doom of misery, infamy, and shame.*

The trials and difficulties which beset the missionary's path were not without their spiritual fruit. They led Mr. Phillippo more simply to the Cross of Christ and to the throne of grace; to a deeper knowledge of his own heart, and of the riches of that grace which sustained him. "They have taught me," he says, "many important lessons which I never should have learned in any other school. By them I have been led to see more of my own insufficiency, and have learned my entire dependence upon God." Strengthened in the inner man, Mr. Phillippo continued abundant in labour, reaping a harvest of blessing which he ever ascribed to God, "to whom only the honour and glory are due."

This chapter of busy and successful toil may fittingly be closed by an extract from a letter to his mother, in which he briefly describes the routine of his daily life. "Our days," he says, "are never too long. On the contrary, I never recollect going to rest without regretting and sometimes feeling angry with myself that the day has not been more devoted to the great purpose of my life. I rise every morning at five o'clock, spend an hour in my study, pass another hour in my garden, or walking about to inhale the freshness of the morning air. I then return to my study, and remain there till eight. Breakfast; conduct family worship, including any persons who may happen to be on the premises. We afterwards go down

---

* In a note dated 1875 Mr. Phillippo adds that the five or six young women redeemed were afterwards respectably married, and, with one exception, became members of the Church of Christ. Three or four became the wives of schoolmasters. One opened a private school, and her son is a solicitor in good practice in Jamaica. Her daughter is the wife of a native clergyman. The families of the rest are numerous, and are much respected.

into the school, which is on the floor beneath us, and which we superintend, and there remain until other engagements require attention. At two o'clock, when at home, I again visit the school, and remain till it is over for the day, concluding it as it was begun, with singing and prayer.

"About half-past four we dine, then get ready for chapel, class-meetings, singing-classes, leaders' meetings, evening adult school, or meetings of some kind or another in town or country every day in the week. They usually commence at six o'clock and continue for an hour and a half. We then take tea, have family prayers, and at nine or half-past retire for the night.

"This is the regular routine, interrupted, of course, on the week days by services in the country, at Old Harbour, thirteen miles distant, and elsewhere, by visits to the sick ; by monthly intercourse with members and inquirers, by experience meetings and church-meetings, by settlement of disputes, and by marriages and burials, &c."

This is truly a scene of active and arduous work, and a key to that large amount of blessing it pleased God to grant to His servant during the early years of his missionary career.

CHAPTER XI.

PERSECUTION—VOYAGE TO THE UNITED STATES—
1828 TO 1829.

THE labours of Mr. Phillippo and his brethren were perpetually in danger of destruction from the besotted folly of the planters. Just as the year 1828 was about to close the Sectarian Committee presented its report to the House of Assembly. It was adopted with only one dissentient. It professed to be founded on evidence furnished by men of various positions in life, among whom were members of the missionary societies. The island was ransacked for the calumnies and slanders that passed from mouth to mouth, among them that one of the missionaries (understood to be Mr. Phillippo) had baptized seventy-five persons in the Rio Cobre, "bare as Nature made them."* The character of some of the witnesses may be judged of by the fact that one witness was brought before the committee by a constable, being in custody on a charge of assault and robbery. A local newspaper even ventured to say "that subornation the most gross must have been resorted to in procuring the

---

*The following is a mild specimen of the abuse lavished on the missionaries by the island press :—" Among the absurd, preposterous, unjustifiable, and irreligious regulations which they have irreverently adopted as the text of their creed is the prohibition of indulgence in dancing, and other innocent amusements of a similar kind; and in doing so they belie their Saviour and imitate the devil himself."

evidence, unsubstantial as it is." The presumed facts
thus ascertained were said to justify the following statements of the report:—"That the principal object of the
sectarians is to extort money from their congregations
by every possible pretext, and by the most indecent
expedients; that they inculcate the doctrines of equality
and the rights of men, and preach and teach sedition
even from the pulpit; that they occasion abject poverty,
loss of comfort, and discontent among the slaves fre-
quenting their chapels, and deterioration of property to
their masters; and such is their outrageous thirst for
gain that they recommend females to prostitute themselves to get money to swell their contributions!" These
monstrous charges were immediately repelled by the
missionaries; but the report was printed in large numbers and sent to England for wide distribution, with the
hope of inducing the Colonial Secretary to pass the
re-enacted Slave Law. Writing to Mr. Dyer on the 5th of
January, 1829, Mr. Phillippo says:—" I do trust that no
exertion will be spared by the friends of missions to
defeat the diabolical purposes of our adversaries and of
the enemies of God. If these men gain their point we
might as well leave the island at once. It may materially
affect the missions of every denomination in every part of
the world. Every denomination should unite in an in-
flexible determination to frustrate such unholy, unjust,
disgraceful, and destructive purposes. Never, perhaps,
has there been such an important crisis as the present in
the annals of missions." Happily, the agent of the colony
at once saw that the circulation of this vile document
in England would infinitely damage the planters' cause.
It was, therefore, prudently withheld from the public
eye, while in the island itself it found many strenuous
opponents. The persecuting clauses of the Slave Law
were withdrawn, but the Secretary of State retained many

others which were used to harass the missionaries and hinder their work.

In Vere Mr. Phillippo had to complain of the persecution of the slaves for holding class-meetings on some of the numerous estates of the parish. The oppression was, perhaps, more grievous than in any other part of the island. The old white man whose house Mr. Phillippo had hired was ousted from his holding by the rector and magistrates, treated with indignity, and threatened with the enmity of the neighbouring planters. On one estate a Negro slave was flogged to death for conducting a prayer-meeting in the class-house, and another was severely punished for the like crime. It was with great difficulty that Mr. Phillippo obtained a licence for the preaching-place. Similar hostility had also to be encountered in the parish of St. Thomas-in-the-Vale.

A few of the more moderate among the planters felt, however, that it was necessary, in some degree, to meet the demands of the English Government for an amelioration in the condition of the slaves. A meeting to consider the matter was called at the Half-way Tree House, at which, says Mr. Phillippo, the following resolution, wholly at variance with the representations of the House of Assembly, was passed :—" That this meeting, observing a progressive improvement in the moral and religious condition of the slave population of this island, is of opinion that they are in a state sufficiently advanced to be permitted to enjoy the civil rights and immunities intended for their benefit by the new Slave Law." But no good came of such resolutions, and the tale of woe continued unchecked. The promoters of the movement did not even attain what was their true object—that of blinding the eyes of the people and Government of England to the real condition of their bondsmen, or to the fallacious nature of the relief, said to be the intention of the enactment, which for so long a time had been in controversy with the home Government.

Multiplied and laborious duties, added to the perpetual anxieties occasioned by the course taken by the planters, at length painfully affected Mr. Phillippo's health. Rest and a resort to a cooler climate for a time became absolutely necessary, and were only delayed until he could safely leave Mrs. Phillippo, after the birth of their eldest daughter, Hannah, which took place on the 5th of April. On the 24th of July Mr. Phillippo set sail from Port Royal, with two very disagreeable passengers as companions. He soon found that the crew of the vessel consisted of a most disreputable lot of men. Even before leaving the harbour his store of provisions was pillaged. The voyage was one scene of disaster to its close. Two of the sailors were concealed pirates, and nearly succeeded in carrying the vessel to the Isle of Pines, the well-known rendezvous of sea brigands. The captain, being possessed of little nautical knowledge, blunderingly sailed into the Gulf of Mexico instead of the Gulf of Florida. The reckoning was lost, and they lay becalmed for ten days, exhausting their provisions and exposed to the fierce rays of a tropical sun. Slowly drifting with the current they came in sight of Havana, and entered the harbour with their flag half-mast high, in distress for water and food. The Cuban authorities treated them as spies upon the expedition of General Santa Anna, just then about to sail for the Spanish main. By a judicious use of money, Mr. Phillippo and one of his fellow-passengers were permitted to land, and to purchase the provisions of which they stood in such great need. But when on shore they were not safe. Passing along a street, they were arrested, as strangers who had violated the law by traversing the city without a passport. After an angry interview the Alcalde allowed them to return on board their vessel. The captain of a Portuguese brig in the harbour next entreated Mr. Phillippo, hearing that he was an English clergyman, to go aboard his ship to console his fever-stricken crew. It was a frightful sight. The sick and dying men lay in a semicircle round the bulwarks with parched and bleeding lips. Their faces were bloated and yellow with disease. " I gave out a verse or two of a hymn," says Mr. Phillippo, " and sang them to the tune of the Old Hundredth, in which some from early recollection tried to join. I then prayed amidst the sobs and hearty amens of all, and spoke to them of ' The Lamb of God which taketh away the sins of the world.' Their eyes were fixed upon me, many were in tears, some sobbed aloud, and the captain at my side wept like a child. It was a solemn moment. All seemed to feel that the hand of death was upon them, and that they were going unprepared before the tribunal of the great Judge of all. The short service over, I stepped into the boat, some raising themselves up and looking over the bulwarks, and invoking blessings on my head."

After another arrest, another visit to the guardship, and to the officer of the port, the vessel was allowed to depart, only to encounter a tremendous hurricane, which lasted for two or three days and nights. The captain and mate were incapable, and, until lights from the shore were discovered, Mr. Phillippo, at the request of his companions, assumed charge of the navigation of the ship. Several days more of anxious watching followed, when on the fiftieth day of their voyage they arrived at Staten Island, to find that, owing to the delays that had been experienced, the ship's owners had given her up for lost, and had obtained the insurance money, and were now highly incensed with the captain for having brought her into port. After a short quarantine, from which he escaped with the assistance of General van Buren, Mr. Phillippo paid brief visits to Philadelphia, New York, Boston, New Providence,

and other places, receiving a hearty welcome from various
ministers of his own denomination, among whom he
briefly mentions the names of Drs. Brantley and Day,
Cone and Maclay, Wayland and Sharp. He was everywhere received with much Christian kindness. His
health rapidly improved, notwithstanding the privations
and dangers through which he had passed. The return
voyage, by way of St. Thomas, though sufficiently trying
and anxious, was not marked by any striking incidents.
As a minister of the Gospel, he was enabled to lead a
fellow-passenger, dying with consumption, to the Saviour's
feet, and to place some check on the unbridled tongues of
the crew. He reached Spanish Town in safety on the
23rd of September, finding his family well. Soon after
his return, he had the happiness of baptizing 129 persons.
Most of them had been accepted as candidates for church-
fellowship before he left for the United States. Many
more, he was happy to find, were seeking " to enter the
gates of Zion," and were ready " to declare what the
Lord had done for their souls."

CHAPTER XII.

SUCCESSFUL LABOUR—ILLNESS—DEPARTURE FROM JAMAICA—1830 TO 1831.

IT will be unnecessary to give in detail an account of the prosperous condition of the stations under Mr. Phillippo's immediate direction during the eighteen months that followed his brief visit to the United States. He has, however, preserved a letter addressed to the Rev. Isaac Mann, of Maze Pond, London, in which he more particularly describes the feelings with which he carried on his manifold and arduous labours. The correspondence sprang out of an arrangement made by the Committee of the Society, by which the missionaries would be brought into more intimate relations with its members. They were invited to confide, more fully than in official letters is usually done, the anxieties, the spiritual experiences, and the trials through which a missionary must make his way. The sympathy thus begotten would, it was conceived, bear fruit in a fuller appreciation of the missionary's difficulties, and in a more prayerful and strenuous interest in his labours. The revelation to a tried servant of God of the heart's emotions would meet with a fraternal and loving response, and the missionary be girded to endure hardness as a good soldier of Jesus Christ.

It was in answer to a letter from Mr. Mann—the first of the series—that Mr. Phillippo wrote on the 19th of April, 1830, portions of which may be given. He first speaks of the prejudicial effect of the climate on his health. "Gibbon was not far from the truth when he styled this land the grave of Europeans. On this side, and on that, it may emphatically be said, mankind fall off like leaves in autumn. The most healthy and vigorous of mankind are cut down at a stroke. Nor are the signals of Death's approach to be detected at a distance. That, indeed, is the interval between the arrest and the execution of his commission. A raging fever touches the brain, or some other prevalent disease seizes the springs of life, and no physician's skill can administer either antidote or cure. Such circumstances have never failed to remind me forcibly of my own mortality; nor have they failed in some measure, I trust, to exert a beneficial influence on my engagements as a minister of Christ. But I never felt myself so much of a sojourner in the world as now. I literally view myself as standing amidst a shower of shot and shell and heaps of slain, every moment liable to receive the mortal wound, and appear before my Judge. I never felt so much before the necessity of personal piety; of diligence, as a student of the records of eternal life; of cultivating the temper and disposition of the Saviour; of working while it is day; and of setting my house in order."

"I think I have already replied to some parts of your very kind letter, and have expressed my gratitude to you for selecting me for your quarterly correspondent. I have wanted an experienced friend at home. There have been moments when I have greatly needed disinterested counsel, encouragement, and sympathy; but, above all, I have wanted excitement to personal piety, as it is that, I conceive, upon which our conduct, character, and usefulness as ministers of Christ so materially depend.

"If I have had no particular causes for joy, I have had, I can truly say, no occasion for sorrow. My bread has been given me, and my water has been sure. I have as tranquil and happy a home as is to be found anywhere in this world of vicissitude. As to spiritual things, 'I know whom I have believed.' The atoning blood and perfect righteousness of the Redeemer are the foundation on which I build all my hopes for eternity, and the source from which I draw all my consolation. Often as I have had reason to mourn over the decay of the graces of religion, both in myself and in others, and numerous and powerful as have been the temptations that have assailed me, yet I have reason to bless God that my faith in Christ, as the only, yet all-sufficient, Saviour of sinners, has never been shaken. Not even in my darkest moments do I remember that I have ever questioned the evidences of my individual interest in the merits of His blood. Though I feel myself more than ever the subject of countless frailties and imperfections—a sinful worm of the earth habitually carrying about a body of sin and death—yet I hope I do not deceive myself when I say, that I am not more certain that the sun shines in the firmament than that I shall be finally presented faultless and spotless before the presence of His glory with exceeding joy."

After expressing his delight in his work, Mr. Phillippo proceeds :—

" The Lord has done great things for us indeed, whereof we are glad. During the comparatively short period since I was permitted to commence my public labours, I have had the high honour of adding unto the church, on a profession of their faith in the Lord Jesus, nearly one thousand individuals ; 145 have been added since the last annual report. The influences of the Holy Spirit have certainly been poured out upon the churches here in no ordinary degree—the effect more especially, I cannot help conceiving, of that spirit of prayer that is poured out upon the church at home. Do but continue your supplications for the outpouring of the Holy Spirit, and, feeble as your missionaries may be of themselves, they will be 'mighty through God.' They will feel no discouragement as to the issue of their exertions ; it will animate them in their work, and fill them with a resolution and confidence of success which the united opposition of earth and hell can never alter or shake.

"At all the stations the prospects are such as to awaken our gratitude and animate our zeal. In every direction new fields for cultivation are rising up to view. My own congregation continues good, and, what I regard as a very pleasing circumstance, our white attendants are on the increase. There is now among that class a disposition to hear. We have sometimes on a Sabbath evening between twenty and thirty gentlemen and ladies present, and an equal number of soldiers. Several of the former (many of whom I regard as regular hearers) are Jews, who not only appear to hear the Word with great attention and seriousness, but who read the New Testament and manifest a willingness for tracts. Pray for them, my dear sir ; let your church pray for them ; and oh ! that the whole Christian world would manifest a more ardent desire for their subjection to the sceptre of Emmanuel ! "

In closing, Mr. Phillippo observes :—" Opposition, you say, can never injure us if we are right. The whole of your remarks on this subject are truly valuable. It is more than ever my conviction that no obstacle can be removed, or any material good effected, by rendering evil for evil. I have never entirely lost sight of the advice with which your letter concludes—I mean, rather, your hint in 1823. I have given myself credit for having acted with considerable prudence as the result of that admonition ; but I must have my trials, and they cannot but be such as I must feel. I pray earnestly that I may be enabled to bear them in the spirit of my Lord."

Among the interesting events in which Mr. Phillippo took part during the year 1830, he specially mentions the formation, in Kingston, of an auxiliary to the British and Foreign Bible Society, and a few days later another in Spanish Town. The first public meeting was held on the 2nd of February, 1831, in Wesley Chapel, Kingston. It was a crowded meeting, and, in Mr. Phillippo's words, " formed an era in the history of the colony, being the first of the kind ever held in the island, and which a short time since could not have been attempted for fear of the hostility it would have excited."

But while fully and incessantly occupied with the pressing duties of his own immediate locality, Mr. Phillippo's active mind was often engaged with the question how best to supply the many openings for Christian labour which offered themselves in the districts around. Writing to Mr. Dyer on the 3rd of December, 1830, he says : " I charge myself with much negligence in not having more repeatedly and powerfully urged upon the Committee the claims of the adjacent parishes. If you cast your eye over the map of Jamaica you will perceive the parishes of St. Elizabeth, Manchester, and Clarendon. All these, with the exception of a small Moravian settlement and one solitary Evangelical minister of the Establishment, are entirely without the faithful preaching of the Gospel." He then indicates a salubrious spot at Black River, in St. Elizabeth, as suitable for a station, and relates his endeavours for six years past to establish stations in various parts of St. Thomas-in-the-Vale. At all these places some hundreds of eager hearers had been collected. In one he had only a mud hut in which to sleep, and often had to return home from others late at night, through long distances, utterly exhausted. In two or three spots land had been offered him on which to erect chapels and houses, but the pecuniary means were wanting. He had frequently gone to St. Thomas-in-the-Vale on a Saturday evening and preached next day in the woods till noon, beneath the shade of a tree. After a brief repast he had then ridden eighteen miles in a burning sun, or sometimes drenched with rain, to preach to a crowded congregation in Spanish Town. This exposure to rain, and sun, and dew had greatly injured his health. "Now," he pathetically adds, "I am good for nothing, surrounded by claims, and I cannot satisfy them." He reminds his correspondent how that at Kingwood the magistrate of the parish, a member of the House of Assembly, had stolen the materials collected for building a chapel, and applied them to the erection of a house for himself. "This justice of the peace," he adds, "is now glorying in his shame, taunting the poor Negroes on his triumph over sectarianism, and threatens to expel religion from the parish.· And shall he expel it? I would ask the Christian world if I had a voice to make them hear. Shall he expel it from upwards of five hundred poor Negroes, who have for years been bleeding under the persecutions they have had to endure for the sake of Christ? I must beg the Committee to reply." But he hopes the people will themselves build a chapel on the site sold him by a noble-minded female of colour, if only the Society will vote a grant for the erection of a house. The need was great, for the parish contained 8,000 Negroes, and no other Christian teaching was within their reach. He concludes his earnest and powerful appeal by reminding the Committee that established stations require continuous support, and that his own decayed state of health must shortly oblige him to return to England, when Spanish Town itself, with all its numerous agencies, must be supplied.

It was this state of things which had led Mr. Phillippo, on more than one occasion, to press on Mr. Dyer the importance and necessity of some arrangement being

made for the employment of native labourers, and the
establishment of a seminary for their education. " I have
now," he says, " five whom I could thrust into the field ;
and, well satisfied of their qualifications for the work, I
have no doubt of their success. I repeat my conviction
that in the interior of the country they would soon be far
more efficient than Europeans." * To Mr. Phillippo
belongs the credit of being one of the first to realise this
necessity, and to insist on the means required to meet it.
The project met with Mr. Dyer's cordial approval, and it
was one of the subjects set down for the consideration of
the deputation which the home Committee at that time
contemplated sending to Jamaica. It was not, however,
destined to be realised till later on in the history of the
mission, and under circumstances more favourable for its
success.

With the opening of the year 1831 it became more and
more evident that Mr. Phillippo must seek re-invigoration
of health in a more favoured clime. The new year, he
remarks, "already begins to proclaim the realities of
which it is the exponent. What a mercy it is that we do
not hear the whole of its utterances, either of joy or
sorrow, at once ; or it might have many things to say
which we could not bear. While time is passing, may my
future opportunities of doing good be more improved
than in the past, remembering that

' Time destroyed
Is suicide, where more than blood is spilt.' "

The urgency of his health compelled the Society to
make arrangements for his speedy return to England, and
the first months of the year were spent in anxious
expectation of the arrival of the Rev. John Griffiths, who
had been appointed to fill his place. Mr. Griffiths landed

---

* Letter to Mr. Dyer, July 14th, 1831.

in Kingston on the 11th of July, only, alas! in ten days to fall a prey to the fatal fever of the tropics. Mr. Phillippo's departure, however, could no longer be delayed. Committing his stations to the care of the Rev. John Clarke, with the full approval of his brethren, and obtaining the island licence to leave,* he sailed for his native land on the 7th of August, taking with him his wife and two children, and the bereft widow of Mr. Griffiths. While full of regrets at this break in his missionary labours, Mr. Phillippo felt thankful that he had so long been spared to labour in the vineyard of his Lord. Whatever might be the will of his heavenly Father, it was his duty joyfully to acquiesce in it, only solicitous to be found walking in the path which His providence and His word should mark out for him. It was amid the loudly expressed regrets of his flock, and tokens of the warmest affection from all classes, that he departed. It will suffice to copy one brief extract from a note received from the Rev. C. Dallas, an island curate. " May the blessing of the God of all grace," says Mr. Dallas, " bless both you and yours, and sanctify your voyage to you! I would come to shake you by the hand once more, but cannot. Be assured I will remember you among my Christian friends and brother servants of the Lord at His throne of grace. May He strengthen and establish you for His work, and send you forth again in health to preach the truth, accompanied by His power! "

---

* At this time no one was allowed to leave the island without advertising his name in the *Gazette* for three weeks, and obtaining a certificate from the Island Secretary's office. Mr. Phillippo's licence was signed by the Governor, and was dated St. Jago de la Vega (Spanish Town), 6th of August, 1831.

CHAPTER XIII.

IT was with a heavy heart, and in silent sorrow, that the parents embarked, for their youngest child was very ill. They hoped and trusted in God that He would disperse the dark cloud which hung over them. The dear child, however, became worse, suffering extreme pain. She required incessant nursing and other care, by night and day, while the vessel afforded anything but comfortable accommodation. In three or four days from Kingston, the little one died, and her precious remains were committed to the " hoary deep." The following extract from Mr. Phillippo's diary well expresses the bitterness of this trial :—"This sweet infant (she was a little over nine months old) had endeared itself to us all in a more than ordinary degree, and the circumstances under which the grim messenger snatched her from our embrace have left a wound which nothing but the Balm of Gilead can heal. During her sufferings my proud heart was at times ready to rebel ; but, O my God and Father, grant me that holy resignation to Thy will which I trust I sincerely desire. Help us both to say from our heart of hearts, ' Thou hast done all things well ! ' The Lord gave and the Lord hath taken away ; blessed be the name of the Lord."

The voyage was long, and by no means a pleasant one. It terminated at Falmouth, then the rendezvous of the Mail Packet Service, on the 5th of September. On landing, they were met by the Rev. W. F. Burchell, the pastor of

the Baptist church in Falmouth, and other friends, and
soon found a welcome and a home amongst the kind and
hospitable members of the congregation. After a few
days' gratifying intercourse, the voyagers re-embarked on
board the Irish packet for London. It was inconveniently
crowded with Portuguese refugees and Irish labourers, and
the voyage was rendered exceedingly unpleasant by the
quarrelling of the passengers, the miserable berths, and the
disgusting habits of the occupants of the steerage. Great
anxiety was felt from the obvious incapacity of the captain,
who ran the ship aground near Plymouth. One amusing
incident tended to relieve Mr. Phillippo's vexations.
Dreading to occupy his appointed berth, Mr. Phillippo
delayed seeking rest till all the lights were out. Having
to step over a portly person who had stretched himself in
the lower tier, he grasped the leg of a man who, as he
for a moment supposed, had by mistake entered the berth
appropriated to him. His cry awoke the sleeper beneath,
who vociferated, "That is my leg. Please give it to me."
"I beg your pardon, I did not know that any one would
occupy that berth." He found next day that it was a
cork leg and thigh, and its owner was that distinguished
personage, the Marquis of Anglesea.

Although Mr. Phillippo's health was much improved by
the voyage home, he was constrained by the advice of his
physician to decline the numerous engagements which
were at once pressed upon him on his arrival in London.
After a brief stay, he proceeded to Chipping Norton,
taking Oxford on the way, to find among old friends and
associations the rest he so sorely required. His enforced
leisure was, however, well occupied in the preparation of
a reply to some strictures on the "Leader and Ticket
system" pursued by the Baptist missionaries in Jamaica.
This paper does not appear to have been published, and
the painful events which took place in Jamaica in the

opening months of the new year (1832) set this and all other questions of missionary policy aside.

It was on the 20th of February that tidings reached England that the island was in a dangerous state; that the Negroes had broken out into open insurrection in the parishes of St. James and Hanover; and that the works and trash houses on numerous estates had been burnt, together with the houses and settlements of many free persons of colour. The militia had been called out, and the regular troops sent to the scene of the outbreak. Subsequent mails brought the further information that three Baptist missionaries (Knibb, Whitehorn, and Abbott) and two Wesleyan missionaries had been arrested—ostensibly because they would not serve in the militia, but truly because they were suspected of being promoters of the insurrection; and that not less than ten Baptist chapels and mission-houses had been destroyed by the enraged planters. Mr. Taylor, the colleague of Mr. Phillippo, was also seized, and his nearly completed chapel in Vere razed to the ground. With this exception, the scenes of tumult and bloodshed were confined to the northern portion of the island. In Portland, a society, consisting of 103 persons, was formed with the avowed object of destroying all the " sectarian chapels." At a meeting of the Colonial Union, convened to take measures to remove all " sectarians " from the island, the following resolution was adopted :—" We, the undersigned, most solemnly declare that we are resolved, at the hazard of our lives, not to suffer any Baptist or sectarian preacher or teacher, or any person professedly belonging to these sects, to preach or to teach in any house in towns, or in any districts of the country, where the Colonial Union extends, and this we do, maintaining the purest loyalty to his Majesty King William the Fourth, as well as the highest veneration for the Established religion."

Seven Baptist missionaries in all were at one time or another imprisoned, until their innocence of all complicity with the outbreak was established. The rebellious Negroes were very speedily overthrown, and the ringleaders shot after a brief trial by Court-martial. The rising began the day after Christmas-day, and by the middle of January the danger was past. Few, if any, white men lost their lives, either in the first rush of the insurrection, or during its suppression; but many hundred slaves were slain or hanged, in the endeavour to loosen from their necks the oppressors' yoke.

The rising was unexpected. In England a planters' rebellion was feared, rather than one on the part of the slaves. Since the disallowance of the Slave Law threats of transferring the allegiance of the colony to the United States had openly been made, even in the House of Assembly. Meetings of delegates were held in several parishes at which this treasonable act was violently advocated, and the slaves were given to understand that, in such a case, they would be slaves for ever. There is no doubt that a general idea prevailed among the Negroes that their freedom had been declared by the British Parliament, and that it was unrighteously withheld from them. Even where the colonists did not sympathise with the violence of many of their number, they regarded the action of the British Government as a mischievous and unjust interference with the rights of property, and as a breach of their political constitution. The proposed ameliorations in the condition of the slaves were held to be most dangerous incitements to turbulence, and calculated to ruin the colony. If improvements were required, it was argued, they ought to come from themselves. The slave-owners were abetted in these views by the West India mercantile body of London, who, on the 6th of April, protested against the Order in Council as "unjust and oppressive, inconsistent with the parliamentary resolutions of 1823, and destructive of the rights of property."

The struggle for emancipation was now transferred to England. The planters would not confer any of the liberties so ardently desired, and their bondsmen could not wrest freedom from their grasp. It only remained to arouse the British people to the sufferings of the slave, and to fight the battle of the oppressed in the constitutional arena of the British Parliament. It is needless, here, to pursue the history of the conflict, which, after stirring the nation to its depths, issued in the emancipation of all slaves held in bondage in any portion of the dominions of Great Britain. It is a part, and a noble part, of the annals of our country. It must suffice here briefly to indicate the share taken in the " good fight" by the subject of this memoir.

Mr. Phillippo's first appearance on the platform as an advocate for the slave was at the anniversary of the Baptist Missionary Society held on the 21st of June, in Spa Fields Chapel. The Rev. William Knibb had arrived from Jamaica a few days before, and, at Mr. Dyer's request, Mr. Phillippo left to his eloquent colleague the description of the true nature of Negro slavery, and the narrative of the insurrection and of the sufferings that he and his brethren had undergone.* It was Mr. Phillippo's duty to dwell on the missionary aspect of their work. The stations, he urged, must not be deserted because of this dreadful interruption ; the chapels must be rebuilt, and the missionary band must be replenished

---

* Mr. Hinton, in his Life of Knibb (p. 144), seems to imply that Mr. Phillippo was silent on the horrors of slavery from a desire to avoid the subject. Mr. Hinton was not aware that this topic was left to Mr. Knibb by pre-arrangement with the Secretary, Mr. Dyer.

and increased.   He testified that the intellectual powers
of the slaves had been awakened ; that their superstitions
were giving way, and that they heard the Gospel gladly.
From fifty to sixty thousand souls had been converted, and
from eighty to one hundred thousand were seeking the
way to heaven, in connection with the various denominations.   He depicted the eagerness of the people to hear
the Word of God ; and recounted the sacrifices they made
for the purpose of attending the house of prayer, and
stated that Christian natives were being raised up to
carry on the ministry of grace among their Negro
fellow-men.   Finally, he anticipated the time when the
quondam slaves of Jamaica would return to Africa, and
carry to the homes of their fathers the glad tidings of
salvation.   For himself, he was ready to return and die
in Jamaica, and did not doubt that the events which
had taken place would be overruled for the furtherance
of the Gospel.

The demand made on Mr. Phillippo by the numerous
meetings now held up and down the country was often
greater than his strength could bear.   Everywhere he had
to encounter the false and slanderous statements of the
Jamaica journals, which were widely disseminated in this
country.   The letters he received from the brethren
Taylor and Clarke, who were supplying his stations, told
him of the indignities to which they and their congregations were subject.   Their lives were in constant jeopardy.
The most deadly opposition to the progress of the Gospel
among the slaves and towards their ministers continued,
and the whole country presented an aspect of discontent
that offered little prospect of a return to peace and
prosperity.

Mr. Phillippo's defence of his missionary brethren, and
his expositions of the character of slavery in the West
Indies, were not confined to his appearances on the plat-

form.* He communicated many facts to the public papers, and in Norwich, at the request of the late J. J. Gurney, Esq. (who took the chair), and other friends, such as the Revs. J. Alexander and W. Brock, and the Sheriff of Norwich, he delivered, in the autumn, a course of four lectures on Jamaica, and on the state of the West Indian colonies. The attendance was very large. The event did not, however, pass away without calling forth strenuous opposition from the friends of colonial interests in the local press. The lectures were not, indeed, without influence in Jamaica. For the Rev. J. Taylor, writing at the end of the year on "the gross and infamous oppression" to which the people were subject, and on the virulent persecution that he himself had to endure, tells Mr. Phillippo "that it would not be prudent" for him to return at present. But the people hoped that his absence would not be prolonged. There were some indications, however, that hostility, in its worst forms, had begun to subside. For Mr. Taylor reported that he was able again to visit some of the stations which he had been obliged for several months to abandon.

At the beginning of the year 1833, Mr. Phillippo's health was so far improved that he could accept the invitations which poured in upon him from all quarters, not from ministers and churches of his own denomination only, but also from those of the London Missionary Society and from the Anti-Slavery Society and its auxiliaries in London and elsewhere. He spoke in Exeter Hall at the meetings of the London Mission, the British and Foreign School Society, the Religious Tract Society, the Sunday-

---

* His state of health at the time prevented Mr. Phillippo from giving the evidence, which he was requested to do, before the Select Committee of the House of Commons, appointed on the 30th of May, 1832, on the extinction of slavery throughout the British dominions.

School Union, and also enjoyed frequent and gratifying intercourse with many eminent men and philanthropists of the day. "My engagements," he says, "at this time were at Portsmouth, Portsea, &c., in conjunction with my friend and brother, Mr. Knibb, where we held very interesting and successful meetings. The venerable Dr. Cox and friends next claimed my services at Hackney, and soon after I went down again to Norfolk to fulfil engagements there. During my short stay I took a last look at East Dereham, the town of my birth, and the residence of my earliest years. I was the subject, more than on my first visit, of a feeling of isolation. I found myself a stranger, unable to say which were the most painful, the things that were changed, or those that were not."

In a letter to his wife he gives us the following brief notes of a tour made in Wales in the month of August. He entered Wales at Swansea.

"Here I called," he says, "on Mr. Roff, the Baptist minister, and was advised by him and others not to stop at Carmarthen, but proceed at once to Milford Haven. I therefore arrived on the following morning by mail. In the afternoon Mr. Stephens, the deputation with me, and some other ministers, arrived. The meeting in the evening was a good one. Next day we proceeded by boat to Pembroke Dock, and there held a meeting also. Saturday I was accompanied by a Welsh brother and Robert Smith, the black brother from Jamaica, to Haverfordwest. Here I preached on the Sabbath to a very large congregation in the morning, and to a still larger one at the Independent place in the evening. On Monday evening was the missionary meeting, when brother Stephens and myself, as the deputation, were specially engaged, and a very interesting and successful one it was. Tuesday we proceeded in a kind of car to a place called Bethlehem. Here brother Stephens preached in Welsh, and I in English. We dined on bacon at a good old farmer's house, which was as dark as a prison, and then went on to Beulah, where we found a meeting of the annual Association for the county. A good old Welsh brother, his head enveloped in a red kerchief, was giving utterance to some of the strangest guttural sounds I ever before heard, and accompanying them with such violence of voice and action as made me almost tremble for his poor frail body. The chapel was crowded, and much devotion appeared to be manifested, although at first it was considerably disturbed by the appearance of Robert Smith, at whom all stared as if he had dropped from the clouds, and been the inhabitant of another world than ours. On the outside of the chapel a stage was erected, where we, the deputation in particular, were to exhibit on the morrow. Very much fatigued, Smith and myself proceeded to the quarters designed for us. After breakfast on the morrow we held a most animating meeting, presided over by the squire of the district and an M.P., and proceeded onward to Beulah. The service was already begun in Welsh. A good old brother and my companion preached in Welsh, I in English. Again we found ourselves on our way, passing through clouds of dust, and narrowly escaping an accident by the breaking down of our vehicle, which compelled us to walk for two or three miles to reach our destination. In the town all soon became bustle and confusion. The shoemaker threw down his lapstone, the carpenter his axe, the blacksmith his hammer—in a word, all business seemed at a stand, the inhabitants rushing to the doors and windows, and into the streets, to see our black companion, having previously heard of him and his history, and some never having seen a black man before. Here at Fishguard we partook of some refreshment and

were again ready for our work. A very large congregation
was present, but a very small collection was made, though
said to be a better one than usual. The next morning we
pursued our course to Newport. Here we held a public
meeting, and stayed at a public-house in the intervals
between the services. The following morning we started
for Cardigan, where I now am. On entering the town, it
being market-day, Smith again excited much interest and
wonderment. We were followed along the streets by
hundreds of men, women, and children to the place of
our temporary abode. And here again came the trial of
our lungs and physical endurance. We each had to
preach twice in the country at considerable distances in
the day, and towards evening delivered addresses from a
platform in a field, where the whole town and neighbourhood seemed to be gathered. Thus far at present. We
are to occupy the same field again this evening, and then
proceed, attending to other claims, to Aberystwith. Now
farewell."

The Negro, Robert Smith, above referred to, had made
his escape from slavery and imprisonment in Jamaica,
and, as a fugitive, reached England, hidden in the hold of
a vessel, to seek redress by an appeal to his mistress. He
had paid a large sum for his freedom to this lady's agent
in Jamaica, who had fraudulently failed to give a receipt
for the money, and to secure for the man his papers of
manumission. Being arrested and in danger of re-sale
because he could not produce his " free papers," allowed
only to visit his dying wife manacled and under guard, he
resolved to escape. This he accomplished, and, landing
in London, found his way to Mr. Phillippo's lodgings at
Clapham.* With much difficulty, owing to her marriage

---

* He was known to Mr. Phillippo as an inquirer, from attending the
classes of the congregation in Spanish Town.

and change of name, Mr. Phillippo discovered the lady's residence, and there strangely enough encountered her agent. He absolutely denied the facts, and in the lady's presence denounced both the missionary and the slave as impostors, threatening both, on their return to Jamaica, with summary vengeance. He was curtly told *that*, at any rate, would be prevented, and that if Smith returned at all it would be as a free man, and that he would most surely be placed beyond his grasp. Smith's history becoming known, it excited the deepest interest. His simple story, supplemented by a relation of atrocities suffered by others still in bondage, deeply touched the audiences he addressed, and helped to swell that great wave of national feeling which broke on the system of slavery with over-whelming force, and swept it from the world-wide empire of Great Britain. While in London Smith was baptized and united with the church in Eagle Street, under the pastoral care of the Rev. Joseph Ivimey. On his return to Jamaica, he settled down as a tradesman at Old Harbour, where, after some years, he died looking for "the mercy of our Lord Jesus Christ unto eternal life." *

As Mr. and Mrs. Phillippo's health was sufficiently improved to justify their return to Jamaica with their two boys, their passage was taken, and on the day before Christmas-day they bade farewell to their friends in London, after a pleasant, though in some respects sorrow-ful, devotional service—sorrowful because they were about to leave behind, not only old attached friends, but their eldest daughter Hannah. "Keen, indeed," says Mr. Phillippo, "was the pang of separation. So great a trial

---

* In a picture painted by Mr. R. Rippingill to commemorate the passing of the Act of Emancipation, the portraits of Smith, and his wife and child, appear, expressing their thanks to the British nation that they are free.

had we not endured since we committed her dear little sister to the deep on our voyage home."

They did not, however, finally leave England till the 7th of February. Their vessel, with many others, was detained in the Channel by contrary winds. The tedium of this delay was pleasantly varied by visits to hospitable friends at Portsmouth and Ryde. In the latter place, they met a band of not fewer than twenty-six missionaries of various Societies, wind-bound like themselves. "We are now, at length," writes Mr. Phillippo in a letter to the Secretary of the Society, "near the Needles, going along delightfully, all our sails spread. The morning is very fine, and the wind fair. Upwards of three hundred vessels, many of which are now around us, are estimated to have left the Wight this morning. Governors for the East and West Indies, admirals, ambassadors, missionaries, emigrants, all proceeding to their several destinations. What a train of interesting reflections do these circumstances create!"

CHAPTER XIV.

RENEWAL OF MISSIONARY LABOURS—1834.

SEVERE gales had to be encountered, and once a dangerous storm of three days' duration, before the voyagers could land at Kingston, on the 13th of March. But their reception speedily effaced from their minds the discomforts of the passage. "Our welcome can be imagined," Mr. Phillippo says, "only by those acquainted with the impulsiveness and affection of the Negro character. On our arrival at the mission-house, they rushed into the premises from all parts of the town, and soon after from all parts of the surrounding country, to bid us welcome. The chapel and the entire mission premises were crowded. The joyous excitement was not exceeded by anything that could be conceived of, even by those who are not strangers to the African race. Our brethren also seemed to vie with each other in their congratulations on our arrival, so long delayed, in improved health and buoyant spirits, and had sent conveyances for us to Kingston. The next day was the Lord's-day, and crowded congregations assembled to greet us, and again to listen to the message of eternal life from the lips of the servant of the Lord."

The old work immediately engaged the attention of Mr. Phillippo. With regard to the state of the church and congregation in Spanish Town, he says: "I feel myself laid under almost inexpressible obligations to brother Clarke. I found everything as I could have desired—the premises, the Sunday-school, the church—everything. He is a dear and valuable brother, nor is his wife less excellent. They are both exceedingly beloved by the church and congregation, and, I may add, by all. I have expressed to them my most cordial thanks, and I should feel very much gratified if the Committee would show that they are not backward to commend where commendation is deserved. Everything begins again to look natural, and I am very far from regretting my return." *

Arrangements were immediately made to place in Mr. Clarke's hands the stations in the parish of St. Thomas-in-the-Vale, having Jericho as the centre of his missionary operations. But Mr. Phillippo speedily endeavoured to establish himself at "Above Rocks" in the mountains, and also at other spots in St. John's. Writing on the 29th of May, he reports his Sabbath-school as more than ever interesting. The children in attendance were principally those of slaves coming various distances from the farms and pens, and exhibiting a strange thirst for the knowledge which should fit them for the freedom now so near. He again organised an adult school, and found that reading-books were in great demand. "Meet a Negro," he says, "on the road, and give him a spelling-book or a tract, and his benediction will follow you as far as you are visible." Influenced by what he had seen in England, Mr. Phillippo soon added a temperance society to his measures for benefiting the Negro, and his example was quickly followed by his colleagues—Mr. Taylor at Old Harbour, and Mr. Clarke in St. Thomas. His congregation in Spanish Town necessarily received the chief attention. On the Lord's-day it was his custom to hold

---

* Letter to Mr. Dyer, May 17th, 1834.

three public services in the chapel, besides occasional church-meetings, and exercising constant supervision over the Sabbath-school.   Monday evenings were devoted to a prayer-meeting, Wednesdays to a Bible-class, Thursdays to the weekly lecture.   Preaching visits were paid to the country, and to the stations at Passage Fort, Red Hills, and in the mountains of St. Catharine.   These employments, together with the pastoral duties imposed by a fellowship of nearly a thousand members and the erection of school buildings and chapels as they were required, demanded incessant diligence, and left little time for relaxation or repose.   But he was cheered and sustained by evident proofs that his labours were not in vain, and that God continued to smile on his "feeble efforts," as he terms them.

It has been seen that from his first arrival in the island Mr. Phillippo gave great attention to the question of education.   It was his conviction that, great as were the advantages of freedom, it would lose much of its value if the slave remained in the degrading state of ignorance to which slavery had doomed him.   During his stay in England he had pressed the subject on the Committee of his own Society, but more particularly on the consideration of the British and Foreign School Society.   In the following letter to Mr. Henry Dunn, dated April, 1834, Mr. Phillippo briefly explains his plans, and narrates the steps he had taken to fulfil his desires :—

"You are aware that before I left England I designed the erection of a school-room for the education of the poor children, chiefly black and coloured, on the principles and plan of the British and Foreign School Society.   Immediately on my arrival I commenced the necessary arrangements, and, on the assumption of the Government by the Marquis of Sligo, I entered into negotiations for the purchase of land for the purpose.

"A few days ago, hearing that both his Excellency and the Marchioness were well disposed towards the education of the people, I thought it would be well to apprise them of my intentions. After a few days, I received his Excellency's reply. In the meantime, however, or soon thereafter, it was currently reported that prompt and decided measures were to be taken for the establishment of a model school on the Madras system, by and under the auspices of the Governor. This report was soon confirmed, as in a day or two after receiving his Excellency's reply an application was made by the Governor's secretary to a person who had been conducting our school to take charge of a similar institution to be established by Government, distinctly stating that it was to be on the Madras system, the secretary being well acquainted with that system, he having witnessed its operation and success in Madras. One of my objects in now writing you is to apprise you of this, and to ask if the funds at the disposal of the Home Government and in the hands of the Governor here are to be applied to one exclusive system. This may not possibly be the wish of the Governor, who is regarded as truly liberal in his views on the subject; but there is danger from the advisers around him. It will either be sustained by patronage, or by pecuniary means on the part of Government, and, after the novelty is passed away, be suffered to languish for want of interest on the part of its quondam friends. As the Negro will not acquire virtue by the simple Act of Emancipation, neither by that Act will the prejudices of the master undergo revolution. What guarantee, therefore, have we of the permanency of such an institution? It is with the conviction that such an institution would be comparatively inefficient, and only in a trifling degree meet the wants of the masses, that I write; but, even if it should succeed better than can reasonably be expected, there will still be room for the exercise of private benevolence.

"Under any circumstances, I am still determined to persevere in my purpose to build the school-room, and even to lay the foundations broader and deeper than at first proposed. It is now my purpose, not only to include boys in my plan, but girls and infants (each department separate), and, if possible, to fit up a room in which the children will have the advantage, as formerly, of being instructed after school - hours in several useful and productive arts, or in the general pursuits of agriculture. To carry out the plan to the full extent, and with the most cheering prospects of success, all that is necessary is to secure the sympathies and aid of that part of the British public which is distinguished by its attachment to the principles of civil and religious liberty."

The erection of the school-rooms on the plan proposed was begun on the 25th of September, when the foundation-stone was laid by the Custos of the parish, the Hon. T. J. Barnard, and P. Watkis, Esq., the latter a barrister and gentleman of colour, and an uncompromising advocate of emancipation, amidst a great assemblage of all classes. The cost of these structures was largely met by the liberality of friends in England; but soon after their completion he was able to announce that a sum of £450, granted by Lord Glenelg (Secretary of State for the Colonies) through the representations of Lord Sligo and two esteemed Friends in England, had enabled him to finish the buildings and furnish them throughout. The schools were two in number, one for boys and one for girls, and were calculated to hold 300 scholars. They ranged with the mission premises, and had a frontage, including a committee-room in the centre, of seventy-two feet. At the same time the chapel was enlarged so as to hold 500 more hearers. The scene at the opening a few months later Mr. Phillippo thus describes:—

"Last Sabbath-day there were more persons present than on the first Sabbath in August. The chapel was crowded almost to suffocation. Between three and four hundred were estimated to have been outside; and multitudes went away, unable to bear exposure to the sun, or to hear the preacher's voice. The members were not only so numerous as to throng completely the lower part of the chapel, but the porticoes also, and the gallery stairs. Four or five had literally squeezed themselves into the little enclosure beneath the pulpit, which I occupy as my stand at my week-day evening services, and to some the sacred elements were handed through the windows. The appearance which this vast assemblage presented in the neighbourhood on its egress from the chapel, exchanging mutual congratulations, and covering the whole face of the ground, was deeply interesting. Some of this multitude came from a distance of ten and fourteen miles, whilst hundreds came from beyond a circle of five miles from the centre of the circuit. It was a high and hallowed day on many accounts. Not only did a thousand (more or less) of us sit down and commemorate the dying love of our once crucified, but now risen and exalted, Saviour, but I had the honour and happiness of introducing to that 'feast of love,' and of giving the right hand of fellowship to, *one hundred and seventeen* persons, who never before enjoyed the privileges of their high and holy relationship, and to whom I had just administered the sacred rite of baptism on a profession of their faith in Christ, in the presence of a great cloud of witnesses.

"Some of these were young and interesting—had been nurtured almost from childhood in our Sabbath-school— had been 'turned from darkness unto light, and from the power of Satan unto God,' chiefly through the instrumentality of instructions there received; and, above all, were among the '*first fruits*' of that blessed institution unto Christ. No less than six of these interesting young persons were before me. Though once *scholars*, they were now *Sunday-school teachers*. And under the influence of feelings and principles which sound Scriptural education inspires, they seemed so fully aware of the nature of the vows they had vowed, and of their deep responsibility to God and to His Church, that they continued bathed in tears during the greater part of my address to them. These circumstances awakened the sympathies of the whole assembly; and, while all eyes were turned towards them, many and fervent, I doubt not, were the prayers offered up that God would preserve them from all the future dangers of their pilgrimage, and at last minister unto them an abundant entrance into glory. There was a third circumstance of interest connected with these youthful converts, and which I must not omit to mention. Three of the females had been slaves; one of them had been redeemed under circumstances of painful interest by friends at Reading; the others under circumstances of interest no less painful by friends in Jamaica. Two of them are the active and efficient school-mistresses in the 'Jamaica Metropolitan School,' and the other is training for the same department of usefulness."

CHAPTER XV.

By these and other plans Mr. Phillippo hoped to prepare
his people for the enjoyment of that modified measure of
freedom enacted by the first reformed British Parliament
in 1833, and appointed to come into operation on the 1st
of August, 1834. The agitation for this humane measure
had proceeded concurrently with the great struggle for "the
emancipation of the people of Great Britain from the rule
of an oligarchy which for two centuries had been the
predominant force in English politics." At the election
which immediately succeeded the passing of the Reform
Act, a large number of members were returned pledged to
the abolition of slavery. It may truly be said that it was
only the intense feeling displayed by the middle and
working classes which forced the Bill on an unwilling
Legislature, and compelled the Ministry of Earl Grey to
attempt the settlement of the question. "A great part of
the nation," says the historian Alison, "including a vast
majority of the urban constituencies, were seized with a
passion on the subject not less strong than that which
carried reform, and more estimable, as being less impelled
by selfish ambition, and more springing from humane
feelings." * The Nonconformist bodies were first and
foremost in this merciful and beneficent agitation.
Every congregation was visited, and the villagers of the

---

* Alison's " History of Europe," vol. v., p. 420.

remotest hamlets assembled in crowds to listen to the voice of the missionaries Knibb, Burchell, Phillippo, and others, pleading for freedom for the slave. It was fitting that Mr. Buxton, a member of the Society of Friends, a Dissenter from the Established Church, which, on this as on so many other occasions, held aloof from the popular agitation for human rights, should bring the subject before the House of Commons. The Government yielded to his urgent representations. Not that the members of it withheld their sympathy from the movement, but, in their opinion, there were many other measures which had long been pressing for settlement, and which seemed to demand their immediate attention. For there was not a department of the State which did not need reform. Nevertheless the Government resolved to listen to the voice of the nation, and to make a strenuous and final effort to remove the blot of slavery from every portion of the empire, and it will ever remain as the especial glory of the first reformed Parliament that many of its earliest hours were given to the accomplishment of this " act of national virtue, unparalleled in the history of the world."

On the 14th of May, 1833, Mr. Stanley, who had become Colonial Secretary, explained to a committee of the whole House the measure on which the Cabinet had determined.* Great as were the pecuniary interests at stake, they were not, he said, to be compared with the moral and social consequences which must result. "The freedom of 800,000 of our own, and many millions of foreign, slaves, the emancipation and happiness of generations yet unborn, the ultimate destiny of almost a moiety of the human race, were bound up with the question." But it was not possible longer to delay a settlement of it in the face of the " growing determination on the part of the people of

---

* Molesworth's " History of England," vol. i., p. 255.

this country at once to put an end to slavery—a
determination the more absolute and the less resistible
that it was founded in sincere religious feelings, and in a
solemn conviction that things wrong in principle cannot
be expedient in practice." *   The Government, therefore,
proposed the immediate abolition of slavery, and the
substitution during a period of fourteen years of a system
of apprenticeship, in which the emancipated slave might
be prepared for the full enjoyment of personal liberty.
After prolonged discussions, the measure ultimately took
the form of a gift of twenty millions to the owners of
slaves, as a compensation for their claims, and the
establishment of an apprenticeship of seven years for
predial slaves, and of five years for all others. This
portion of the Bill met with strenuous opposition from
Mr. Buxton, Lord Howick, and other friends of the Negro,
but was advocated by Lord Macaulay, and by the members
of the Government and their supporters.†   " Against this
part of the scheme," says Mr. Phillippo, " I strongly
protested at a meeting held by the Anti-Slavery Society in
the Guildhall Coffee House, and would have done so
publicly at the meeting, in the conviction that the greater
part of the slaves would be worked to death before the

---

* Alison, vol. v., p. 421.

† Lord Palmerston's views are stated in a letter to the Hon.
W. Temple, under date of June 25th:—"Both West Indians and
saints are moderately dissatisfied with our plan for the abolition of
slavery. To be sure, we give the West Indians a tolerably good
compensation. I really believe that the twenty millions are about the
whole value of all the estates, at the present market price ; so that
they will receive nearly the value of their estates, and keep those
estates into the bargain. I must say, it is a splendid instance of
generosity and justice, unexampled in the history of the world.
People are sometimes greatly generous at the expense of others ; but
it is not often that men are found to pay so high a price for the luxury
of doing a noble action."—" Life of Lord Palmerston," vol. ii., p. 163.

fourteen years had expired; but I was persuaded to be silent by an influential member of the Society of Friends. I also undertook to declare my conviction, as representing the whole slave population, that they would sooner remain in bondage than accept the boon proposed. I made my protestations known to several of the gentlemen present, who seemed to think it would be unwise to throw any impediment in the way likely to postpone a settlement of the question; that we must be thankful for what we had got, and not risk a certainty for an uncertainty." We shall presently see how completely subsequent events justified the forecast of one who so thoroughly understood both the Negro and his master.*

Still, extravagant and imperfect as were the terms, slavery had received its death-blow; and great were the preparations made to welcome the day on which the first gleam of freedom should shine. Mr. Phillippo has given us a lively and graphic account of the events of the day at Spanish Town, and it is a fair example of the rejoicings which took place in all parts of the island.

" According to previous arrangement among our missionary brethren generally, the day was to be set apart as a day of devout thanksgiving to Almighty God. On the joyful morning, a morning (notwithstanding the suffocating closeness of the atmosphere and the threatening aspect of the clouds the day before, exciting apprehensions of a hurricane) as serene and beautiful as ever shone out of the heavens, the apprentices were seen at an early hour clothed in clean and neat attire, flocking from all parts of the country into the town. Most of them repaired to the houses of their respective neighbours and friends for rest

---

* Mr. Stanley, when Lord Derby, in a speech in the House of Lords on the 7th of February, 1838, stated that the apprenticeship was only a system of modified slavery.—Hansard, vol. xcvi., p. 175.

and refreshment, after which thousands hastened to the different places of worship open to receive them—almost literally as "doves to their windows." At ten o'clock the chapel was so crowded that I could scarcely find my way into the pulpit; and, by the time the service was commenced, multitudes could not get within reach of the doors or windows. This was before intimated to be a meeting of devout acknowledgment to God for the great boon the principal part of my sable congregation had that day received; and never shall I forget my feelings when I saw them for the first time in my life standing before me in all the consciousness of freedom.

" It seemed as if I was in a new world, or surrounded by a new order of beings. The downcast eye, the gloomy countenance, and, strange as it may seem, even the vacant, unintellectual physiognomy had vanished. Every face was lighted up with smiles, and I have every reason to believe that every heart rejoiced. After such an introduction as the occasion would naturally dictate, I called on several of my sable brethren to lead the devotions. Their addresses to the Divine footstool, which they approached with great reverence and self-abasement, were a mingled flow of supplication and gratitude, adoration and love. There was scarcely a tongue in the vast assembly that did not respond to every sentiment and utter a hearty Amen. Those I had chiefly fixed upon to engage in these holy exercises, being more immediately interested in the great event that blessed morning had ushered in, might be expected to have dwelt with peculiar emphasis on the subject of their present altered condition and future prospects as to this present world; but it was not so. These considerations seemed lost in the overwhelming importance attached to them in reference to things spiritual and eternal.

" Said one : 'O Lord, our gracious Saviour, what we is

meet togeder for dis mornin' when we don't usual do so
dis day of de week? We is come to bless and to
magnify dy great and holy name dat dou has done dis
great blessin' unto us, to bring us out of de house of
bondage dis day. O Lord, what is dis dat we eye see,
and we ear hear? Dy Word tell we dat king and prophet
wish to see de tings dat we see, and to hear de tings dat
we hear,. and die without de sight. O Lord, if we
desperate wicked and tubborn heart won't prais dee as
dey ought, pluck dem up by de root! Here, Lord, we
give dem up unto dee; melt dem wid de fire of dy lov,
wash dem in de pure fountain of dy blood, and make dem
what dow would have dem to be.'

" ' Blessed Lord,' said another, ' as dou so merciful pare
we, to let we see dis blessed morning, we want word, we
want tongue, we want heart to praise de. Debil don't do
de good to us, but dou do de good to us, for dou put it
into de heart of blessed European to grant us dis great
privilege! O derefore may none of we poor sinner praise
de debil by makin' all de carouze about de street, but
fock like dove to deir window to praise and glorify dy
great name.'

" ' Since dou has don' dis great ting,' said a third, ' O
dat we may love dee and dy Gospel—may we neber turn
dy blessing into a curse, may we be diligent in our proper
calling, fervent in spirit, serving the Lord. O Lord, now
do dou make thine arm bare, and turn de heart of all de
people unto dee. We bless dee dat dou has incline so
many poor dyin' sinner to come up to dy house dis day.
O Lord, teach deir heart—turn dem from deir own way,
same as dou did de city of Nineveh! Now make dem
trow down deir rebellious weapon, fight against dee no
more; for dou says, Who eber fight 'gainst dee, and
prosper? Our eye is up unto dee, we cannot let dee go
except dou bless us wid dy grace—dou only canst change

de stubborn heart, turn it like de river of water is turned, dat all may serve dee from de least even unto de greatest.'

"Among the hymns sung on this deeply interesting occasion was one which, as missionaries, had we ever given out before, would have subjected us to a charge of treason. It was sung in loud chorus, the vast assembly simultaneously rising up on the repetition of the two first lines :—

> 'Blow ye the trumpet, blow,
> The gladly solemn sound!
> Let all the nations know,
> To earth's remotest bound,
> The year of jubilee is come ;
> Return, ye ransom'd sinners, home.'

"The service concluded, Mrs. Phillippo having a considerable number of pin-cushions, bags, &c., sent by kind friends from England, left on hand after the sale, I gave notice that I would distribute them as far as they would go among the female part of the congregation, on condition of their keeping them in commemoration of the day, and that on presenting them when the term of their apprenticeship expired (*i.e.*, those who survived) they should each be presented with a gift more worthy their acceptance. Happy should I have been to have distributed among the more intelligent part of them the munificent gifts voted them by the British and Foreign Bible Society ; but they had not arrived.

"By this time (nearly two o'clock) the children, to the number of four hundred, had again assembled, and had seated themselves in the centre of the chapel, they especially having been led to expect some little memento from Christian friends in England on this never-to-be-forgotten day. They were clothed in their best attire, and looked remarkably clean and neat. We distributed among them medals, pin-cushions, bags, and books, completely exhausting the stock of these articles we possessed. The closing devotional exercises being attended to, they then returned in an orderly manner to their homes. After a short interval for refreshment and rest, the hour arrived for evening service. The congregation was again overwhelming, and exhibited, as usual, every grade of colour, and, I was about to say, every diversity of creed, and circumstance, and character. I preached as well as my exhausted energies of both body and mind allowed, and thus closed the services of one of the most interesting and glorious days that has ever adorned the page of history."

The following Sunday was even a more remarkable day. With slavery, Sunday markets were abolished. All the shops were accordingly closed, and thousands upon thousands of the newly enfranchised peasantry came from all parts of the country to their sanctuaries. "It was a high day," says a missionary; "a Sabbath long to be remembered, a foretaste of better things to come."*

Mr. Phillippo was soon confirmed in his belief that greater atrocities than ever would be committed on the slaves by their owners, "in order to make the best (the worst?) of a system forced upon them, as they considered, by their enemies." During the few months antecedent to the 1st of August, persecution was especially directed against slaves connected with Baptist missionaries. In February, 1834, Mr. Phillippo reports that, while some Negroes were engaged in prayer after returning from a funeral, their merciless proprietor came to the house, demanding in a rage that the individual who had been praying should be delivered up to him. The man escaped, but the occupant of the house was immediately seized, handcuffed, and made fast in the stocks. Next day he

---

* Gardner's "History of Jamaica," p. 301.

was sent to Rodney Hall Workhouse to be further punished. The female slave of the same house was also laid on the ground and severely flogged. On the 30th of April several slaves and free persons of colour were indicted at the quarter sessions for attending a so-called illegal meeting of slaves held for the purpose of hearing the missionary preach. The slaves were found guilty, admonished, and discharged. The free people, four in number, were fined, and on refusing to pay were sent to gaol. But these acts of inhumanity were only a prelude to the far worse cruelties that were to come. In November eleven apprentices, for some trifling offence, were publicly flogged in the market-place of Spanish Town. The culprits were marched to the place of punishment under an escort of police, and the special magistrate improved the event by an address to the spectators. The sufferers were then paraded, with their backs lacerated and bleeding, about the town, and before Mr. Phillippo's door—"a spectacle," he adds, "I had never seen in the worst times of absolute slavery." "The atrocities committed under colour of law," continues Mr. Phillippo, "were greater than I had ever known. I wrote to Lord Sligo (the Governor of the island) and to friends in England, stating some of the cases of severe flogging, by order of special magistrates, for the most trifling offences, and stated my conviction that, if the system was not soon abolished, the slaves—for such they really were—would be goaded to an insurrection more general and far more disastrous in its consequences than had ever yet occurred. This communication was read in the House of Lords, and was noticed by Lord Brougham. There is reason to believe that at the same time it influenced Lord Sligo shortly after to set his apprentices entirely free. With this determination, he appointed two gentlemen and myself to see that his purpose was carried into effect." Lord Sligo had replaced Lord Mulgrave in

April, 1834, with the especial view of carrying out the Emancipation Act. Numerous special or stipendiary magistrates were appointed under the Act, who appear to have been selected with little care, for some of them proved to be more cruel and ignorant than the planters themselves. It is said of one, records Mr. Phillippo, a navy officer, that, in conversation with a gentleman who had offered him advice, he thus expressed himself:—"The fact is, sir, that we have entered on a new area, that corrosive measures must be used, and that there must be mutual condescensions on both sides!"

The course taken by the House of Assembly, and the spirit displayed in the Session of 1834-5, more than justified the apprehensions of Mr. Phillippo. A Bill was brought in for the infliction of corporal punishment for minor offences. "Messrs. Hodgson and Fowler thought flagellation a very laudable practice, and that no occasion should be lost of allowing it in reasonable measure. Mr. Hylton conceived it to be a most unnecessary waste of fine feelings to spare the apprentices, whom he designated as a set of barbarians only fit to be cudgelled. Here and there only a member was found sufficiently bold to protest against the wild talk of his colleagues." A Mr. Watkins, a gentleman of colour, intimated his opinion that these civilisers of barbarians might themselves be benefited by an application of the lash on their own backs, "as it was the only chance of making them wise legislators." Every attempt, however well-meant, on the part of any member of the Assembly to meet the necessities of the hour in a fair spirit, was met with contumely and indignant reproach. In a letter to a friend, Mr. Phillippo thus describes the state of things shortly after the system had come into full operation :—

" When with you in London, I ventured to predict, as you will remember, that the apprenticeship would not work. Nor does it! Nor can it be made to do so. Both the Governor and the planters are at their wits' end to know what to do. The whip, it is feared, has only changed hands, and what matters it to the sufferer by whom that instrument is wielded? 'The Negroes will not work,' say their masters. ' Massa give me no lowance ' (allowance), says the apprentice. ' He no give me Friday—no make leave off four o'clock good' (viz., at the proper time), 'make me work when me no able—old man, old woman, and piccaninney, all work.' Under such circumstances, can tranquillity and peace be expected? Almost everywhere there is confusion and every evil work. May God avert another insurrection! But before I can expect this devout wish to be realised I must pray, and the friends of the African and of humanity must pray, and work more earnestly than ever until this accursed species of *quasi*-slavery be completely abolished."

By many friends in England these fears were thought to be exaggerated. Remonstrances were addressed to Mr. Phillippo against the forwarding of what were said to be "excited tales" of the atrocities committed under the new *régime*. It was declared to be inconceivable that the planters should so recklessly act in the teeth, as it seemed, of their own interests. But the exasperation of the planters and masters of the apprentices increased in violence against the Home Government as well as against the philanthropists of England and the missionaries. Stipendiary magistrates who endeavoured conscientiously to fulfil their duties with justice and impartiality were bitterly assailed. "They were denounced," says Mr. Phillippo, "in the House of Assembly in the most disgraceful manner, and in the coarsest language. Another order of that august body was issued to the missionaries to appear before a committee of that House to answer such questions as they might think proper to propose.* This investigation was owing to the action of the Baptist missionaries in endeavouring to promote the social interests of the people in opposition to the oppressions and exactions of their former owners. On this account they were more virulently than ever, if that were possible, denounced as political parsons and demagogues. They were told that it was their duty to preach the Gospel, and to leave to statesmen, legislators, and judges the enactment and administration of civil laws."

Mr. Phillippo, however, did not thus limit his conceptions of his duty, and he continued to adopt such measures as seemed to him best adapted to elevate the Negro, to collect such facts as would illustrate the state of the people, and to forward the result of his inquiries to parties interested in the success of the Act of Emancipation. He also willingly united with his brethren in the publication of a protest against the Report of the Committee of the House of Assembly to which the inquiry into the causes of discontent had been referred. This curious document asserted that a pernicious influence had been " exercised by sectarian clergymen over the minds of the head people on the plantations, who were led to believe that they were violating the principles of their faith and their duty to God " by obeying the laws ! In their reply the missionaries declare these statements to be false. They affirm that the Assembly was acting on unsupported statements or on garbled and *ex parte* evidence, and that their untiring

---

* The order to Mr. Phillippo ran as follows :—" You are hereby required to attend the committee appointed to inquire into the causes of the discontent among the apprentices—their reluctance to work as formerly, even during the limited time prescribed by law, and the almost universal determination on their part not to work for wages during their own time—on Wednesday, the 12th inst., at ten o'clock, in the Assembly Room."

efforts were "directed towards the preservation of the peace of the community."

It had been the cherished hope of the Home Government that the planters would make the best use of the interval provided by the apprenticeship, to pass such measures of legislation and social improvement as would prepare the way for the period of full liberty. Never was hope more painfully disappointed. The result cannot be better expressed than in the following portions of a speech addressed by the Marquis of Sligo to the Assembly in February, 1836 :—

"The very extraordinary nature of the message I have received from the House of Assembly compels me to point out to the Legislature of Jamaica the position in which the conduct of one of its branches has placed the colony; to that branch, therefore, must I more particularly address myself, while I review its proceedings during the present Session—while I point out what *disposition it has evinced to meet the wishes of the mother country.*

"I pressed on you the establishment of more Courts of Assizes, so strongly recommended by the presentment of the Grand Jury. You took no notice of it. A revision of the laws affecting the discipline of gaols, and other places of confinement, was recommended to you. All these subjects have remained unnoticed. The *whipping of females*, you were informed by me, officially, was in practice; and I called upon you to make enactments to put an end to conduct so *repugnant to humanity, and so contrary to law. So far from passing an Act to prevent the recurrence of such cruelty, you have in no way expressed your disapprobation of it.*

"I informed the House that, in the opinion of the British Government, the taxation imposed by the local authorities on the property of apprentices was quite illegal; *you totally disregarded this suggestion.*

"I sent you down no less than four messages on the subject of an extended system of education; as no measure on the subject has emanated from the House, can I do otherwise than conclude that you are indifferent to it? I informed you that £25,000 sterling had been voted by England for the support of education in the colonies, with the promise of still further assistance being afforded, and *you have taken no steps to make it available.* I transmitted to you despatches from the Secretary of State, recommending the repeal of the 33rd Clause, *with a view to increase religious instruction in the colony;* you have not attended to the recommendation.

"I recommended the introduction of an Emigration Bill; I pointed out to you the injury done to the poorer classes of the claimants for compensation by the schemes of interested persons; I communicated to you the circumstances, arising out of your own decision, relating to the Police Bill; *you have taken no notice of it.*"

"Thus," says Mr. Phillippo, in a letter to the *Morning Chronicle,* "they have positively treated with contempt and scorn every benevolent and wholesome recommendation of the parent Government, and continue venting their malignity against the Executive, as the organ of the Government, in a shameful and unparalleled degree. Nothing can be more evident than that, even at the time they were giving their sanction to the Abolition Act, our legislators were determined to nullify every provision of it which wore a favourable aspect to the Negro. It is out of all reason that such a course can any longer be pursued. What will the British Government do in this extremity? Their course is plain. They must either arm the Governor with full powers to enforce obedience to their own wholesome and holy determinations, annihilate the local legislature, or, although last not least, at once and for ever subdue our political strifes and heart-burnings by proclaiming our peasantry totally and unconditionally free."

In a subsequent page the issue of this conflict will appear.

CHAPTER XVI.

IT has already been seen that Mr. Phillippo gave much attention to the question of education, and made unceasing efforts to promote it within the range of his personal action. In January, 1835, we find him replying at some length to a series of questions forwarded by the Secretary of the Society, and it was very gratifying to him to learn that his proposal for the establishment of an institution for the training of young men for the ministry was favourably viewed by the Committee. Its necessity became daily more evident to the missionaries, from the rapid growth of the mission, and from the altered social condition of the people. Some idea of Mr. Phillippo's own exertions may be learnt from his reply to a message from the Government of the island on the subject. He states that he had in his charge the following schools :—

"IN SPANISH TOWN, connected with the Metropolitan establishment. One boys' school, one girls' school, and one also for training teachers, as a normal school; a Sunday-school for boys and girls, an adult Sunday-school, and an adult daily and evening-school for both sexes.

"AT HIGHGATE OR SLIGOVILLE. One day-school on the plan of Fellenburgh, one boys' and one girls' day-school, a Sunday-school, an adult Sunday-school, and an adult evening-school for apprentices of both sexes.

"AT PASSAGE FORT. A day-school for boys and girls,

a Sunday-school, and an adult day-school for apprentices of both sexes."

A still wider range of influence was opened to him by a communication from the Marquis of Sligo on the 29th of June. Lord Sligo, from the commencement of his administration, had shown himself much interested in the education of the labouring classes. He now requested Mr. Phillippo* to lay before him a plan of general education, having special application to the circumstances of Jamaica, in which there existed so many people attached to religious denominations other than the Establishment. It was desirable that the plan adopted should not interfere with the peculiarities of any.

The important document forwarded by Mr. Phillippo is too long for insertion here; but it may be briefly summarised. In the first place, Mr. Phillippo commends the plan of the British and Foreign School Society as liberal and comprehensive, while its simplicity and economy are unrivalled. It knows no creed, recognises no sect, teaches no catechism, but takes as its fundamental principle the common Christianity of Christendom, and adopts the Bible as a class-book. The discipline of its schools is cheerful and inspiring, and encourages habits of industry. Mr. Phillippo then proceeds to point out its adaptation to

---

* Lord Sligo wrote as follows :—" Highgate, June 29th, 1835.—Dear Sir,—As I know you have turned your mind to the education of the poor Negroes, I should feel much obliged if you would communicate to me any plan of general education, without reference to any peculiar religious opinions, which you may have formed. I have been for some time endeavouring to collect information on the subject, and to form some plan ; but, up to this day, I have not been able to hit upon any system which is at all likely to answer, without so enormous an outlay as I do not think the Government at home would find the House disposed to agree to. Will you, therefore, be kind enough to communicate to me any such plan as you may think feasible?—I remain, my dear Sir, your faithful Servant, SLIGO."

the needs of Jamaica, and advocates, after suitable inquiries, the formation of a central Government school, with
dependent parochial schools, under mixed committees of
all colours and creeds. He further estimates the cost at
£250 for each school of 100 children, most of which
would be obtained from the school fees, supplemented by
the liberal support of the friends of education. But he particularly urges, as indispensable, the immediate formation
of a model school in Spanish Town for the training of
teachers, without which, in the then condition of the
island, no local schools could be furnished with suitable
schoolmasters or mistresses.*

Wise as these suggestions appear, the Governor was
unable to induce the House of Assembly to take the subject into consideration, nor was it until after the Disturbances of 1865–66, and the voluntary suicide of the House
of Assembly, that the Government of Jamaica was able to
introduce into the island a general system of elementary
instruction. The efforts of the Home Government were
equally unavailing.

In October, Mr. Phillippo was busily engaged in replying, at the request of Lord Sligo, to a despatch from the
Colonial Secretary of State, Lord Glenelg, as to the possi-
bility of educating adult Negroes, and the prospect there
was of employing them in the instruction of their fellows.
In the long and important paper supplied to the Governor,
Mr. Phillippo treats the subject from every point of view,

----

* The Governor replied as follows : —" Highgate, July 3rd, 1835.—
Many thanks, my dear Sir, for your prompt attention to my wishes on
the subject of education. I shall, if you will allow me, keep the books,
&c., for some time, till I collect the whole of the information I am
seeking for, as I confess myself quite at sea on the matter, and have
seen so many objections to those that have suggested themselves to
me that I have as yet decided on none. I hope, however, ere long to
be able to hit on something, when I will probably have to trouble you
further on the subject.—My dear Sir, your faithful Servant, SLIGO."

more especially urging the necessity of an immediate attempt to educate the Negro in order to remove from his mind and habits of life the pernicious effects of slavery, and to fit him for a life of patient, continuous, and successful toil as a free man. The paper is an able statement of the entire case, and deserved the commendation it received from Lord Glenelg,* to whom it was sent by Lord Sligo, with strong expressions of approval, and a recommendation that the plans suggested should be adopted. Mr. Phillippo did not, however, approve of a compulsory system of education, either for children or adults, which, in a subsequent despatch to the House of Assembly, was advocated by Lord Glenelg. No doubt these circumstances contributed largely to the favourable reception of the memorial which, about this time, was addressed to the Lords Commissioners of His Majesty's Treasury by Mr. Phillippo, and supported in the strongest manner by Lord Sligo. It was a request for help in the erection of the buildings of the Metropolitan school. The sum of £500 was immediately granted, and with expressions of pleasure by Lord Glenelg highly gratifying to Mr. Phillippo.

The encouragement he received prompted Mr. Phillippo to establish schools in every place within his reach, and he also interested himself in bringing to the notice of the Government the schools of his brethren that were

---

* Lord Glenelg's despatch is as follows : — "Downing Street, January 1st, 1836.—My Lord,—I have the honour to acknowledge your lordship's despatch, No. 174, of 25th October, enclosing a communication from the Rev. Mr. Phillippo on Negro education. I have perused these papers with the interest which they well deserve, and I beg to thank your lordship for the information they contain. My thanks are also due to Mr. Phillippo for the valuable suggestions which his experience of the Negro population in Jamaica has enabled him to make.—I have, &c., &c., GLENELG."

needing aid.*   He also laid before his friends in Jamaica and England the plan of a college, similar in some respects to those established in India at Serampore and elsewhere, for the culture of the Negro race in the higher departments of learning.   His report of the issue of his endeavours for this object is, " that the scheme was regarded with the utmost apathy," and that his efforts, both in Jamaica and in England, with respect to it were in vain. The object, however, long possessed his mind, and in his volume on " Jamaica, Past and Present," published in 1843, he has inserted in the Appendix his plan in full detail.   Since then some attempts have been made to accomplish it, both by the Government and by private individuals or societies; but in its main features the scheme remains unfulfilled.

About this time Mr. Phillippo addressed an interesting letter to Mr. James Cropper, of Liverpool, on the establishment of an orphanage for both sexes on some salubrious spot in Jamaica.   The subject had been discussed with Mr. Cropper when he was last in England.   Mr. Phillippo now gave that gentleman the results of his inquiries, earnestly recommending the adoption of the plan, in the conviction that it might be highly useful, and might be made self-supporting.   He also pointed out a spot near Highgate, in the mountains above Spanish Town, as eminently adapted for the experiment.   This project, however, amid the pressure of other events, was laid aside, and never carried into execution.

Some extracts from a letter addressed to his generous friend, Joseph Fletcher, Esq., in the month of September, 1835, will suitably close the above record of Mr. Phillippo's educational labours during the period under

---

* As in the case of the Suffield school-house at Falmouth, then in course of building by the Rev. W. Knibb.

review.   After referring to the prosperous condition of his
school undertakings in Spanish Town, he proceeds : " I
have intimated that his Excellency the Governor is
favourable to religious instruction.   A few days ago I had
the pleasure to receive a letter from him, stating, among
other things, that the plan embraced by my communication was the most eligible that had come before him, and
that it should have his most earnest recommendation to
the Government.   I, of course, urged the voluntary
principle. His Excellency, indeed, has expressed it
verbally to me as his decided opinion that the general
establishment of schools would be one of the most important and salutary acts of beneficence to all classes
of the community that could be conferred upon the
country.

" The addition to our chapel has been long since
completed ; but, had I made it twice the present
dimensions, I should by no means have exceeded the
provision required. Our chapel on a Sabbath morning is
usually crowded to excess, and seldom is it the case but
that multitudes are obliged to sit or stand in the yard,
unable to gain admittance within the walls. The addition
was principally intended for the Sabbath-school, and will
seat between four and five hundred children and teachers.
Almost every Sabbath I find on my descent from the
pulpit full fifty boys and girls sitting upon and about the
staircase, where it is impossible for them to benefit by the
service. We have lately had a gratifying increase of
respectable and efficient teachers, principally the sons and
daughters, or relatives, of respectable merchants in the
town, or persons of independent circumstances. One of
them was a teacher in Surrey Chapel Sunday-school for a
period of twelve or fourteen years.

" At Passage Fort the foundation-stones of a chapel and
school-room were laid last week. Groups of children came

from Kingston and Spanish Town to witness the ceremony and pass the day. Besides the children, no less than five hundred spectators were present. Many were overseers, proprietors, and others, who came to testify their good-will to the undertaking. If no other good was effected on the occasion, it was one of the greatest triumphs achieved over vulgar prejudice that was perhaps ever known in the West Indian colonies. Respectable persons of almost all colours met around the same table in acknowledged equality. At the table at which I had the honour to preside was a magistrate, a candidate for parliamentary honours, a solicitor, a merchant, a doctor and his lady, several missionaries, and a considerable number of ladies, some white, some brown, all mingled together as members of the same great family. On a comparison with the state of society a few years ago, I could not forbear reflecting on the wonders which the Gospel effects in the civilisation of mankind, and in the restoration of that peace and harmony among them which sin has so fatally disturbed.

"A school will be attached to the station (as to each of the others), and, from the favourable disposition manifested by the overseers, managers, and others, I apprehend no lack of scholars. There are about three thousand apprentices within a distance of three miles of the location, the greater part connected with my church and congregation. I have no doubt means will be forthcoming. The silver and the gold are His, under whose direction and smile we have, we trust, begun the execution of the plan."

CHAPTER XVII.

THE numerous demands on Mr. Phillippo's energies from without by no means rendered him unmindful of the spiritual necessities of the people under his special charge. In January, 1835, he is writing in the most urgent terms to the Secretary of the Mission to supply him with means for the extension of the Gospel in various parts of the parishes of St. Catherine and St. John. The claims of Passage Fort, of Highgate, and of Red Hills are pressed in detail. The people, he states, are urgent for instruction; and the more anxiously does he seek for aid since "the feeling of the lower classes in these districts is universally in favour of the Baptists." "I most earnestly hope," he adds, "the Committee will give the question their very serious consideration ; I, indeed, implore them to do so." If, however, he found the Committee unable to meet his wishes to the fullest extent of his needs or desires, he yet gratefully records that their grants were kindly and liberally apportioned. On the 8th of August he returns to the subject. "The whole land is before us," he says, "and when once we take possession of it, which we as a denomination are doing in a most unexampled manner, the warfare to a great degree will be over. After a few years more of patient, persevering, and zealous effort on the part of the Society and their agents here, I much question if the Baptists do not outnumber all other religious societies. By a letter just received from brother

Burchell, it appears that he preached on the 1st inst. to a congregation of seven thousand persons. A communication from brother Knibb furnishes accounts almost equally delightful. I was on that memorable day at St. Thomas-in-the-Vale, and laid the foundation-stone of the chapel there being erected by brother Clarke, and the attendance, and everything, indeed, connected with the event, was most cheering. On the following day, brother C. baptized, as I understand, 184 persons. Brother Taylor baptizes to-morrow."

In the month of May he records, in a very graphic manner, the baptism of forty-eight converts at Passage Fort. "It was a high and hallowed day," he says, "to that part of my sable flock whose earliest associations were connected with the place. Such general solemnity, or so great a degree of interest, I never saw exhibited before. The whole scene was delightful—I might have said inspiring. The majestic, but (at that early hour of the morning when the preliminary hymn was sung) half-developed outline of the Liguanea Mountains stretching themselves before me in all the glowing depths of shade; the deep purple of a mass of retiring clouds overhead, tinging with a darker hue the already dark-blue surface of the sea; the solemn stillness of the atmosphere, the gently languid ebbing of the waves upon the beach, added to the deep-toned feeling of devotion which such an occasion may be supposed to create in every pious mind, exerted an influence upon my spirit which I seldom feel. I seemed to breathe the atmosphere of love, combined with an almost indescribable sensation of reverential awe. Surely God was with us. And have we not the promise of His special presence, and of the peculiar manifestations of His grace, if we seek Him in His ordinances?

"At half-past ten a.m. I found myself standing amidst a congregation amounting to 1,500 or 1,600 persons. The premises contained three large dilapidated sheds, which stood originally detached, but which, by the exertions of the candidates the day before, were now united by a roof constructed of the branches of the cocoa-nut and mangrove-tree. This afforded a tolerable shelter for nearly the whole mass; but the entire range of buildings, if buildings they may be called, being situated so closely to the water's edge, and indeed of such irregular and novel construction as to render a sight of all impossible, it required no small effort to make myself distinctly heard.

"Here, too, as at the solemn ceremony that had just been witnessed, circumstances were of an unusually interesting character. The very spot on which we were now assembled was the old Spanish Fort, from which the village derives its name; and of this we had sufficient proofs from the decayed rampart which encircled us, and the heavy pieces of artillery that were planted here and there. Here it was that a handful of our countrymen, under the command of Colonel Jackson, long before the conquest of the island by Penn and Venables, are reported to have effected a landing, from which they advanced to St. Jago de la Vega (now Spanish Town), the capital, plundered it of its wealth, and put again to sea. Within these very battlements, over which the proud and bloody ensign of Spain so long floated, and where, amidst the disgusting scenes of riot and debauchery that were exhibited, her impious sons often chanted the Salve Regina, and other hymns, was planted the peaceful standard of the Cross, and were sung, but we trust in higher and holier strains, the high praises of Immanuel. On such an occasion, and under such circumstances, it was natural that a train of reflection should be awakened in my bosom as to the contrast with those bygone days now exhibited before me, and that I should embody them in my address to the dense mass that hung upon my lips. The effects produced seem to have been salutary. May they be permanent, and God shall have all the glory!"

Later in the year the new chapel at Sligoville was opened for Divine worship. Although numbers present had scarcely ever been in a place of worship before, the greatest possible seriousness and attention were visible on every countenance. All were cleanly and neatly attired. They returned to their homes highly gratified by the interesting and impressive services of the day. The chapel was built on a spot of great picturesque beauty, and could be seen from long distances around.

These large and rapid additions to the churches of persons so lately living in a bondage in its very nature degrading and immoral, naturally awakened the fear in many thoughtful minds that they could not be in all cases the subjects of Divine grace. It was also supposed that the discipline of the churches must suffer from the want of efficient supervision where such large numbers were concerned. Mr. Phillippo was perfectly aware of these presumptions, and, on their being stated to him by a friend, at once set himself to reply. The most important portions of his letter are the following :—" When individual churches comprise such numbers as are comprised in most of our churches in Jamaica, and when it is taken into account that most of our converts have suddenly emerged from a state of semi-heathenism, it is scarcely to be expected that they should endure a critic's eye, or that there should not be found amongst them occasional inconsistencies and sins; this the more especially as from the influences of unjust and oppressive laws we, as ministers, have been precluded access to the dwellings of our flocks, and have been unable to see the influence of religion on them in their families. Any instances of dereliction among them each missionary deplores as deeply as the pastor of any other church, and

I feel confident that none could more diligently labour, both in the pulpit and out of it, to prevent them.

" In the admission of members, it is impossible for us to be more cautious. I hesitate not to say that we carry matters in this respect to an extreme. Seldom is it the case that we admit any one to communion under a two years' probation, whilst it is the common case that they have been three, four, five, and even seven years."

After citing various cases as illustrations, Mr. Phillippo then proceeds to remark on the methods by which discipline was maintained :—

" So much for the admission of members—now for discipline. Most of us have a church-meeting every week ; and having one or two deacons (or those who act as such, by assisting us in the discharge of our pastoral duties) on almost every estate, numerous as our churches are, scarcely a single act of serious discrepancy can arise without our knowledge. Things, indeed, of the most trivial nature, and others less trivial, but which are connived at at home, are brought for adjustment before our churches here. As soon as any one is convicted of being in the indulgence of actual sin, the preliminary steps, of course, being taken, he is instantly excluded, and the cause of that exclusion is publicly proclaimed. To show to the world our intolerance of sin, in whomsoever it is found, we have been apt to exceed the apostolic command ; hence 'suspensions ' are very little known amongst us, and of those who are the subjects of excision, scarcely one in ten turns back again into the world. So far as my own church is concerned—and I have a right to presume that others of the same standing are equally uncorrupt—I am persuaded that a purer church, under the same circumstances, does not exist in any missionary station in the world. I might have gone farther, and put it on a footing with the churches with which I am acquainted in England and America.

But if the churches in Jamaica are inferior to them in piety and sound Scriptural knowledge, what has been the cause, and who are to blame? Not the missionaries and their flocks, but British Christians, in so scantily supplying the field with labourers. I, for inṡtance, have a church amounting to nearly 1,500 members, with perhaps an equal or a greater number of inquirers—this, together with preaching at three subordinate stations, exclusively of regular week-day services at Spanish Town, with marriages and funerals, and chapel and school-house building, &c., &c. I can, therefore, scarcely be supposed to perform so many pastoral visits, or to possess so many opportunities for communicating private instruction, as a pastor at home, who has less than one-third of such duties to perform.

" Our incessant and earnest cry to Britain, as missionaries, has ever been, ' Come over and help us; for the harvest is great, and the labourers are few.' "

The assistance here called for was indeed most urgent. The modified measure of freedom allowed by the Emancipation Act had been followed by an enormous increase in the congregations throughout the island. The missionaries were overwhelmed with the demands on their time and strength. They were regarded as the only true and sincere friends of the oppressed, and were resorted to in every case of distress. Their interposition in cases of cruelty was prompt and frequent, and the gratitude of the people showed itself in their most ready acquiescence in the wishes of their pastors, and in the most liberal consecration of their earnings to the cause of God. In his letter to the Association which met at Kingston in March, 1836,* Mr. Phillippo speaks with enthusiasm of the

---

* This Association had been broken up by the persecutions of 1831-2, but was revived at Rio Bueno in 1835.—"Voice of Jubilee," p. 89.

"delightful prospects of usefulness to the Church of God" everywhere apparent. "Obligations of the deepest gratitude to the Head of the Church," he said, "were laid upon them by the extraordinary success with which it had pleased Almighty God to crown the efforts of His ministers and people." As a proof of this, Mr. Phillippo proceeds to mention that since his return from England 435 persons had been added to the church by baptism in Spanish Town alone, which, after deducting deaths and exclusions during the year, left a clear increase to its fellowship of 401. The spiritual state of the church he thus describes:—"We have been in the almost uninterrupted enjoyment of peace. Attendance upon the outward ordinances of religion has been increasingly regular and punctual. A spirit of Christian love, manifested in acts of kindness towards each other, is more and more visible. The personal and relative duties of our holy religion have been more faithfully and perseveringly performed. The discipline of the church has been more strictly and impartially administered, and a growing attachment has been manifested for the local interests of religious truth, and for its diffusion throughout the world. Both in our collective and personal capacity we have deeply to lament our barrenness and unfruitfulness in the knowledge of God; but at the same time we trust we do not deceive ourselves when we express the hope that, forgetting the things that are behind, we are pressing forward towards the things that are before—' towards the mark for the prize of our high calling of God in Christ Jesus.' With many of our dear friends we have had to part through their removal by death. The last moments of all were peaceful, and of some it may be said they were triumphant. Angels seemed to beckon them away, or waited to convey their happy spirits to the purchased possession." Mr. Phillippo then records the interesting fact that in the year and seven

L

months that had elapsed since his return from England
he had celebrated between two and three hundred
marriages ; distributed 1,500 copies of the Scriptures, sent
as gifts by the Bible Society to the apprentices who
could read ; circulated thousands of tracts, and kept the
books of two libraries in constant use amongst the intelligent members of the congregation. He closes his
interesting letter with the following words :—"Thus
blessed with abundant means, everything with us is cheering in an unexampled degree. The fields all around us,
as we have been led to anticipate is the case in almost
every district of the island, are white unto harvest. That
holy influence, without which we are deeply sensible all
human efforts for the final happiness of man must prove
abortive, seems not only to follow, but to go before us,
preparing the soil for the seed of the Kingdom ; so that
whatever may be the difficulties and anxieties with which
we go forth to our labour, we return again with rejoicing,
bringing our sheaves with us."

It was a spring-time of bright hopes, and full of promise
for the future. No cloud had yet arisen in the horizon
to threaten the glorious harvest time in view.

N.B.—The following are the statistics of the Baptist churches and
schools in Jamaica for the year ending March, 1837, under the care
of sixteen missionaries and schoolmasters :—

Number baptized during the year	2,950
,, of Members	16,821
,, of Inquirers	16,146
Clear increase of Members	2,800
Total number connected with the Mission	32,966

SCHOOLS.

Number of day scholars	1,622
,, of evening scholars, adult	451
,, of Sunday scholars	5.594

CHAPTER XVIII.

SUCH were the oppressions to which the apprentices continued to be subject that, at the suggestion of Mr. Phillippo, and with his aid, a petition was sent to the House of Commons by those living in and around Spanish Town, setting forth their grievances, and praying earnestly for the abolition of the system. They found it to be more galling than slavery itself. It was goading them almost to madness. They were charged, often most unjustly, with neglect of duty, disobedience, and insolence, and for the slightest offence flogging in its worst forms was inflicted both on men and women. During the first year of the apprenticeship, upwards of 25,000 punishments were adjudged in various parts of the island, and in the first eight months of the second year 27,000 more were recorded. "During two short years," says Mr. Phillippo, "60,000 apprentices received in the aggregate one quarter of a million of lashes, and 50,000 other punishments by the tread-wheel, the chain-gang, and other modes of legalised torture. But for the influence exerted by the Governor, the missionaries, and some of the special magistrates, the exasperation produced by these enormities would, in all probability, have broken out into open and general rebellion." Rumours, indeed, were rife that the apprentices were preparing on the 1st of August to assert their freedom, especially in the parishes of St. James and Hanover, so that, on the 27th of July, the Marquis of Sligo addressed a note to Mr. Phillippo requesting him to ascertain through his brother missionaries how far such rumours were true. The fears of the planters, justified indeed by their cruelties, were found to be the real source of their anxieties, the more so as some of them notified to their apprentices that they were not to make a holiday on the 1st of August, which by law the apprentices had every right to do. From Messrs. Knibb, Burchell, Abbott, Thomson, and others, replies were received, expressing astonishment at the rumours referred to, which they declared to be utterly groundless. "If there be anything of the sort," replies one of them, " it has not come to my knowledge, notwithstanding all my opportunities of knowing. But on Friday last I did hear from Mr. Knibb that somebody, having authority, had given intimation on his estates that yesterday, the 1st of August, was not to be, and was not in law, a holiday. Mr. Knibb, however, declared the contrary to the people, and intended to see that nothing should hinder them from enjoying their right." The day passed in perfect peace. Neither military forces, nor a ship of war, as asked for, were sent, and Mr. Phillippo had the gratification of receiving the thanks of the Governor for the information he had acquired. "It was suspected," he adds, "that the demand for a preventive force was really meant to intimidate the apprentices into the acceptance of a mere nominal rate of wages, the result of a combination of planters, who, by their princely hospitality to the Governor's informant, had thus induced him to aid them in their object."

The breach already existing between Lord Sligo and the planting interest now became irreparable. His liberality, his impartiality, his resolve that the provisions of the abolition law in favour of the apprentices should not be infringed, were unpardonable offences. His appeal to the

House of Assembly to reconsider some decision respecting the Act was treated as a breach of privilege. This, and the wavering support he received from the Colonial Office, at length caused him to resign his post, amidst expressions of the profoundest regret and gratitude from the people whom he had endeavoured, so ineffectually, to protect and serve.

A meeting was held in Mr. Phillippo's chapel to invite the Marquis to reconsider his decision. It was violently and illegally interrupted by a magistrate, and the Riot Act read, though the assembly was in perfect order. The meeting, however, under Mr. Phillippo's guidance, maintained its right, and the memorial was adopted. A similar address, drawn up by Mr. Phillippo, was also presented to Lord Sligo on the part of the Baptist missionaries. On the 30th of August, Sir Lionel Smith arrived in Jamaica as his successor, and with instructions, if possible, to harmonise the clashing interests of the planters with the plans and purposes of the British Government. As an old West Indian Governor, the planters formed high expectations of the favourable results to their interests which would flow from Sir Lionel Smith's presumed sympathy with their claims ; and some of his first actions seemed to justify their confidence. But as the true character of the position came to be understood, and as the hopes that his coming had inspired were proved to be fallacious, the hatred and hostility endured by his predecessor soon fell upon him.

In his first speech to the House of Assembly indications were not wanting that Sir Lionel Smith was a friend to humanity and progress. He had the boldness to commend the missionaries to their esteem. " The first object," he said, " is to instil the doctrines of Christianity. . . . I firmly believe that the assistance of the missionaries is most necessary to this end. Gentlemen, you have hardly four more years to watch over the experiment of apprenticeship. Give every facility you can to the missionaries' labours. Banish from your minds the idea that they are your enemies. I will answer with my head for their loyalty and fidelity. Encourage their peaceable settlement among your people. Let every four or five contiguous estates combine for the erection of chapel-schools; and knowing, as you well do, the attachment of the Negro to the place of his birth and the burial-place of his parents, you may, I sincerely believe, by these means locate on your estates a contented peasantry."

It was in vain. The House of Assembly was in no mood to listen to words of moderation and wisdom. "The system of apprenticeship," says Mr. Phillippo, "was unsatisfactory to all parties, and beneficial to none. It was the source of the most unparalleled difficulty, labour, and obloquy to the noble-minded individuals under whose eventful and successive administrations it was carried on. It therefore failed—and failed signally. It was obnoxious to the master, hateful to the slave, and perplexing to the magistracy. Slavery will admit of no modification." The strong representations which reached the friends of the Negro in England led, in the Parliamentary Session of 1836, on the motion of Mr. Buxton, to the appointment of a Committee of the House of Commons to inquire into the working of the system. The charges of cruelty were fully substantiated; yet on the whole the Committee thought that the system worked not unfavourably. The conduct of the apprentices generally was declared to be good, they worked for wages, were, in most cases, fairly treated, and were more industrious than in slavery. But this admitted good conduct on the part of the labourers only rendered it the more intolerable that they should be so often unjustly and so cruelly dealt with. It was no wonder that the Anti-slavery party should oppose the decision of the Committee to allow the system to continue till the close of 1840, the period determined by law, or that they should resolve to put forth their utmost efforts to bring a system so productive of evil to a speedier end.

The earlier cessation of the apprenticeship was due in a very large measure to the calm, exhaustive, and irrefutable report of a deputation which visited the chief islands of the West Indies in the cold season of 1836-7. It consisted of Mr. Joseph Sturge, Mr. Thomas Harvey, William Lloyd, Esq., M.D., members of the Society of Friends, and of Mr. John Scoble; but the report was the work of the first two gentlemen. They visited Antigua, Montserrat, Dominica, St. Lucia, Barbadoes, and Jamaica. It was on the 22nd of January, 1837, that they reached Jamaica. Six days afterwards they visited Spanish Town and made the acquaintance of Mr. Phillippo. Of a visit paid to the Metropolitan Girls' School, on the 7th of February, they thus speak :—"There were ninety children present, many of whom were the coloured offspring of overseers. There were at one time in this school four or five children of a late Governor, the Duke of Manchester; and one of its present teachers is the daughter of the Duke's *celebrated* secretary, Bullock. Her freedom was purchased some years ago by the English patronesses of the school. The dreadful state of social disorganisation in Jamaica is legibly written even on the surface of society. Its ' bad eminence ' is doubtless to be attributed, in part, to the corrupting influence of the long administration of the above-mentioned Governor. Many of the children are apprentices, of whom fourteen coloured girls are sent by their attorney from a single estate in the neighbourhood. They are intended to become teachers of estates' schools. The principal teacher, a

coloured young woman, was purchased and made free by
an old Negro, her grandfather, who is still himself an
apprentice." *   The "bad eminence" here alluded to is
derived from a remark of Sir Lionel Smith to the deputation, to the effect that he considered the Negroes of
Jamaica far more degraded than those of Barbadoes,
or the other islands of which he had been Governor.
Even during the administration of his predecessor no
progress had been made in preparing the people for
freedom, for the time had been lost in " squabbling "
with the planters.

On the 19th the deputation attended the various Lord's-
day services of Mr. Phillippo. The meeting-house was
densely crowded, chiefly by apprentices, whose attention
and decorum much pleased them. Of the deacons and
leaders, some were free, but others were estate-hands and
apprentices. With these men, whom they considered to
be fully equal to English peasants in intelligence and
information, they had, at Mr. Phillippo's request, considerable intercourse. One informed them that he was a
constable. It was difficult, he said, to act according to
his oath, as he was expected to do everything for his
master, and nothing for the people. He had frequently
to remonstrate with the overseer about the oppressions he
practised. The regular allowances of clothing and food
were capriciously withheld, and the overseer often took
away their time whenever he wanted it. " On our asking
whether the people would be willing to work after 1840,
he said, ' Nothing was sweeter than for a man to labour
for his own bread ' — a sentiment to which all present
responded." Many had been flogged or sent to the treadmill who had never been punished during slavery. One
poor woman present, the mother of eight children, in

---

* " The West Indies in 1837," pp. 181, 183.

declining years and health, had been sent to the treadmill because she could not keep her place in the field-gang. In slavery she had lived in comparative ease, but her house had been pulled down since the commencement of the apprenticeship. All complained of the difficulty of securing an impartial trial before the magistrates.

On the 20th of February the deputation record, " On several occasions we have seen the penal gang of men and women, in chains and collars, in the streets of Spanish Town, and to-day observed two pregnant women chained together in the gang." * On another day they met in the streets of the town seven women handcuffed, who had been apprehended as runaway apprentices. They were free women, and had been illegally taken from their houses and avocations without the shadow of a reason. For this outrage no compensation was given them.† The general conclusion to which these gentlemen came must be stated in their own words :—

" Not a single slave-owner can complain of being defrauded in whole or in part of his share of compensation. The sum of twenty millions sterling has been paid with accumulated interest, and free of all charges. The nation has fulfilled its part of the compact, and even exceeded its stipulations. The Negroes, though no parties to the agreement, have yet fulfilled all its onerous and unjust conditions. But, on the other hand, in every essential particular it has been violated by the planters, with the connivance, and even the active participation, of the Executive Government. Each succeeding Colonial

---

* " The West Indies in 1837," pp. 197, 199.

† *Ibid.*, p. 277. These cases have been selected from the mass of similar cruelties with which the pages of the report are filled ; because, taking place in Spanish Town, they illustrate the accuracy of Mr. Phillippo's representations to his correspondents at home.

Minister has trodden in the same steps, and the conceal-
ment and defence of successive errors have led to the
establishment, by authority, of the new system such as we
have described it.   At the present moment, the shelves of
the Colonial Office groan under accumulated evidence of
the wrongs and sufferings of the Negro." *

In a letter to the Rev. John Dyer, soon after the departure of the deputation, Mr. Phillippo thus refers to their
visit:—"Of our English friends, Messrs. Sturge and Harvey
I know most, as they did me the honour of abiding at my
house during their residence in Spanish Town, and I cannot but say that I not only esteem them very highly for
their work's sake, but also for their personal virtues, for
their purity of motive, their singleness of eye to the
Divine glory and the good of men, which shone out so
conspicuously in all their plans and efforts for the accomplishment of their object.   In further accordance with
your wish, I also afforded our friends every opportunity
of informing themselves as to the state of my church,
congregation, and schools.   Of the results of the mission
of these benevolent men, as to its main object, I shall
say but little.   Nor need I, as I am persuaded that ere
this reaches you the appalling disclosures will have been
made.   A man must have an iron heart not to sympathise
with the poor apprentices in the sorrow they are enduring;
and as my sensibilities, notwithstanding all my familiarity
with oppression, are not yet paralysed, most earnestly do
I hope that no time may be lost, nor effort spared, in
securing the destruction of the last vestige of that
accursed system by which, under the name of liberty, the
people are enthralled and bowed down.   'Disguise thy
form as thou wilt, still, Slavery, still thou art a bitter
draught!'"

---

* "The West Indies in 1837," p. 372.

Immediately on his arrival in London, May 30th, 1837, Mr. Sturge laid before an assemblage of the Society of Friends, of from 1,500 to 2,000 persons in number, gathered from all parts of the United Kingdom, the documents and facts with which he was burdened. After two hours' discussion, the assembly came to the unanimous conclusion that they would exert all their influence to urge the people of England to demand the abolition of the apprenticeship system at the earliest possible moment. The fire quickly spread. The press raised its powerful voice, and within six months deputations of varying magnitude gathered in London from all parts of the country. Downing Street and Westminster Hall were besieged. Petitions were presented, signed by upwards of a million persons—a mighty host, marshalled and led on by the piety, talent, learning, eloquence, and philanthropy of the best portion of the community—in which the abolition of the system was imperatively demanded, on the ground of the violation of the contract by the planters.*

The motion of Lord Brougham in the House of Lords on the 20th of February, 1838, that the apprenticeship should cease on the 1st of August, was supported by only seven peers ; † and in the Commons the same motion, made on the 29th of March, was lost, the Government opposing it, by a majority of fifty-four in a House of 484 members. But a bolder proposal was brought forward on the 22nd of May, viz., that the Negro should at once, and for ever, be free. It took the Government by surprise, and the motion was carried by a majority of three. Although a week later the

---

* Phillippo's " Jamaica : Past and Present," p. 174.

† In the course of this debate, the Marquis of Sligo quoted letters which he had received from Mr. Phillippo on the treatment of the apprentices.

resolution was virtually rescinded, it was evident that the cause of the oppressor was lost.*

The Legislature of Jamaica, after an adjournment, met on the 5th of June. The Governor called their attention to the uncontrollable agitation existing in the mother country. It was evident that the Government of England itself was unable to ensure the continuance of the apprenticeship as an act of national obligation in the face of the national protest. The Negroes also were in a state of excitement, expecting that the 1st of August would set them free; so that the Administration was sending circulars to the missionaries entreating them to use their influence to quiet the agitation. In some of the other islands the local Legislatures had already decreed the abolition, and there were proprietors, like Lord Sligo,† in Jamaica itself, preparing to release the predials and non-predials on the same day; while the amending Acts of the British Parliament threatened to override the free action of the House of Assembly. Thus pressed, the House, on the third day of their sitting, read for the first time a Bill to terminate the apprenticeship on the 1st of August. After a brief adjournment it was read a second time, and on the next

---

* Mr. Kitson, writing Mr. Phillippo, thus refers to this incident: "Our joy is turned into mourning, on account of the failure of all our efforts for the abolition of the apprenticeship next August. Our harps are on the willows; but our hope and trust is still in God. Though our petitions and addresses are disregarded by our earthly Sovereign, our supplications will rise up to the King Eternal that He may arise and plead the cause of the oppressed; and who can resist His power!"

† Mr. Phillippo, writing to Lord Sligo on the 29th of May, reports that the Marquis's declaration in the House of Lords that he should set free all his apprentices on the 1st of August had produced "an astonishing effect" in Jamaica. It had been hailed by the people with enthusiasm, but with a mixture of "despondency and bravado" by the pro-slavery party. Their hopes of perpetuating the system were irrevocably gone.

day, a few amendments being made in committee, a third time, and was passed. It quickly ran its course through the Council, and on the 16th of June it received the Governor's assent. The grace of the concession was in some measure dimmed by the protest that accompanied the Act. The House declaimed vehemently against the interference of the British Parliament with the internal affairs of Jamaica. It was declared to be illegal and unconstitutional; they " would neither assume the responsibility, nor exonerate the public faith." Nevertheless, freedom was secured, and the three hundred thousand bondsmen of Jamaica were made absolutely free.*

Mr. Phillippo was not without some expectation of this event. Writing Mr. George Stacey on the 14th of April, 1838, he says :—" Lord Brougham's speech has created the most extraordinary sensation here. Let the Government now be firm, and the planters will give up the system in August next, it is my firm opinion, without a struggle. All of tyrannical character are heartily tired of it, and I am persuaded would much rather freedom were universally proclaimed than agree to the provisions proposed by Lord Glenelg. I most earnestly hope that the friends of freedom will succeed in securing a universal jubilee in August next."

Mr. Phillippo was present as a spectator at the opening sitting in which this important measure was proposed, and, in a letter to Mr. E. Sturge, has, in a very lively manner, described the scene :—" Our local Legislature met on Tuesday, the 5th inst., according to announcement. The Governor's speech was straightforward and to the purpose. Sir Lionel read his speech to both Houses distinctly, and in a firm tone of voice—in a manner altogether indicative, as I thought, of a determination not to

---

* Gardner's " History of Jamaica," pp. 315, 317.

be trifled with any longer. He stated with much frank-
ness his own conviction that, as the law stood, it was
impossible that the apprenticeship could go on. When
the tidings of Lord Glenelg's amendments of the Emancipation Act first reached us here, I understood it to be the
determination of the members of the Assembly generally
to abolish the apprenticeship themselves, and thereby
prevent the infraction of their charter, as well as avoid
the degradation of an abject submission to a power they
could no longer resist. The Governor, however, by
attending strictly to his orders from Downing Street, and
issuing the proclamation within the given time after its
reception, was supposed to have created a reaction, and it
was, therefore, with considerable anxiety that I mingled
with the crowd, and followed this august body from the
Council Chamber to the arena where the general feeling
would be disclosed. The rules of the House having been
read, a member, from whom it was least to have been
expected, to my great surprise moved that the speech
should be made the order of the day for the morrow, in
the hope that arrangements might be made for abandoning
the system on the following Sunday! His proposition,
however, was overruled, and the committee for the consideration of the speech was appointed, as customary.
The address in answer to the speech was soon prepared,
and from the debate on it I was no longer in doubt as to
the general determination. The only point, indeed, that
seemed to arise regarded the time when the proclamation
of liberty should be made. Would it not be well to terminate the unnatural system at the close of the present
week, on the coronation day of their youthful Queen?
Or shall it be deferred until the 1st of August? These
questions were asked with deepest interest. The members
in general manifested more moderation than was to have
been expected. Only two individuals broke in upon

this feeling. The ravings and wailings in which these
gentlemen indulged were disgraceful in the extreme, and
as I looked towards the French Commissioner, who witnessed the exhibition,* I could have wept for our national
honour. One who had lately sold his estates at a good
profit indulged in such invectives against Mr. Hill, the
member for Trelawney, as to excite general indignation.
The whole House was thrown into confusion and uproar.
The monster Slavery was now in his final agonies, and it was
natural that his pangs should be manifested in his most
sensitive members. A few amendments were made, and
the address was ultimately carried by a small majority.
The member for St. Catherine immediately gave notice
that he would, on the following day, introduce a Bill to
abolish the apprenticeship system on the 1st of August
next, which was responded to by hearty cheers outside the
bar. I did not hear the few words that immediately
followed, but I soon ascertained that a decision had been
come to that the Bill should emanate from a committee."
The issue has been already told. "When," continues
Mr. Phillippo, "the result of the Bill could not be mistaken, I held a meeting for thanksgiving to Almighty God
for the joyous event. The hearts of the people seemed
filled with gratitude to overflowing. On the 1st of August I
expect we shall have a joy unparalleled in the history of the
world. What shall we render unto the Lord for all His
benefits? These, my dear friends, are the results, under
God, of your benevolent visit to our shores." In a brief
note to Mr. Kitson, Mr. Phillippo refers to the same event.
"Since my last letter, the Bill for full and unconditional

---

* This gentleman, M. Chevalier, who was commissioned by the
French Government to report on the condition of the apprentices in
Jamaica and the question of emancipation, was at the time on a visit
to Mr. Phillippo.

emancipation has passed the Legislature here without a dissentient voice, and, but for some little amendment by the Council, it would have been borne by the present mail, as on the wings of the wind, to the Colonial Office. Every humane and feeling heart is filled with gratitude at the result, and the tongue of every bondsman will soon sing for joy. To God be all the glory. Amen and Amen."

Although the die was cast, and slavery, whether real or disguised, was doomed in a few weeks to extinction, there were not wanting some individuals among the overseers and book-keepers and others on the estates who, for purposes of their own, seemed determined to annoy the people by insulting behaviour, and by threats of expulsion from their little holdings except on the most oppressive conditions as to rent and labour. Happily, this conduct was by no means general. Mr. Phillippo has given us, under date of July 7th, in a letter addressed to the Rev. John Dyer, an interesting account of the feelings with which the day of absolute freedom was awaited and prepared for.

"It cannot be dissembled, that many proprietors and managers, to their disgrace be it spoken, seem to manifest every disposition to annoy and impose upon the people under them by idle threats of expulsion from their properties, and by disgraceful proposals for their future services. As a consequence of the dissatisfaction occasioned by these circumstances, and others of a similar kind, occasioned by misrule, I have often within this last week or two been ready to sink beneath the fatigue of travelling from place to place, for the purpose of securing permanent and general good-will.

"A day or two ago I visited almost every estate and penn in the neighbourhood in which I understood the least excitement prevailed—assembled the people privately in their towns, and at their work, and, with all the earnestness and arguments I could exercise and command, entreated them, even under the most trying circumstances, to manifest the patience, forbearance, and respectful demeanour of true followers of Christ. Nor, in any single instance, were these efforts unavailing ; all with one voice declared their resolution to take off the crops without delay, to agree to whatever was equitable, and to cultivate future habits of industry and peace. But, while I have thus judged it advisable to apprise you of the real cause of any discontent that may possibly reach your ears, I would, at the same time, guard you against the apprehension of anything extreme. The 1st of August, I doubt not, will pass over with all the peacefulness and sanctity of a Sabbath ; and the majority of planters, I am persuaded, acting in accordance with the spirit and changes of the time, will secure the willing services of the people on the following Monday. This, however, I may say, I have obtained almost as a pledge from the whole apprentice population by whom I am surrounded, both in town and country, amounting probably to 10,000 individuals. Some of the proprietors and attorneys, and these among the most wealthy and respectable, have submitted for my remarks their calculations relative to a scale of wages, &c.; at the same time declaring their determination, as ultimately most advantageous to themselves, to act towards their labourers upon the strictest principles of equity. Terms acceptable and beneficial to all parties once concluded upon one or two of the principal properties in this parish, under the management or in the possession of persons heretofore reputed liberal and humane, I have cheerfully offered my services to facilitate their universal adoption as far as my humble influence extends ; and I have no doubt, from the character of the persons with whom the proposals originate, and from the importance and influence of the parish, that such an impetus will be given as will secure their speedy adoption more or less extensively by the mass.   As the effect of the changes that are so rapidly progressing, and as illustrative of the ease with which men regulate their policy by their interests, I must not omit to inform you of the bright and glorious prospects which are now opening up to us for the prosecution of our glorious work.   I am persuaded that there is now scarcely a proprietor or manager of any extent, in the whole district which I occupy, but who would be glad to afford me all the encouragement in his power in imparting religious instruction to his people.   At the present moment I have invitations from not fewer than a dozen of the most influential individuals in town and country to establish schools and preaching in the vicinity of their estates, accompanied, in almost every case, by an offer of land and materials for the purpose of a religious establishment.   The people in general are looking forward with intense interest to the 1st of August.   The very wilds are already fascinated with the productions of their own native muse, and as to the towns there is no moving for the poets which the occasion has created.   I have no doubt but the event will prove the most interesting that ever transpired in the annals of the world.   British Christians, come, or send over, and help us!   What is to be done must be done quickly, for the fields are ripe and the harvest is great."

The following letter from the Marquis of Sligo is so honourable to that nobleman, and so illustrative of the influence enjoyed by Mr. Phillippo, that it cannot be omitted from the history of the events recorded in this chapter.

From the Marquis of Sligo to the Rev. J. M. Phillippo.

London, April 8th, 1838.

My dear Sir,—The last packet will have brought to you an account of my resolution to emancipate my Negroes on the 1st August next.

I was considering the matter since last spring, and did not come to the determination without much doubt and difficulty. Even now, I am not without misgivings that I may have been wrong. It is on account of this feeling, and to try and obviate such danger, that I now address you. My fears have been that the Negroes of the estates surrounding mine may be led to think that they are illegally kept in servitude when they see mine set free on the 1st of August, and I have had considerable uneasiness in my mind as to my conduct producing any bad effects of that sort. I know well your influence with your flock, and I have conscientiously done you justice as well in my writings as in my speeches; I do hope you will repay me in the only way I ask for any repayment, by exerting that influence to prevent any injury arising from my emancipating my Negroes. I am anxious that my own Negroes should continue to conduct themselves properly after being emancipated; that the Negroes of those estates around mine should not show any signs of discontent, but should continue in their labour quietly and properly. They must feel that I have made a great sacrifice to promote their freedom two years sooner than it would naturally come to them. I don't wish any repayment for that, except that I should have influence enough over them and their comrades to prevent their committing any either *active* or *passive* breaches of the law. I am anxious to point out to them that much of their future prospects as regards legislation in the Colonies, and the approbation here of those laws, depends upon the manner in which they shall comport themselves on this trying occasion. There are many other points, which will suggest themselves to you much more advantageously than I can name them, which I am most desirous should be impressed on them by their pastors. I am quite confident that Mr. Taylor, or whoever is in charge of the Old Harbour district, might effect a great deal by impressing these sentiments on them *continually till the* 1st of August, by pointing out to *mine* that, having been selected for the experiment, it behoves them to show that they are fit for it, and to the surrounding ones that much of the future position of the Negroes depends on their tranquil and willing obedience to the laws. It is unnecessary for me to say more. I am sure that we have but one feeling, and that is mutual, a desire to do the greatest possible quantity of good. From the prominent part which I have taken in this case, I am perhaps morbidly sensitive on the result of my conduct, and I may, therefore, bore you by all this; but I should not be tranquil did I omit doing anything to contribute to produce the effect I desire, and most uneasy shall I be till I hear the result of the 1st of August. I hope that you will find time to write to me *before then*, as to what your opinions are of the way it will be received, and your general views of their conduct on the occasion, and also to write me a few lines after August how the day has gone off, and your opinion as to their future conduct.—My dear Sir, most truly yours,

SLIGO.

Bernal of Cherry Garden was the man, as I hear, who proposed at the West India meeting that they should all follow my example. I am told that they almost kicked him out of the room. He deserves great merit for the attempt, and it ought to be known.

The unexpected action of the House of Assembly happily rendered unnecessary the precautions here suggested. Unconditional freedom was decreed for apprentices of every class.

CHAPTER XIX.

CELEBRATION OF FREEDOM—1838.

The 1st of August, 1838, dawned amidst scenes of intense excitement. Thousands of people had gathered in the chapel and on the mission premises on the previous evening, and many more kept pouring in from all quarters throughout the night. Appropriate and deeply interesting services of mingled prayer and praise, interspersed with addresses, were held until dawn; and when the sound of the clock striking six was heard, one universal shout burst forth from the lips of the multitude within the building, echoed by the greater multitude without. " Freedom's come! Our wives and our children are free! Glory to de God for dis blessed day!" Hymns prepared for the occasion were sung in strains that showed unmistakably the melody of the heart, and none with fuller emotion than the opening hymn, beginning with the verse :—

> Joy! for every yoke is broken,
> And the oppressed all go free :
> Let us hail it as the token
> That our much-loved land may be
> Blessed of the Lord Most High,
> Ruler of the earth and sky.

Another service, with a sermon, commenced at ten o'clock ; and at eleven, according to an arrangement made with his Excellency the Governor, a procession, with numerous banners having appropriate mottoes, and with bands of music, Mr. Phillippo at its head, marched to the

Parade, in front of the King's House. The entire population of the town were present, and, with the multitudes from the country, were addressed by Sir Lionel Smith, surrounded by the Bishop, the Chief Justice, and his personal staff, in a speech full of feeling and paternal advice. The deep impression it made was quite remarkably seen in the attention, the respect, and the gratitude with which it was received. It is due to Mr. Phillippo to quote the remarks of an observer describing this affecting scene. " The writer is free to confess that he can hardly refrain from polluting with feelings of envy the admiration with which he beheld a man who had brought forward an immense portion of the population, who were ready to acknowledge themselves indebted under God to him for having been rescued from barbarism and sin, and received at his hands the blessings of religion, morality, and education." During the delivery of the speech, his Excellency was greeted by reiterated and enthusiastic cheers as their friend and benefactor, and, with three closing cheers for the Queen, the mass attended their pastor to the mission-house, saluting him in the most enthusiastic manner. The close of the day's proceedings must be given in the words of an eye-witness.

" Arrived in the immediate neighbourhood of the chapel, the multitude surrounded him, grasped him in their arms, and bore him, in the midst of shouts and caresses, into his house. The enthusiasm of the multitude being now wound up to the highest pitch, they declared themselves unwilling to separate without greeting the different flags ; and flags and banners were accordingly unfurled, and for nearly an hour the air rang with the shouts of exultation that were thus poured forth from thousands of joyous hearts.

"The school children had remained behind to sing several airs before the Government House, and just as the

mass were cheering the last banner, upon which was in-
scribed in large capitals, ' We are free, we are free ; our
wives and our children are free ! ' they all entered, and,
adding their shrill voices to the rest, created an acclaim
that seemed to rend the air.

"The whole scene which the mission premises presented
on that day was delightful, and will never be forgotten.
Over the two principal entrances to the chapel were three
triumphal arches, decorated with leaves and flowers, and
crowned with flags, bearing the several inscriptions of—
' Freedom's come ;' ' Slavery is no more ; ' ' Thy chains
are broken, Africa is free ! ' while in addition to these,
and the flags and banners borne by the procession, one
was seen waving from the cupola of the Metropolitan
School, with the motto, ' The 1st August, 1838.' "

On the following Thursday and Friday a bazaar was
held for the benefit of the schools ; and an examination
of the children on the Saturday, attended by the Governor
and his suite, closed the proceedings of this memorable
week—a week unequalled in the annals of the country,
and unstained, as far as was known, by a single act of intemperance or violence.

During the ensuing weeks the event was celebrated by
the members of the church and congregation in a very
becoming manner, on several of the different penns and
estates around. At Dawkin's Caymanas the late apprentices gave a banquet to the Governor and several special
magistrates. In all cases the ever-memorable day was
celebrated with the utmost good feeling towards their late
owners on the part of the people. To Mr. and Mrs.
Phillippo these gatherings were of intense interest.
Nothing could exceed the reception they met with. Over-
powering congratulations everywhere attended their steps,
and from Cumberland Penn they were accompanied home
by an escort of the newly enfranchised peasantry on horse-

back. " The whole scene," says a writer in the *Jamaica Gazette*, " was deeply interesting, and the order and propriety observed would have done credit to Christians of the most civilised country in the world. The conduct of the people in this district generally, in other respects also, is such as to entitle them to the highest commendation. Well knowing the inconvenience to which their masters' customers would be otherwise reduced from a want of food for their horses and cattle, they voluntarily went out to work on the second day, and in some instances on the following, and supplied the usual demand of the market, presenting their labour thus voluntarily given as a free-will offering to their employers."

" God," says Mr. Phillippo, " was universally recognised as the Giver of the bounties enjoyed, and from first to last He was regarded as the Great Author of their deliverance from bondage."*

---

* Fuller details of these celebrations may be seen in Phillippo's " Jamaica: Past and Present," p. 175; and also in the " Missionary Herald " under date. Engravings of the scenes before the King's House, and of some others, were also published at the time.

CHAPTER XX.

THE three years following entire emancipation were to Mr. Phillippo years of intense, arduous, and exciting labour. Scarcely had the people quieted down after the stirring events of August, 1838, than we find him recording that the enfranchised peasantry were working admirably, and in the most generous manner devoting their earnings to the erection of schools and chapels, and the extension of the means of grace. From the commerce carried on between the towns and country, and from the appearance and manners of the people, it was evident that the enjoyment of freedom was acting as a stimulus to industry and enterprise. The people were cheerful and happy. They seemed to exist in a new world, and to breathe a new atmosphere. The happy effects of the change surpassed the hopes of their friends, while many opponents to freedom became converts to its advantages. Hence the missionaries were welcomed on many estates formerly closed to them, and the opportunities for extended operations opened on every hand so rapidly and widely that Mr. Phillippo expresses the opinion, towards the close of the year, that " if the Society could but aid us in our struggle for two years longer, with men and with increased means of a pecuniary kind, they might then leave us to ourselves. There is scarcely an estate or property of any kind, for miles around, upon which I have not been invited to establish schools and erect a place of worship. If I have had one acre of land offered me for this purpose

I have had a hundred, and in almost every case accompanied with the offer also of building materials, and a part of the labour requisite in the erection."

In his endeavours to meet this state of things, Mr. Phillippo involved himself in large pecuniary liabilities, so that we find him constantly appealing to friends in England for aid, especially for the maintenance of the numerous schools he was encouraged to commence. The congregations formed before freedom was complete had to pay off the debts incurred on the buildings in Spanish Town, Passage Fort, and Sligoville, so that little help could be rendered for the present need. "Men of Israel," he exclaims, "help! It must be painful indeed to a missionary to labour among a people who manifest no disposition to listen to his message; but I often persuade myself that it is still more so where he is unable to satisfy the insatiable appetite of hundreds hungering and thirsting for the bread and water of eternal life. What is to be done, 1 really cannot tell. Wants requiring pecuniary means arise on every hand. In addition to the need of new chapels, all those already erected require enlargement. Spanish Town and Passage Fort scarcely hold half the congregations."

The assistance rendered by the Committee of the Society, though again and again acknowledged by Mr. Phillippo to be generous, was far from meeting his necessities. The same cry came from all parts of the island, and the resources of the Society were taxed to the utmost to supply only a small part of the demands that came before them. There can be little doubt that the extraordinary liberality of the Negro congregations * in some

---

* In a letter to Mr. Dyer on the 28th of December, 1840, Mr. Phillippo warns his correspondent that this extraordinary liberality was owing to the exceptional circumstances of the case, and could not be expected to continue.

measure disguised from the churches at home the need of immediate and unstinted action ; but it may be questioned whether, if these requirements had been met, the difficulties which afterwards arose would not have been intensified.   Burdened on every side, Mr. Phillippo nevertheless pressed onwards, and new congregations, new chapels, new school-houses, sprang up with extraordinary rapidity.   A brief extract from a letter to the Rev. John Dyer, dated February 25th, 1840, will give some idea of the pressure upon his energies, both of mind and body.   After stating that he had been compelled to draw on the Treasurer, he says, " The facts of my condition are briefly these.   I have had upwards of £100 to pay this year for doctors' bills.   Nearly £500 for the last addition to the chapel out of £1,000, the total cost.   £500 towards liquidating the debts on the chapels at Passage Fort and Sligoville.   Full £500 for the salaries of schoolmasters ; £150 for land at St. John's (on which the people of the district have offered to build a chapel, principally by their own labour), and I am full £700 in debt.   I have indulged the hope that, after all, I might be able to obviate the necessity of an application to the Committee, by an appeal to the inhabitants of the town in general ; but, the calamity at Savanna-la-Mar happening just at the time * I was contemplating it, I was, of course, induced to forego my own appeal in favour of brother Hutchins and his people, on whose behalf I obtained £250.   For the payment of the £700 I am now pressed to such a degree that I am driven to draw £100 upon the Committee by next packet, to which, under the circumstances, I feel confident they will not object."

---

* On the night of the 23rd of November, 1839, a fire broke out in a store, and soon reached the new and beautiful chapel built by Mr. Hutchins, at a cost of £4,000 currency, and completely destroyed it. —" Voice of Jubilee," p. 114.

A little later, May 13th, he writes : "I am greatly harassed for means to carry on my various schools. My people are now about making an effort to refund my advances, but I am almost afraid to press them. Our new chapel at the Red Hills is already begun, and next week I contemplate preparations for the enlargement of that at Sligoville, which is to be twice its present dimensions. Thus I have more labour and anxiety in prospect than ever. With these incessant building engagements, with their attendant anxieties, added to the cares and labours of more direct ministerial duty, I must again inform you that I am almost worn down. To go on much longer as I am now doing will be impossible."

With all this he was unable to resist the appeals that were made to him. He reports, among others, frequent deputations from the parish of Manchester, begging, with tears in their eyes, for a minister to be settled among them, and promising to provide all the expenses of the station if the Committee will send them one. "This," says Mr. Phillippo, " is probably saying more than can be done ; but I have no doubt they would support a minister comfortably after twelve months, if not before, their energies being directed during that term to the erection of a dwelling-house and the completion of their chapel."

The appeal made to the Committee met with a very cordial reception ; but their arrangements did not meet his case. Writing to the Secretary on the 1st of October, he says : "The resolution of the Committee with regard to the terms on which they will consent to supply us with additional labourers are ruly generous. But I deeply regret to say that it is out of my power to avail myself of their advantages. First, because in a week or two's time, although the debt incurred by the erection of the building is scarcely liquidated, I must begin an addition to the chapel at Passage Fort that will involve an expense of

£500.   Secondly, because I have already begun the erection of a large place of worship at the Red Hills, or Kitson Town, that will probably involve a still larger sum; and thirdly, because I am now in the midst of pecuniary claims to a large amount for an addition to the chapel at Sligoville—far larger than I shall be able to collect from my people. Add to this the heavy and pressing demands of my schools, eight in number, and which cost little less than £14 a week, to say nothing of incidental expenses and the support of my family.   For the latter items I am dependent on the Spanish Town portion of my church, and the uncertain assistance afforded by benevolent friends in England.   These have always been inadequate to my wants, as well as uncertain, and occasion me no small degree of anxiety and pain.   These things I have never felt more keenly than at present, as it has been my resolution, if possible, to accomplish my building plans independently of foreign aid.   It will require my most strenuous efforts to extricate myself for two years to come at least.   But help I must have, or I must either sink beneath my labours and responsibilities, or subject the Society and myself to the reproach of doing the work of the Lord imperfectly.   To my load of cares and responsibilities, already far too numerous, I have just added the purchase of a property called Kensington, consisting of 350 acres of land, for the purpose of forming another township and missionary station.   In a few weeks I expect the whole will be sold to the poor peasantry of the district, and the money be in possession of the salesman."

The Committee so far relaxed the terms of their proposal that, in January, 1841, Mr. Phillippo was joined by Mr. and Mrs. William Hume, to act with him as assistant-minister and schoolmaster; and in the following April Mr. John Williams arrived from England to relieve Mr. Phillippo of tne charge of the work in Manchester, where, in the interval, at Porus, he had gathered a congregation.

The pecuniary difficulties of the Society towards the close of the year led the Committee, in order to economise their agencies, to contemplate the removal of Mr. Hume to Westmoreland. It did not take place till the beginning of 1842, when the Rev. Thomas Dowson came to his aid. The proposal, however, called forth an earnest and eloquent remonstrance from Mr. Phillippo, and led to the following description of his necessities and the extent of his labours :—" I have been alone in this district for the last seventeen years and upwards. I have eight stations, some of them full twenty miles distant from the central one, each of which requires the services of a regular minister at least once a month on the Sabbath, as well as occasional meetings on a week-day. Eight schools are under my superintendence, and are solely dependent on me for support. I have three new chapels in building, and one being enlarged, the cost of which, full £3,000 sterling, I, in some way or other, must meet. I have services to maintain three times on the Sabbath invariably in Spanish Town, and a church-meeting and Sabbath-schools to attend, besides two week-day services, all of which probably involve as much mental labour as in a respectable town in England ; with marriages and funerals, visits to the sick, and a thousand other pastoral duties to discharge arising in churches of between two and three thousand members in town and country. The Spanish Town station, except during the enlargement of the chapel, has supported me for years. To the utmost of my ability, and even beyond it, I can most conscientiously declare I have endeavoured to avoid being burdensome to the Society. The number of stations that I have been instrumental in forming and carrying on for a time have not been fewer than seventeen. Some of these stations, such as Jericho, Springfield, Old

Harbour, Vere, and others, have become the parents and centres of surrounding ones, and are now among the most important of any in the island. I think the sums had for these stations were peculiarly small, while for those still under my care I have been in the habit of receiving from the Society only the proportion of £30 per annum for each. The whole of the stations under my charge do not raise for one benevolent object and another less than £2,000 sterling *per annum*—I mean objects connected especially with our own denomination, such as chapel-building, support of schools, the African Mission, and others of a local kind."

It is not possible to conceive of these exhaustive labours as other than most trying to the constitution and spirits of the healthiest and strongest man working in the tropical climate of the West Indies, and it will be no surprise that Mr. Phillippo should utter, towards the close of 1841, the following touching words respecting it :—" My health, and spirits too, have given way beneath the pressure of these engagements and anxieties, sustained for so many years. I am indeed now laid almost totally aside by the failure of my voice, occasioned by its almost incessant and too violent exercise for years past in and out of doors. My medical adviser positively tells me that, unless I cease altogether from public speaking for two or three months, I shall lose its use in public. My dear wife also, having shared my anxieties and labours, and borne a large family of nine children, five of whom have been torn from her by death, and often sicknesses which many times have brought her to the very gates of the grave, is now in such extremely delicate health and bad spirits as to be obliged to reside almost entirely at Sligoville, where I must leave her, as it were, in solitude the greater part of each week. Thus, from the moment of my arrival in the island until now, I have scarcely known a respite from distracting care and exhausting toil."

But his exertions were not without an ample reward in the Divine blessing that accompanied them. Each year bore witness to his success, in large additions to the fellowship of the churches, and in the growing intelligence and piety of the members. A few extracts from his letters and reports will suffice to show the gracious approval of his Lord on his manifold labours. Writing on the 28th of February, 1838, he says: "God has been pleased to bless the church in Spanish Town with prosperity as to members; nor has He left us without such tokens of His grace as have visibly promoted the growing influence of vital piety over the minds and habits of the church in general. The nature and extent of the Divine requirements with regard to the Sabbath are more generally understood, and the duty of regular and punctual attendance upon the public worship of God is more regarded. Brotherly love continues, and peace and harmony prevail amongst us. Owing to the regular preaching of the Word at Passage Fort and Sligoville, and the late dismission to the latter station of 218 members, the congregation here is somewhat diminished; but our place of worship is still as full as it will conveniently accommodate, and is often so crowded as to render a separate service in the school-room necessary. God has not only been with us, but in His holy influences He has gone before us, preparing the hearts of the people to receive the seed of the Kingdom." During the year he had baptized nearly three hundred persons, and the number of members in communion at the three stations was 2,191. The nineteen schools he supported contained 1,588 scholars.

Writing again on the 16th of April, 1839, nine months after the enjoyment of complete freedom, after reporting that the churches had suffered some losses by defection, he proceeds to remark that, amidst the excitement attending the celebration of freedom, it would have been no wonder if many had been betrayed into intemperance and other excesses at variance with their profession, and the habitual self-denial required of the disciples of Christ. But, "in no case," he says, "have these fears been realised. The conduct of our friends and brethren was such as became the followers of our Lord and Saviour Jesus Christ, uniformly modest, sober, and devout, their enemies themselves being judges. In every instance, when treated with the consideration due to human beings, and in the prospect of fair remuneration, have they been diligent in business, fervent in spirit, serving the Lord. From general imperfection, and from individual acts of sin on our part, as a Christian society, we by no means consider ourselves exempt. But as the pastor of the church, in some degree, I trust, aware of my awful responsibility to God, I most solemnly declare, in opposition to all that may have been insinuated to the contrary, that wholesome discipline and the most vigilant oversight have been anxiously and unremittingly maintained. The habitual exercise of wholesome discipline I have regarded as in every way advantageous to the prosperity of the church, and this I have ever found it. By its exercise, a greater dread of sin has been inspired, the weak have been strengthened, the backslider reclaimed, and the purity of the church and the glory of God preserved.

"The increase of our stated congregations since the great boon of freedom has been enjoyed has been so great that a third enlargement of our chapel at Spanish Town has become necessary, and also of those of Passage Fort and Sligoville. Such, indeed, is the desire on the part of the poorer classes of the people generally for the Gospel, and of the late apprentices in particular, that if each of the chapels I have already built were twice its present dimensions, and half-a-dozen more could be erected, I have not the least doubt of all being filled."

The net increase of his churches during the year had been 326 members, while no less than 2,598 children and adults were under constant instruction.

A similar bright picture may be given of the Christian work of the year 1840; but with some brief excerpts from the report of 1841 this chapter shall be closed. They are taken from a letter dated 1st of February, addressed to the ministers and messengers of the associated Baptist churches about to assemble at Falmouth. Mr. Phillippo writes :—" The chapel at Spanish Town, which has been a third time enlarged, is too small for the numbers that usually flock to it on the Sabbath. On the first Sabbath of the month, on which day the Lord's Supper is administered, although a separate service for the children is held in the school-room, the members present so far exceed what the chapel will accommodate that from one to two hundred communicants are sometimes obliged to sit outside. Our Sabbath morning prayer-meetings are still maintained, having been carried on without intermission during a period of seventeen years. We have also a similar service on the Monday evening. The contemplated establishment of a mission to Africa by our Society, the interest felt in the enterprise by British Christians, and the actual devotion of our beloved brethren Clarke and Prince to the object, have especially contributed to the spiritual warmth and vigour which we trust we now enjoy with reference to the extension of the Redeemer's Kingdom. There is generally manifested amongst us a growing acquaintance with the truth as it is in Jesus, and an increased relish for spiritual enjoyments. Peace and harmony remain unbroken. Love to God, to one another, and to the whole household of faith, it is hoped, continues to increase. The sacred Scriptures, by being more widely diffused, are more generally read, and consequently better understood, whilst personal and relative duties have been more correctly discharged.

" Removals by death have been comparatively few, and with respect to every one of them evidences were afforded of their having entered into rest.   Holy and exemplary in their lives, they exhibited in their last moments a tranquillity which death could not ruffle, and a confidence that the King of Terrors could not shake.

" Many have betrayed symptoms of a backsliding state which have demanded the exercise of discipline.   Yet few have remained hardened in impenitence, and a considerable number have been welcomed back again to a participation of the privileges of Christian communion.

" At the close of the year the membership numbered 2,551 persons, and at all the stations, both principal and subordinate, the attendance on the means of grace was increasing.

" Thus," concludes the letter, " amidst many discouragements, it is evident that the blessing of the Lord our God has been upon us, prospering the work of our hands. With this conviction, let us animate each other to increased energy and perseverance, forgetting the things that are behind, and pressing on towards things that are before, looking for and trusting unto the day of God." Thus, " in weariness, in painfulness, and in watchings often," Mr. Phillippo pursued his arduous work, sustained by the assurance that the Lord was with him, giving effect to His Word, and crowning his efforts with success.

CHAPTER XXI.

THE system of apprenticeship was scarcely carried into effect in 1834 than disputes arose between the planters and their apprentices as to the wages which should be paid for their toil; and when full freedom came in 1838 little or no progress had been made in settling this important question. To this day it can scarcely be said to have reached a final and equitable decision. There were, however, not a few proprietors of estates who at once endeavoured to meet the case in a fair spirit, and who requested the missionaries to exercise the influence they possessed with the labourers to bring about an amicable settlement. Mr. Phillippo especially mentions, among other large proprietors and attorneys who took this course, the Hon. A. Bravo and the Hon. T. J. Bernard. As a representative of the people, he was present, by desire, at a meeting of the agents of these gentlemen with their apprentices to consider the proposals of the estate-owners. After long discussions, these proposals, with some modifications as recommended by Mr. Phillippo, were adopted to the satisfaction of all parties. But these mutually beneficial conferences were the exception, and not the rule. Other meetings, not so gratifying in their result, took place, of one of which Mr. Phillippo has preserved the following lively account. It was held in St. Thomas-in-the-Vale, and was marked by the presence of the Governor. His Excellency, finding there would be no one there to represent the people, invited the services of Mr. Phillippo for the occasion. "A very large assemblage of both parties," says Mr. Phillippo, " were at the tavern where the conference was to be held. I arrived before his Excellency, and found myself in a large room filled with planters and others of the ruling class, including the rector and curate of the parish. I was treated with superciliousness and contempt. The Governor had no sooner entered than he was surrounded by the planter-complainants, who occupied him for upwards of two hours in efforts to prejudice him against the labourers. The people, who had crowded round the entrance to the house, expressed their dissatisfaction to me. Their complaints, they said, were disregarded, and they handed to me, over the heads of the crowd, in the cleft of long sticks, receipts for the rent of houses and grounds, some of which amounted to more than the wages given them, rent being charged for almost, if not quite, every member of the family. These I investigated, amid the rude insults and threatenings of one or two roughs of overseers, who were watching my movements. I then forced my way to his Excellency, and told him that the labourers outside were afraid that they would not be allowed to make their complaints or defence. He at once followed me into the yard, and seated himself under the shade of a tree. The people gathered round, and put into his hands their papers. Both by word and gesture his Excellency expressed his indignation against the perpetrators of the injustice and oppression, and then, ordering his carriage, hastily withdrew and returned home. The planters started for Rodney Hall, where they re-assembled, and passed resolutions condemnatory of the Governor, and especially that he had insulted the rector, and through him the church and the whole parish, in treating a sectarian minister as his chaplain and counsellor.

They further embodied their complaints in a document which they forwarded to the Colonial Office."*

On many estates the people were cajoled by promises never intended to be performed. Relieved by the Emancipation Act of 1838 from the stringent clauses of the Act of 1834, the planters were entirely at liberty to pursue any course they saw fit, and the most despicable arts were frequently resorted to to obtain labour for almost nothing. If the miserable remuneration was refused, the cottages of the recalcitrant labourers were pulled down, the estates' cattle driven into their provision grounds, and the growing crops destroyed. Homeless and houseless, great numbers, whether in health or sickness, old or young, were driven to the bush for shelter. A standard of a day's labour and its value had gradually been formed during slavery, and it was naturally expected by the apprentices that their remuneration would be laid accordingly. Some efforts were put forth by the Government, in connection with committees of planters, to establish a tariff of work and wages, on the principle that a free man would be sure to labour more heartily, and give a better return to his master, than a slave. But these tariffs generally failed of adoption, the planters preferring perfect freedom of contract, which would allow them to exercise any pressure within their reach on the necessitous labourer. They were altogether unwilling to pay such wages as the new circumstances of the Negro

----

* Mr. J. J. Gurney thus speaks of the usefulness of the Baptist missionaries :—" The Baptist missionaries in Jamaica, for many years past, have been the unflinching and untiring friends of the Negro. No threats have daunted them ; no insults or persecutions have driven them from the field. They are now [1840] reaping their reward in the devoted attachment of the people, and the increasingly prevalent acknowledgment of their integrity and usefulness."—" Winter in the West Indies," p. 120

required. For with enfranchisement came a demand for better dwellings than the miserable huts of the estate in which they had hitherto been housed. Greater comforts and conveniences were sought after, and the social, moral, and intellectual elevation of the enfranchised people required larger provision to be made for its attainment.

Foreseeing these difficulties, Mr. Phillippo, shortly after 1834, with several of his missionary brethren, assisted by some wealthy gentlemen in England, began to purchase land for the settlement of the labouring classes. The lawlessness and tyranny to which they had been subject taught them that they could not be sure of a home unless they possessed freeholds of their own. The opportunity of relief from this oppression was eagerly seized on the arrival of emancipation, and the allotments made on the properties thus purchased were immediately bought. Estate-hamlets were abandoned, and free villages and townships sprang up in all parts of the island. The acquisition of land was rendered more easy by the large number of properties that came into the market. This arose partly from the impracticability of working with profit many of the estates in the interior now that unpaid and forced labour could not be secured ; and partly from proprietors who had received compensation for their slaves, which, as Lord Palmerston said, in many instances was an amount equal to the value of the fee simple of the land itself, abandoning the cultivation of sugar, and the island altogether.

Mr. Phillippo was among the first to make provision for the large emigration from the estates that took place. Early in 1835 he purchased twenty-five acres of land, which were afterwards increased to fifty, in the mountains above Spanish Town, in the first instance to form a mission station. It now became the nucleus of a settlement. The position was unrivalled for beauty and salubrity, and stood in the midst of a district entirely destitute of religious privileges. The settlement was named Sligoville, in honour of the Marquis of Sligo, whose country residence was near at hand, and who, with his family, took great interest in its formation, as the first town to arise on the ruins of slavery. When purchased, the land was an unreclaimed wilderness. It was covered with masses of rock, and with a rank luxuriance of vegetation that obstructed the prospect. The first building erected was a chapel and a school-room under one roof. It was begun in the month of October, 1835. A larger building soon became necessary. This was completed in July, 1838, immediately preceding the close of the apprenticeship system. About two months before the proclamation of entire freedom, the first lot of land was purchased by Henry Lunan, formerly a slave and head-man on the Hampstead plantation adjoining. The remainder of the land was rapidly bought by the apprentices of the neighbourhood, and on the 12th of June, 1840, the settlement was formally opened by a religious service in the chapel. The township then contained about 100 families; but when all the purchasers had built their houses and entered on their tenancies they would be increased to 200. Though surrounded with many difficulties incident to the first settlement of such a spot, there was every prospect of a prosperity as conducive to the interests of the colony as to those of the labourers and artisans themselves, all of whom gradually found employment at moderate wages on the properties around.

The township was visited by Mr. Joseph John Gurney, attended by Mr. Phillippo, on the 7th of March, 1840. Mr. Gurney thus describes his impressions :—" We spent [here] several hours. It is located on a lofty hill, and is surrounded by fifty acres of fertile mountain land. This property is divided into 150 freehold lots, fifty of which had already been sold to the emancipated Negroes, and had proved a timely refuge for many labourers who had been driven by hard usage from their former homes. Some of them had built good cottages; others, temporary huts; and others, again, were preparing the ground for building. Not a hoe, I believe, had ever been driven into that land before. The people settled there were all married pairs, mostly with families, and the men employed the bulk of their time in working for wages on the neighbouring estates. The chapel and the school were immediately at hand, and the religious character of the people stood high. Never did I witness a scene of greater industry, or one more marked by contentment for the present and hope for the future." *

A medical gentleman visiting the town some two years later, and remaining there a week, thus speaks of what he saw :—" Every allotment of land is now sold, and many of the people are applying in vain for more. The canes, provisions, and fruit are equal, if not superior, to any in the island. Many of the settlers had not a penny when they came; but they have worked and paid for the land by its produce. They have erected comfortable cottages, and are now living in perfect happiness, as far as human happiness can be perfect. They have no anxieties; and are eminently grateful, both to Christians who worked for, and to the God who gave them, freedom."

Sturge Town, situated about seven miles from Spanish Town, and named after the eminent philanthropist Joseph Sturge, was the next township formed. The land was purchased by Mr. Phillippo, with moneys supplied from England, and formed part of a large estate of a thousaud acres, the whole of which was purchased in the following

---

* " A Winter in the West Indies," by Joseph John Gurney (London : 1840), pp. 115, 116.

year. At the other extremity of the estate, the village of Kensington was afterwards built, and opened in August, 1841. By this purchase some loss was incurred by Mr. Phillippo, as a few of the planters, finding they would be altogether deprived of labourers if they refused them homesteads, offered portions of their outlying lands for sale, and at a price less than that which Mr. Phillippo could afford.

The lands of Kitson Town, eight miles from Spanish Town, consisting of 195 acres, were bought with assistance found on the spot, in August, 1839, and were sold chiefly to labourers who had been turned off from estates. The township was situated in the midst of a dense agricultural population, and was opened with a suitable ceremony on the 3rd of July, 1841.*

Clarkson Town, the fourth township in order of settlement, was commenced by Mr. Phillippo in 1839. It is distant eight miles from Spanish Town, in a glade near an estate called Taylor's Caymanas. The mountains on either side of the long valley rear their summits to the clouds and nearly meet at their base. The town was divided into three principal streets, one of which, by an angle in its centre, became two, named respectively Victoria and Albert. Along these streets, leaving a piece of garden ground in front, the cottages were ranged on either side, at equal distances. The township was opened with a very interesting ceremony on the 12th of May, 1842. "At the appointed hour," says Mr. Phillippo, "the words 'Come to prayers' being vociferated two or three times by one of the most robust and active of the villagers, who ascended the summit of a detached hill for the purpose,

---

* Tradition reports that the settlement was on the site of a large Carib settlement called Guanaboa. Indian utensils and other remains are often found in the woods.

every individual in the settlement was seen wending his way to the rural sanctuary, under the widespread branches of the trees, fixed upon for the service. The aged and infirm came supporting themselves on a staff, and others more vigorous climbed the steep ascent with quick and eager step. They were seated in semi-circles, on planks affixed to uprights placed in the ground." A sermon was preached by the Rev. T. Dowson, followed by an address from the pastor, who proceeded afterwards to name the streets of the town. " May this infant township," were his closing words, " rise under the blessing of Almighty God ; and may its inhabitants to the most distant posterity, united in bonds of Christian love and fellowship, be as one family, with one feeling to prompt and one principle to govern ! "

Visiting this township on his return from Sligoville, Mr. J. J. Gurney says :—" We returned towards Spanish Town by a very wild path, over stones, and through brakes and briars, until we came to Clarkson Town. Here we were refreshed by the hospitable people with draughts of lemonade. We found them industriously engaged in cultivating their own freeholds. Many of them had long been labourers on a neighbouring estate, from which they had at last been forced away by ill-treatment. Their cocoa-nut trees had been felled, their huts demolished. What could they do but seek a new home ? They crowded round us, and expressed the most entire willingness again to work on the property if they were but treated with fairness and kindness. They were well known to my friend Phillippo, being many of them members of his church, and a better-conditioned or better-mannered peasantry could not easily be found." *

In December, 1840, Mr. Phillippo opened the sixth of

---

* " Winter in the West Indies," pp. 116, 117.

these townships at Porus, in Manchester. This property was bought by a combination of the people among themselves, but laid out by Mr. Phillippo, who named it Vale Lionel, after the excellent Governor, Sir Lionel Smith, who on the site of it had addressed the people previous to freedom. It is at the present time a populous place, and the seat of a large coffee market.

In 1842, Mr. Phillippo calculated that the above settlements contained about 3,150 individuals. To these should be added several villages or townships the formation of which, more or less, he directed or superintended. It is difficult, if not impossible, he adds, to ascertain the number of similar settlements which sprang up within five or six years of emancipation. Lord Stanley stated in the House of Commons, in 1840, that in one parish alone there had been acquired by the enfranchised peasantry 7,340 freeholds, consisting of houses and lands of various extent. A hundred thousand acres of land must have passed into the hands of the people in that short space of time, and a very large number of labourers were thus permanently withdrawn from sugar cultivation on the estates.*

In a letter to Mr. Sturge, dated October 30, 1841, Mr. Phillippo thus sums up the general condition of the people :—

"The labouring population are in the most striking manner falsifying the planters' loud predictions respecting their conduct. The sloth and idleness which were imputed to them by anticipation turn out a mere dream

---

* Among the numerous free villages established by Baptist missionaries may be mentioned, Bethel Town and Mount Carey, by Mr. Burchell; Kettering and Hoby Town, by Mr. Knibb; Wilberforce and Buxton, by Mr. Clark; Victoria, in St. Thomas-in-the-Vale, by Mr. John Clarke; and the Alps and Calabar, by Mr. Dexter.

of fancy. The mass of the people are truly industrious; and, I am persuaded, there is as much labour performed in the island, in the aggregate, as ever there was in slavery; the failure in the last two years' crops is not attributable to want of labour, but solely to the calamitous drought with which the country has been afflicted.

"So far as steady industry, sobriety, and honesty of conduct, and mild and peaceable demeanour are concerned, the 'grand experiment' has in this island, not only perfectly succeeded, but has proved a universal and unalloyed blessing.

"In some parts of the country there is still a cry for labour; the real want, however, is confined to a very limited number of estates in particular localities, and, in most instances, it originates in the gross mis-management or tyrannical conduct of the parties themselves; the great bulk of the planters find no difficulty in procuring all the labour they require, if prepared with the means of paying the regular market price for it; great numbers have not the necessary command of cash, and, unwilling to confess their own poverty, dishonestly impute their failure to deficiency in the labour market.

"The true meaning of the outcry of the planters is not that labour is deficient, but that cheap labour is required; they declare that one shilling or one shilling and sixpence per day is more than they can afford; they flatter themselves that by means of immigration they may reduce the market price to sixpence or ninepence per day—a palpable delusion; if they could even succeed in introducing fifty thousand immigrants, I am persuaded it would not be the means of reducing the price of labour one penny."

Mr. Phillippo's intimacy with Sir Lionel Smith afforded him many opportunities of serving the cause of the oppressed, which he was not slow to embrace; but his exertions brought upon him no small amount of abuse.

" I was called," he tells us, "'the notorious parson Phillippo,' 'the principal adviser of the Governor,' 'the fabricator of apprentices' petitions,' 'the political parson,' ' arch agitator,' &c., &c., all which, by-the-by, from the character of the sources from which they spring, I regard as the highest compliment I could receive."   Sir Lionel Smith left the island on the 1st of October, 1839, amid the profound regrets of the people, and was succeeded in his office by Sir Charles Metcalfe, who was able, though with considerable difficulty, to obtain from the Legislature various Acts suited to the changed circumstances of the times.   Amongst these new laws was one to legalise, register, and confirm marriages by Dissenters and others not members of the Established Church, in the progress of which through the Assembly Mr. Phillippo took deep interest.   With the united aid of his brethren,* changes were made in the original form of the proposals, by which the ministers of all denominations were able to work in harmony with its provisions.   Within four years of the passing of the law, the Baptist missionaries alone cele- brated three thousand marriages, and took their full share in the endeavour to remedy the enormous mischiefs of the system of concubinage, which, until slavery was abolished, had prevailed throughout the island.

Among the incidents of the commemoration of the first anniversary of freedom in Spanish Town, in 1839, Mr. Phillippo especially mentions the formation of a branch Anti-Slavery Society in connection with the English Society formed in the previous April in Exeter Hall, to promote the abolition of slavery throughout the world. The speech he made on this occasion was published.   It is an animated address on the progress made since

---

* Mr. Phillippo was examined by a Committee of the House of Assembly on the subject.

1811 in the overthrow of slavery and the slave trade, and urges at length the necessity which still existed to seek the destruction of this enemy of human rights in all parts of the globe. "It cannot be," he said, "that the sons and daughters of Africa in Jamaica and the other British islands of the West, now enjoying freedom, that best earthly gift to man, can be indifferent to the liberties of their brethren and friends. Well may you determine to tell the merciless tyrants who ravage your fatherland that the days of their guilt are numbered, and that their ill-gotten gains are at an end. You will tell them that Africa is about to become her own guardian, and to avenge her own wrongs by the devotion of her own sons and daughters, now disenthralled, to the sacred cause of her liberty; and that her freedom they will have, whatever be the labour, and whatever the sacrifice." It was most gratifying to the feelings of Mr. Phillippo that his people should heartily cherish the hope of assisting the down-trodden in their fatherland, and be so ready to help, in however feeble a manner, to dry up at their source the evils from which they had so recently escaped.

CHAPTER XXII.

DURING the year 1841 the strifes and dissension between the planters and their labourers were to some extent allayed, and a better understanding was established. Individual instances of wrong and oppression were not indeed infrequent; but the mass of the population was happy and prosperous. The conciliatory conduct of Sir C. Metcalfe, the Governor, towards the House of Assembly largely contributed to the passing of measures suitable to the altered condition of the country; while the improved well-being of the people enabled them to bear without much suffering the drought with which the island was visited. The exertions of Mr. Phillippo during the anxious months immediately following entire emancipation had greatly impaired his health, so that a period of rest had become absolutely necessary; but he was not able till the close of the year to seek the relaxation he required.

A recognition of his labours received in the month of June gave him much satisfaction. It consisted of a diploma of membership in the "Council of the Institute of Africa" in France, accompanied by a very flattering estimate of his services to the cause of freedom. In his reply he says :—"Although I fear the kindness and partiality of friends have led them greatly to overstate the influence I have been enabled to exert for the general benefit of the African race, and thereby multiplied the

claims I possess upon the consideration of your honourable Committee, yet I flatter myself I may affirm, without
suspicion to the contrary in the breasts of those around
me, that the temporal and spiritual interests of this
oppressed and benighted people have long been a subject
of my most ardent solicitude. I cannot but regard
association with your Society in the benevolent designs it
contemplates as a distinguished privilege and honour.
The nature and extent of my engagements will, I am
apprehensive, preclude the probability of my rendering
material service to the Institution in the way of official
correspondence; but I hope, by practical efforts for the
furtherance of its designs, I shall not wholly disappoint
the expectations that have been formed of my qualifications
and character."

It was with no little pleasure that Mr. Phillippo saw
and encouraged the desire of his congregations to share
in the plans now in course of preparation by the parent
Society for an evangelistic mission on the Western Coast
of Africa.*   At the missionary meeting held in the chapel
at Spanish Town on the 2nd of August he read to them the
letters of Messrs. Clarke and Prince, then on a tour of
exploration, and contrasted with great effect the condition
of Jamaica with that of their fatherland. His address
called forth the warmest expressions of sympathy, and a
resolve that they would not be behind their brethren in

---

* At the annual meeting of the Western Association in Brown's
Town, 1840, it was resolved to request Mr. Knibb, then about to visit
England, to bring before the Committee of the Baptist Missionary
Society the importance of a mission to Western Africa. The project
was favourably entertained by the Committee, and they engaged the
Rev. John Clarke, then in England, and Dr. Prince to undertake an
exploratory visit to the coast. They left England in October, 1840,
and arrived at Fernando Po on the 1st of January, 1841.—" Voice of
Jubilee," p. 119.

other parts of the island in energy and zeal for the promotion of this sacred cause.

It was on the 9th of December, 1841, that Mr. Phillippo was at length able to leave his charge and to go on board the *Firefly*, one of H.M.'s steamers, to seek that relief to body and mind now become imperative. The vessel was bound for Barbadoes. The brief stay of the steamer at the various ports on the route allowed but few observations to be made on the condition of their inhabitants; but he was charmed with the beauty and grandeur of the scenery as they coasted along the shores of the numerous islands that form the breakwater of the Caribbean Sea against the waves of the Atlantic.

The first port to be reached was St. Jago, in Cuba. Mr. Phillippo did not venture to land, well knowing the hatred of the Spaniards to all friends of liberty to the slave. Threats of assassination had only recently driven from the island a Wesleyan minister, an agent of the Bible Society, then on a brief visit to Havana. Slavery existed in Cuba in all its horrors, and the decay everywhere visible in the town and its surroundings, as seen from the ship, bore ample evidence to the wretchedness which follows its hateful presence.

A short hour's visit to Porto Rico did not afford much matter of interest, but at nine o'clock the same evening they reached the Island of St. Thomas, where the next day was occupied with rambles about the city, visiting the stores, and climbing the mountain side which dominates the small but beautiful harbour.

Two days and a-half were spent in Barbadoes while waiting for the return steamer. " Barbadoes," he says, " is very different in appearance to Jamaica, being all under cultivation, and presenting none of the bold mountain scenery which characterises the West India Islands generally. Bridge Town, the capital, is much more regularly built, and much more in the style of English towns, than any town I have seen in these colonies. At each extremity of the town, and in the interior of the island, are the very beautiful villas and residences of the merchants and others of the more wealthy inhabitants, embosomed in groves of fine trees and lovely flowering shrubs. I collected a few seeds of plants new to me, but the time was unfavourable to my making a good collection."

The longest stay was made in the Island of Haiti, where he stopped on his return voyage. He landed at Cape Henry on the 30th of December, and, possessing letters of introduction, he received a hearty welcome from the Commandant, General Bottex, and his son, Captain Bottex. On reaching the palace he found the General in bed, but was immediately admitted to his chamber, and received a most hearty welcome as the friend of the slave. "The General," he relates, " spoke with great enthusiasm of the philanthropists of England, many of whom he named, and of the noble generosity of the Government. On retiring he grasped my hand with much apparent cordiality and affection. His son, in conversation afterwards, expressed himself strongly in favour of Protestantism, denouncing the errors of Popery and the conduct of the priests as tending to lead intelligent men into Deism. He said that Christophe at the commencement of his reign sent to England for schoolmasters, and established schools on the Lancasterian system. I was present one evening at a *soirée* in the palace. Most of the company were, of course, coloured and black. Their costume and manners were exact reproductions of the French. All was in Parisian fashion, but the greatest propriety was observed throughout the evening.

" I found in the city of Port au Prince only one Protestant congregation, a very small community of Wesleyans, under the care of the missionary, the Rev. Mr. Bird. There were also in the town a few American Baptists, who held services among themselves. To Mr. Bird and his excellent wife I needed no introduction, as I had known them in Jamaica. Mr. Bird very kindly took me about the city, and explained the causes of the dilapidated condition of the forts, the public offices, and many of the best private buildings. The city is beautifully laid out. The houses are mostly two and three stories high, with trellises, covered with flowers, the entire length of the galleries in front of the houses. But many of the houses are un-roofed, the street paving is broken up, and the whole city tells the sad tale of the desolation and horrors of war.

"The proprietor of the estate, which was once the principal country residence of Christophe, invited me to take a day's excursion to see the advantages of the Metairie system of cultivation on his property. He accordingly buckled on his sword, and we started, passing on our way through rivers haunted by alligators. The estate had no doubt been a splendid one, as the ruins of the house and the magnificent gateway, with its avenue of palm-trees, testified. But I was not enamoured of his system. He paid the labourers their share of profits in kind, which was mostly spent, before it was earned, in intemperance. I said, 'This plan, while it might do well for the master, ruined the labourer.' He replied, 'I have nothing to do with that; every man must do the best for himself.'

"In the evening I rode out into the suburbs of the city with Mr. Thompson, who showed me the remains of a residence of Christophe's, where he had committed so many murders, the dens into which the bodies had been thrown, his palace, which he did not live to finish, and the ruins and grounds of the Jesuits' College. He also pointed out to me the spot hallowed by the memory of Toussaint l'Ouverture."

The principal object of this brief sojourn in Haiti may be gathered from the following extract from a letter to the Rev. John Dyer, dated Spanish Town, the 21st January, 1842, a fortnight after his return to Jamaica :—— " I passed the interval of a packet at Cape Haitien, availing myself of letters of introduction from gentlemen here to personal acquaintances. I was hospitably entertained and most kindly treated by them, especially by the British Consul and the Governor. My communications with the latter related almost entirely to the moral and religious state and prospects of Jamaica and Haiti, and I am happy to say as the result that Haiti presents an open door to the preaching of the Gospel by Baptist missionaries—the most ample protection being afforded by the Government to ministers and Christians of all denominations." Encouraged by the representations of Mr. Phillippo, the Society shortly after commenced its interesting mission in Haiti, at Jacmel, a town on the seacoast on the south side of the island, and a port frequented by the English mails on their route to Jamaica.

CHAPTER XXIII.

MATTERS of great importance engaged Mr. Phillippo's attention immediately on his return. The continuation of the letter just quoted will best describe them. " I arrived in Spanish Town about a fortnight ago, very shortly before the meeting of our Annual Association, I am thankful to say the better for the trip, although the disease of which I complained is yet far from being removed. Several matters of importance were attended to at the Association, some of which I will briefly notice.

" I.—It was unanimously resolved (to the effect) that, after the 1st of August next, no further drafts be made on the parent Society in aid of the Jamaica Mission, and that the amounts required by any brother previously to that time be ascertained and forwarded to the Committee.

" Although I and others of my brethren who are not in the secrets of the Western Union had some cause to complain of the circumstances under which this resolution was proposed, yet so glorious in all respects would be its results, if carried into effect, that, deeply involved as I am in a pecuniary way, I not only cordially approved the resolution, but publicly expressed the honour I felt in presiding on the occasion. I, therefore, as the senior missionary here, on the assurance that the Committee would not object to the grant of a loan in relief of present liabilities, at once set the example to the brethren similarly circumstanced with myself, of entirely relinquishing all further drafts on the Society, except under very peculiar circumstances, from the commencement of the present year. The consequence of this will be, as I then stated, a suspension to a very considerable degree of my chapel-building operations, and a diminution of the number and efficiency of my schools; and this will, of course, greatly increase and protract my anxieties, as well as involve no ordinary sacrifice of feeling. Impossibilities cannot be done, and if in the 'last great day' I shall be accounted faithful over the few things committed to my trust it will be enough.

"II.—The Institution.—After some debate it was carried, as an amendment to an original resolution, that, no premises having been found more central, Calabar, near Rio Bueno, be fixed on as its seat, until others more eligible can be found. The opinion of those on the south side is, decidedly, that Kingston, the neighbourhood of Spanish Town, or the centre of the parish of St. Ann's are in all respects preferable; and I fear, if any attempt be made to continue it at Calabar, where it would be almost exclusively under the influence of the Western Union, it will lead to very unpleasant consequences.

"III.—The subject of the African Mission scarcely admitted of a difference of opinion. All engaged to help it forward to the utmost practicable extent. Brother Merrick—subject, of course, to the approval of the Committee—goes to join his beloved pastor (the Rev. John Clarke) in Africa. As a neighbour and friend I shall deeply regret his loss; a more pious, devoted, and amiable man cannot be found in the mission.

" IV.—A long discussion ensued as to the matter of the calumnies circulated against us as missionaries and our churches, on which it was resolved that some one of our brethren should be appointed a deputation to England for the especial object of disproving them, and counteracting their influence on the public mind. As brethren Abbott,

Oughton, and Clarke intimated their intention, or desire, to return home during the summer, it was resolved, after a prayer-meeting for Divine direction in our choice, that the individual should be selected by ballot. The lot fell upon brother Knibb, who had eleven votes out of the nineteen given ; and, as it was represented that he was sent for by the Committee to attend the Jubilee of the Society, and as at the same time some anxiety was expressed that his appointment should be unanimous, all coincided in the decision.

" I regret to hear, what I sincerely hope is incorrect, that the Committee have at length recognised both the Western Union and the Annual Association in their associate capacity, as power may thereby be acquired which may not only be extremely injurious to the happiness of individuals and the general welfare of the mission here, but which may operate materially against the Society at large, of which it is possible the Committee themselves may become the first victims, or, at all events, which they might find it very difficult to control. If anything like a Presbytery is countenanced, our bond of union is dissolved, and the citadel will be desolated by foes within.

" If ever there was a time in the history of the Jamaica Mission that particularly called for the exercise of prudence and discretion on the part of the Committee, it is now. I would reiterate it to the Committee with earnestness. Continue to maintain your legitimate influence over the Jamaica Mission, and be jealous of the least usurpation of your rights. I throw these out as hints, considering that in doing so I am only fulfilling an obvious duty."

It is clear from this letter that Mr. Phillippo had a full perception of the importance of the measures taken by the Association. The resolution to cut the mission adrift from the funds of the Society did not meet with his entire approbation ; and it is due to him that a note appended to the copy of the above letter in his journal, and dated so late as the year 1876, should be given. "Thus, not to stand in the way of accomplishing the object (that is, the complete cessation of drafts on the Society), if it could be done, as was confidently affirmed by Messrs. Knibb and others, I, however, opposed the resolution as premature, and as likely to be a death-blow to the mission, proposing a diminution of the drafts first. One or two of the brethren also entered their protest. I only agreed on the condition of loans being granted by the Committee. I now record (in 1876) that our mission began to decline from this day onwards to the present time."

Leaving to subsequent pages to justify or otherwise the concluding words of this note, it is matter for surprise that neither at the time, nor for two years afterwards, until the necessities of the brethren forced attention to the subject, was there any attempt made to define the future relations of the missionaries to the Society, or to arrange those many questions of detail which were necessarily involved in this momentous decision. That the churches in Jamaica would at some period become independent of the funds of the Society, and be thrown on their own resources for the maintenance of the Gospel of Christ in their midst, was not indeed a new idea. The proved capability of many of the churches to support their pastors, as in the case of Mr. Phillippo himself, who for several years had drawn his stipend from the church in Spanish Town ; the frequent assertion of such representative men as Mr. Knibb,* Mr. Burchell, Mr. Dendy, and

---

* Thus, in relation to the support of the African Mission, Mr. Knibb said to the Home Committee, "I will pledge my church to £1,000, and I will get it in a week. I will pledge Mr. Dendy's church for £500 or £600, and he will get it in a few days. I will send to Jamaica, and I am sure we shall get our money as soon as you get yours."—Memoir, p. 364. And this in addition to the ordinary contributions of the people.

others, that the churches were both able and willing to undertake this duty; and the large sums that were raised for new chapels, manses, and school-houses frequently led the Committee at home to inquire whether, and how soon, the Society could be relieved from the burden and responsibility of their support.   The drain on the revenue of the Society for Jamaica objects* could not be met without incurring constant and increasing debt, nor without neglecting the obligations the Society was under to its older missions in the East; so that the pressure from home was not inconsiderable to realise the bold and sanguine forecasts of the Jamaica brethren.   The demand for relief to the home treasury became in 1841 more urgent than ever.   It was absolutely necessary to escape in some way from the embarrassments which the rapid growth of the requirements of Jamaica brought upon the Society.†   The Committee at home, therefore, hailed with joy the resolution of the missionaries; and, if in any minds there were doubts of the wisdom of the measure, they were quieted by the manifest proofs which the Jamaica churches had given of their ability to fulfil their pledge. This was the more confidently relied upon since the demand for new chapels was rapidly being met; and, although debts of considerable amount remained to be liquidated, there was at the time no sign that the prosperity the island then enjoyed would meet with an early check, or that the means of the people would undergo a rapid and painful diminution.

---

* In 1839, the cost to the Society of the Jamaica Mission was £6,514; in 1840, £6,870; in 1841, £9,016; in 1842, £9,701.

† In 1839 the debt of the Society was £2,631; in 1840, £3,341; in 1841, £1,958; in 1842, £3,943; notwithstanding that during the first three of these years £4,610 had been contributed by the British churches to remove the yearly accruing deficit.   The average income of the Society for the four years was only £16,944, to support all its missions both in the East and West.

The wish expressed by Mr. Phillippo that the parent Society should retain some control over the future development of the churches does not seem to have met with any sympathy from the majority of the missionaries, nor was it ever brought before the Committee as a desirable object to secure. Indeed, under the laws which usually govern Baptist churches, it is difficult to see how the Society, when it had ceased to furnish pecuniary aid to the congregations in Jamaica, could claim or exercise any authority or control over their proceedings. Arrangements were made shortly afterwards to secure by the trust deeds the permanent use of the property of the churches for the purposes for which it had been acquired, by giving to the Missionary Society the reversion in case of any future abandonment or misappropriation ; but, beyond this, Baptist principles forbade any interference on the part of an extraneous body with the internal development or practices of the churches. Thus independence of pecuniary support from without carried with it independence of control from without ; and no one would have been more jealous of interference on the part of the Society than the brethren who felt themselves able to carry forward the work of Christ's Kingdom in Jamaica without the necessity of seeking its pecuniary aid. As it was, the chief hesitation to enter on this new stage in the mission on the part of Mr. Phillippo and those who thought with him arose from the difficulties they were then experiencing in the payment of their chapel debts.

The warning given by Mr. Phillippo in the closing paragraph of his letter has special reference to his fear that efforts would be made in Jamaica itself to interfere with the lawful independence of the churches. On more than one occasion in former years he had expressed anxiety on this point, arising from what he thought were symptoms of " Presbyterianising " on the part of the

Western Union and the Annual Association. Of the Union he had long ceased to be a member; but he continued his alliance with the more general body, the Annual Association. Thus, in a letter to the Rev. John Dyer, dated September, 1837, he says that he fully agrees with the Committee "in their opinion as to the impolicy of recognising the brethren here (in Jamaica) as an associated body, and of corresponding with them in their united capacity. You will remember that I have more than once in my letters seriously deprecated such a recognition, as likely to entail serious consequences both to the Committee and to the independence of our respective churches." In the following passage from his diary, under date of 1837, he more particularly refers to the origin of the above remarks :—" Several attempts have been made by some of the brethren to form an association of ministers and churches, assimilated to a Presbyterian synod, and thus to concentrate in a few of the brethren the power of an executive body, destroying the individuality of the churches and the independence of their action, as also that of their pastors. I felt the importance of standing out against this innovation for several years, and succeeded to a considerable degree in preventing its adoption and in neutralising its occasional exercise." Mr. Phillippo's fears were not altogether imaginary, and subsequent years have testified to the wisdom and discretion he displayed in opposing the existence of a power that would undoubtedly have shaken the mission to its foundation.

The establishment of an institution for the training of Jamaica Christian men for the ministry had for many years been a favourite object with Mr. Phillippo. It has already been referred to. But in 1837 he pressed the matter on the Committee in an elaborate letter, in which he fully entered on the various aspects of the question.

On the employment of a native agency, he says : " I have almost hitherto imagined that I have been in advance of the Society in this particular. Hence I have at this time, and have long had, the services of upwards of forty subordinate agents, each of whom has a class-house, or place of worship, in which he conducts the regular worship of God one or two evenings of the week. I refer to my leaders and deacons, being naturally the most intelligent and worthy members of my churches, who are in almost every sense of the word as much native assistants, or local preachers, as some of the converts in Hindustan. They have not been ordained to the work of evangelists for various reasons. Most of them are apprentices, and not more than two or three of them can read intelligibly. From their circumstances they are not eligible to the office of pastors. I have, however, already applied to the Committee for assistance in support of three or four young men who may be employed to advantage, having received a tolerably good education, and proved their qualifications for the work by their disinterested labours and addresses in our Sabbath-schools."

The abolition of the apprenticeship opened the way for the education and employment of such young men as these, and in 1840 the missionary brethren arranged that one of the senior missionaries, the Rev. Joshua Tinson, should commence the work. Six young men, who gave promise of becoming useful preachers of the Gospel, were selected ; but the sudden failure of Mr. Tinson's health brought the effort to a premature close. Encouraged, however, by the promise of aid from the Jubilee Fund of the parent Society, the subject was not permitted to fall into abeyance, and, as the statement of Mr. Phillippo shows, the institution was now determined upon. The premises at Calabar, on the north side of the island, were purchased, and the college buildings erected at the cost of the

Society. It was opened on the 6th of October, 1843, under the presidency of Mr. Tinson, who had returned in good health from England, with eight students, to whom *four* more were added before the close of the year. Here Mr. Tinson continued to labour till his lamented death in December, 1850. The formation of such a "school of the prophets" had become essential, in order to supply pastors to the numerous churches which had sprung up in all parts of the island, and the more so since there was no prospect that the Society would continue to send labourers from England, either to open up new spheres of labour, or to fill vacancies which death or other causes might bring about. In the last years of the Society's grants for the support of the mission, a considerable number of men, both as schoolmasters and missionaries, had been sent out.* But it seems now to have been understood on all sides that, with the independence of the churches, they must be left to their own resources to multiply pastors and ministers of the Word.

It will be noticed in the above extract from Mr. Phillippo's letter on native agency that reference is made to the employment of a large number of uneducated and untrained men as leaders to conduct Divine worship in the numerous class-houses belonging to his congregations. The leader-system was adopted throughout the island by the Baptist missionaries, and sprang out of the necessities of the time. Slavery had no compassion for the ignorant, and rare indeed were the instances in which a slave-owner attempted to instruct his slaves, either in the art of reading or in the knowledge of salvation. Some organisation was required, however rude or imperfect, to watch over and control the multitudes who crowded to the churches

---

* In 1840 ten new missionaries were sent out in answer to the eloquent appeals of the Rev. W. Knibb, who visited England for the purpose, at a cost of more than £2,000.

and filled the ranks of inquirers. The missionaries, from necessity, fell back upon the more intelligent among their slave members, and placed them over their fellow-slaves, both because the overseers of estates regarded with extreme jealousy the visits of strangers to the homes of the slaves on their properties, and because no others could be found. For some years, especially after the apprenticeship was abolished, representations were made by various persons, for the most part inimical to the mission, that the missionaries displayed great carelessness in the selection and oversight of these agents, and that as a class they were ignorant, superstitious, and often immoral men ; that the tickets which were given to recognised inquirers and church members were regarded as passports to heaven ; and that the missionaries baptized great numbers of unconverted men. It added to the authority, if not to the gravity, of these charges that two or three of their own brethren in some measure combined with ministers of other bodies to affirm their truth. It was certainly not requisite that the missionaries should assert that there was no truth at all in the accusations. The known conditions of their work rendered it impossible that there should not be here and there individual adherents worthy of reprobation. Yet there can be no doubt, on the other hand, that the general implication that the entire system was fatally and wilfully faulty was untrue, and a calumny on the noble, generous, and disinterested efforts of multitudes of good men, trained indeed in slavery, but whose earnest desire it was to lead their fellow-bondsmen to Christ. They exposed themselves to bitter suffering and persecution, and even death itself. To this day there are living old men who bear on their persons the marks of the deadly whip, or the gunshot wound received in the service of Christ. By far the greater part of them proved by their Christian lives and happy deaths that they were Christians indeed.

The brunt of this attack had to be borne chiefly by the missionaries on the north side of the island. Hence the selection of the Rev. W. Knibb to represent them in England, and whose triumphant vindication now renders any further explanation unnecessary.* Mr. Phillippo, however, shared in the defence, and, though unable from his ill-health to unite with Mr. Knibb in the public justification of himself and brethren on the platform, yet with his pen, in the various periodicals of the day, he bore his testimony on behalf of truth and righteousness. It will be sufficient to quote the deliberate judgment of the Committee, after a very diligent examination into the whole subject, given in their parting address to the churches:—" We have been rejoiced on all occasions to find that these accusations cannot be substantiated. The unsolicited testimony of men of unimpeachable judgment and impartiality — we refer to the published works of Messrs. Gurney, Sturge, and Candler; the well-attested results of your own church discipline, as apparent in the annual return of the Association; and the maxim of Divine authority, that a tree is to be known by its fruits, have concurred with our specific inquiries to satisfy us of the general falsehood of the charges which have been brought against you."

On his return from the Windward Islands Mr. Phillippo had hoped for a long spell of earnest and continuous work. But after a few Sabbaths of labour the former symptoms of ill-health returned, and he felt himself constrained to accept the invitation of the Committee to assist in the Jubilee services at Kettering, which he had at first declined, and to seek in England a season of rest. He could leave his charge with satisfaction in the hands of the Rev. Thomas Dowson, who reached Jamaica in

---

* See " Memoir of Knibb," by Rev. J. H. Hinton, pp. 423-426.

the early part of the year. The churches were flourishing. In February he had baptized at Passage Fort, in the River Cobre, near its mouth, " twenty-eight individuals who had for some time previously given evidence of repentance towards God and faith in our Lord Jesus Christ, in the midst of hundreds who crowded the beach, and multitudes in canoes, which formed a semi-circle around the place of baptism." His schools generally were prosperous, and a most interesting and successful examination of the metropolitan schools had been held in the presence of the Hon. T. J. Bernard. In April he opened the new chapel at Sligoville, and in the following month the new township called Clarksonville was ready for settlement. A brief extract or two from a letter forwarded to him by the deacons of his church well expresses the feelings with which they viewed his departure :—" We earnestly hope that the blessing and peace of God may attend you, your dear wife, and all who go along with you, and we would entreat you never to lose sight of your promise, or suffer any other thought to take root in your mind, than that of coming back to labour among the people that you have for so many years been the instrument of turning from nature's darkness to the saving knowledge of our Lord and Saviour Jesus Christ, and some of whom are the subjects of sorrow at parting with you, and exhibit the utmost concern for your safety by their earnest supplications to Almighty God. They cherish the hope that you will soon have recovered your wonted strength and ability, and that not many months shall have passed before they have the privilege of seeing you again in the flesh."

Mr. Phillippo, with his wife and his younger son, Edwin, sailed on the 12th of June in the *Rawlins*, and, after a long and, on the whole, pleasant passage, arrived in London on the 9th of July.

CHAPTER XXIV.

MR. PHILLIPPO had scarcely arrived in London than very numerous applications were pressed upon him to give his services at missionary and anti-slavery meetings. He had hoped to take part in the jubilee meeting of the Society at Kettering in the autumn of the year, as well as to communicate to public assemblies his rich stores of information on all matters relative to Jamaica and the results of emancipation. In this he was painfully disappointed. During the eighteen months of his sojourn in England, the occasions were rare in which he was able to appear in public, and though he enjoyed in private intercourse frequent opportunities of meeting leading ministers and philanthropists, and of conferring with them on many points of interest and doubt, he felt deeply the seclusion to which he was consigned. The doctors whose advice he sought—and among them were some of the most eminent men of the day—one and all prescribed rest and entire abstinence from public speaking. The organs of speech had been so sorely tried in the overwhelming duties of his work in Jamaica that his future usefulness was imperilled should he fail to obtain relief. In a letter from Norwich to his life-long friend, the Rev. J. P. Mursell, he thus describes the condition of his health :—" My throat is in so relaxed and inflamed a state that I am here with my brother, undergoing a course of treatment for it which binds me to his surgery, and positively forbids the slightest degree of exposure or excitement. Every physician, moreover, whom I have consulted expresses it as his full conviction that, unless the treatment I am now under is continued without interruption for some months, and unbroken silence is observed, the probability is that my public duties will be or are at an end. This would be a very painful consequence, and one, I am sure, neither you nor my Leicester friends would wish me to hazard on any consideration. From the same cause I cannot go to Ireland with you, which you will believe me when I say it is to me a source of real and painful regret. A good cause, plenty to say, physical vigour and health at disposal, but the lips sealed! No one can tell the sacrifice it is to me. But I must not murmur!" From Norwich he went to Hastings, where he spent most of the autumn and winter, though to little purpose, and it was not till towards the close of 1843 that he was pronounced equal to a moderate amount of public employment.

He found some consolation in the warm welcome he received from his many friends; among whom none exhibited more watchful care and constant attentions than Joseph Fletcher, Esq. To this gentleman he had been, moreover, greatly indebted for numerous liberal gifts towards the support of his schools. Their friendship was now confirmed and deepened yet more, and bore generous fruit. Mr. Fletcher's was the strong arm that nobly sustained Mr. Phillippo during those coming years of trouble and distress, the shadows of which even now at times seemed to throw their gloom over his mind in his retirement. The following brief but characteristic note preserved by Mr. Phillippo will sufficiently indicate the warm interest in his welfare displayed by this staunch friend :—

"Shooter's Hill, August 29th, 1842.—My dear Sir,— The dispensation is trying, and you need *all* that faith and patience which are promised to the believer, and are sufficient to perfect his strength by a communication from the Almighty, who does not anything in vain. You must strictly be obedient, and waive present gratification for the hope of future enjoyment. Act the Christian philosopher, armed by a power the Grecians never knew. If ' enter not into temptation ' had been rightly understood, you would not have been seen in the large party at J. J. Gurney's. The chaplet of flowers, ornamental to the victim, was to it no compensation for the sacrifice; and where you will meet one who will understand that friend Phillippo MUST not talk, you will find a thousand who will prefer hearing *our friend* to his safety and future usefulness. Say not that I am censorious. The truth I write (being a libel upon man, which sages say means woman also) is a truth nevertheless. I trust that much good will come out of your affliction, and that you will be rendered the means of opening the eyes of the public to the delusion under which they so long have suffered. May you be preserved and directed; all you do being under a holy influence, and being caused to bear upon the best interests of men. We all return to Mrs. Phillippo and to you our kindest remembrance, and shall be happy when you renew your visit under circumstances of less privation and more enjoyment."

The " censorious " remark of Mr. Fletcher met with a very complete justification at the Annual Meeting in April, 1843. Mr. Phillippo was introduced to the assembly by the Rev. Dr. Brock as an old missionary lying under a strict injunction not to attempt to speak. But the injunction availed nothing; he was compelled by the warm expressions of sympathy called forth, and by the urgency of some brethren sitting near him, to rise and address a few words to the assembly. He said that he " should have been glad to advert to the extraordinary change which had been effected in the entire aspect of society in Jamaica since the commencement of missionary operations, to have adduced facts and anecdotes illustrative of the purity of the churches, and to have urged these successes as a stimulus to more persevering and vigorous effort for the extension of the Gospel throughout all the West India Islands, South America, and Africa." But he was bound to abide by the decision of his physician, and listen to the urgent objections of friends around him. Happily, the fruits of his experience were not lost to the Christian Church. The chief employment of Mr. Phillippo in his enforced leisure was the preparation of the work which he published in the autumn of 1843, under the title of " Jamaica : its Past and Present State."* The work was entered upon after much consultation with friends, and in a spirit of devout dependence on Divine aid. In the following lines he expresses the feelings with which he undertook the task :—

> " If Thine, Great Spirit ! is the cause I plead,
>   Then deign my erring mind and pen to guide :
> For well I know the wisdom which I need
>   Can only be by Thine own hand supplied ;
>   Without Thee, I am lost in thought's wild tide.
> Oh ! let no love of self my work impair ;
>   I would be well content Thy voice to be :
> Make me like pearly dew, or morning air :
>   From love of power, and vain ambition free :
>   Unseen and lost, except when serving Thee."

The book was well received, and had a large and remunerative circulation, three editions being rapidly exhausted. The earlier portion of the volume is devoted to a sketch of the geography and history of the island, its physical aspects, vegetable and mineral productions.

---

* The full title is " Jamaica : its Past and Present State. By James M. Phillippo, of Spanish Town, Jamaica ; Twenty Years a Baptist Missionary in that Island. London : John Snow. 1843."

Mr. Phillippo next describes the population, the government, and the divisions necessary for purposes of administration. After a brief account of the white and free coloured portions of the population, he gives an animated picture of the condition of the slaves, which naturally introduces an account of the slave trade, the establishment of the apprenticeship system, and the final overthrow of slavery by the great Act of Emancipation on the 1st of August, 1838. Interesting disquisitions follow on the intellectual character and social condition of the Negroes under slavery, with a description of its dreadful effects on the moral life of society. Several chapters are then devoted to the state of religion in the island, its spread through the labours of missionaries of various Christian denominations, and its blessed results on the life and conduct of the people. The work closes with an appeal to the sympathies and benevolence of the Christian world to complete and perfect the work so well begun.

The volume is an excellent specimen of Mr. Phillippo's powers as an author. His taste for scenery, and his delight in the study of natural history, are apparent throughout. It is never tedious. It is enlivened in parts by quaint and sometimes pathetic anecdotes illustrative of the Negro character. Their proverbs, their superstitions, their African usages, find a place in his picture. Their conduct under both slavery and freedom is brought distinctly before the reader; and there is given the fullest information as to the causes and results of emancipation. The style is here and there ornate, with an occasional poetical phrase, somewhat diffuse, but in the main simple and direct, while every touch and sketch bears the marks of the writer's truthfulness and integrity. Highly as his work was commended in the various publications of the day, perhaps not one testimony to its interest and value pleased its author more than that contained in a brief note from the venerable Clarkson, who said: "I have read the book with no ordinary pleasure. To the Abolitionist it will afford a great treat, because he will see in the conduct of the emancipated slaves all that is praiseworthy beyond all his former ardent expectations; and to the Christian it will afford a rich feast of joy whenever he thinks on the subject."

The work was published at an opportune moment. The first steps of freedom had been safely taken. The people, the planters, and the churches were yet untried by the painful and unforeseen events which tested to the uttermost the faith and hope of the friends of the Negro, and gave to the enemies of free labour apparent grounds for denying its value and success. For, however advantageous may have been up to this time the results of freedom to the slave, the years 1842 and 1843 witnessed another of the ever-recurring periods of depression in the sugar industry of the island. At the request of Mr. Clarkson, Mr. Phillippo wrote a paper on the subject. It is too long to be given here; but, in the judgment of Mr. Phillippo, the difficulties of estate owners were to be traced to the vicious system of management which, prevalent under slavery, was still adhered to; to the absenteeism of proprietors; to the want of capital, and the high rate of interest for loans; to the dishonesty of agents; to effete methods in use in the cultivation and manufacture of the sugar; to the mortgaged condition of the produce; and, in frequent cases, to the unsettled relations between the labourer and his employer.

The tedium of Mr. Phillippo's retirement was further relieved by the favourable news he received of the progress of his stations. Letters from some of the teachers gave him the liveliest joy; while their assurances of sympathy and desire for his return filled him with gratitude. But he was more especially pleased by the setting apart of

Mr. Alexander Fuller for mission work in Africa, though, to his deep regret, his medical advisers refused him permission to be present at the solemn service. This coloured man was a member of his church in Spanish Town, and came with him to England. For some months Mr. Fuller was placed under the instruction of the Rev. Wm. Salter, of Amersham, who bore high testimony to his Christian character. His course in Africa was short, but his speedy removal has been more than supplied by the vigorous and successful career of his son, Mr. Joseph Fuller, who as a lad went out to his father in the *Chilmark* with the native band of helpers that Jamaica gave to the work of Christ in their fatherland.

But the father's heart was more deeply touched when his beloved daughter, Hannah, whose piety had long been manifest, " put on Christ " by a public profession of His name in baptism, which was administered by the Rev. John Aldis, of Maze Pond. She united in fellowship, however, with the church at Brixton Hill.

The relief afforded to the funds of the Society by the cessation of drafts from Jamaica, and the noble and generous response made by the denomination to the appeal for contributions that should be worthily commemorative of the fiftieth year of the Society's labours, enabled the Committee to hasten its measures for the achievement of the plans contemplated in raising the Jubilee Fund. These embraced not only the relief of the Society from its indebtedness, and the erection of a Mission House in London that should become the centre of denominational activity, but also the establishment of the proposed mission on the West Coast of Africa and the extension of the mission to other islands of the West Indies. The Rev. John Clarke and Dr. Prince, both of the Jamaica Mission, had pioneered the way in Africa. The Committee now turned to Mr. Phillippo to assist them in their plans for the West Indies. He was invited to spend some months among the Windward Islands, to report fully their condition, and to inquire as to the prospects they held out for evangelistic effort. An incidental advantage would be a further period of relaxation, during which Mr. Phillippo's health might become thoroughly restored.

Furnished with the requisite instructions, Mr. Phillippo set sail for the West Indies in the mail packet on the 2nd of December, taking with him Mrs. Phillippo, his little girl, and his youngest son.

CHAPTER XXV.

MR. PHILLIPPO found among his fellow-passengers on board the *Trent* the Venerable Archdeacon Trew and Mrs. Trew, on their way to the Bahamas, and the Rev. R. Young, a Wesleyan minister, and deputation to Jamaica. Calling at Madeira, he had an interview with Dr. Kalley, then incarcerated in a filthy prison for speaking on religious subjects and distributing Testaments and tracts among the Portuguese, who desired to hear and know the truth from the pure fount of the Word of God.

At Grenada, he parted from his wife and daughter, who went forward to Jamaica, and proceeded, on the 27th of December, to Trinidad, which was reached on the evening of the same day. From this point the letters and reports of Mr. Phillippo contain very copious accounts of his inquiries. His reports to the Society have already been printed in full, and may be found in the Annual Reports for the years 1844 and 1845. It is therefore unnecessary to reproduce them here. They were exhaustive and satisfactory, and guided the action of the Committee with respect to the missions that were afterwards established in Trinidad, the Bahamas, and Haiti. It will, however, be interesting to extract a few personal notices from the copious materials at hand.

Of the visit to Dr. Kalley's prison he writes, December 23rd:—" I went in company with Dr. Trew and Mr. Young. Dr. Kalley was cheerful, but was looking with great anxiety for his acquittal and release. Through the kindness of an influential friend or two in the island he has been removed from the loathsome cell to which he was condemned, and was occupying two or three commodious rooms above the prison. He, however, continues to distribute tracts ; and visitors of all classes, which will appear surprising, are allowed access to him in twos and threes at a time. The sympathy of the people with him in his persecution is astonishing, and justifies the hope that a light is kindled here which the world, the Pope, and the devil will not be able to extinguish. Dr. Kalley has now been imprisoned for several months for his noble testimony to the truth, and, without the exertions and prayers of the Christian Church on his behalf, he may there remain as many years."

The approach to Trinidad he thus describes :—" The high mountains of Cumana on the South American continent on the one side, and the magnificent Gulf of Paria like a polished mirror, at the extremity of which stands Port of Spain, the capital, were before us. We anchored at some distance from the town, from the shallowness of the water occasioned by the vast quantities of mud brought into the gulf by the waters of the Orinoco. Mr. Cowen met me at his gate, and both himself and wife received me kindly, and insisted on my remaining with them during my stay. I have attended his little place of worship two or three times, and have addressed the people, about fifty in number, more than once without injury to my throat."

" On New Year's Day I witnessed the gew-gaw exhibitions at the papal cathedral, when my spirit was really stirred within me. I have walked a good deal about the town, and, excepting the awful ignorance and superstition of the people, am pleased with it, nor do I doubt the success of Protestant missions in the island.

" On Monday afternoon I went in company with Mr.

Cowen to a place called Tacarigua, where is a settlement of disbanded soldiers of the 1st West India Regiment. I slept in a hammock for the first time in my life, and returned last evening after a fatiguing ride of thirty miles on horseback."

"If you look at the map of Trinidad you will see a place marked on it, ' Mission — Savanna-la-Grande.' Here I have been several days among the native Indians and American settlements of disbanded soldiers. While in the neighbourhood I visited the mud volcano, and have taken a rough sketch of the place, which I shall want my dear Hannah to fill up and complete for me under my direction."

A lively description of this natural curiosity is con tained in a letter to his two boys :—" The people call the mud volcano—for what reason I could not ascertain—' The Devil's Woodyard.'   It lay in the midst of an im mense forest of palm and other trees, which was so dark, and at the same time so dangerous from the badness of the roads and the immense creepers, which like ropes of all dimensions threw themselves from tree to tree across the path, that I began almost to despair of reaching the place. I came suddenly upon it.   The top of the crater formed a circle of about a hundred yards in diameter.   The sur face was flat, with a number of mounds scattered over it from two to four feet in height, much like a cone flattened at the top.   About every ten minutes one or two of them threw up a quantity of soft mud of a sulphurous smell. Within the crater scarcely any shrub was known to grow, but outside its limits magnificent trees and stately palms formed a most splendid amphitheatre.   I left the neigh bourhood with regret, because the people seemed anxious to hear the Gospel."

In another letter he continues the journal of his visit :—

"The minister of the Scotch church here [Port of

Spain] is exceedingly friendly, and is anxious for a whole batch of Baptists to come from Jamaica. I have spoken occasionally at the different meetings I have attended, and last Sabbath evening I preached for the Presbyterian minister, at his earnest request. I am not the worse for it by any means, but I will still be careful. Many very respectable people were present, anxious to hear the Baptist Bishop, as I am called. I have been strongly urged to deliver a lecture or two on Jamaica, or to speak at a public meeting, but I have steadily declined. I have been collecting some seeds of different plants, which I hope to forward to you before I see you."

From Trinidad Mr. Phillippo proceeded to St. Vincent, "where," he says, "I met with a considerable number of black American Baptists, or rather from New Providence, in the Bahamas. They said they had been praying for years for a Baptist missionary to be sent among them. They were brought here by a Colonel Brown. There were originally about three hundred of them, but are now reduced to one hundred and twenty. They are still residing on their old master's estate. I held a very interesting service among them, and promised to intercede for them with the Committee. I had also repeated interviews with some Caribs descended from the original inhabitants of the island. I also visited the volcano, and stayed for this purpose two or three days under the hospitable roof of the Rev. Mr. Moister, Wesleyan minister. I had a very pleasant tour of the island, and it was also successful as far as my object was concerned. I was very much pleased with St. Vincent. It is more beautiful (not magnificent) than any of the islands I have previously seen. I shall write to urge the Committee to send out one or two missionaries without delay."

The next visit was paid to St. Lucia. "I embarked for St. Lucia on the afternoon of the 5th of February, in a small sloop passing along the eastern side of St. Vincent, and the still more enchanting scenery presented by the western shore of the former island. The lofty mountains of St. Lucia, covered with majestic forests, their spiral tops appearing above the stratum of clouds that rolled their dense masses along their precipitous sides ; its gentle undulations and spacious valleys clothed with the vivid green of the sugar-cane, contrasting beautifully with the dark purple of the surrounding heights ; and its steep and hoary cliffs, ascending abruptly from the sea, presented a picture which, indisposed as I was, could not fail to attract my attention and fascinate my eye. I landed about nine o'clock in the evening at a small town called Sauffrere, passing between the celebrated Pilons, the magnificent spiral mountains which rise like pyramids out of the sea at the entrance of the bay, and which, but a few hours before, were spanned to the very bosom of the dark blue waters with a rainbow of the most perfect form, and of the most splendid colours, I had ever seen. Next day I proceeded in a passage boat to Castries, the capital, about twenty miles distant, situated on the western side of the island.

" Here I was most kindly entertained for several days by the Hon. W. Muter, one of my fellow-passengers on board the *Trent*, during which I called on the Governor, a pious, excellent man, whose wife had been the widow of a Congregational missionary in India. On breakfasting with them one or two mornings, in company with the rector, the only Episcopal or other Protestant minister in the island, I was requested to conduct family worship. Government House is beautifully situated on a hill called the Morne, from which not only the town of Castries, but also Martinique and another island or two, are distinctly visible, presenting a scene to which no description can do justice. Mr. Muter took me to see two or three of his estates, and also to different parts of the island. He lamented that, with one or two recent exceptions, no attempt had been made to establish even a school in the colony. Mr. Muter had imported several mechanics from Scotland, and settled them on his properties in comfort ; and had several young men, also from Europe, in his mercantile establishments. The result of my inquiries was this : There could hardly be found an island in these seas in greater spiritual need, or one in which there was a greater prospect of success. I gave in my report to Fen Court accordingly."

He left St. Lucia by the mail steamer, and reached Dominica on the 11th of February. Here he stayed eight days. He found a home in the hospitable residence of Mr. Gordon, the superintendent of the schools sustained by the Mico Charity. "There is," he says, " a good opening in this island for a missionary or two; but they would have very hard work, with little encouragement, for several years, all the people being Roman Catholics and speaking the French language."

Among other curious places, he visited the " Sauffrure," or Sulphur Hill. " I walked over a mountain of burning sulphur, which is supposed to be perfectly hollow beneath. Water was bubbling up in various spots, and flowing in streams hot enough to boil in a few minutes almost any article of food. Sometimes we were completely enveloped in clouds of vapour that proceeded from the boiling fountains. In the town, the fumes of sulphur are some-times so strong as to render the place almost uninhabitable. This excites considerable alarm, as it is caused by the extension of the boiling streams of a souffrure to the westward arising from subterranean action. Almost everything is turned black in the houses, and it is scarcely possible to keep anything clean. On this account, the inhabitants of the different islands are very much afraid of an explosion, but the Dominicans are perfectly unconcerned respecting it." In a letter home he reports :—

"I am, blessed be God, quite well in health, but very, very anxious to be with my dear wife and family. When once I find myself on the way from Grenada to Haiti, I shall be half at home. Be sure you take care of yourself. I can scarcely trust myself to think of the happiness I shall enjoy on finding myself once more in possession of my happy home, and in the presence of her who makes it so. My voice is very much improved, for I am very careful. I have but little time for writing, so that you must beg my brethren, Dowson and Lynch, as well as my dear people, to excuse my apparent neglect of them. Soon I hope to see them, and then I will try and make amends for all neglect. Cease not to pray for my health and success and safe return, and beg an interest in the supplications of all my friends for the same end."

Mr. Phillippo reached Jacmel, in the Island of Haiti, on the 15th of March, but, on landing, he found the inhabitants in a state of great excitement from an apprehension of war between the French and Spanish portions of the island. A strong detachment of militia had just left for Port au Prince, and upwards of five hundred refugees had come into Jacmel from the disturbed districts. The insurrection was reported as everywhere prevalent. Acting under the advice of the authorities, he thought it best to postpone his investigations to a later period, and accordingly returned on board the steamer to proceed to Jamaica, where he landed on the 20th.

Writing to Dr. Angus on the 1st of April he says, in closing the account of his deputation : "I arrived here a few days ago amidst the almost overwhelming gratulations of my beloved people, and had the happiness to find my dear wife and family well in health. Nor was I less delighted, nor, I trust, less thankful to God, for the state

and circumstances in which I found my church and different congregations throughout the district. My highly
esteemed brethren, Dowson and Lynch, to whose oversight my stations were committed, have done their utmost
to promote their interests, and, although I am aware it is
God's blessing alone that renders human instrumentality
successful, yet I feel that I should be chargeable with a
want of affection for my flock and of proper concern for
the Divine glory were I not to express to you the deep
obligations of gratitude under which I feel myself laid to
them."

Thus, after an absence of nearly two years, with health
very much improved, having fulfilled with great ability
and success the commission entrusted to him by the
Society, and restored to the home in which his affections
enjoyed unalloyed happiness, Mr. Phillippo resumed his
labours as a missionary, only too soon to enter on a
period, prolonged through seven years, of constant anxiety
and distress.

CHAPTER XXVI.

THE LAW SUIT—1844 TO 1851.

THE amicable arrangements made by Mr. Phillippo with
his two assistants were soon interrupted by the departure
of Mr. Dowson for England on a matter of private
interest; and not till his return, six months after, in
the month of November, did Mr. Phillippo become
aware of a change in the feelings of that gentleman
towards him. Till now, the most entire confidence
had subsisted between them. During Mr. Phillippo's
stay in England, he had received from Mr. Dowson and
from the churches many letters "of kindness and affectionate gratitude, such as perhaps few ministers could
produce, and which were most creditable to himself
and them."* On Mr. Phillippo's arrival in Jamaica, he
was welcomed with every show of cordiality, and the
resumption of his work as pastor was in every way
facilitated by Mr. Dowson. No change was thought
of, or spoken about as desirable, in the relative positions
they had hitherto occupied. Mr. Dowson had scarcely
settled down on his return before he put forth the claim
of being the pastor of the church in Spanish Town.
Efforts were made to alienate the affections of the
people from Mr. Phillippo, and Mr. Dowson unhappily
succeeded in gathering round him a band of sympathisers

---

* These words are those of the Vice-Chancellor's judgment.

who demanded possession of the chapel. To give colour
to these proceedings, a meeting of the seceders, increased
in number by the most unjustifiable extension of the rights
of membership to others, was held in a booth that had
been hastily constructed, at which Mr. Phillippo was
deposed from the pastorate, and Mr. Dowson was elected
in his room. One of the two trustees remaining in the
island, without reference to his co-trustees in England,
next created a new trust-deed, on the faith of which
turbulent, and even violent, attempts were repeatedly
made to obtain possession of the mission premises by
excited mobs. Legal proceedings were therefore necessarily resorted to by Mr. Phillippo for the protection of
the property, and the securing of the position he had
for more than twenty years sustained.

It is unnecessary, as it is also undesirable, to enter into
the details of the protracted litigation which ensued.
In the course of the conflict, Mr. Phillippo's character
was unsparingly assailed by portions of the press, as well
as by his adversaries, in order to induce him to quit the
island in disgust. His advocacy of the cause of the slave
and his exertions to obtain emancipation were now remembered against him, and the occasion seized to his
injury by those whose hostility his benevolent action
had aroused. But the warm and cordial support of his
brethren was not wanting to him; with two or three
exceptions, they and their congregations came to his
aid. But especially did he find the most generous
sympathy in the unfailing regard of his friend Joseph
Fletcher, Esq., and in the aid rendered by an English
Committee, of which Mr. Fletcher was treasurer. The
suit brought into view most of the leading ecclesiastical
principles of Baptist churches, and had the effect of
placing on a foundation of colonial practice and law
the legal rights of Baptist congregations. It made

clear the meaning and extent of the independence
assumed by the churches and their pastors, for it was
held, as expressed in a letter from the Rev. J. Angus,
the Secretary, addressed to Mr. Phillippo on the 4th of
June, 1845, that, "the Committee having given up
mission work in Jamaica, there is no propriety in their
interfering at all in points in dispute between churches
and ministers." An unfortunate intermediate judgment
of the Vice-Chancellor, at an early stage of the suit,
greatly contributed to delay its decision for nearly six
years, but the courage and persistence of Mr. Phillippo
in the maintenance of his just rights were at length
rewarded by complete success. The cost was great.
His pecuniary resources were crippled by the secession
of so many members of his congregation, as well as
by the general depression which had set in in the
agricultural and commercial condition of the island.
The heavy expenses of the suit, though largely met by
generous friends in England, pressed most heavily on
his congregation, and entailed personal distresses and
sacrifices scarcely to be borne; still the weary months
and years, incessantly occupied with research, with the
collection of evidence, with the copying of innumerable
documents, and with consultations with his legal advisers,
came to a close.

On the 4th of November, 1850, the suit reached its
end, when the judgment was given in the High Court of
Chancery of the island by the Vice-Chancellor. "To
describe the feelings," says Mr. Phillippo, "excited
thereby in my own mind, and in the minds of others most
interested in the successful result, would be impossible.
It was the Lord's doing. No wisdom or power but His
could have prevailed against the wicked and powerful
conspiracy that was formed against the cause of truth
and righteousness. The congratulations of friends were

warm and flattering to a degree that could not fail to excite the sincerest expressions of esteem and gratitude, such that I doubt not I shall carry with me to my grave. Friends in need! Among those in this country who encouraged and applauded my resolution, though unostentatiously, to abide the issue were persons of property and influence, as well as nine-tenths of the class to whom the anarchists belonged." But although sustained by the sympathies and generous aid of many friends, both in Jamaica and England, Mr. Phillippo felt most acutely the defection of a few brethren from his side, some of whom appear to have thought all law-suits illegitimate in a Christian missionary. It was therefore a source of intense gratification to him to receive the unanimous congratulations of the Committee of the Missionary Society, and their recommendation to the friends of the Society to assist him in the disbursement of the costs. In publishing this resolution, the circular, signed by the Rev. J. Aldis, says : "It is matter of devout thanksgiving that the oldest missionary in Jamaica has thus been sustained in his important position, and that property which cost £10,000 has been rescued from lawless misappropriation. It is yet more important that this esteemed servant of God has been enabled to pass through a severe trial with honour to himself and the missionary cause, while the interests of the Jamaica churches have been greatly promoted."*

The decision of the Vice-Chancellor was not, however, immediately followed by security. Two more riotous attempts were made by the defeated party to obtain possession of the mission property, the last of which

---

* The funds collected by this Committee were chiefly expended on the repairs of the mission premises. The costs of the suit were almost wholly borne by Mr. Fletcher.

for some hours threatened the lives of Mr. and Mrs.
Phillippo and their daughter, with those of the missionary
brethren Teall and Hewett, who happened to be staying
with them. Much damage was done, both to the chapel
and the mission-house, but the administrators of the law
at length secured a peaceable termination to the strife.
Mr. Phillippo and his people, by the close of the year
1851, were able to worship in peace, and to resume those
ministries of grace and truth which these lamentable events
had so long interrupted.

There can be no doubt that the painful incidents of
this conflict greatly affected Mr. Phillippo's judgment
of the Negro character. The bright side had ever presented itself to him in the early years of his missionary
life. He had hitherto known the people as remarkably
accessible to kindness, and to the influence of those who
had sought their freedom and the advancement of their
highest interests. He had seen them as peculiarly im-
pressionable to Divine teaching, docile to those in
authority, and grateful for sympathy under their oppressions. But now he had to learn that slavery could
not be abolished without leaving behind a legacy of
evil, and that its mischievous effects were not to be at
once removed by the righteous act of emancipation. He
had with grief to discover that even liberty could not
by a breath of sweetness melt away the uncorrected
tendencies of barbarism and savage life, or remove
habits peculiar to the "vile institution" of slavery. The
saying of the old Greek poet seemed on the eve of
verification in the face of Christian hope itself. "Half
our virtue," says Homer, "is torn away when a man
becomes a slave, and the other half goes when he becomes
a slave let loose." To use Mr. Phillippo's own words,
he was compelled to recognise with the bitterness of
disappointed feeling "a state of society for which he

was not prepared. The people," he continues, "have not spirit to struggle against poverty; too many give themselves up to abject melancholy. They are subject to extremes of joy and sorrow, as well as to love or hatred ; of strong, ardent, and impetuous feelings and passions, they can do little except under excitement. Ardent for a time in what they undertake from benevolent motives, they as quickly cool. It is hard work to keep them to duty even when voluntarily undertaken." He speaks of the change in some as " awful ; " the worst passions of half-civilised men were let loose, and the town itself for a time was given over to anarchy and sin. The change in the condition of the people appeared to be for the worse, and not for the better. The want of employment, the absence of all provision for helpless poverty, the dense ignorance which the Legislature made no real effort to remove, the cruel banishment of the peasantry by many of the estate owners and managers from the little holdings and cottages in which they had been born and bred, provided an abundant field for the operations of evil-minded men.

The ten years from 1842 to 1851 was a period of intense anxiety, suffering, and trial to every interest in the island. The wonder is that, with a hostile Legislature, a feeble Executive, and every class of the community depressed by the decay of cultivation and decimated by the fatal pestilence which swept through the island in 1850, emancipation did not become a disastrous failure. To one who had laboured as Mr. Phillippo had done, the disappointment of so many bright hopes was great. If the people were free, it was also evident that long years of patient labour were yet needed to bring to maturity the seeds of truth and righteousness, purity and order, which it had been his aim and that of many other benevolent men to sow.

This biography would not be a faithful picture of Mr. Phillippo's life were it to pass over the severe spiritual struggles to which these events gave rise. Although of a happy and sanguine disposition, there were moments when his faith and hope in God were well-nigh gone. It may not be that the veil should be entirely drawn aside from those scenes of dark trial and conflict through which he was called to pass; yet a few passages may be culled from his diary which will sufficiently indicate his mental sufferings. At first, when the hope of a speedy settlement of the affair was in prospect, he bore the trial with equanimity and fortitude, so that he could say, " Blessed be God, I have a consciousness of having done everything for the best, for the promotion of God's glory, and the good of the Church. Therefore I enjoy peace of mind." But as the evil days came more thickly, and unfolded their dark burden of sorrow and anxiety, the shadows deepened over his spirit. At the dawn of day his mind would be hopeful. " Calm and composed," he says ; " scarcely ever more so since these troubles commenced. Communed with my own heart upon my bed, and was still. It seemed as though I was sure God would not allow the enemies of His truth to gain their object. I therefore felt myself strong in the Lord, and in the power of His might." But the shades of evening would bring a different phase of feeling. " May God mercifully deliver us from our long and distressing troubles, and grant us again peace and prosperity! O Lord, support and strengthen me in this arduous conflict, if Thou shouldst not see fit yet to deliver me from it. My heart is lifted up to Thee. Leave not my soul desolate!" But this was in an early stage of his troubles. A little later he writes (October 18, 1846): "I lay awake long before day, under a very heavy depression of mind. My way appeared more hedged up than ever. A hundred fears

took hold upon me. My heart fainted within me, and
out of the depths I cried unto the Lord, though with a
mixture of dissatisfaction, unbelief, and confidence. I
was, however, enabled to say, ' Mine eyes are ever toward
the Lord, for He shall pluck my feet out of the net. Turn
Thou unto me, and have mercy upon me, for I am desolate and afflicted.' " Then, in a day or two, he comforts
himself by the example of Henry Martyn, whose memoir
he was reading. " What contempt and scorn had he to
endure at Shiraz ! And how meekly did he bear it all
for Christ. May I feel and say as he did :—

' If on my name, for Thy dear sake,
Shame and reproaches be ;
All hail reproach, and welcome shame,
If Thou remember me ! ' "

More especially does he feel the depressing influence of
his circumstances when, on a Lord's-day morning, he has
to meet, in the school-rooms, the large congregation
which still attended his ministry. " June 27, 1847. Sabbath morning.—My mind still oppressed with care and
apprehension as to the future, but had, as usual, recourse
to God in prayer. Poured out my heart before Him. Oh!
how mysterious His providences are respecting me.
Darkness still besets me round. Preached in the evening ; my mind very gloomy. Felt little unction throughout
the whole service. What happy seasons I once enjoyed !
How sweet their memory still ! O Lord, I am oppressed ;
undertake for me." And a day or two later he exclaims :
" Show me, O Lord, wherefore Thou contendest with me,
and hidest Thy face from me. O Lord, Thou hast been
my helper ; leave me not, neither do Thou forsake me,
O God of my salvation ! I have acted, as I hope, for Thy
glory and the good of Thy Church. Be not, therefore,
far from me. Let not my enemies triumph over me." Not
always, however, was he thus cast down. Some act of

kindness from his people, some hopeful incident in the progress of the trial, or a few bright words from his correspondents at home would induce a more cheerful tone. Thus, under date of February 26, he writes: "My mind was disquieted yesterday by some gloomy apprehensions; but I am thankful to say they have not been realised. It is true I knew not what awaited me, but I knew whatever befell me depended on the government of an infinitely wise and gracious God. I know the love He bears me. I am comforted by His mercy. Were I to doubt of the gracious providence of my God, all my past days would witness against me and reprove my folly, distrust, and ingratitude. All nature would make me ashamed. Every bird, every insect, would reprove my unbelief, and heaven and earth would appear against me as witnesses of Providence. Almighty Ruler of the world, my God and Father, I will not dishonour Thee by my anxious cares. I will commit them all to Thee. As a child, with tender love I will look up to Thee, and with joyful confidence expect from Thee every good."

Thus was Mr. Phillippo led into deeper acquaintance with his own heart's necessities, and to cry earnestly to God for more growth in grace and holiness. "I am dissatisfied," he says, on the 13th of March, "with my want of faith, and zeal, and holy love; with my frequent impatience under my trials. Oh, that it were otherwise! that I could bear, not with patience only, but with pleasure, what my heavenly Father has appointed me to bear; the same when concealed from public observation as when exposed to the gaze of multitudes; that I may be a priest who presents himself a living sacrifice to God; that I may feel the sanctity and height of my calling; that my sympathies may be more tender, my zeal more fervent, glowing, and energetic. May I make the Lord's own words in some measure the motto of my life : ' I must work the works of Him that sent Me while it is day, for the night cometh.' "

One more extract will suffice to reflect the changeful experience of these days so burdened with anxiety and care. " My mind is greatly depressed, and it doubtless gives its tinge to my communications home. I felt sad, and at times almost in despair. I tried to pray, but could not. Language failed me. I could only sigh out my feelings, and thus relieve my oppressed heart. And this oppression clung to me, diverted for a time by occupation, but recurring as soon as thought was no longer absorbed by a different subject of interest. I turned to the 46th Psalm, to Luther's Psalm, and read over the experience of David. My mind became more calm, more disposed to trust. ' God is my refuge and strength, a very present help in trouble.'

> ' O Thou, who driest the mourner's tear,
>   How dark this world would be
>   If, when deceived and wounded here,
>   We could not fly to Thee !
>
>   *   *   *   *   *
>
> ' Oh ! who could bear life's stormy doom,
>   Did not Thy wing of love
>   Come brightly wafting through the gloom,
>   Our peace-branch from above ? ' "

Looking back over this troublous period, he could at last joyfully recognise the gracious leadings of the Divine hand in it all. At the close of the year 1851 he writes : " At its opening my cup was full of bitterness and my prospects were gloomy in the extreme. How different now ! This is the Lord's doing ; it is marvellous in my eyes." The chapel had been restored, though in a damaged state, to his possession. Larger congregations than ever hung upon his lips, and with a sanctified feeling of joy and desire he concludes the diary of the year :

"Here I raise my Ebenezer.   Bless the Lord, O my soul,
and forget not all His benefits.   Oh, that I had more
reverence for God, more of a sense of His presence and
superintendence, more of trust in Providence, more of submission to His will, more of consciousness that He doeth
all things well!"

CHAPTER XXVII.

THE events narrated in the preceding chapter interfered to a painful degree with the evangelistic labours of Mr. Phillippo. For a large part of the time, his Spanish Town congregation could only meet in the school-rooms, which, happily, being large, would hold from twelve to fifteen hundred worshippers. But his ministry was not without many gratifying evidences of the attachment of his people ; and he thankfully records that many Sabbaths were marked by the Divine presence and blessing. Thus, on April 12th, 1846, he writes : " Sabbath Day. Early prayer-meeting. Well attended. Sabbath-school also. At half-past ten, chapel literally crowded ; persons coming from all parts of the country in carts, on horseback, &c. Not fewer than thirty horses in the burial ground and yard, besides those left in other and different parts of the town. Preached from Mark xiii. 12, 13, 14. Felt very much at liberty, and people seemed greatly interested. Administered the Lord's Supper. About one thousand partook of it ; a very interesting service, the most so I have experienced for many months. People full of animation. Refreshed myself and attended a church-meeting. Preached in evening. A large congregation also." Again, on the 7th of June, he writes : " Rose before daylight. At six o'clock went to prayer-meeting. Held conversation with several of the country people for nearly an hour. Numbers of people pouring into the school-room from all quarters ;

some coming on horseback, some in carts, &c.   Preached
from Gen. xxviii. 22 : ' And the stone which I have set
for a pillar,' &c.   Felt aroused and animated by the congregation, so large and so attentive, that I preached with
great fluency and comfort, and I hope not without benefit
to my audience.   They literally seemed to hang upon my
lips, and by their looks and gestures appeared ready to
lay down their lives for me.   That they have borne so
much obloquy with so much Christian fortitude and
forbearance, as well as made so many sacrifices, is
sufficient to redeem the black and coloured people as
a mass from the imputations with which they are
charged in consequence of the conduct of some towards
me.   On the dispersion of the multitude, which filled the
whole three apartments of the school-house, it seemed
immense, crowding the streets in all directions."

These scenes were more especially seen on the days
devoted to the administration of the Lord's Supper.
Nevertheless, at other times, and even when the prospect
of success in the suit was problematical, the congregations were large.   Amid the deepening distress of the
people he continued to receive manifold proofs of
personal affection and regard.   So that, writing on the
18th of October, 1848, he could say that, while accounts
from all the West India Islands spoke of ever-increasing
depression, and which were fully corroborated by his
brethren in Jamaica, yet, " however torn and embarrassed
the church at Spanish Town has been, it appears to be as
truly prosperous in all respects as any one in the island."   If
this was the case during the dark time of trouble, it may
readily be conceived with what joy the pastor and his
people re-entered their disused sanctuary on the execution of the Vice-Chancellor's decree.   This longed-for
event took place on the 7th of February, 1851.   Writing
on March 4th, Mr Phillippo says : " After the customary

morning meeting, the chapel doors were thrown open. A very large congregation assembled at half-past ten o'clock. The preliminary part of the service was conducted by brother Teall, and I preached from 2 Cor. viii. 5. The afternoon was devoted to the interests of the Sunday-school. We closed the day with grateful thanksgiving to God for our success. Great, indeed, it was! I cannot doubt that it was gained by the interposition of God. 'Not unto me, not unto me, O Lord, but unto Thy name be all the glory!'" Similar blessings were enjoyed on the following Lord's-day. "My mind and the minds of all my people overflowed with gratitude to God in the belief that our deliverance was complete. I preached from 1 John iv. 10: 'Herein is love,' &c., and felt great pleasure and more at liberty than for some time past in the delivery of my message." One more extract from his diary will show the joy and comfort with which the resumption of his work in the sanctuary that he had built filled his heart. "April 20, 1851.—Easter Sunday. Expected a large congregation this day, and was not disappointed. The early prayer-meeting was well attended, and before ten o'clock the people came in streams from every quarter, so that the attendance was greatly increased. A larger number of children were also present at the Sabbath-school. I visited it between the morning services, and was highly gratified. Especially was I delighted to see the long line of them, attended by their teachers, going from the school to the chapel. It called forth the recollections of long past times. The school bell rang merrily in my ears, and told of our being active and vigorous again. I looked to see the children pass along, until tears of thankfulness and pleasure filled my eyes. The Lord has done great things for us, whereof we are glad."

Besides the services in Spanish Town, Mr. Phillippo visited, at more or less regular intervals, the stations at

Sligoville and Passage Fort. Sligoville had fallen much into decay during the years of trouble from his inability to supply its wants. But as he now frequently occupied a small farm residence in the neighbourhood he was able to give more time to its interests, and was rewarded by witnessing a revival of its temporal and spiritual prosperity.

Passage Fort enjoyed throughout a fair measure of prosperity, and he often mentions large congregations, interesting Sabbaths, social gatherings of his flock, and baptismal times as giving him unalloyed pleasure and satisfaction.

The incessant demands of the law suit on his attention, the labours incident to the stations, and his pastoral visitation of the sick and aged left Mr. Phillippo little time to devote to the extension of the Gospel in the surrounding districts. Still he often shared with his ministerial brethren the more general engagements which the welfare of the mission throughout the island required. Thus the 1st of February, 1848, he is met with at the meeting of the Association as chairman, when numerous questions relating to the state of the mission were discussed. Later in the year he is at Calabar, taking part in the annual examination of the students, then under the care of the Rev. J. Tinson. At another time he visits Vale Lionel to assist in the formation of a new church.

These excursions were a great refreshment to his spirit. Always fond of scenery, he delighted in the mingled grandeur and beauty of the mountains and deep valleys of Jamaica among which he journeyed. Gorgeous visions of colour and celestial softness would alternate with tempest and storm, the echoes of the rocks being awakened with appalling sounds by the terrific thunder that accompanied them. A few extracts from his diary will express the enjoyment he derived from these scenes, and also illustrate his powers of description. This from his mountain home. February 18, 1848—"Two showers of rain fell during the middle of the day. The black, lowering clouds to the north-east and south indicated an abundant fall, but it fell on the plains embracing Kingston, Spanish Town, Old Harbour, and Milk River. In my rambles I was struck with the beautiful appearance of the clumps of coffee-trees, covered with pearly white blossoms, in fine contrast with the deep-green, laurel-like leaves. The little supply of water that has been received has attracted the birds hither from the lowlands. Large flocks of teal flew past as I was gazing on the splendid scenery that lay before me in the short twilight, with the sound almost of a hurricane, produced by the rapid vibration of their wings. The moon is at the full, and the evening star hangs brilliant on the verge of the western horizon, and gives an indescribable charm to the sky. The night is bright and clear of clouds, except to the south, and the atmosphere is at rest." Rising at sunrise the next day, he says, "I took a long walk, gun in hand, hoping to meet with some birds that would supply the morning meal. Heard for the first time for some weeks the cooing of the wild dove, but saw nothing except the loggerhead. The woodpecker was tapping at the trees like a ship's carpenter; the ground dove, the beautiful green todie (*Iodus viridis*), the nightingale, and the humming-birds, which are very numerous, were gambolling on every side in the dewy freshness of the morning. The dew was abundant, dripping like rain from the trees, and sparkling in the morning sun like globules of crystal. The forests were tinged with the rays of the luminary of day, a stillness reigned that might be felt, and colours, like those of an English forest in autumn, gave an entrancing interest to the scene, and I could but exclaim—

> ' These are Thy glorious works, Parent of good, Almighty :
> Thine this universal frame, thus wondrous fair ;
> Thyself how wondrous then ! '

It is remarkable that few trees hybernate in the tropics, and those that do are the softest and least valuable of woods, such as the bombax ceiba, the baobab, the Spanish plum, &c. These, and several others of the deciduous species, being now leafless, add to the charm of this autumnal scene."

A very different outlook is recorded on the 27th of May, 1850. " A more dreadful night of storm I have never known. The rain descended as though the vast floodgates of the sky were suddenly opened for the purpose of overwhelming us. But the terror inspired came from the lightning and thunder. The flashes were incessant during the whole night, illuminating the entire hemisphere, and in the innermost chambers of the house it streamed over myself and family as we lay in bed. I rose to look at it. The thunder shook the house, and once or twice it literally rocked to and fro like a cradle. Added to this war of elements a high wind increasing to a hurricane arose, driving the rain into the house and deluging it. The streets were filled with water, and for hours were well-nigh impassable after the storm had passed away."

Another brief extract describes a ride between Clarksonville and Brown's Town, in company with his dear friend the Rev. John Clark, of the latter place, on the 11th of August, 1852. " It was late in the afternoon when we started, passing through a more picturesque district than I had seen before, as also a more fertile one, although the greater number of fine properties along the road were abandoned to ruinate. We passed along a splendid ravine, at the foot of which rolled a celebrated river that loses itself underground, and re-appears after some miles as an impetuous torrent. It is reported that, as a gentleman and his servant were once driving rapidly along the steep road leading to Clarksonville, the horse dashed down the precipice into the river. They were afterwards found at the distance of many miles from the spot, having been carried by the torrent along its subterraneous course. We passed by Bethany Chapel, another of brother Clark's stations, and arrived at Brown's Town at dark, a journey of fifteen miles."

One more description of the incidents of tropical life may be interesting. " Wednesday, July 7th, 1852.—While sitting in my study intent on reading a book that had absorbed my interest, I was aroused by a loud shaking of the doors and windows; but thought for the moment it might be caused by the carpenters that were at work in the house, or by some passing cart or wain. I then felt the house rocking, and, rising from my seat, was nearly thrown down. I felt an extreme nausea, like that of sea-sickness. It continued for a minute or two, and I went downstairs. The vibration continued, alarming the whole family, the house seeming literally to rise and fall like a wave of the sea. It was a shock of earthquake. I went afterwards to Passage Fort, and about five o'clock the shock was repeated, and I took occasion to refer to it in my address." The next day the diary continues :—" The earthquake is the subject of universal talk. The Jews, as usual, flew to their synagogue, and at other places thanks-giving meetings were held. The intervals between the shocks, or the few minutes that pass after the first shock subsides, are minutes of awful suspense, and sometimes, especially in the dead of night, of awful terror. On this occasion there were two distinct shocks, passing from north to south. The first was a tremulous motion, which lasted for some fifteen or sixteen seconds. The second was an awful heaving of the earth, like the pitching of a ship in a heavy sea, and its duration was about thirty seconds. In some houses the chandeliers swung to and fro for ten minutes. Pictures were moved on the walls. An iron bridge rose and fell so as to appear falling prostrate upon the river. Bells rang, clocks stopped, and the water in reservoirs was agitated so much as to overflow the brim. Walls were thrown down, and the inmates of some houses were precipitated into the streets."

The general state of the mission during these years gave Mr. Phillippo the gravest concern. At the Association that met in the month of February, 1848, at which he was called to preside, he records that the gathering was one of "melancholy interest." Many congregations were reported to be without pastors. Many missionaries had either left, or were on the eve of leaving, the island, from the inability of the churches to support them.* "After prayer, long and very interesting," he says, "were the discussions on the state of churches. Various were the causes assigned for their present condition, and as various the propositions made for their revival ; but as all the other denominations share equally the depression, though differing so widely in church government and discipline, I was of opinion that what had been said were but the adjuncts of some great evil existing which was not discovered, an evil by which the Spirit of God had been grieved, and which must be found out and renounced before He would again return to us."

There can be little doubt, now, that the chief cause of the evils deplored was the general state of poverty, and the decay of trade and employment from which every class of the population was suffering. Scarcely was the resolution of the missionaries to rely on the resources of the churches for their support carried into effect, before pecuniary difficulties, arising from the distress of the people, began to press upon them. To this cause must

* In his diary at this time, Mr. Phillippo writes : "About sixteen missionaries and schoolmasters have either left Jamaica or are dead within the last few years, and some of the brethren on the north side of the island are starving "

be added the action of the planters in breaking up the villages on their estates, and turning out the occupants without any provision for the sick and needy; difficulties arising out of the question of labour; the purchase of small properties by the peasantry, which absorbed their savings, and taxed their earnings to meet the cost of the erection of cottages in the newly founded townships, and the clearing of the land. All these things drew largely on the resources of the people, so that contributions to the service of Christ began to decline; besides which, the moneys needed for the completion of manses and chapels were necessarily devoted to the support of the pastor, so that debts were incurred or left to accumulate. A time of widespread sickness also set in. The health of many brethren needed a change which they were unable to secure, while unanticipated emergencies sorely beset the ministers of the smaller congregations. Such entries as the following again and again recur in Mr. Phillippo's diary. "What will become of the mission I cannot, nor can any one else, conjecture, except that in four or five years' time, if vigorous measures are not used, it will become a complete wreck. All are dispirited. Several speak of returning to England" (December 30, 1847). "The future is dark and gloomy. The country is increasing in poverty, and religious feeling is rapidly declining. But the Lord reigneth, therefore will I hope in Him" (October 20, 1852). "Many of my brethren are even in greater straits than I. Says one in a letter written from a bed of sickness, to which both himself and his wife, with almost all his family, were then confined, ' We have been without money and almost without food, little as we have required for our own use; but what time the last fowl was boiled another has come in, and, when the last piece of yam has been used, more has come in just as it has been wanted. So you see, though we are cast down, we are not destroyed, neither have our perplexities driven us to despair. We shall have a new song put into our mouth, even praise unto our God'" (September 23, 1849). "I am daily becoming convinced that the apparent indifference of the people, and the decay of their old liberality, are attributable entirely to their poverty" (May 19, 1850).

This state of things could not but awaken the deepest anxiety in the minds of the friends of the Mission at home. It was absolutely necessary to render some aid to the ministers thus struggling with debt, and with perplexities of various kinds springing out of the social changes freedom had entailed. The first step was taken in 1845, when the Committee of the Society resolved to raise a sum of £6,000 * to assist in the liquidation of the debts existing on the manses and chapels to the extent of £18,000. In the distribution of this fund care was taken, by mutual consent, that nothing should be done to interfere with the independence of the pastors and their congregations. With that one and only condition the money was freely bestowed.

Important as was the help thus rendered it did not touch, except incidentally, the personal circumstances of the missionaries. The later months of 1845 and the early part of the following year added to their difficulties, and the most pressing representations were sent home of the absolute need of further assistance. The general condition of the island was worse than ever. The deaths of the Revs. W. Knibb and T. Burchell increased the gloom, and intensified the forebodings of evil which found expression in the letters of the sufferers. In October, 1846, the Committee of the Society therefore resolved to invite the Revs. Dr. Angus and C. M. Birrell to visit

---

* The sum actually contributed reached £6,300.

Jamaica "to confer with the brethren," and to make the fullest inquiry into the condition of the mission. For their personal relief Sir Morton Peto, one of the Treasurers, most generously placed £2,000 at the disposal of the deputation.

It was an important part of the duty of the deputation to ascertain whether it was desirable to interfere with the state of independence which had been established. Some of the missionaries, and Mr. Phillippo was one of them, with many friends in England, were inclined to think that the absolute freedom of the congregations from home influence and control was injurious to them, that they were still in an immature state, and too weak in faith and purpose to be left safely to their own guidance and strength. No doubt the trial of the voluntary principle in this case was a severe one. It was put to the test under circumstances of the greatest possible difficulty. But, with all the facts before them, the deputation were unable to counsel a change in the action of the Committee. It was held that the Baptist churches in Jamaica were generally stronger in number and resources than the majority of Baptist churches in England, and that, by co-operation and mutual help, they might well sustain the cause of Christ in their midst. Only such aid, therefore, should be expected from England as might be rendered in cases of great and unforeseen emergency.

Towards the close of 1849 numerous and painful appeals were again addressed to the Society for relief. The necessity was fully acknowledged by the Committee, and arrangements were made to give some temporary aid. The assistance was, however, rendered from independent sources, on the ground that the missionaries themselves as well as the Committee felt it to be " most undesirable that the Jamaica churches should be thrown into a position of unconditional dependence on the funds of the

Baptist Missionary Society." The result has established the wisdom of this decision. The churches in Jamaica have largely increased in number, and, barring unexpected calamities, there seems no reason to doubt that they are generally well able to sustain the ordinances of the Gospel and the means of grace.

One of the most urgent of the questions pressed on the attention of the deputation was the need of ministers to fill the numerous vacancies existing in the pastorate of the churches. Immediately after emancipation the Society resolved to attempt to raise an indigenous ministry, and the Institution at Calabar, near Rio Bueno, was formed for the purpose. This object had the warmest support from Mr. Phillippo. He never doubted the capacity of the Negro to receive and respond to the training that might fit him to become a preacher of the Gospel and a pastor of souls. The progress at first was slow. Few of the emancipated people were found to possess even the elementary knowledge requisite to enjoy the advantages of the Institution. But Mr. Phillippo never lost heart. Thus he says, under date of February 10, 1848 : "If the cause of missions is to be maintained here it must be by the efforts of native labourers, and how great soever the difficulties that may be in the way, and however unpromising at present the agents, yet this object must be pursued, and the sooner it is begun the better. On this account I earnestly hope the Institution at Calabar will be maintained." After referring to the arrival of the Rev. J. Tinson, the tutor, who had been on a visit to England, he says, under date of July 11th, 1848: "The Institution is progressing prosperously. This ought to be kept up as the only means of preventing, if I may say so, the complete extinction of the Baptist cause throughout the island, as I am persuaded still that scarcely a white minister will be in the island in two or three years to come, unless some sympathy and aid are experienced from England very shortly."

It is beyond the scope of this Memoir to narrate the measures taken by the Society at various times to maintain a certain number of European ministers in Jamaica. It is sufficient to say that Mr. Phillippo's fears have not been justified by the events. He lived to see his hope of an indigenous ministry amply fulfilled, and a large number of Jamaica's own sons are now filling with credit, honour, and success the pastorate of many of its numerous congregations. A large number of schoolmasters have also gone forth from the Institution, and obtain their fair share of the grants-in-aid by which the Government now seeks to render universal the instruction of the children.

CHAPTER XXVIII.

THE STATE OF THE ISLAND—THE CHOLERA—
1849 TO 1850.

THIS incessant occupation with the affairs of the Spanish Town chapel and church, and the trying condition of the mission in which he so largely shared, withdrew Mr. Phillippo's attention, to a degree unusual with him, from matters of public interest. So far as the free-trade legislation of the English Parliament affected the sugar cultivation of Jamaica, he sympathised with the planters. He believed, beneficial as that legislation might be to the general welfare of the empire, that it was fraught with destruction to the protected interests of the West Indies. In his journeys he could not but notice, with regret, estates formerly the scene of a flourishing industry abandoned to neglect and decay. Thus he notes in his diary on the 29th of June, 1849: "Since the passing of the Emancipation Act, of the 653 sugar estates then under cultivation in the island, 140, containing 168,032 acres of land, have been abandoned and the works broken up. They employed, when in full operation, 22,553 labourers. Many of the poor, who from 1839 to 1844 were paid at the rate of 1s. 6d. per day, are now glad of employment for sixpence."* On the 8th of December, 1848, he writes: " Great complaints exist among all classes of the population as to the pressure of the times. Estates continue to

---

* The authority for Mr. Phillippo's statement was a committee of the House of Assembly appointed in 1849 to inquire into the extent of agricultural distress. The same authority states that, in the same space of time, 465 coffee plantations had been abandoned, containing 188,400 acres of land, and which employed, in 1832, 26,830 labourers.

be thrown out of cultivation, and every day adds to the
list of those for sale. This has been owing evidently to
the admission of the produce of slave labour into the
British market. And yet this policy, which must issue in the
ruin of the sugar colonies, is persisted in by the present
Government, and, what is worse than all, it gives a powerful
impetus to the slave trade."

Although Mr. Phillippo declined to attend the numerous
meetings which were held to protest against the removal
of the duties on sugar, he used what influence he possessed
to induce his people to be present at them. In the
following sentences he states in a brief form the reasons
which actuated him :—" The fact of the distress of a
country is not the ruin merely of holders of property. It
involves the poverty and oppression of the labourer. You
cannot ruin the former without entailing poverty on the
latter. In no country can you make men, hitherto
wealthy, impoverished, without rendering the labourer a
beggar. This measure [that of 1846] will not only do
this, but will seriously retard the progress of civilisation
among the people." His interest in the question arose
chiefly, if not entirely, from its bearing on the well-being of
the peasantry. His solicitude was mainly on their account.

Writing in 1840, Mr. Joseph John Gurney fully anticipated these results from a policy which was then only in
prospect. " Once equalise the lower duty charged on the
sugar produced in these islands, the sugars of Jamaica
will lose their market, the planters will withdraw from the
production of sugar, the labourer will lose his employment and his wages, the merchant and the shop-keeper
will feel their sources of profit cut off, and the Abolitionist
will discover with dismay that a fresh impetus of vast
force is given to slavery and the slave trade." *

---

* " A Winter in the West Indies," p. 240.

The first measure in which the principles of free trade were applied by Parliament to the sugar-growing colonies of Great Britain was passed, under the Government of Lord John Russell, in August, 1846. The object was to provide for the immediate reduction and the speedy abolition of the heavy differential duties then levied on all foreign sugar. A slight reduction had been made in 1844 in favour of countries in which slavery did not exist. Full effect, however, was not given to the Act of 1846 till 1848. Then sugar from all countries, whether the product of free or slave labour, was admitted into this country at equal duties.* This is not the place to discuss the merits of the question of free trade as against protection. One thing is certain, that neither protection nor the enforced labour of slaves had ever given prosperity to Jamaica even in its palmiest days; for the records of Parliament are crowded with incessant and clamorous appeals from the " ruined interests " of Jamaica for still further privileges. The Legislature of Great Britain did, however, attempt to lessen to the utmost the injury it was affirmed that free-trade legislation would inflict, which, perhaps, was inevitable, on the islands of the West.† Among these measures must be mentioned the Act that allowed the colonies to admit foreign goods on the same terms as

---

* The price of sugar fell from the average of 37s. 3d. per cwt. in 1846 to 24s. 6d. in the eight following years.—" Slavery and Freedom," by Charles Buxton, Esq., M.P., p. 33. For further explanation of the causes of the depression in the sugar colonies, reference may be made to this excellent paper.

† " A severe temporary pressure upon all concerned in sugar cultivation was no doubt to be anticipated while the change of policy was in prospect; but, until it had been accomplished, it was certain that society in these colonies could not be placed in a sound and healthy condition; and the longer it was delayed the more painful would be the crisis which must be passed through."—" The Colonial Policy of Lord John Russell's Administration," by Earl Grey, vol. i., p. 60.

British goods. They also benefited by the complete repeal of the Navigation Laws. Increased and successful efforts were also put forth to suppress the slave trade on the coast of Africa. The Government, moreover, listened favourably to the schemes of immigration urged upon them by the planters, which in some cases were scarcely distinguishable from slavery itself. But these schemes were condemned by the Anti-slavery party in England, and met with strenuous opposition from the missionaries, in the interest of the emancipated peasantry. "The papers," writes Mr. Phillippo, under date of January 29, 1848, "are filled with accounts of meetings held to petition the British Government against immigration, £15,000 more of the public money having been voted by the Assembly for the purpose. I might well have said wasted; it is worse! The evils of it are awful. Of the hundreds, if not thousands, of coolies imported, all are dead, or soon will be. Now, none but Africans are desired—the hapless men who were so long calumniated as the most ignorant, depraved, and idle of all the human family." And on the 6th of March he records the presentation of a petition to the Governor, for transmission to the home Government, against the system. This he had prepared, and it was adopted at a meeting at which he took the chair.

On the other hand, the Jamaica House of Assembly refused to listen to any measures proposed by the home Government for the improvement of the condition of the people. "The statute-book of the island," says Lord Grey, in 1853, "for the last six years presents nearly a blank, as regards laws calculated to improve the condition of the population and to raise them in the scale of civilisation."* In fact, the people were utterly uncared for by the ruling power in the Assembly. In the country

---

* "The Colonial Policy," &c., vol. i., p. 173.

districts they were left to perish miserably for want of medical aid. Agricultural as well as other instruction was entirely neglected, and every possible measure was passed that tended to check the spirit of independence. The finances were scandalously mismanaged, and often misappropriated. The ordinary supplies were refused, on the plea of the necessity of retrenchment, and to force the Government to yield to the reckless demands of the Assembly. The plans of the Government were thwarted, and justice was administered in a grossly partial manner. The educational schemes brought forward were so arranged as to advance the interests of the Established Church, and to throw obstacles in the way of the schools founded by the missionary bodies. One of the measures pressed upon the Government was an "Orphan Asylum Bill," which, though professedly for the benefit of the orphans of those who had fallen a prey to the cholera, was so framed as to re-introduce the system of predial apprenticeship; and to expose the youth educated in the asylum, and afterwards placed under masters, to a modified species of slavery. The intention of the Bill was evidently to secure a supply of forced agricultural labour. To this measure Mr. Phillippo gave the most strenuous opposition. He prepared memorials to the Governor and the English Legislature on behalf of his congregation, and, in an interview with the Governor, urged its inexpediency and injustice. It met with the opposition of the Nonconformist bodies throughout the island, and of the friends of freedom at home, and was at length laid aside. Irreparable injury was done to the island, and at a time when it needed the highest wisdom to meet the new condition that emancipation had introduced, as well as to improve the position of the Negro population, and to prepare them for the exercise of that influence and power to which it was obvious they must at some time necessarily advance.

Early in 1850 Mr. Phillippo, nevertheless, writes: "Things are, I hope, a little improving here. A great demand is still made for colonial produce in England—sugar, coffee, pimento, and logwood; this latter scarcely ever found a better or more remunerative market. An impulse is also given to the growth of cotton, which it is hoped will in some degree restore prosperity. Among other improvements which necessity has induced it is pleasing to see the attention now paid to gardening."

The closing months of the year were, however, a period of extreme suffering. The cholera swept over the land, sparing neither sex nor age. Not less than 20,000 persons fell before the blast of the pestilence in three months, and, before its ravages ceased on the following year, it is calculated that at least one-tenth of the population became its prey. Agricultural operations came to a stand, and labour almost entirely ceased. Mr. Phillippo records, under date of October 11th, that he had just heard of its appearance at Kingston. "I trust," he says, "that it will induce greater cleanliness in the towns." On the 13th he reports that he was shocked to hear of several deaths in Kingston and Port Royal, and that boards of health had been formed to encounter the fell disease. On the 16th he himself is nominated a member of the board appointed for Spanish Town. With his colleagues, the next few days are fully occupied in perambulating every street, visiting every court, removing nuisances, and making arrangements for an immediate supply of medicine.

The first case was reported on the evening of the 19th, and he thus describes the effects of the seizure:—"The agony suffered by the subject of this malignant disease was intense. It is indeed the pestilence that walketh in darkness, and the destruction that wasteth at noonday. It is the most fearful form of disease that ever visited man. It is sudden. I thought of the 91st Psalm as an antidote against the fear of it, and a precious antidote it is." In spite of every precaution the pestilence daily multiplied its victims, and heartrending were the scenes into which his duties led this fearless servant of Christ. Even when there were symptoms of its crossing his own threshold, he did not shrink from the post of danger. In conjunction with the Vice-Chancellor, to whom, with himself, certain wards of the city were apportioned, he visited the sick daily, dispensing medicines, comforting and praying with the smitten, and watching their closing moments, and often accompanying their remains to the tomb.

One or two extracts from his diary will suffice to bring these sorrowful events distinctly before the mind, and exhibit the character of Mr. Phillippo at such a time of fear. On the 27th of October he writes that, having just returned from a funeral, he heard of the seizure of Miss McNeal, one of the most pious and interesting young people of his church, and of her mother, on their return from chapel the previous evening. " I went almost immediately, and found both of them in great agony, but both sensible. Eliza knew me, and addressed me. At intervals her countenance was benign and heavenly, and she often expressed her gratitude to me as the instrument of her salvation. She surrendered herself to her Saviour, in body, soul, and spirit, in language and with looks and gestures that drew tears from all present. From hence I accompanied Dr. Morales to the hospital. And what a sight was here! Two lying dead, and about sixteen or seventeen more rapidly following them. The nurses were once of my flock, and so were the people. I asked them if they wished me to pray. Several of the dying cried out, almost choked with the vehemence with which they uttered the words, ' Yes, minister, yes!' I did so, kneeling on the floor in the middle of the room, the poor creatures lying on mats around me. Numbers were attracted from all parts of the hospital as soon as I began, and all responded with sighs, ejaculations, and tears."

One more entry will suffice. The next day was the Lord's-day. "Sunday: Went to prayer-meeting as usual. A large congregation. Heard of the death of Miss McNeal and her mother. Went to Passage Fort. Called at several houses. Saw several persons dead and dying. Called at the hospital and found more dead there, and the hospital in a filthy state. Preached to a thin congregation, owing to the great mortality in the neighbourhood. Called again at the hospital, and ordered a nurse to be procured. From thence went to Cumberland Pen ; several cases of the disease existing, and several deaths. The Kraal Pen had been in a dreadful state, but was somewhat improving. The Farm Pen, the property of Lord Carrington, was rapidly decimating ; several had been interred without coffins, and numbers were being taken with the epidemic every hour. I prayed with all the patients, and returned to town at dark. Preached in the evening to a large congregation."

Thus, day by day, with unwearied step and unshaken courage, this servant of Christ carried the balm of consolation to the dying, and sought to cheer their closing minutes with words of salvation and hope. The strain was great for the few weeks during which the mortality was greatest ; but, towards the end of November, the pestilence began to abate in Spanish Town and its vicinity, and by Christmas the south side of the island was nearly free of its ravages. About 2,500 persons fell victims to the pestilence in the parish of Spanish Town, while in the city of Kingston, fourteen miles away, 10,000 were stated to have perished. Through the gracious Providence of God, not a missionary in the island fell a prey to the disease ; so mercifully was fulfilled the promise, " A thousand shall fall at thy side, and ten thousand at thy right hand ; but it shall not come nigh thee." The Baptist churches in England raised nearly £2,500 for the assistance of the sufferers in Jamaica. Large quantities of medicine were also sent out. In the distribution every class of the population was assisted, and very welcome aid given to the pastors, whose privations were scarcely less painful than those with which the poor people were afflicted.

The closing days of the year had an additional tinge of sadness added to them by the decease, after a long and painful illness, of the Rev. J. Tinson, the tutor of the Calabar Institution. It was the sorrowful duty of Mr. Phillippo to preach his funeral sermon, on the 18th December, before a large congregation. Mr. Phillippo afterwards embodied his reminiscences of his very dear friend in a brief memoir, which was inserted in the *Baptist Magazine* for May, 1851.

CHAPTER XXIX.

TIMES OF REFRESHING—1852 TO 1853.

WITH the opening days of the year 1852, Mr. Phillippo's prospects began to brighten ; and he was able to resume in all its departments, his pastoral and evangelistic work. January 5, 1852, he writes : "This morning I was privileged to administer the ordinance of believer's baptism to sixty-three persons, chiefly young and intelligent. It took place at Passage Fort, and the whole of the previous night was occupied by a prayer-meeting, I giving an address at frequent intervals. The chapel and yard were crowded, and all the services were deeply interesting. On the following Lord's-day the baptized, with eight others who had sought restoration, I had the happiness to receive into the church, and to introduce to the table of the Lord. It was indeed a delightful day—'a time of refreshing from the presence of the Lord.' I can truly say that, all things considered, appearances of prosperity were never greater at any previous period of the church's history."

The people entered heartily into the plans for the repairs of the chapel and the manse. Some gave their ser vices gratuitously as masons and carpenters ; others, of the better class, cheerfully superintended the progress of the work. Subscriptions to the amount of £200 were sent in during the first six months of the year. The people at Sligoville and at Kensington built kilns, and burnt lime sufficient for the entire restoration. "And they came, every one whose heart stirred him up, and every one whom his spirit made willing, and they brought the Lord's offering to the work of the tabernacle of the congregation" (Exod. xxxv. 21). At Sligoville, he says, "about thirty-seven turned out to work with the greatest hilarity and energy, some cutting down trees for firing, some collecting stones, others breaking them. The scene was really inspiring. They had a mind to work; and, before the close of day, the foundation of a very large kiln was laid, which rose three feet from the ground. A still larger number turned out the next day. Glad should I have been had some of those been present who affirm the impossibility of getting the peasantry to work, except for a very high rate of wages, as well as to see the effect of the voluntary principle. Altogether, fully a hundred hands were employed. I, besides superintending the gangs, felled about a dozen trees myself, to show that I was willing to bear a hand with them." Ten days later he records: "Both kilns finished to-day, and set fire to. They blazed beautifully, as seen from the elevation the house commands."

Later on, Mr. Phillippo records that these appearances of prosperity were not deceptive. "Sunday, March 10, a good prayer-meeting, and about the best congregation I have ever seen in the chapel for years—the first Lord's-day in January not excepted. The sight was deeply interesting; and I should have been ungrateful indeed had I not magnified the Lord for His goodness. The great number of decently dressed, intelligent young people especially interested me. I never saw so many before. At no former time, indeed, have so many been connected with us. This is a source of great encouragement as to the future."

His congregation at Sligoville also participated in this pleasing revival. "March 17—Sunday: A very excellent congregation. I scarcely ever saw a better; so many young persons, and so good a Sabbath-school." "May 10—A very large congregation, notwithstanding the rain which had deluged the mountain district for some weeks previously. People all in good spirits."

The effect on his own spiritual feeling, too, was most cheering. Thus, under date of June 11, he writes: "Had, I trust, some profitable thoughts and meditations this day on the text, 'Seeing then that we have a great High Priest, that is passed into the heavens, Jesus the Son of God,' &c. (Heb. iv. 14, 15). O Thou Light of the world, enlighten our souls. Teach us to know more of Thy infinite, unsearchable riches, Thou great God-Man, that we may love Thee with an increasing love, and serve Thee with an increasing zeal, till Thou bringest us to glory.

> " 'Give me Thyself, from every boast
>   From every wish set free ;
>   Let all I am in Thee be lost,
>   But give Thyself to me.
>   Thy gifts, alas ! cannot suffice
>   Unless Thyself be given ;
>   Thy presence makes my Paradise,
>   And where Thou art is heaven.' "

His delight in nature and natural objects burst forth with new freshness. "June 18. Up long before day and listened with indescribable sensations of delight to the concert of the birds, the mocking bird leading the choir, and his liquid melody heard above all, the rest being like an accompaniment. The birds are very numerous now, being, as I suppose, so little disturbed, especially the nightingales. Their song is almost incessant in the immediate neighbourhood of the house. Sometimes one sings on a tree just before the door at nine o'clock, and on moonlight nights until midnight. The humming birds, too, are greatly increased in number with my increased stock of flowers and flowering shrubs, and other birds also, less known to me, but not less beautiful."

The general and happy influence of the severe trials through which the church had passed he thus summarises:—"Sunday, June 27. Our difficulties, our long and great difficulties, are surmounted ; but, like the Israelites when they achieved the conquest of Canaan, many Canaanites lurking about the walls of our Zion give us annoyance, and are permitted occasionally to hurt us. This we may expect for years to come. We are now placed in our right position as a church in relation to the world. The line that separates the two has now become distinctly visible. We never were so before, and perhaps no section of the Church in this island is in the same situation. We are the first in Jamaica that are really separated from the world. It is fit it should be so, that such a reformation should take place under the oldest missionary and in the metropolis of the island." With the secession the most unworthy members of the flock had been carried away.

It was with no little joy that, the repairs being completed, the chapel was re-opened on the 1st of August. For some days previous the several classes of the church were busy in cleaning and beautifying the neat but spacious edifice. At an early hour of the day a prayer-meeting was held, presided over and addressed by Mr. Phillippo. The prevalent sickness to some extent diminished the attendance, but throughout the day the people, with " an exuberant " joy beaming on every countenance, flocked to the various services. The interest was both deep and devout. The morning service was conducted by the Rev. D. J. East, who had a few months before arrived in Jamaica to take charge of the Calabar Institution. His " excellent " discourse was founded on the words of the 13th verse of the 102nd Psalm. In the evening, a scarcely less impressive sermon was preached by Mr. Phillippo's staunch friend, the Rev. W. Teall. In the afternoon, a

service, commemorative of the Act of Emancipation as
well as the re-opening of the sanctuary, was held, and
the happiness of the occasion found expression in several
addresses from the pastor and others present to share in
their gladness. In a note referring to the proceedings of
the day Mr. Phillippo says: "The chapel and the whole
premises, being just repaired and painted, looked neat
and beautiful, in great contrast with the desolation and
ruin they so lately exhibited. These improved aspects
of the outward condition of the church, added to the
happy circumstances which these services especially
commemorated, excited in the minds of all, not only deep
and lively gratitude, but also the devout and earnest
aspiration of the Psalmist, 'Save now, I beseech Thee, O
Lord; O Lord, I beseech Thee, send now prosperity.'"

Towards the close of the year the small-pox spread as
an epidemic throughout the island, and, although it was
not so fatal as the cholera, it added to the distress which
still prevailed. But Mr. Phillippo and his congregation
were more especially affected by the sudden decease of
their tried friend, Joseph Fletcher, Esq. The painful
tidings was communicated to Mr. Phillippo by the Rev.
John Cox, of Woolwich, Mr. Fletcher's pastor, and it is
due to the services rendered by Mr. Fletcher that the
reply should be recorded here, expressing as it does Mr.
Phillippo's estimate of their value:—"Spanish Town,
December 23rd, 1852.—My dear Friend,—It was with
deeper sorrow than I can express that I received your letter
announcing the death of my beloved and venerated friend,
Mr. Fletcher. I felt deeply for myself, for Mrs. Fletcher,
and for the beloved family, and for the Church of God.
We have each and all sustained a loss never again, at
least in two of these respects, to be supplied.

"For myself and family, and, I may add, the whole
church at Spanish Town, we feel that we are bereaved.

We have lost a faithful, kind, and generous friend—a father; and our poignancy of sorrow may be in some measure conceived. His name and generous actions are engraven on the hearts of thousands in Jamaica, and his memory will be cherished here to the end of time. God has honoured him to accomplish a work for us that no other man could or would have effected."

"I am extremely obliged to you for the details you have given me of the last moments of our revered friend. I shall read your letter on next Lord's-day, and I will venture to say that it will call forth feelings that I shall be unable to withstand."

"None, perhaps, but you, myself, and a very few others know what our beloved friend was in the domestic circle, and none, therefore, can so fully estimate their loss. He was, without exception, the kindest, most loving, and beloved father of a family I ever knew. Beneath his roof, amidst the tender, generous hospitality of himself and his beloved wife and children, myself and those dearest to me have enjoyed some of the happiest hours of our existence, and it is a pang in our sorrow, that we shall never cease to feel, that our earnest hopes, so fondly cherished, of seeing him once more in the flesh are broken off and disappointed."

Mr. Phillippo subsequently prepared a brief sketch of his friend's life, which appeared in the *Baptist Magazine* of the year 1853.

Apart from these sad events, the spiritual growth of his congregation filled Mr. Phillippo's heart with gratitude and joy. The schools in Spanish Town, re-opened in 1847 under the care of Mr. O'Meally, who had been his faithful helper in all his troubles, gave him unalloyed pleasure. The following letter, written in the early part of the year 1853, presents a very pleasant picture of the busy and successful pastor :—

"I am thankful to say that our peace and prosperity as

a church and congregation continue.   On the morning of the new year I had the pleasure of adding to the church, by baptism, thirty-two persons, and on the following day, being the first Sabbath of the new year, they were received into the fellowship of the church in the presence of a very large and deeply interested assembly.   The greater number of those thus received were, as has been usual of late, young persons, the children of pious parents, who have mostly been taught the first rudiments of education in our schools.   It is gratifying also to notice that not fewer than eight or ten of the number attributed their conversion to God to services that were held during the prevalence of cholera.   Among the young people was an African girl, some short time since, together with some twenty or thirty more, rescued from a slave-ship and placed on an estate in the neighbourhood.   She gave such clear and, in every respect, such satisfactory evidences of her piety as both interested and astonished me.

"I have had the great happiness of adding to the church by baptism since I have been restored to full possession of the chapel, including a period of about two years, upwards of one hundred and fifty members, and have received about fifty who had from various causes previously discontinued their attendance on the public means of grace, or who had gone to other places of worship, making a total of full two hundred.

"Yesterday, in accordance with previous announce-ment, I preached a sermon to young people, when the chapel was crowded, and more strangers were present than I have seen for many years past; some, indeed, were present who, I believe, were never in our place of wor-ship before.

"Although great poverty is experienced by the people in general, in which we, as ministers of voluntary churches, of course largely participate, we have much to encourage us. May God graciously, in His own good time, afford us temporal as well as spiritual prosperity !

"As soon as we can get a little free from the remainder of our embarrassments I hope to hold a missionary meeting here, to try what we can do for Africa and the Calabar Institution. We shall, however, have much to do for some time to come in the repairs of the mission premises at Sligoville and Passage Fort, which have suffered much during our long struggle and consequent inability to preserve them from decay. Another object that claims our anxious concern and most vigorous efforts are our schools, which have been injured also from the same causes. We have, indeed, much work before us, and I pray God to give us grace to do what we have to do with all our might.

" Both myself and people are much gratified and cheered by the kindness of the different individuals and churches who have so readily and generously assisted us by their donations towards our repairs at Spanish Town, as also to the brethren by whom our cause has been espoused and advocated."

The meetings referred to in the above letter were held in the month of July in Spanish Town, Passage Fort, and Sligoville. They proved to be gatherings of the deepest interest, and called forth strong expressions of wonder and gratitude from Mr. Phillippo and the numerous friends who assisted him. A friend from England, Mr. D. Haddon, occupied the chair on each occasion. The meetings were crowded to excess. In addition to the great numbers of the inhabitants of the town, many hundreds came from various parts of the country, some on horseback, and whole families in carts. The utmost order and decorum prevailed. There was not the slightest interruption, either within or without doors, during any of the services. This series of meetings, says Mr. Phillippo, " were a matter of grateful astonishment to me. I could not but regard the presence of many as a token of their regret at the share they had taken in my troubles. Everywhere the most marked deference is manifested towards me. This clears the atmosphere around me, and will do wonders. I have now a smooth sea before me, and I may put more canvas on my bark. This is the Lord's doing. O Lord! keep me from pride and vainglory; but more than all from forgetfulness of Thy mercy and goodness. I may truly say, What has God wrought!"

His active participation in public affairs was now much sought after. He entered very warmly into a proposal that was made to the missionaries, that they should nominate representatives to join a mission of delegates to England, to lay before the Queen's Ministers the decayed state and perilous condition of all the interests of the country, and made several journeys to the north side of the island to confer with his brethren on the matter. He was summoned (March 9th, 1853) by the House of Assembly, to attend and give evidence before the Committee "appointed to inquire into and report upon the moral and social condition of the labouring people of the island since 1845, the educational wants of the juvenile population, and whether the future good of the island would be best consulted by making education compulsory."*

On this last topic the interest of Mr. Phillippo was deep. From the beginning of his life in Jamaica he had devoted much time and energy to the spread of instruction amongst the people. Next to the preaching of the Gospel he regarded it as the most effectual method for promoting their civilisation and well-being. Among his numerous references to this subject, he has left the following brief compendium, written at this time, of the views he entertained :—

"The friends of education may be divided into two

---

* He had been summoned in the previous February to give evidence on the necessity of a bridge over the Rio Cobre.

classes. First, those who hold that the spread of education should be left to the voluntary action of the people. These may again be divided into two sections : (1) Those who dislike the principle of Government interference in all matters affecting the moral interests of the community; (2) Those who distrust the *working* of such measures.

"The former deprecate any plan not religious. The latter fear that Government interference would in its immediate results be injurious to the interests of religion, and, perhaps, ultimately lead to tyranny by the controlling power it would give to the inculcation of the opinions of the governors.

"By the first of these a Government plan would be opposed as unjust ; by the last, as inexpedient.

"2. The advocates of State interference may in like manner be divided into two parties : (1) Those who wish to see both original and controlling power vested in a central board ; (2) Those who would confine the function of Government to the aid of schools already in existence, or to the establishment of new ones in connection with local effort on fixed and understood principles."

Mr. Phillippo then proceeds to state his own conclusions as follows :—

"1. If Government interfere at all in the education of the people, it must do so rather by aiding and promoting voluntary efforts than by centralisation and direct control.

"2. That education, in order to be useful, must be moral and religious, without being sectarian or exclusive.

"3. That the Bible is better adapted than any other book for general use in schools, its introduction without note or comment involving us in fewer difficulties, and offering greater advantages, than any other plan that has yet been devised for the religious instruction of the population.

"If these points can be successfully established, the

path of duty will be plain. Good men of all parties must unite to lay the foundation of public virtue and private worth in the general education of the people on Scriptural and comprehensive principles. A system of instruction established on any other basis would be a public calamity, since it would not only supersede voluntary efforts, but convert public instruction either into an engine for the promotion of spiritual tyranny, or into a channel for the propagation of latitudinarianism."

These views were by no means acceptable to the ruling authorities in Jamaica, and no real effort was made or attempted to provide for the instruction of the peasantry. The discussions in the local journals were frequent, often bitter, and on not a few occasions did Mr. Phillippo vindicate in the press the enlightened views he held. Twelve or fourteen years had to elapse, and a frightful calamity fall upon the island, before the education of the masses was brought home to the minds of the rulers with a force and necessity they could no longer withstand.

Among other matters of lighter interest we find Mr. Phillippo delivering, in April, a series of lectures on Cuba and other islands of the West Indies, to a literary and reading society which had been recently formed in Spanish Town. Later in the year he was engaged in preparing a reply to a series of questions on Jamaica addressed to him by the secretary of the Statistical branch of the British Association.

The year closed with the reception of the very gratifying news that their eldest son had passed his examination in Edinburgh, and had attained the degree of M.D. It was a joy to his parents that he soon after commenced practice in Spanish Town, and that their declining years were cheered by his filial care.

CHAPTER XXX

THE WORK OF FAITH—1854 TO 1855.

BETWEEN three and four years of pleasant and successful labour were now granted to Mr. Phillippo. With renewed energy and diligence he gave himself to the ministry of the Word, and reaped the fruit of his labours in constant additions to the churches under his care, and in their steady growth in Christian knowledge and faithfulness. The difficulties of previous years were at an end, and he often wondered as he witnessed the favour which God gave him in the eyes of all classes. He records with especial pleasure the incidents that attended the observance of the 1st of August, 1854, as showing that his "expectations with respect to the cause in Spanish Town were not disappointed." The commemoration of the day of emancipation was preceded by missionary services on the 16th and 18th of July, in connection with the Calabar Institution and mission work on the Western Coast of Africa. The day itself was observed with a baptismal service at Clair Park Pen, near Spanish Town. The attendance was larger than on any previous occasion, the people flocking in during the night from all parts, encamping under the trees, and with bonfires illuminating the scene. At daylight, a thanksgiving meeting was held. The booth which had been erected proving too small for the crowds, this solemn act of worship was conducted in the open air. The candidates for baptism were then seated under the branches of a wide-spreading tree, the spectators standing around. After Mr. Phillippo had addressed them, they proceeded to the river-side. Here the pastor delivered an impressive discourse on the subject of baptism, and after singing and prayer the candidates, forty-two in number, were baptized. "The place selected for the observance of the sacred rite," says Mr. Phillippo, " was a truly beautiful one, the wooded banks rapidly ascending from the river's bed on both sides, giving the appearance of a vast amphitheatre, thronged with people. The greatest silence and solemnity prevailed throughout, and numbers were deeply affected. The lawn before the house was covered with horses, carts, gigs, and all kinds of vehicles." Interesting and striking indeed must such a scene have been even to an indifferent spectator; but to those who knew what slavery had been, who had seen the degradation and cruelty that attended it, who had become acquainted with the persecution that some of these very people had suffered for professing their love to Christ; but more especially to Mr. Phillippo himself, the veteran advocate of freedom and fast friend of the enslaved—such a sight must have excited emotions too deep and thrilling for words to express. At the re-ception of the baptized into the church on the following Sunday at the table of the Lord the chapel was crowded to excess, and the services seem to have created a revival among the strangers, as well as the usual congregation present on the occasion.

A similar delightful season is recorded on the last Sab-bath of the year, when forty-three, chiefly young and intel-ligent, people were baptized in the Rio Cobre. Mr. Phillippo writes : " It seemed as though the whole town and neighbourhood had poured forth their population to the spot. On fronting them from the river's bank, I beheld a compact mass of heads upwards and on each side, as far as my eye could reach. The address was listened to throughout with an interest and attention that could not be exceeded. I had previously requested that none of the spectators should move from their places until I emerged from the water and pronounced the Benediction. This request was implicitly obeyed ; not one stirred from the spot or broke the universal silence, until I gave the signal, when they moved away with the same decorum and order as they had exhibited in coming, and during the whole ceremony. The circumstances altogether were deeply solemn and impressive—such as a few years since I could not have anticipated ; while I have reason to believe that many present were spiritually benefited ; many were in tears. Others who had been undecided added their names to the list of inquirers ; and some who had backslidden promised a renewed dedication of themselves to God and His cause."

Such days as these do not stand alone in the records Mr. Phillippo has left behind. Again and again it was his joy to receive into the church individuals of all ages, who testified to the saving power of the Gospel irrespective of race or station. But nothing gave Mr. Phillippo greater happiness than to learn that men who had formerly been his bitterest adversaries, as well as the greatest oppressors of the slave, had become the servants of the Master he loved. Referring to one such case which happened at this time, he says : " How marvellous are the works of God ! Mr. L., the magistrate who did his utmost to prevent the introduction of the Gospel into his parish, who interrupted the surveyors engaged in measuring the piece of land purchased by the slaves, and some others of the people who were free, for the purpose of building a chapel ; who ordered the materials collected to be carted away to his own premises ; and who was one of the greatest enemies in the country to missionary operations, has returned to Jamaica ' a new man in Christ Jesus.' He now attends the place of worship which he aimed to destroy, and is a contributor to the cause he laboured to overthrow."

The year 1855 was marked by much sickness and mortality among the members of his flock, some of the most pious and useful being amongst those who entered their rest. And although this year did not bring additions to the community, yet " the state and prospects of the church and congregation were most pleasing." He adds : " We have a considerable number of young people who are anxious to unite with us in Christian fellowship. Some of them are of unusual interest and promise, whom we hope to baptize in a few weeks. Our peace and harmony continue unbroken. Prejudices and other unfavourable circumstances seem to have entirely disappeared, and everything indicates future repose and prosperity, consisting in the devotion of heart and life to God. We have had two or three deeply interesting missionary meetings during the year, which were most numerously and respectably attended."

The large school in Spanish Town, on which he had expended so large a measure of time and cost, gave him much satisfaction. At the examination conducted by Dr. Morales, the Speaker of the House of Assembly, that gentleman observed "that the children had acquitted themselves in a manner that reflected great credit on themselves and their teacher. And to you [turning to Mr. Phillippo] great praise is due for the indefatigable zeal you manifest in raising and continuing these institutions. You, I believe, were among the first in this island to set in operation institutions for popular education. This school is associated with many pleasing recollections of my past career. So far back as twenty-five years I had the pleasure of visiting it, and it is still more gratifying to me to learn that the present master, Mr. O'Meally, was educated here, whose work is worthily seen in the efficiency of the scholars I have had the privilege of examining to-day."

The crowning happiness of the year was, however, the tidings that his two younger sons had been baptized and united in fellowship with the churches at Lucea and Mount Carey. "Thus," he records, "my three sons and only daughter, in the morning of their days, relying on strength and grace from above, have given their hearts to God, and have consecrated their lives to His service."

The general affairs of the mission had also a full share of Mr. Phillippo's attention. As a consequence of his previous connection with many of the churches and his long experience as a missionary, he was not unfrequently requested to mediate in matters of importance beyond the circuit of his own ministrations, and to reconcile both individuals and churches between whom causes of strife had arisen. He was eminently a peacemaker, and sought to infuse in every association with which he was connected his own spirit of gentleness and respect for the views of others. He gladly took part in the management and in the annual examinations of the Calabar Institution, and gave his hearty support to the enlargement of its usefulness, which took place in 1854, by the formation of a normal school department.

The death of the greatly esteemed Treasurer of the Society, W. B. Gurney, Esq., early in the year, called forth a warm expression of regard and esteem from the missionaries assembled at Calabar. In forwarding their resolutions to the Committee, Mr. Phillippo seized the opportunity to give his own personal sentiments. "To say our late Treasurer was a great and good man is not enough. He was one of the princes of the people, and of the heads of the elders of Israel. In personal, practical devotedness to the cause of God, and real benevolence in its support, it seems scarcely possible that he could have a superior. His habits and the whole tenor of his life proved that the good of souls and the advancement of Christ's Kingdom in the world were his meat and drink, his study and his recreation, the goal towards which his efforts, his prayers, ever seemed to tend. Oh! that many who have similar capacities for usefulness may catch his fallen mantle. The Society has great cause for thankfulness that the successor [Sir S. Morton Peto] of their late honoured Treasurer is a man of like spirit; but we want such men multiplied a hundredfold. Mr. Gurney died, it seems, just as it was expected he would, his mind calm and serene, not trusting in his own righteousness or depending upon his good works, but as a sinner looking for the mercy of God through our Lord Jesus Christ. ' Let me die the death of the righteous, and let my last end be like his.' "

CHAPTER XXXI.

EARLY in 1854 an important change was made in the government of Jamaica, by the formation of a salaried Executive Council of three persons, who should act as responsible advisers of the Governor, and with whom all money Bills were to originate, instead, as heretofore, with individual members of the Assembly. A much-needed check was thus placed on the extravagant expenditure so frequently authorised at the instance of interested parties. Under the administration of Sir Henry Barkley, who succeeded Sir Charles Grey in October, 1853, these changes worked well; and a brief period of political repose aided the growth of the general industries of the island. The value of all kinds of produce increased, and an impetus was thereby given to trade. The sugar estates were slowly falling into the hands of resident owners, and were being cultivated, especially on the north side of the island, with a spirit and success unknown for many years. The Governor's visits, during April and May, to various parts of the country filled him with pleasure. He could not but be pained to witness the large number of estates still lying ruinate; but the indications of progress among the peasantry were an ample compensation. If their education had been neglected by the propertied classes, he found others active in the cause, and bore willing testimony to the energetic and successful labours of the various missionary bodies. Still, the subject was one that called forth incessant discussion. In February, 1854, Mr. Phillippo was requested, by a communication from the Governor, in common with other missionaries, to supply returns annually of the state and progress of education at his stations ; and, shortly after, the House of Assembly took up the question, and made an effort to pass a Bill which, in the judgment of Mr. Phillippo and his colleagues, was calculated to jeopardise mission schools, and to give an undue prominence and control over public instruction to the clergy of the Establishment.

The measure was hurried through the House of Assembly in order to prevent any remonstrance from the Nonconformist communities. " I attended," says Mr. Phillippo, "a meeting held in Mr. H.'s office, to prepare a memorial to the House, and to the Governor in Council, against this renewed attempt to ignore and obviate the good being done by missionaries. The Bill appears to have secured the favour of the Council, since it was brought in by the acting Attorney-General, although a professed Liberal. Such was its nature that one of the brethren writing to me thus expressed himself: 'If that Bill becomes law, I think all of us had better put ourselves in a posture ready for flight at a moment's notice, as any rabble may immediately cause us to be ousted from our homes, and the protection of the law be completely taken away from us.' Being in the metropolis, and having the opportunity of seeing the members of the Council, I was expected to do all in my power to arrest the progress of 'this monstrous Bill.' The measure was arrested by the combined action of the Nonconformist missionaries. I furnished them particulars respecting its provisions and their operation, and waited on the Governor with an address, being deputed by the body for the purpose."

The subject of education continued also to be much agitated in the press. Mr. Phillippo published several letters in the *Watchman* and the *Standard* newspapers, which were afterwards reprinted in a collected form, and obtained a wide and useful circulation.* Mr. Phillippo's own schools were conducted on the system of the British and Foreign School Society, and supported entirely by voluntary contributions. He therefore strongly opposed another Bill brought into the House of Assembly, in 1856, at the suggestion of Lord Glenelg, the Secretary of State for the Colonies, which would have enforced a compulsory system of education throughout the island, for which it was totally unprepared. It was Mr. Phillippo's conviction " that the machinery proposed would involve a mischievous waste of public money, that the grants would be perverted to private gain, and that they would augment the evils which the system professed to correct and obviate."

Not less strenuous was his opposition to the scheme, which, in the session of 1854-5, found favour with the House of Assembly, for making appropriations from the public funds to any and every religious community that would receive them. "Grants," says Mr. Phillippo, " were lavishly made, not only for the support of the Established Church and the Church of Scotland, but were also offered to the Moravians, the Wesleyans, the native Baptists (the latter unconnected with the organised body of Baptist missionaries), and Roman Catholics, and would possibly have been given to any other sect had they existed in sufficient numbers to be thought worthy of such consideration."

" The Roman Catholics seem to have had special advocates in their favour in the House ; and such persons were commended by them and the press for their liberality

---

* The pamphlet was entitled, " A Plea for Education on the Voluntary System. In Letters addressed to the Members of the Honourable House of Assembly, Jamaica, 1856."

of sentiment. No doubt the Jews, United Presbyterians, Congregationalists, and Baptists would have been equally successful, if they could so far have forgotten their principles, and bartered their spiritual rights and independence. With regard to the Roman Catholics, the Nonconformists had lifted up their voice year by year against such a prostitution of the public money by a professedly Protestant Legislature. Our Presbyterian brethren acted nobly in the matter, giving expression to the sentiments of their Synod in strong language, as did others, asserting that such grants were an endowment of Popery. My correspondence with brethren on this subject was very considerable, as may be supposed from the locality of my residence."

At Mr. Phillippo's suggestion, the Baptist missionaries, when assembled at the annual meeting of the Calabar Institution, opened communications with the Presbyterian missionaries, expressing their great willingness to co-operate with them in suitable measures of opposition to all grants for religious purposes from the island treasury. But these grants were not finally withdrawn or discontinued till the measure for the Disestablishment of the Church of England in the colony was passed in 1870.

One other public matter much occupied Mr. Phillippo's time in the years 1855-7. The old Clergy Bill, by which the salaries and *status* of the island clergy were fixed, had yet some four years of its original term of fourteen to run. But, as the Legislature seemed in a compliant mood, the partisans of the Establishment resolved, if possible, to secure their position for a longer time, and to perpetuate their privileges for another like term at the close of the current period, even though, to secure it, they might have to submit to some reduction in the stipends then payable. Mr. Phillippo and his colleagues thought it an opportune moment to raise the general question of the need of an Establishment at all. He commenced a series of letters in the *Watchman* newspaper, and carried on an active correspondence with his Nonconformist brethren throughout the island. "Now," he says, "as the Clergy Bill was likely to dispel all hopes of Disestablishment for many years, a conference of all the ministers of voluntary churches was thought necessary, and I forwarded circulars for the purpose." The conference was held in the Metropolitan school-room, in Spanish Town, and a memorial, both to the Governor and to the Colonial Office, was adopted. But it was of no avail; and in January, 1857, "this scandalous Clergy Bill," as he terms it, "passed into law."

CHAPTER XXXII.

On the 9th of June, 1856, Mr. Phillippo embarked in the
Robert Lush, Captain Graham, for a brief visit to the
United States. For some time it had been evident that
the strain of the last twelve years of anxiety and labour
had greatly affected his health. A change was eminently
desirable, if not absolutely necessary. The voyage, which
was attended by fine weather throughout, had its customary
invigorating effect on his constitution, and he arrived in
Baltimore, on the 25th of June, in safety and improved
health. He at once found himself in the midst of friends,
among whom he specially mentions the Baptist ministers
of the city, and Mrs. Kingdon, the widow of a former
missionary and colleague in Jamaica.

Learning that the Congress was in session, he hastened
to Washington, "the city of magnificent distances,"
finding everywhere a welcome, and enjoyed brief intercourse with some of the leading celebrities of the State.
During a short visit to Philadelphia, he renewed his
acquaintance with Dr. Belcher, an old English friend
who had transferred his ministry to the United States,
and with whom he consulted concerning the publication
of his work on the United States and Cuba, which for
some years he had been busy in his more leisure moments
in bringing to completion. He availed himself of every
opportunity which his journey afforded to increase his

stores of information and to test the accuracy of his views. Another English acquaintance whom he met was the Rev. Mr. Berg, who had been for some time settled at Williamsburgh, and for whom he preached. A few days after he reached New York, and in an interesting letter to his wife, dated Brooklyn, July 13th, he thus refers to the state of things around him :—

" I am thankful to say that the affection of my voice is much better than when I left. I have preached only once on each of the two Sabbaths I have been here, although I have much to do in replying to questions about Jamaica and its people on each day of the week; that is, in correcting the misrepresentations and in counteracting the slanders that are put abroad here by the pro-slavery party respecting the results of emancipation in our island. Some are astonished and gratified; others look suspiciously, and evidently do not like my reports. I went to the Anti-slavery office the other day, and saw Lewis Tappan, Esq., the Clarkson and Sturge of America. He heard my representations of the real state of things in Jamaica with great interest, and expressed much anxiety that I would embody my statements in an article which he would place in some of the leading periodicals. This I could not possibly do then, but I promised to comply with his request, if I can command sufficient leisure to do so, on my return from Canada. The subjects of Slavery and Freedom are the all-absorbing ones at this time in America. Everything seems to hinge upon and take its colouring from them. Nothing else scarcely, except business, is thought or talked of. Slavery is most certainly doomed ; —the only fear is the results of the conflict for its abolition to the integrity of the union in relation to North and South. From all I hear I am of opinion that disruption would not follow this great measure of justice to the African race. The alliance between these two portions of the union is too complex and powerful both socially and commercially. I think the free States have only to place the helm of the State in the hands of Fremont, and he will guide the vessel safely, though not without loss and danger, into port. Party feeling runs high in relation to the next President. The candidates are Buchanan, Filmore, and Fremont. The latter is against the institution of slavery—the others advocate or tolerate it. The principal chances, it seems, are between Buchanan and Fremont. Filmore is the idol of the ' know-nothings,' and is said to have no chance of success."

In a postscript, he adds, very characteristically, " Please tell Mr. Hall, and all the deacons, leaders, and people, both in Spanish Town, Sligoville, Passage Fort, and all round the country, that I feel sometimes very anxious about them, and that I most earnestly hope they will be regular in their attendance at the chapel and on all the means of grace, and otherwise conduct themselves in such a manner as to cause me no pain on my return. I have here to listen sometimes to very great misrepresentations, both of the people and the state of things generally in Jamaica, but I unfailingly make known the truth."

From New York Mr. Phillippo proceeded to Canada, making a delightful voyage up the Hudson to Albany, and thence by rail to Niagara. Here he met Mr. and Mrs. Landon, with whom he sojourned for a few days, enjoying the recollections and amenities of their old friendship in Jamaica. He reached Montreal by way of the St. Lawrence, and has preserved the following graphic description of his shooting the rapids of Lachine:—

" At a small Indian village we pause a moment to receive on board our steamer an Indian pilot, who takes complete control of the vessel. Four men are at the wheel. There is hardly a breath of air stirring, everything is calm and quiet, and our steamer glides as noiselessly

and gently down the river as she would along an ordinary
canal. Suddenly a scene of wild grandeur breaks upon
us. Waves are lashed into spray, and into breakers of a
thousand forms, by the dark rocks they are dashed
against in the headlong impetuosity of the river. Whirlpools, narrow passages beset with rocks, a storm-lashed
sea, all mingle their sublime terrors in a single rapid. In
an instant we are in the midst of them ; now passing with
lightning speed within a few yards of rocks, upon which,
were our vessel but to touch, she would be reduced to an
utter wreck before the sound of the crash could die upon
the air ; again shooting forward like an arrow towards a
rocky island, which our bark avoids by a turn almost as
rapid as the movements of a bird. Then from crests of
great waves rushing down precipices our craft is flung
upon the crests of others as they recede ; she trembles to
her very keel from the shock, and the spray is thrown far
in upon her decks.

"Now we enter a narrow channel hemmed in by
threatening rocks, with white breakers leaping over them ;
yet we dash through on our lightning way, spurning the
countless whirlpools beneath us. Forward is an absolute
precipice of water ; on every side of it breakers are thrown
high into the air. Where shall we go ? Ere the thought
has come and gone we mount the wall of wave and foam
like a bird, and glorious, sublime science lands us a
second afterwards upon the calm, unruffled bosom of a
gentle river. The seemingly dangerous Lachine Rapids
are left behind us, and onward we come ; the fear and
excitement of our apparently perilous descent gives way to
admiration, as we gaze upon the gigantic structure before
us spanning the river, the ' Victoria Bridge.' "

During the few days devoted to Montreal, he enjoyed
the hospitalities of Dr. and Mrs. Davies, meeting with
many friends " from Yorkshire, Leicestershire, Hastings,

and elsewhere." "All along my route," he continues to his wife, " I have met with friends and acquaintances from England and Jamaica almost innumerable. I scarcely stop in a place for a day but I meet with many persons I have known before, and even in places where I am not personally known, to my great surprise, oftentimes it is said my name has for years been a household word."

This delightful intercourse, however, necessarily came soon to a close, and after a short visit to the Grand Ligne Mission he passed through Boston and Rhode Island to New York, where he embarked for Jamaica, having in company the young lady to whom his youngest son, Edwin, was about to be united in marriage. They arrived in Jamaica on the 6th of October.

This short holiday did not, however, produce all the beneficial results which Mr. Phillippo hoped would follow. In his reply to a very cordial letter from the late Dr. Brock urging him to visit England, dated February 24th, 1857, he announces his intention to adopt the advice of his friend, and says :—" My principal object will, of course, be to seek renovated health. I have now been in this climate nearly three-and-thirty years, and, not having been idle, nor without my share of the anxieties and cares to which flesh is heir, it will not appear surprising that my constitution should begin to betray signs of decay. I have not been really well for several months past, and my symptoms are such that I feel persuaded if I do not get away from my work here, and find a more bracing atmosphere for a time, my future usefulness will be greatly diminished, and probably my life be jeopardised. I have been home twice during the three-and-thirty years, but both times I delayed doing so till my health and strength were so prostrated, or disease had become so seated in my constitution, as almost to preclude the hope of recovery, even after a residence of years. I was better for my hasty visit to the States ; but the advantage was only temporary. At the same time, as it appears now pretty evident that the will of God is for me to find my grave in Jamaica, and as I am so far verging towards the common limit of human life as to preclude the prospect of bidding farewell to my relatives and friends if I postpone my visit much longer, my wife and family unite in urging my visit as a duty I owe both to myself and them, and to the cause of God in Spanish Town. Under these circumstances, added to your kind invitation to your hospitalities, you will be among the first to whom I shall present myself on my arrival."

Mr. Phillippo accordingly sailed for England in the *Atrato* on the 26th of March, accompanied on board by his sons Cecil and George. On the previous evening a fare-well, but deeply interesting, prayer-meeting was held by his flock to commend him to the care and blessing of God.

It is unnecessary to say that he received a hearty wel-come from Dr. Brock. On his arrival at Southampton he was greeted by a letter from him, and, lest Mr. Phillippo should not take him at his word and proceed at once to his house, Dr. Brock sent his son to bring him thither. He was scarcely settled comfortably in the cheerful home of his warm-hearted host and hostess than he was over-whelmed with applications for his services at missionary meetings, to most of which he sooner or later responded. He was also called upon by several influential members of the Liberal party in London, and by his friends of the Anti-Slavery Society, anxious to hear from his lips some authentic evidence on the state of affairs in Jamaica.

The views to which he gave utterance he at length embodied in three letters, which appeared in the columns of the *Freeman* in the month of June, and, as they con-tain his matured judgment on the various matters referred to in them, it is due to his memory to give some general outline of their nature.

The objections or statements he had to encounter took generally the following form :—It was affirmed that the emancipated peasantry had fallen into a state of deeper degradation and immorality than that which existed anterior to the era of freedom ; that Obeahism and Myalism, and other kindred superstitions, had greatly increased ; that idleness had become a painful characteristic of large masses of the population, and that no wages would tempt them to steady and continuous labour; that the grossest immorality and licentiousness were unblushingly practised ; that anarchy and resistance to lawful authority were on the increase ; that irreligion was increasing on every side ; and, finally, that the Negro exhibited no inventive faculty, and no desire for social progress or material improvement.

Mr. Phillippo's reply to these allegations consisted of two parts : of an explanation, and of a statement of facts drawn from his own experience.

By way of explanation, he points out that it was natural to expect that, when the pressure of a slavish condition was removed, the true character of the Negro would become more visible ; that many of the evils deplored were the sure result of the wicked system from which the slave had so recently escaped ; that the Legislature had placed no check on the increase of gambling-houses and taverns, where the means of intoxication were cheap and abundant ; that many superstitions which were dying out had been re-awakened in power by the introduction of liberated slaves from Africa, and of emigrants from India and other heathen lands.   He freely admits that riots and other breaches of the laws had become not unfrequent, but traces them to the action of a few demagogues and others who, at elections, by the most unworthy means, sought the electoral support of the rising class of free-holders. He regrets the increasing neglect of the ordinances of the Gospel, but remarks that it was partly owing to poverty, and still more to the subsidence of the excitement which attended emancipation. At all events, it had one beneficial result—there was less hypocrisy and fewer unworthy members of the churches bearing the name of Christian. But more particularly he traces many of the evils and difficulties under which Jamaica was then suffering to the mortgaged condition of many estates, to the decay of cultivation;* to the competition of the slave-grown sugar from Cuba and elsewhere in the English markets; to the great increase of taxation, which was made to press with unfair weight on the peasantry; and, as the consequence of all this, the diminished means of the better classes and the resulting poverty of the labourers. He calculates the loss which the island sustained from these causes at not less than £800,000 a year, for the most part borne by the labouring classes. "It cannot," he concludes, "be difficult to conceive that this combination of circumstances must have had a powerful effect on the whole country in producing the poverty described, and the utmost ruin to its agricultural and commercial interests, as well as in the deep injury that must have been inflicted by their operation on the ministers of the Gospel, and on the religious and school establishments dependent upon the voluntary contributions of the humbler classes for support."

But there was another side to the picture. The condition of Jamaica was not all dark. If the moral and social condition of the people was not altogether satisfactory, or even if it had in some respects retrograded,

---

* He states that out of six hundred estates under cultivation previous to emancipation three hundred had been abandoned and become ruinate.

nevertheless, "considering," he says, "the demoralising influence of the system to which the masses were subject for so many generations, it is my opinion that the degree of their advancement in the moral and social scale during the last ten or twelve years is without a parallel in the history of any country. The masses are advancing steadily onward towards that higher state of civilisation and morality to which I believe them destined by nature and Providence."

He then goes on to affirm that some of the indications of deterioration referred to are rather evidences than otherwise of progress ; they are the effect of "the decline of superstition," of "their recovery from intellectual prostration," and "the effervescence of freedom in minds suddenly let loose from sullen and ancient depression." The charge of idleness he declares to be "decidedly and palpably untrue. In all my journeyings through the extended district under my superintendence, in which there are sugar estates, coffee and pimento plantations, and several extensive villages, I have scarcely seen an individual at any time loitering about, *or indisposed to labour for reasonable wages duly and punctually paid.*" On this point Mr. Phillippo lays great stress, as it was notorious that in numerous instances this condition was "shamefully violated." He then proceeds to remark on the improvements he had witnessed in the style and manner of living, on the increase of well-built and well-furnished houses; surrounded by land purchased with the savings of the people, and cultivated in sugar, ginger, and other tropical and profitable products of the soil. In numerous cases these freeholds were gradually assuming all the features of sugar estates, small mills rising up, and the manufacture of sugar increasing year by year. In fact, a very considerable portion of the sugar consumed on the island was produced by these small cultivators, while hundreds of

U

barrels were exported to England and America. He mentions one parish as having produced at least a thousand barrels for export.

These improvements, he affirms, were largely owing to the increased pastoral visitation on the part of the missionaries, the easier access to the people in their own homes enjoyed by ministers and teachers, the pressure of church discipline, and, above all, the instruction constantly and strenuously imparted in church and school. There had been indeed a great falling off in their contributions, "not occasioned to any extent by decreased inclination on the part of the people to contribute to benevolent objects, but to their real inability from the prevalence of poverty." But there had been a remarkable display of liberality by these recently enfranchised slaves. " I am of opinion," he concludes, " that, since 1845, more than two-thirds of the full amount required for perpetuating the operation of these agencies, including schools, the erection and repairs of places of worship, and the support of schoolmasters and ministers, have been raised on the spot."

"In conclusion, emancipation has increased the opportunities of the people for improvement, induced in them a relish for the comforts as well as the necessaries of life, aroused them to a sense of the value of property, and brought about habits of industry. The path has been opened by which all the highest, and best, and noblest human possessions may be obtained by the once despised and oppressed bondsmen of Jamaica."

This exposition of the condition of Jamaica was everywhere warmly welcomed, and, happily, though Mr. Phillippo's health was sorely tried by the numerous engagements which pressed upon him, he was able to visit the chief centres of population and intelligence, and to convey to many parts of the kingdom a true picture of the results of the great boon of freedom. He further aided the cause of Jamaica by becoming a member of a deputation, promoted by the committee of the Anti-Slavery Society, to wait on Lord Palmerston on the subject of African immigration. His practical knowledge of the question led to his being put forward as the chief speaker on the occasion. The deputation, he says, "was most graciously received, and Lord Palmerston promised to give his best consideration to the subject."

The general affairs of the mission also called for his constant attention, the Committee of the Society embracing the opportunity of his presence, with that of the Rev. W. Dendy and others, to confer with them on the interests and well-being of the churches and their pastors. These conferences bore fruit in after-years; and he strongly expressed his grateful appreciation of the cordiality with which his views and suggestions were received by the Committee, and by the friends of the mission in all parts of the country.

Towards the close of October he spent some happy days with his relatives in Norfolk, where his aged mother still lived to rejoice in his usefulness. Having accomplished, beyond his expectations, the objects which brought him to England, Mr. Phillippo embarked on board the mail-steamer *Parana*, at Southampton, on the 2nd of November, and bade farewell once more to his native land. After a somewhat unfavourable voyage of twenty-four days, he landed in Jamaica on the 26th.

"I journeyed," he says, " the following day to Spanish Town in safety and health. I need not say that my return was cordially welcomed by the people. My own thankfulness and joy were especially excited by the health of my beloved wife and family, and the happiness they expressed in finding me once more amongst them. The means of grace had been regularly maintained at my several stations during my absence, and uninterrupted peace and harmony had prevailed." But Mr. Phillippo found that the advance of years was not without its powerful influence on his energies, and he adds: " One thing, however, occasions me deep regret, and this is my sense of inability to perform the work of former years. My district embraces a circle of full fifty miles, and requires constant labour in travelling, preaching, and pastoral supervision, to say nothing of superintendence of the schools."

CHAPTER XXXIII.

THE agreeable and extended visits paid by Mr. Phillippo to the large circle of friends he formed in the United States and in England brought upon him on his return home a constant stream of correspondence on various subjects connected with the well-being of Jamaica. Among his American correspondents, Mr. Tappan, the well-known opponent of American slavery, is particularly mentioned ; and in the month of April, 1858, he had the pleasure of entertaining in Spanish Town the brother of that gentleman, and of introducing him to his congregation. The distinguished Abolitionist was anxious to possess information on the working of emancipation, and this Mr. Phillippo gladly supplied. The editors of several newspapers in the States frequently asked his aid, and threw open their columns to his exposition of island affairs. At the same time he maintained an active interchange of letters with various parties in England, more especially keeping the leaders of the Anti-slavery Movement informed of the progress of events under the administration of the new Governor, Captain Darling, who, having been long resident in the colony, and employed as secretary under Lord Sligo and Sir Lionel Smith, possessed in a special degree an acquaintance with the wants of the country. To several of his friends, from whom he had received assistance for his schools, and enjoyed marked proofs of personal regard, he forwarded collections of the fauna and flora of Jamaica, to the study of which he had devoted many leisure hours during his long residence. Referring especially to a collection of land shells that he had made, he says: " I was for some years ignorant of these beautiful fabrics of insect manufacture, but, when aware of their variety in form and the splendour of their colouring, it became so fascinating a study, and so interesting to collect them, that it beguiled many a walk and journey, and occupied what might have been useless minutes to obtain and classify." He also soon became involved in the discussion of many matters of local interest. On the 1st of April he is the spokesman of a deputation to the Governor, congratulating his Excellency on his assumption of the high office he was called to fill. Next he is making urgent applications to the local authorities to increase the facilities needed by the people to convey their produce to market, and to improve the condition of the roads. He presses on their attention the destructive inundations caused by the overflowings of the Rio Cobre in and around the village of Passage Fort, the chapel and mission-house being at times rendered unapproachable, except by boats. A few days after he is taking part in a large public meeting, which was held at his mountain home, to consider the impassable state of the roads in the district between Sligoville or Highgate and Spanish Town. The memorials adopted at these meetings were laid before the House of Assembly in order that the money needed might be obtained. Of a more general nature were the efforts he put forth, in common with his missionary brethren, to prevent the adoption of an immigration law, which they held to be both unnecessary, in the presence of the large amount of unemployed labour in the island, and unfair to the newly emancipated peasantry dependent on their daily toil.

Soon after his return Mr. Phillippo had the pleasure of receiving copies of his new work on "The United States and Cuba,"* which had just issued from the press at home. The book quickly ran into a second edition, and was received with much commendation, both in England and the United States. The substance of the volume, during several years, had been delivered in a course of lectures before various literary and scientific societies. The materials were drawn from every publication within his reach, corrected, enlarged, and enlivened by his personal recollections and observations. The scope of the volume is very wide, embracing almost every conceivable subject connected with the United States. The discovery of the country, the history of the States, their geography, government, laws, measures, customs, education, social and religious life, natural phenomena, geology, zoology, and other subjects, all in turn find a place in the panoramic picture he has drawn. The work has seldom been equalled for completeness. If in some parts it is too statistical, these dry matters are relieved by descriptions of scenery, and a pleasant account of the various sorts of people which formed the mingled population. The volume overflows with information carefully compiled, and conveyed in a style at once fluent and clear. An American authority pronounced it to be the best work that had ever appeared on the subject ; and another critic speaks of it as a book which "deserves the widest circulation in Great Britain, America, and the West India Colonies." Time has in some measure deprived the work of its value. The twenty-two years that have elapsed since its publication have added immensely to the resources of the States, and witnessed the growth of innumerable cities in magnitude

---

* "The United States and Cuba." By James M. Phillippo. London: Pewtress & Co.

and wealth.   The great war of emancipation has changed the entire aspect of its civil and social life.   But Mr. Phillippo's book may always be consulted with profit, and will remain a valuable and trustworthy description of the country at the time to which it relates.

At the meeting of the association of the churches held in Falmouth on the 31st of March, Mr. Phillippo met with a very hearty welcome, and an address, signed by all the ministers present, twenty in number, was presented to him.   "We are not unmindful," they say, "of your long-tried and faithful services, of the wisdom and experience you have acquired by them, nor of the immense advantages that experience is calculated to confer on the mission. We highly appreciate your untiring efforts during your sojourn in England to promote the best interests of our own mission, and our educational institutions in particular, and to promote the welfare of the people generally.   For these self-denying labours accept, dear brother, our united, hearty thanks.   Our hope is that we shall yet reap no small profit from them."

During his stay in England, Mr. Phillippo was able to obtain considerable promises of support for his schools, so that on resuming his labours they were both revived and strengthened.   In a letter to a friend he thus reports upon them, under date of February 1, 1859:—"The metropolitan schools were re-opened soon after my return to Jamaica, amidst demonstrations of joy throughout the town, and are now amongst the best conducted and most efficient institutions of the island.

"These schools already contain one hundred and six scholars of both sexes, of which number ninety-five are in daily attendance.   They are conducted by Mr. and Mrs. O'Meally, who, though once slaves, and received their education in the schools over which they now preside, are among the best qualified teachers in the country.   They were for many years teachers of these schools before their discontinuance; they subsequently kept a respectable private school; and Mr. O'Meally was latterly second master of a free grammar-school in the town, to which, in all probability, he would have succeeded as principal but for his inability to produce the testimonials of a graduate of one of the English universities. Mr. and Mrs. O'Meally are also exemplary members of the Christian Church, and their character as well as their literary qualifications are unquestionable.

"The country schools, three in number, containing upwards of two hundred children, and presided over by four teachers, male and female, are not only still in existence, but have been brought into greater efficiency since my return, I having been enabled, by the increased means afforded, to secure in two of them better qualified teachers than those previously employed.

"Altogether, my most sanguine expectations with regard to the efficiency and general prosperity of these schools, as the result of the generous subscriptions and donations of the friends of the Negro, have been hitherto more than realised, and, in reliance upon the faithful performance of the promises of friends made for the two succeeding years, I flatter myself still that the chief difficulties in the permanent maintenance of these institutions will be overcome."

Not less vigorously did Mr. Phillippo labour for the spiritual welfare of his people. Three weeks later he writes :—" The church here (Spanish Town) has continued in peace, and has been blessed with some degree of prosperity. Fourteen, chiefly young persons, have been added to it by baptism, and several more who have given evidence of repentance towards God and faith in our Lord Jesus Christ have signified their desire of putting on Christ by a public profession of His name. The attendance on the public worship of God during the former part of the year was not encouraging, but we are thankful to say it has latterly been more in accordance with our desires. The ordinances have been duly administered, and outdoor services have occasionally been held in the suburbs of the town and other adjacent localities. The Sunday-school suffered awhile from various causes, but it is now supplied with a sufficient staff of teachers, and the prospects of future prosperity are encouraging. The day-schools here, and those in connection with this station at Passage Fort and Caymanas, are well attended and efficient. But constant efforts, here and at Passage Fort, for the repairs of the premises have diminished our ability to aid foreign objects.

"At Sligoville, the church and congregation are in an encouraging condition. Thirteen young persons have been added to our number by baptism, and many to our list of inquirers, while the congregation has very considerably increased. The day-schools here and at Kensington have fluctuated as to numbers, but the Sunday-school is large, interesting, and efficient. The teachers make good use of their library, and are anxious to purchase another from the Tract Society."

In a letter to a friend in the United States he enters more fully on the general state of the mission. "Our churches here, as you know, were in a highly prosperous condition for some years. Hundreds, I may say thousands, of persons were added to them year after year. Indeed, during the thirty-five years of my missionary life, I have baptized and added to the churches under my own care several thousands who were, I have reason to believe, truly converted to God.

"The religious excitement that formerly prevailed has, I regret to say, considerably declined during the last few years, which was to have been anticipated; but we are thankful to say, looking at the field before us in its full extent, and calculating all the circumstances connected with our population, that we have no cause for discouragement. Our chapels are in general well filled with attentive hearers, and there are being added constantly to our churches such, we have every reason to believe, as will be saved.

"The Baptists, as a denomination, are, perhaps, in some respects the least flourishing at present, owing to difficulties they have had to encounter in consequence of their entire dependence upon the voluntary contributions of their people for support.

"But they have sanguine hopes that they will be able, with the temporary aid of the parent Society, or with that of the ministry and churches at home still interested in our welfare, to overcome these difficulties and become more really prosperous than ever.

"We have lately held our annual Association, and it may not be unacceptable to you to be furnished with a few statistics of our present circumstances and condition.

"We have connected with us, as a union or association, fifty-two chapels, accommodating 38,565 persons; attending the ministry, 44,704; average attendance, 28,192—*i.e.*, sixty-five per cent. of adherents; fifty-seven out-stations, fifty-three assistant preachers, seventy-seven deacons and others conducting services in the absence of pastors; sixty-one day-school teachers, about 5,000 day scholars, 730 Sunday-school teachers, and 8,746 Sunday scholars. Members, 15,682. Inquirers, 2,043.

"Added to these items, we enumerate 140 class-houses on estates and in Negro villages, twenty-eight dwelling-houses or pastors' residences, school-rooms separate from chapels accommodating 450 hearers.

"We have raised altogether for missionary purposes this year upwards of £600, besides amounts for the repair of premises, building new chapels, and support of ministers.

"I must not omit to observe that these statistics do not include all the churches and congregations connected with our denomination on the island, as several are not associated with us as a union, and are therefore not reported."

Successful as had been the exertions of the missionaries, there were nevertheless many reasons for anxiety as to the future well-being of the churches, partly occasioned by the general condition of affairs, but more particularly arising out of the progress that had been secured.

The question of sending a second deputation to Jamaica to inquire into the condition of the mission had been brought before the Committee of the Baptist Missionary Society in 1857 by a letter from ten of the most influential of the European brethren. This desire had still further been earnestly pressed upon the Committee by Mr. Phillippo and Mr. Dendy, during their stay in England in the following year. It was not, however, until the close of 1859 that the Committee were able to secure the services of the Rev. J. T. Brown, of Northampton, and myself for this important task. At the request of the Committee, in the months of September and October I visited Trinidad and Haiti, and Mr. Brown joined me at Kingston, in Jamaica, on the 25th of November. This is not the place to recount the investigations of the deputation, which lasted over a period of five months, or to give the conclusion to which they were led on the manifold topics that received their attention.* The stations at

---

* By those interested in these questions, reference may be made to the Reports of the Society for 1860-61 ; to the *Missionary Herald* of December, 1860; and to the following work: "The West Indies : their Social and Religious Condition. By Edward Bean Underhill. London : Jackson, Walford, & Hodder, 1862." Also, "Emancipation in the West Indies : Two Addresses by the Deputation at a Public Meeting held at Willis's Rooms, February 20th, 1861. London : 1861."

Spanish Town and its vicinity were the first visited, and the last public meeting in which the deputation took part was held in Mr. Phillippo's spacious chapel, a member of the Government occupying the chair, and the audience a large one, consisting not only of the congregation usually attending Mr. Phillippo's ministry, but of the most influential persons of the town.

It may, however, be interesting to give Mr. Phillippo's account of the visit, and the impressions produced on his mind. They are found in a letter he addressed to the Rev. Mr. Berg in the month of June, 1860.

"A few weeks since I forwarded you a few lines to introduce my friend Mr. Brown, who had been sent as a deputation to our churches here at the request of the missionaries generally. Owing to the misrepresentations of self-interested and prejudiced persons, much misconception had arisen in the public mind in England as to the state of things amongst us. At the same time, owing to the changes that had taken place in the condition of the people connected with our churches, and in that of the missionaries also, and the necessity of some modification of existing plans to meet the exigencies that had arisen, the Committee were persuaded to depute the Rev. J. T. Brown, and one of the secretaries, to visit us, and report to their constituents the result.

"The brethren were most cordially welcomed by both ministers and churches throughout the island, and were well received everywhere by the proprietors and managers of estates, and by gentlemen of respectability. At public meetings held at some of the principal towns, the attendants at which comprehended all classes of the inhabitants, they gave full and free expression to their views. These were very favourable as to the condition of the island socially, morally, and religiously, and their opinions were heartily acquiesced in by all the various classes comprising these assemblies. At a missionary meeting held in Spanish Town, their sentiments were endorsed by several of the most influential members of the Legislature who were present, one of whom occupied the chair. Their opinions of the state and character of the masses of the people in a religious aspect appear to have been much higher than those entertained by them previously to their visit, and to those formed by Christians at home. In a word they seem to think that a greater work has been accomplished in the island than the Christian world supposed, high as was the estimate they in this respect had formed; that Jamaica stood indeed unrivalled as a field of successful missionary enterprise; and that, with continued sympathy on the part of British Christians in relation to schools, and in some other ways, no cause would exist for apprehension in the future."

"Our annual Association was held this year at Montego Bay, in the month of February, and was one of unusual interest, especially from the presence of our brethren, the deputation. Several interesting and important papers were read relating to the present state and prospects of the churches, as also to the theological institution for the training of native young men of talent for the ministry and for day-school teachers. The statistics of the churches, though gratifying in some instances, were not on the whole encouraging, and resolutions were unanimously adopted that a week should be set apart specially to invoke the influences of the Holy Spirit with a view to the revival of religion amongst us. Among the encouraging incidents recorded were the erection of new chapels, the repair of old ones, and the generally increased attendance on public worship. The contributions to our local missionary society were very gratifying, showing a considerable increase in the year. We have long wished to raise at least £1,000 a year for home and foreign mission work; the amount this year was exceeded. Day and Sunday-schools are in most cases connected with our congregations, and the latter contain 10,000 scholars.

" The number of brethren assembled was greater than usual. Our public meetings were large and deeply interesting, and our conferences were marked by much good feeling, and tended greatly to our mutual profit. The special conference with our brethren deputed by the parent Society, to which we mutually looked forward with some anxiety, was everything, in regard to the manner in which it was conducted, that we could have desired. Messrs. Brown and Underhill acted towards us with the greatest urbanity and kindness, at the same time in a manner frank and generous, so that confidence in them was inspired from the outset. We found at once that, while they would think and act for themselves, they came bolstered with no prejudices, and were influenced by a simple desire to ascertain the real state of things as they exist among us—to afford counsel and advice under difficulties, and to give their opinions as to the best practicable means to ensure the future progress of the work."

The visits of the deputation to Mr. Phillippo's stations gave them unmingled pleasure, while the kindness and hospitality of their reception, the Christian intercourse they enjoyed with him, his admirable wife, and other members of his family, remain a fragrant and grateful memory. They could not but admire the manly character of their friend, tempered as it was with Christian courtesy and affection. They rejoiced to witness the high esteem in which he was held by every class of the community.

CHAPTER XXXIV.

THE earliest indications of the result of the meetings resolved upon by the annual Association were communicated to the Society by Mr. Phillippo, under date of the 23rd of June, 1860. Writing to me he says :—

"Since you left our shores we have held the revival meetings as decided on at our meeting at Montego Bay. I have carried them on from the last Sabbath in April to the present time throughout the extended district in which my stations are scattered. In the chapels at my different stations, in the class-houses, and in private houses, both in town and country, prayer-meetings have been held, in most cases morning and evening, I going first to one and then to another, to encourage the masses attending them (especially in the country) by out-of-door addresses, accompanied by my wife and daughter. The results, I regret to say, have not been such hitherto as we desired ; but they have been far from discouraging. In addition to greatly increased congregations, there is evidently a deeper tone of religious feeling prevalent, an indication, as we trust, that God the Holy Spirit will yet again pour out His blessings upon us like showers that water the earth. Added to the agency already named, a committee for tract distribution has been formed, and among the applicants for these silent messengers of mercy are several respectable planters and their wives and families. More than this—and I record it as an evidence of God's purpose to bless and to bring into the fold of Christ some even of the class so long at enmity with the cause of God and truth—three or four attorneys and managers of properties have requested me personally, and by messages by the people employed on the different estates and pens, to preach at their residences. On one large property in this parish, having published my intention to preach in the Negro village near, the manager sent to request me to hold the meeting in a booth he offered to erect in front of the great house, that I might address the assembly from the steps or a window, that himself, family, and domestics might have an opportunity of being present. With this request I could not then comply, as a large congregation had then assembled on my arrival at the Negro village. His wife and family accompanied us, however, and after the service expressed their willingness to become tract distributors and Scripture readers among the people of the district. I have since heard that this lady meets with the people in their class-house, and does all in her power to encourage them by her presence and efforts. I have promised to repeat my visit to this property as soon as possible, when I have consented to occupy the manager's house. Last week I received a message from an attorney of several sugar estates requesting me, when I repeated my visit to the property on which he resided, to occupy his house as the place in which to hold the service; or that, if I will hold service occasionally on the Sabbath-day, he will erect a temporary place of worship in the immediate vicinity of the works. In a word, all opposition on the part of planters and others against the progress of the Gospel has ceased, and everything seems to indicate that the set time to favour our Zion again is near. God grant that our hopes may be fully realised!"

Shortly after it became evident that the Divine blessing was about to manifest its power in a remarkable manner.

X

The first striking display of the gracious influence of the Spirit of God took place at a station of the Moravian mission, in one of the southern parishes. It quickly spread to the eastward, and its effects were briefly sketched in a letter from Mr. Phillippo on the 25th of December:—

"You have probably heard before now that the revival for which we as ministers and churches here have been so long praying and labouring has at length been realised in numerous districts of the island. On its occurrence in Manchester and Clarendon some weeks ago I went down to these parishes to the assistance of brother Claydon, and there had sufficient evidence that the work was of God. Since then it has, though at present in a more moderate manner as to its external manifestations, found its way to Spanish Town; so that our places of worship are thronged, and services are continued in them, I may almost say, from morning until night of every day of the week. Intelligence of the rapid extent and wonderful concomitants of this awakening are reaching us by every post. On this south side of the island it has extended itself from Savannah-la-Mar to Old Harbour and Spanish Town ; and on the north, from Bethel Town and Mount Carey, onwards through Montego Bay, Falmouth, Stewart Town, Brown's Town, to St. Ann's Bay. It is spreading and rolling onwards like a mighty river, and will no doubt cover the whole island. The results, as in Ireland and elsewhere, are not altogether unmixed with evil ; but wherever the movement has been under the guidance of pious and devoted ministers of the Gospel the fruits are such as demonstrate them the production of the softening, converting, almighty operation of the Spirit of the Lord of Hosts."

Under these circumstances, the customary New Year's Day services, and the baptismal service accompanying them, were of unusual interest. The concourse of people was immense. They poured in from the surrounding district. It was a beautiful morning, and, amidst the deepest emotion, twenty-four persons submitted to the sacred rite. "Such," says Mr. Phillippo, "was the seriousness and propriety observed that nothing occurred to disturb the solemnity of the service from its commencement till its close."

"On the following Lord's-day the newly baptized, together with several others who had long been separated from the Church (making an addition of sixty during the year), were admitted to Christian fellowship. Gratifying as the attendance on the public worship of God had been since the commencement of the religious awakening in the town, the spacious chapel was now filled to excess— the aisles, the porticoes, the gallery stairs, the children's gallery behind the pulpit, all were occupied, and many were out of doors. Full two thousand persons were supposed to have been present.

"During the morning service considerable excitement prevailed. Numbers cried out for God to have mercy upon them, and others gave expression to their feelings in sobs and tears. There was nothing, however, witnessed or heard that was unbecoming the sacredness of the place or the services—nothing, except for a short time, that obstructed the regular performance of worship. Upwards of a hundred of all sexes were present who were under conviction.

" In the afternoon, Divine service was also held in the school-rooms, there not being room in the body of the chapel for those who had been the subjects of excitement in the morning."

In harmony with the meetings for prayer held during the first days of the year all over the world, the first fortnight of January was devoted to religious meetings with the most happy results. " All the meetings," says

Mr. Phillippo, "have been numerously attended, and such has been the apparent sincerity—such the earnestness and appropriateness of the petitions presented to the Throne of Grace—as to leave no doubt in any Christian's mind that they were heard in heaven. Of this, indeed, we have had abundant evidence. They were quickly followed by the revival influences experienced in other parts of the island ; and, almost simultaneously with them, hundreds in the town and neighbourhood have been under deep concern for their souls' salvation, and have cried aloud for mercy and forgiveness.

"It has not, however, reached the haunts of profligacy and general wickedness either in this town or in Kingston. Neither has the awakening been characterised by the degrees of physical excitement described as so common in other parishes. But it doubtless will come here with power, for it is still progressing, notwithstanding the counteracting influences consequent on the visit of Prince Alfred to our shores.* Scarcely a day passes but we hear of numbers in different parts of the district arrested, sometimes suddenly, in their career of sin, while not a Sabbath-day closes but instances of conviction and conversion occur.

"Among these are numerous persons, chiefly young, who were once united to our congregations as inquirers, but who had abandoned their profession, or had relapsed into a state of carelessness and spiritual insensibility. Of this latter class, principally, I baptized on the morning of Good Friday last forty-two, kindly assisted in the services on the occasion, which were deeply interesting, by brethren J. E. and G. Henderson, the former of whom,

---

* Prince Alfred arrived in Jamaica on the 24th of March, but was summoned home by the death of the Duchess of Kent. He left on the 6th of April, suddenly cutting short the great preparations made for his reception.

on the first Sabbath in this month, received them into the church, and conducted the other services of the day, I having been at length laid aside by sickness—from which, though now nearly a month has passed, I am but just recovering.

" It will thus be seen that, in the course of a few months, upwards of a hundred careless, thoughtless, and, in some instances, abandoned sinners in connection with our church and congregation have been brought to the feet of Jesus, clothed and in their right mind ; these, however, we trust, are but the first-fruits of the revival here."

The movement extended to all the stations under Mr. Phillippo's care : at Kitson Town, Caymanas, Passage Fort, Sligoville, and at almost every settlement and class-house in the district. At Sligoville, he says, "On approaching the chapel, I heard singing, in which all hearts and voices appeared to be engaged. This subsided soon after I entered. The converted were arranged on benches before me, some with countenances beaming with joy and peace, others expressing deep sadness and sorrow of heart. Most of them I found to be young people. Some of them prayed with an eloquence and earnestness I never heard excelled, one little girl especially—she could not have been more than ten years of age. Every one seemed melted to tears by her entreaties for the pardon of herself, her parents, brother, and sister, and all around her. The commencement of the awakening here was on the preceding Sunday, when the chapel was crowded to excess ; and meetings have been held night and day ever since, most of the people remaining to the present time almost without food or sleep."

In a brief account of a very crowded meeting held in the large chapel in Spanish Town, Mr. Phillippo has preserved a vivid picture of the scenes frequent on these occasions. " The building was filled from top to bottom,

and soon after the service commenced the greatest excitement prevailed. In one direction were poor unlettered
Africans pouring out their supplications in some such
language as this, and in the words of one of them with
the utmost earnestness, his voice heard above the tumult;
'O Lord, have mercy on me poor soul. O Lord, me
heart black like me kin (skin); wash him in dy precious
blood. O dear, precious massa Jesus, take kale (scales)
off me dark eye. Dow sa come and dead to save poor
sinner from death and hell. Lord, save me—me a sinner—
me a drunkard, me de tief, me de Sabbat-broker. For-
give me for mercy-sake. O Jesus, save me by dy precious
blood.'

"Another cries out in another direction in great apparent distress, 'What must I do to be saved? Lord
have mercy upon me! Jesus, dow Saviour of sinners, I
look to de. Oh! save me, else me perish.'

"A third rises up under great anguish, uttering un-
earthly moans and piercing cries, which, once heard, can
never be forgotten: 'What, what must I do to be saved?'
His whole soul was in the question, nor could he rest till
completely satisfied by the minister's exhortation to cast
himself entirely on Jesus. Heaven, hell, Christ, salvation
were now no longer uninteresting, unmeaning words and
notions, but living, substantial realities, which rang in the
ears and burned in the hearts of the people.

"While the countenances of some expressed the most
childlike submission and perfect trust, others proclaimed
aloud, with all the animation of perfect sincerity, their
full assurance of God's mercy through Christ, their full
joy struggling for expression. Love, peace, gratitude,
and adoration welled up spontaneously from their hearts,
prompting them to tell to others what great things the
Lord had done for them."

With the advancing months of the year, the fervour of

the early portion of the movement declined, but the lasting benefits were seen in the increased attendance on the house of God, and a more general regard for the ordinances of religion. If many fell away from their first love as the excitement ceased, the gain in genuine discipleship was large, and it became from year to year evident that it was indeed a time of refreshing from the presence of the Lord.

Mr. Phillippo thus sums up the issues of this great movement :—

" The direct religious results have been such as to leave no doubt on the minds of Christian men who have been familiar with it in all its phases, that it originated in the wonder-working power of God. On the part of the churches, it has been a revival of Scriptural knowledge, vital piety, and practical obedience, an unusual warmth of attachment to each other, and to all who love our Lord Jesus Christ in sincerity, added to visible, zealous, persevering efforts for the salvation of their careless and impenitent fellow-creatures. It may be said of our members in general, but especially of the more intelligent among them, that they *laboured* for the promotion of this good work night and day, through many months. Their efforts were distinguished by familiar conversation, more general visiting from house to house, more direct and earnest labour in Bible and inquirers' classes, a deeper interest in the operations of Sabbath-schools, addresses at prayer-meetings, the distribution of religious tracts, a sympathetic regard for the wants of the necessitous, the tempted, and the stricken ; by family devotion and discipline, and, individually, by exemplary conduct and character."

" These agencies, in addition to direct and more frequent ministerial efforts, were followed, as may be supposed, by vastly increased congregations, by demands on the part of the converts for private Christian instruction, and by the multitude generally, both in town and country, for multiplied prayer-meetings and the regular worship of God—services that were conducted in streets and lanes, class-houses and public thoroughfares in general. Nor must it be forgotten, in the enumeration of these results, that an anxious, earnest desire was everywhere expressed for the possession of religious books and tracts, but especially to read, understand, and possess the Book of God."

" With reference to the multitudes who had been living without Christ and without hope in the world, and who, in numerous instances, had seldom—in some cases, perhaps, *never*—been within the walls of a place of worship, the manifestation of Divine influence in inclining such to throng the houses of God, to manifest such sincerity and earnestness of desire for pardon, peace, and salvation —to unite themselves to the people of God, and to walk in a course of holy obedience—is, perhaps, without a parallel in the modern history of the Church. Thousands of sinners of all descriptions of character, among whom were numbers distinguished for profligacy of manners and for overt general wickedness—men sunk in immorality and obdurate in crime—reclaimed from such enormities, subdued, converted, animated with joy and peace in believing, not to mention others less ostensibly depraved and vicious! Thousands of these, together with many a conceited Pharisee and rationalist, 'plucked as brands from the burning,' have been added to the different churches within a few months, and as many have enrolled themselves on the list of probationers for church-fellowship.

" To an intelligent observer the power of God cannot but be visible in the effects produced. A striking change is observable in the conversation, temper, deportment, and even in the very countenances of the converts. In the immediate localities where this awakening has been most powerfully and efficaciously manifested there is scarcely a person to be seen on the Sabbath, except going to or returning from some place of religious worship, or on week evenings, unless on their way to or from a social prayer-meeting, or some place to listen to the reading of the Scriptures and religious tracts. Profane conversation and indecent jesting, drunkenness, gambling, quarrelling, concubinage, and the superstitious practices of Obeahism and Myalism, which presented so great a barrier to the progress of the truth among the more ignorant and depraved of the population, and which operated so fatally to the peace and purity of the churches at large, have in a great measure ceased. In some districts the unnatural custom of wakes, where assemblies were gathered on the decease of neighbours and friends, and where whole nights were spent in noisy mirth and superstitious vigils, have been discontinued, or the revolting practices of such occasions substituted by religious conversations, reading the Scriptures and prayer, with the usual vocal accompaniments of psalms, and hymns, and spiritual songs.

" The minds of some were for a time unsettled, and cases were not rare in which appearances of insanity were visible; but, like the Apostle, the subjects of such paroxysms appeared to solace themselves with the conviction that, if they were beside themselves, it was for God.

" As a final remark, it may be said that nothing has ever occurred in the Christian Church so calculated to promote a spirit of union and harmony of co-operation among ministers and people of different denominations. Were revivals universal, the Evangelical Alliance would embrace the whole Church on earth. Like the rainbow of the Covenant, it would indeed include within the arch of its promise and the glory of its protection the whole family of God in earth and heaven."

The additions to the Baptist churches were a striking testimony to the remarkable influence of the revival throughout the island. The returns at the close of the year from fifty-nine out of the sixty-one churches in union state that 3,757 persons were baptized, while there were restored to fellowship from a backsliding state no fewer than 1,570. The net increase to the churches exhibited a total of 4,422, bringing up the membership to 20,026 persons of all ages. The classes of inquirers were also largely filled, and numbered 6,058 individuals. The testimony of nearly all the ministers of every denomination was that the revival was a real blessing and a permanent good. "It was," concludes Mr. Phillippo, " like a tempest passing over, and with one blast purifying the atmosphere, and calling into new life a thousand beauties over the Christian landscape. It was, indeed, a dispensation which, with all its attendant evils, there are few ministers or churches who would not wish for its recurrence. It gave a higher tone of piety to the churches generally, it excited attention, induced prayer and unwonted zeal. In one word, it was an awakening from spiritual death."

CHAPTER XXXV.

THE three or four years following the revival were years of patient toil. The large additions to the churches required the pastor's watchful care, so that Mr. Phillippo was unable to pursue that wide evangelistic labour which had in so marked a manner characterised his ministry. Besides, the advance of years was making itself felt, and the conviction was pressed upon him that his energies were becoming unequal to the strain they had hitherto successfully borne. This was especially manifest with regard to his schools, which languished for want of more regular support. For although his correspondents in England, more especially those belonging to the Society of Friends, and other supporters resident in Jamaica, liberally answered his appeals, the correspondence involved and the uncertainty of the supplies were an incessant trial of his faith and patience.

To one of his friends in Jamaica he addressed the following letter, November 3rd, 1861:—"I received your kind note yesterday with its enclosure, and scarcely know in what terms to express my sense of obligation. I have five schools in the district, for the support of which I am alone responsible, and I find it hard work to carry them on from year to year. I am, however, with you, deeply convinced of the great necessity of education to the progress and prosperity of this country, both temporal and spiritual. I have for upwards of thirty years devoted myself to the work. I have laboured on through many difficulties and discouragements, but have the satisfaction (the purest, perhaps, that can be experienced in the present world) to know that some thousands of my fellow-creatures have been benefited by my efforts. My chief difficulty of late years, in the support of these schools, has arisen from the conviction of many in England that Jamaica ought now to support its own institutions. As I could not bear the thought of relinquishing them, I am constrained to ask your aid, and that of all the friends of their country who I thought were likely to lend a helping hand."

One of the modes in which he sought to sustain his school operations he thus refers to in his diary, under date of May 10, 1863 : " Having become, almost insensibly I may say, much interested in the study of conchology and ornithology, I made offers of forming collections for gentlemen on condition that they would aid me in the support of my schools. With this object in view, I had frequent communications with W. T. Marsh, Esq." To a friend at Newcastle, who had requested various specimens, he writes : " Both myself and my daughter tried for some time to procure and preserve the different specimens you request, but I have found great difficulty in doing so." He then goes on to describe his work : " In addition to my regular ministerial and pastoral duties, extending over a very large district, I have to bear the ever-multiplying cares and anxieties created by the insufficient means I possess of supporting my schools. It is a perpetual struggle to preserve their existence. I am often driven to such shifts for money to pay the teachers that the close of the institutions, one and all, at times seems inevitable. But, hoping against hope, I have hitherto, most providentially, been able to continue them to this day. Among

the whole mass of philanthropists in England, the Society
of Friends only have steadily pursued their course, and
to them is due the honour of having been the main
instruments in securing the happy results of freedom
visible in the social happiness that exists around us.
Happy is it amid many depressing influences to reflect
that the Lord reigneth, and that, whatever may be present
discouragements, His cause must and will go on. What
cause have we to pray that our faith and hope may not
fail ! "

But if the difficulties in carrying on the schools were
great, Mr. Phillippo had the gratification of knowing that
his exertions were fully appreciated by intelligent observers
on the spot, and that his exertions were rewarded by the
progress made by the children under his care. "That
venerable and highly esteemed gentleman," said a well-
informed person in Spanish Town, "it is well known, has,
during the whole period of his lengthened career as a
missionary on this island, interested himself, with an
energy, activity, and perseverance worthy of all praise, in
the work of advancing popular education, and many are
the living witnesses of the great good which has resulted
from his philanthropic labours in this direction. With
unabated zeal, he is still doing what he can to further the
cause of popular education, although under difficulties and
trials of no ordinary kind. Many in positions of respectability in our island have to thank these institutions for all
they are worth, mentally, morally, and materially. May
they go on and prosper ! May the venerable servant of
Christ, who has taken so much interest in them for so
many years, see abundant proofs arising around him from
time to time that his labour has not been in vain ! "

Nor was Mr. Phillippo without many pleasing indications that his ministry was blessed to the effectual
calling of many into the fold of Christ. Writing April 17,

1865, he says: "You will be pleased to hear that on Friday morning last (Good Friday) I had the happiness to add to my church here by baptism twelve young persons. Some of them had for years been connected with the congregation as inquirers or catechumens, and all the others had been on probation during several months. They were, of course, carefully examined as to their religious knowledge and experience, and the evidence they afforded of true conversion to God was of a very gratifying character."

"The administration of the ordinance was arranged to take place soon after dawn in a very secluded and romantic spot on the river, between one and two miles from town. For those members of the congregation coming from a distance, as lodgings could not be obtained for them, it was arranged that services should be conducted in the chapel during the entire night. They commenced at ten o'clock p.m., at which time great numbers began to pour in. I delivered in the intervals of singing and prayer three addresses, occupying until long after midnight. At four o'clock a.m. the masses began to move, and by five all were on their way to the place appointed, forming an immense procession, with such order and quietness that many of the inhabitants of the streets along which they passed were not aware of the movement. I followed in the rear. Arrived at the chosen spot, the multitude arranged themselves without the least confusion or disorder on the high banks of the stream, while I placed myself in a position which with little inconvenience could command the whole assemblage. After a hymn and prayer I addressed the concourse, after which, while singing the favourite hymn, ' Jesus, and shall it ever be ?' &c., I administered the sacred rite in the name of the Holy Trinity. It was a very solemn and interesting scene. Many were in tears. Not a word was heard, not a gesture seen, so far as I could learn, that was not in harmony with the solemn character of the service in which we were engaged."

" I have since heard that not only were some of the spectators deeply moved, but that two or three at once enrolled themselves as inquirers after the way of salvation."

" On the first Sabbath of the coming month these brethren and sisters in Christ will be privileged for the first time to commemorate the dying love of Christ at His table, and I trust it will prove 'a time of refreshing from the presence of the Lord.' "

Among the persons baptized about this time was Mr. George W. Gordon. This event took place on Christmas-day, 1861. "Of the number who on this occasion followed their Lord," writes Mr. Phillippo, " by submitting to the solemn and impressive rite of baptism, was a merchant and large landed proprietor of the island. He was the last of sixty who on that lovely morning were immersed in the gently flowing stream. When, standing by his side, in front of the vast assemblage that covered the river's bank almost as far as the eye could reach, I asked him if he felt any shame or reluctance to put on Christ by this public and open profession of His name, his heart was too full to allow him to reply in words, but his looks and gestures were not to be mistaken, and, like the Ethiopian eunuch, he rose from the liquid grave, and went his way rejoicing." The unuttered words were afterwards expressed in a brief note to Mr. Phillippo on the same day. "This day," he writes, "the Lord witnesses the actions and motives of us all who have made an open profession of Him. But the secret of the Lord is with them that fear Him, and He will show them His covenant. I pray to-day that henceforth my life may be 'hid with Christ.' May His grace keep and defend me in running the race which is now before me ! "

Although baptized by Mr. Phillippo, Mr. Gordon continued to maintain his connection with the United Presbyterian Church; but on various occasions he sought Mr. Phillippo's advice, and rendered important services in the promotion of the Gospel in the parishes in which his property lay. He took a prominent part at the missionary meeting held at Spanish Town on the 1st of August of the same year, and in the April following he is found consulting Mr. Phillippo with regard to some religious meetings in which he desired Mr. Phillippo's assistance. "May the Lord," he exclaims, "bless all these [services], and may the seed be flourishing many years hence! Oh, how much yet to do! What fallen land yet to break up! May the Lord have mercy, and early manifest His glory in all the earth, and particularly in Jamaica!" In March, 1863, Mr. Gordon announced to Mr. Phillippo his election as a member of the House of Assembly for St. Thomas-in-the-East, and expresses the hope that the Lord will grant him "wisdom, patience, and grace to guide" him in the intricate future. After referring to his obligations to Mr. Phillippo, he further tells him that he has given much attention to the native Baptists, and attributes to them his election. "See what the Baptists have done here, the poor native Baptists, by peaceable means; they have raised at last a representative for the Baptist people and churches of all classes in this island. You know I was honoured by being baptized by you, my dear friend; and I found you liberal and unselfish in your views, not discouraging me from going among the poor natives, but encouraging always to every good work. May the Lord bless and keep you always in this spirit!" In his diary, under date of January of the following year, Mr. Phillippo records: "G. W. Gordon, Esq., has occupied himself in preaching and doing good openly and in various ways, and I recommended him to originate

an independent cause under his own superintendence. He
has met with much persecution, is denominated a hypo-
crite, and by some, of whom better things might be
expected, 'a troubler in Israel.'"

It is interesting to preserve these notices of the man who
in less than two years was falsely accused of treason to
the State, and illegally, and contrary to all right, executed
as a rebel against the Sovereign whom, in common with
all his people, he venerated and loved.

The annual meeting of the Jamaica Baptist Union was
arranged to take place at Montego Bay in the beginning
of the year 1864, on the spot where just fifty years before
the Rev. John Rowe commenced his labours as the first
missionary sent to the island by the Baptist Missionary
Society. It was resolved to celebrate the occasion as a
jubilee. An immense concourse of persons, estimated at
more than ten thousand, gathered to take part in the
festive services. All the free places of worship in the
town were thrown open, and were crowded with the
multitudes that flocked to them. Mr. Phillippo left home
on the 17th of February, accompanied by several members
of his family, and arrived at Montego Bay on the 20th.
On the following day, the Sabbath, he preached in the
spacious chapel erected by that estimable missionary, and
Mr. Phillippo's beloved friend, the Rev. Thomas Burchell.
The jubilee meeting was held in the same place on Tuesday, July 23rd. "Being by some years," he says, "the
oldest missionary on the island then living, I was honoured
to occupy the chair on the occasion. The congregation
was immense. The large chapel was filled to excess, and
numbers could hardly obtain a standing-place, even outside the building." Mr. Phillippo's address does not
appear to have been preserved, but from the other
addresses delivered we learn that since the commencement
of the mission 106 Baptist missionaries had been engaged,

and the fruit of their labours was seen in the seventy-four churches that had been organised, one or more of which might be found in every parish in the island. The membership in these churches consisted of about thirty thousand persons, and for twenty years, notwithstanding the difficulties through which the island had passed, the converts had not only built numerous chapels, many of large dimensions, with manses and school-houses, but had also supported their ministers and the means of grace without foreign aid. Nineteen of the forty-one pastors in active service were natives of the island, and had received a suitable education in the college at Calabar, near Rio Bueno. The institution also embraced as one of its objects the training of masters for the day-schools, which numbered about ninety, and contained 3,500 scholars. If to this number were added the children of the Sunday-schools, there were not fewer than ten thousand under constant instruction. Nor was the missionary spirit wanting among the people. About £1,200 a year were willingly contributed for home and foreign work. Besides the overthrow of slavery, social and temporal blessings of no common value had been secured. Sunday markets had been abolished. Equal civil rights had been granted irrespective of colour or race ; marriage had come to be regarded as a necessary and honoured institution ; many thousands of the people had made themselves possessors of freehold lands, and were independent of estate cultivation ; education, though not so extensive as desirable, was unfettered ; persecution for conscience' sake was stayed, and the superstitious and wicked practices of Obeahism and Myalism had been driven into dark places. Thus the Gospel of God's grace had proved its wondrous power— first in the regeneration and salvation of multitudes of bondsmen, and then in the social reformation it had accomplished during the years of liberty.

The papers prepared for this gathering were afterwards collected into a volume entitled "The Voice of Jubilee," Mr. Phillippo contributing to its pages an elaborate "Argument and Appeal for Christian Missions." This treatise extends to more than a hundred pages, and embraces a full statement of the magnitude, claims, facilities, successes, and blessings of the missionary enterprise. Nor does Mr. Phillippo fail to show the reflex blessings which flow from the devout pursuit of this great object on the Christian character both of individuals and communities. Speaking of the Baptist churches in Jamaica, he says: "Think of thirty thousand souls converted to God in this our island alone! Every one of them once depraved, but now regenerated sons and daughters of Ham, together with the thousands now before the throne of God and the Lamb; and thousands more gathered into the fold of Christ through the instrumentality of other societies, altogether amounting, on a moderate calculation, to little less than two hundred thousand souls, had it not been for missionary exertions, would, in all probability, have been still either sitting in darkness and the shadow of death, or have entered upon a state of hopeless and interminable woe."

These great results Mr. Phillippo had been privileged to witness, all of them secured during the period of his missionary life, he, himself, being not one of the least eminent of the noble band who, in the hands of God, had achieved them. Other good and great men shared with him in the blessedness and joy of these triumphs of the Cross; but it was his happiness, of all the pioneers of the mission, to live to tell at the jubilee "the generation following" what great things the Lord had done.

Notwithstanding occasional attacks of illness, Mr. and Mrs. Phillippo were able to carry forward their great work during these years without much interruption. Towards the close of 1864 they were permitted to rejoice in the call of their second son, George, to the bar in England, and his hearty reception by the bench and bar of Jamaica on his commencing practice in the courts of his native land.   Their happiness was also increased by the marriage of their daughter to the Rev. W. Claydon, missionary in Clarendon ; while from all their children they enjoyed much assistance, combined with a very large amount of filial reverence and affection.   The progress of years was, however, made only too apparent by a slow but real dimi-nution of the energies with which their labours in the cause of God had hitherto been pursued.   But the love and respect which gathered about their home, and the happiness inspired by the " blessed hope " of the Gospel, brightened their days and filled their hearts with peace and joy.

CHAPTER XXXVI.

On the 14th of April, 1865, Mr. Phillippo makes the following entry in his diary:—"A list of questions was this day received from the Governor relative to the condition of the peasantry in the country, as a consequence of Dr. Underhill's letter to the Right Hon. E. Cardwell, Colonial Secretary of State, to which I replied, and sent a copy of my reply to the Secretary of the Union for the perusal of the brethren, to be forwarded to his Excellency with their approval." The Letter which called forth Mr. Phillippo's explanation was sent to the Colonial Office on the 5th of the preceding January. Its object was to call the attention of the Colonial Minister to the lamentable condition of Jamaica, and to entreat an early interposition on its behalf. For two or three years the most painful representations of the poverty and sufferings of the people, and consequently of the pastors, had been received by the Missionary Committee. Two years of drought had desolated the provision grounds and deprived the peasantry of their usual food. The American War, and increased taxation on imports, made costly the supply of breadstuffs, employment necessarily failed, and the moral and spiritual improvement of the people had come to a stand. Other matters affecting the well-being of the population were also brought to the Minister's attention. The increase of crime, owing to the prevailing poverty, was alarming. Work on the estates was scarcely to be had; nor had the estate owners capital to employ the labourers, who, since slavery, had rapidly increased in numbers. The Legislature made no effort to improve the condition of the people. Its members were elected by a mere fraction, and they legislated in favour of their own class, imposing the burdens of the State unequally, and refusing just tribunals.*   "It is more than time," said the Letter, "that the unwisdom (to use the gentlest term) that has governed Jamaica since emancipation should be brought to an end—a course of action which, while it incalculably aggravates the misery arising from natural and, therefore, unavoidable causes, renders certain the ruin of every class, planter and peasant, European and Creole."

This letter was forwarded by Mr. Cardwell to Lieutenant-Governor Eyre, with instructions to report on its contents.

In the course of a few weeks, it was sent by him direct to the custodes of parishes, to the judges and magistrates, to the Bishop of Kingston, and through official channels to the clergy and ministers of all denominations. It was accompanied by a circular requesting these various parties to furnish his Excellency with the materials for his report to the Colonial Office. It was but natural that the subject, under such circumstances, should almost exclusively occupy public attention. The columns of the press teemed with articles, and, as the Governor took no steps to ascertain from the people themselves the nature of their complaints, or the causes of the distress under which they groaned, meetings were called in almost every parish, attended by orderly and patient crowds, to record their

---

* Lord Grey's observations on this point are very remarkable: The Assembly "have used their power to spare their own friends, and to burden severely those who were opposed to them. The affairs of the administration were distinguished by corruption, jobbing, and they exhibited a total want of judgment in the local authorities in adapting their measures to the existing state of things."

grievances and to ask for redress. In every case these "Underhill meetings," as they were called, "endorsed" the statements of the Letter. At the Spanish Town meeting, on the 16th of May, at which Mr. Phillippo was present and gave his hearty sympathy, but in which he took no part, "the present depressed state of the inhabitants of the colony" was deplored; and it was stated that "the meeting views with alarm the distressed condition of nearly all classes of the people from the want of employment, in consequence of the abandonment of estates, and the staple of the country being no longer remunerative, caused by being brought into unequal competition with slave-grown produce." The third resolution expressed sympathy "with the distressed state of the mechanics, who are suffering from the injustice done to them by the Legislature having imposed the same import duty of $12\frac{1}{2}$ per cent. on the raw materials as on the manufactured articles imported into the island." The fifth resolution gives, as an example of distress: "That there are in Spanish Town, the capital of this island, nearly 150 carpenters, 60 masons, 91 shoemakers, 127 tailors, 772 sempstresses, and 800 servants—that is, about 1,900 individuals out of an adult population of 3,124 of all classes, many of whom are without knowing where to obtain their daily bread, and all of whom are suffering more or less from the high prices of food and raiment and excessive taxation." A seventh resolution "corroborated Dr. Underhill's statements," and thanked him for "the sympathy he evinced towards suffering humanity in this island."

The reply of the Baptist missionaries to the Governor's circular was a document of great value and importance. It consisted of returns supplied by almost every Baptist missionary, both coloured and European, and deals with nearly every part of the island. It is remarkable for its

moderation and candour, for the carefulness with which
the facts were collected and its conclusions formed.
The missionaries were possessed of the best means of
information. Their congregations were in the main
composed of the labouring classes, and, from their
intimate relations and constant intercourse with them,
they had every opportunity of knowing the truth. From
the facts thus accumulated, it was but too painfully
evident that the distress was not confined to any one class
of the community, and that the proprietary and peasantry
were suffering alike. It was beyond controversy that the
number of estates under cultivation was yearly becoming
less, and on those in work the cultivation was considerably
diminished. The small settlers, by their industry, frugality,
and thrift, were better off; but even they felt the unjust
pressure of taxation. The landless labouring classes were
stricken down by poverty, low wages, irregular employment, and the high price of food and clothing. The evidence of Mr. Phillippo, from his long residence in Jamaica,
and his known moderation and truthfulness, was particularly
valuable. He states that within the range of his observation there was very great poverty. Cases of real distress
were very numerous. The clothing of the people, both
as to quality and quantity, was not so good as formerly.
Numbers who formerly possessed horses, breeding mares,
mules, donkeys, and small stock were now unable to keep
them. "I think I am within the truth in saying that
upwards of a hundred of the labouring classes in this
parish who used to keep horses and carts have been
obliged to part with them or to discontinue their use within
the last two or three years. I have seen from thirty to
forty horses and carts frequently on the mission premises
on a Sabbath-day, by which whole families were conveyed
to the house of God and the Sabbath-school. Within the
last two years they have been reduced to a third of the

number. Many who manifested a blamable fondness for dress are now in rags, while numbers are scarcely ever seen at public worship from insufficiency of necessary apparel. Nearly one-half of my congregation absent themselves from this cause alone."

On the causes of this distress Mr. Phillippo is not less explicit. "They are," he says:—"(1) Long-prevalent epidemic sickness, measles, whooping-cough, small-pox, and fever of a malignant type; at one time excessive rain, then droughts, with unpropitious seasons, the first rotting provisions, the second withering them. (2) Heavy taxes on the working stock of the peasantry. (3) Excessive dearness of imported articles of food. (4) Want of employment. (5) Inadequate wages. In the lowlands of the parish the people have suffered much from heavy imports on their taxable property, particularly on their horses and carts. On the imposition of the exorbitant tax on their carts and horses the death-blow was given to the commerce and resources and aspirations of the growers of provisions. The market fees are also high and capriciously collected, while the confidence of the people in their representatives had been shaken by their mistaken policy."

The excitement created among all sections of the community by the Governor's distribution of the Letter was greatly increased among the poorer classes by the issue from Government House of two placards purporting to be the "Queen's Advice" to the peasantry of Jamaica, in reply to an appeal for her sympathy and aid. The existence of distress was not denied, but the peasantry were assured that they were labouring under misapprehension as to the better condition of the similar classes in other countries, and that they had only to exercise their own industry and prudence in order to enjoy the means of prosperity within their reach. This "Advice" was felt as a mockery of their distress. It added to the irritation and mistrust already existing. Many Baptist ministers refused to publish the placards, as they were requested to do by the Executive, as only likely to aggravate the universal discontent.

"A bundle of these proclamations," says Mr. Phillippo, " was sent to me to be posted up in every public place of the district I frequented, accompanied with the request that I would read it, with suitable observations, to my congregations. But I did neither—first, Because the people were perfectly peaceable ; secondly, Because doing so would be likely to exasperate such as might be dissatisfied ; and, thirdly, Because they would think the proclamation was the result of 'lies' told to 'Missis Queen,' which they said the Governor and the House of Assembly were always doing, to destroy their character. I was censured for my disobedience by some in authority ; but I judged that I acted right to let well alone. There are few things that disturb and irritate the people here more than the impression that the authorities endeavour to give them a bad character to the Queen." *

* In a letter, written to Dr. Underhill, dated September 8, 1865, Mr. G. W. Gordon thus refers to this "Advice" :—" Mr. Eyre, the Governor, has issued a letter of Mr. Cardwell as the ' Queen's Advice.' This document is extensively circulated and sent to all the ministers of religion.　By several it has been accepted and read in the churches for effect, so that the poor people begin to think that there is no hope for them.　The planters rejoice over it, and seem delightfully encouraged in their acts of unreasonableness and oppression. The condition of the people continues deplorable, especially in the sugar districts, and nowhere that I have been more so than in the parish of Vere.　The state of matters here is really serious—children naked and starving, and coolies too ; adults in misery, and not having raiment even to come out to the meeting. From these causes the places of worship are nearly empty, and the schools badly attended, so that, in point of fact, the social fabric is giving way." He further gives a deplorable picture of the way in which the poor were treated by the planter magistracy, and no redress could be obtained from the Governor.

The climax was reached on the 7th of October, when a court of petty sessions was held at Morant Bay. An unsatisfactory and partial decision of the magistrates led to the release of the prisoner by a disorderly mob, and then to the issue of warrants against Paul Bogle and others who had taken part in the fray. Resistance was made to the service of the warrants on the following Monday, the police were seized and beaten, and only released on their taking an oath to side with the people. The next day but one the people came from their mountain homes to the meeting of the Vestry in great numbers, some of them armed. In the confusion that speedily arose the Riot Act was read, stones were thrown, and the volunteers, who had been unwisely called out, fired on the crowd, some of whom fell. An attack on the court-house immediately followed. A school-house adjoining and the court-house were set on fire, and, as the parties within attempted to escape, they were set upon and killed. The number of persons who fell a prey to the violence and passions of the mob appears to have been eighteen, and the number of the wounded thirty-one. A wild scene of destruction and disorder ensued. Stores were broken into and ransacked, the prison was assailed and fifty-one prisoners were released.

If resistance to the execution of the unjust decisions of the magistrates was at all preconcerted, which seems doubtful, there can be no doubt it was occasioned by the despair of the people of being treated with justice. In a letter addressed to the Governor, with respect to the events of the 7th, and which he received before the subsequent military excesses began, they pathetically say: "We call upon your Excellency for protection, seeing we are her Majesty's loyal subjects, which protection if refused to will [*sic*] be compelled to put our shoulder to the wheel; as we have been imposed upon for a period of twenty-seven years with due obeisance to the laws of our Queen and country, and we can no longer endure the same."

The flame of the rising immediately spread to the country around. Several estates were ravaged and some of the occupants wounded, but it does not appear that any person was killed, though several seem to have narrowly escaped with their lives.

It is not within the range of this work to describe the methods taken for the suppression of this outbreak. If the riot at Morant Bay was attended by many circumstances of horror, the retribution was frightful. The innocent and guilty suffered alike, and large numbers of persons, without even the mock trial of the courts-martial that were set up, were flogged or shot down, or hanged, to glut the cruel thirst for blood which animated the avenging soldiery. The Royal Commissioners ascertained that at least 439 persons were put to death, and a thousand dwellings of the peasantry destroyed. Six hundred men and women were subjected to cruel floggings, in some instances intensified in cruelty by fine wire inserted in the lash. No condemnation can be stronger than the plain, bare, concluding statements of the Royal Commissioners : "The punishments inflicted were excessive." "The punishment of death was unnecessarily frequent." "The floggings were reckless, and at Bath positively barbarous." "The burning of a thousand homes was wanton and cruel."

The letters of Mr. Phillippo at this time are, as may be supposed, filled with details of these lamentable events, as they came to his knowledge. His first communications to the Mission House appear to have been intercepted by the authorities, so that it is not until nearly the end of December that we obtain a glimpse of the state of things around him. He says :—

"We are still in the midst of a very sad state of things,

which you will have found by the newspapers, notes, and enactments of the House of Assembly I forwarded you by the two last mails—that is, if they have reached you, as it is here understood that all letters suspected of containing anything likely to reflect on the Government authorities here are opened at the post-office; and that, in such cases, the writer is subject to arrest at any hour for sedition, and his papers ruthlessly searched.

"On that account it is that I have addressed you through the medium of Mr. Baynes, and for the same reason you will not at present learn the full particulars of the RIOT in St. Thomas-in-the-East, and the circumstances connected with it. I perceive from the *Evening Star*, kindly sent to me by Mr. Snow, that the matter begins to be seen at home in its true light. I say *begins*, as the intelligence since received will, I have no doubt, open the eyes of the public still wider, and, as I trust, force them to the resolution to have the whole matter most thoroughly and impartially investigated from first to last.

"This must be done in justice to your calumniated missionaries, and for the future good of the island, temporal and spiritual. No effort or expense must be spared to this end, especially by the Christian and philanthropic portion of the people of England. And if activity and determination are more necessary on the part of one section of the Christian community than another, the Dissenters are that portion, as it is evident that every effort will be made, and is now being made, to swamp them.*

---

* Mr. Phillippo here alludes to the violent measures, following on the proclamation of martial law, taken by the House of Assembly to destroy civil liberty, the liberty of the press, and the teaching of all religious bodies, except that of the Churches of England and Rome, the Kirk of Scotland, and the Jews, under the plea of preserving the worship of God from scandalous abuses, superstitious practices, and sedition.

"As an evidence how little we have to expect, it is only necessary to refer to the Bill brought in by the Executive Committee, and, as would seem, with the approval of his Excellency the Governor, but which was rejected, with apparent disdain even, by the House of Assembly.

"One consequence of the new Act since passed will inevitably be, under existing circumstances, that the hope of reduction or removal of the taxes for State-Church purposes is utterly extinguished. Little doubt, indeed, can be entertained that they will be greatly increased by the change.

"With reference, again, to the Public Worship Bill, I herewith forward you the substitute for one which was withdrawn. I am informed that this was drawn up or received the sanction of ministers of different Dissenting denominations (Wesleyans included) in Kingston. It may be as well for me to say that *I had nothing to do with it, entirely repudiating,* as I do, all laws restrictive of full religious liberty. Of the acts of which an ignorant and superstitious Ministry may be guilty I am fully aware; but I believe, irrespective of higher considerations, that such restrictions would be impolitic, and would only increase the evil they propose to cure.

"The Martial Law Bill I forwarded you by last mail, and I am anxious to know what the British public think of it, as it has actually passed into law. By this, the liberty of the press is destroyed, and public opinion, judged so necessary in England to good government, is struck dumb; while, the term 'sedition' being undefined, no one is safe if he make an observation on occurrences around him—none less so than ministers of the Gospel, who have supposed sympathies with the labouring population. They are at the mercy of any ignorant, unprincipled informer to whom five shillings would be a temptation. The evidence of such men may fail to convict the accused, but he may be set upon by the harriers of the press, may have his papers rifled, and, in violation of the Act, may be publicly flogged, or sent to Morant Bay to be tried by court-martial and hanged.

" Is it possible that the British Parliament will sanction such a state of things ?

" Nor is this all. There are Acts passed or in progress equally subversive of liberty and dangerous to the expression of public opinion, to which pray call the attention of some of your legal and philanthropic friends, particularly that, as you will do, of our invaluable Treasurer.*

" I trust you have received the list of the more respectable persons arrested, which I sent you a few weeks since. This, however, was only a part of the number arrested. I will, if possible, forward the entire list, with some particulars respecting the parties, that it may be known how far the *Times* and any other slanderers of the Baptists are implicated in the calamity in St. Thomas-in-the-East.

" I think I before informed you that, among some other efforts I had made on behalf of brother Palmer,† I sent a letter to his Excellency the Governor, asking if any charge was made against him ; if so, as to its nature, and when proceedings would be taken, in order to secure counsel for his defence ; otherwise, that he might be released from his imprisonment, which had then extended over a month (now to nearly two), in a filthy dungeon at Morant

---

* These Acts were disallowed by the home authorities, and ultimately the Legislature of Jamaica itself surrendered all its powers, charters, and privileges into the hands of the Crown. From that time to the present the island has been governed as a Crown colony.

† The Rev. E. Palmer was a coloured Baptist minister, and the pastor of Hanover Street Church in Kingston. He was arrested on the charge of sedition, having attended and spoken at an " Underhill meeting." He was put in irons on board a man-of-war and taken to Morant Bay. After a cruel imprisonment of nearly two months, without trial, he was brought back to Kingston.

Bay. Mrs. Palmer also wrote me, and I replied at once, that her husband should not be victimised without a fair trial. I accordingly advised her to place his case in the hands of Mr. Thomas Oughton, who had previously interested himself in the matter, promising to do my best towards meeting any reasonable expenses, as also to speak to my son, the barrister, to undertake his defence.

" A day or two since both Mrs. Palmer and Mr. Oughton waited on me on the subject, when it was decided not to go to the expense of a ' Habeas Corpus,' but to wait the result of proceedings in the case of the editor of the *County Union,* who had also been arrested on a similar charge, for whom my son was engaged as counsel. The case was argued before the Chief Judge yesterday; and the accused were at once admitted to bail.* I understand that the argument of counsel for the defence was such, supported as it was by the highest legal authority, that, if correct, it vitiates all the past proceedings both as to the declaration of martial law and all its consequences—yes, consequences—the destruction, as is now stated or

---

* Mr. Phillippo himself became one of Mr. Palmer's sureties. Under a law passed by the House of Assembly in its last moments, a Special Commission Court was formed, before which Mr. Palmer was indicted in February—first, for seditious language at an Underhill meeting held in Kingston, five months before the outbreak; and, secondly, with others, for .conspiracy. One indictment was quashed from informality in the impannelling of the jury. It was renewed before the same jury. A conviction was obtained, and a sentence of eight weeks' confinement passed. Up to the day of the trial the terms of the charge were kept from the knowledge of the .prisoner and the defence. The construction of the court and the jury, and the desperate efforts made to secure a conviction in order to gain some apparent justification to the plea of the Governor before the Royal Commissioners, deprived the conviction of all moral value. The indictment for conspiracy broke down altogether, and, at the suggestion of the court itself, was abandoned. Mr. Palmer is still the honoured, though now aged, pastor of the church in Hanover Street.

rumoured, of upwards of 3,000 (!!) of the population of the district and the adjoining ones in which the outbreak occurred.*

" I am happy to say that every part of the island is in peace, and, as it would seem, the revolutionary plots against the white and more respectable coloured inhabitants are entirely without foundation. So also, as would seem, is the complicity in them by the exiles from Haiti, as no evidence has been substantiated against them.

" A Mr. Davis, of the Customs, who was said to have secreted stores of gunpowder beneath the floor of his house, and was arrested on this supposition, and some others under similar circumstances, have been set at liberty, and Mr. Davis has been restored to his office. So with a considerable number of others, after an imprisonment of from six to eight weeks, fed only, if reports are true, on bread and water.

" The Maroons (who committed frightful outrages in St. Thomas-in-the-East) are to become a regular organised force. They have been marched through the island on a visit to their brethren in the different districts of their location, and have everywhere been received with enthusiasm, and feasted to satiety by a certain class of the population. Some ask if this is wise or politic, and, it

---

* The inquiries of the Royal Commission happily reduced this number. Speaking of these events, Professor Goldwin Smith said, at a missionary meeting held in Oxford on the 17th of December, 1866: "The vast atrocities which in the first wild paroxysm of alarm were imputed to the Negro, and which formed a pretext for the most dreadful severities, were afterwards disproved. On the other hand, the worst atrocities imputed to the whites unfortunately cannot be disproved, for they are attested by the damning evidence of their own reports. An English colonel boasts of having forced his wretched prisoners to hang each other. He tells you how he put up a prisoner at four hundred yards as a mark for his riflemen. And then he says that nothing can endear a man to the Established Church so much as a campaign in Jamaica."—The *Missionary Herald*, January, 1867, p. 3.

may be, not without reason.   Detachments of the military
are also sent to most of the principal towns on the sea-
board, and, in some cases, into the interior—in some
instances to the astonishment, and in others, as would
seem by Colonel Whitfield's letter to the Governor, to the
displeasure, of the labouring population."

A month later, January 5th, 1866, Mr. Phillippo continues his narration in the following letter :—

" I have been kindly favoured with several of the English
papers, and am rejoiced to learn from most of them that,
while they naturally deplore and condemn the atrocities
committed by the people on the authorities at Morant Bay,
they condemn in still stronger terms the fearful massacre
that has resulted from the means used for the repression
of the riot, and that indignation has been roused throughout the country by the cold-blooded murders that were
perpetrated in the name of justice after the riot was
quelled.

" I now set myself to the task of jotting down a few
more particulars, which, coming from the neighbourhood
of the late scene of slaughter, may not be uninteresting.
We, even here, are yet without any very definite idea of the
predisposing causes of the outbreak.   They, however,
appear to me more remote and more numerous than
persons at a distance are aware of.   Complaints have
been made of the paramount influence of one family,
which was used adversely to the interests of the people ;
of injustice in the petty courts, of summary ejectments,
of insufficient and unpaid wages, and many other annoyances or grievances too numerous to detail.   These
evidently culminated in the determination of the mis-
guided mass to take the law into their own hands, and
inflict summary punishment upon those they regarded as
their oppressors.   It does not appear that they originally
intended to take away life, or to destroy or appropriate

property; their spirit of revenge was not aroused until fired upon by the volunteers or the police.

" I must not, however, omit one or two other important considerations, tending to account for the dissatisfaction that appears to have prevailed in the minds of the peasantry in St. Thomas-in-the-East, viz., Mr. G. W. Gordon's treatment by his Excellency the Governor for his complaints of the wretched condition of the prison, and of the conduct of some of the authorities—specially of the conduct of the Custos in ejecting Mr. Gordon from his office of churchwarden, and the *extraordinary circumstances* of persecution that followed, all which, considering that it was the result of opposition to *them*—they regarding Mr. Gordon as their only friend—tended naturally to increase the dissatisfaction.

" Nor was this all ; the only remaining friend they had, owing, it is said, to a complaint he, as a special justice, felt himself constrained to make of some exactions by individuals in office, and on some other accounts, was removed, so that they felt themselves abandoned to injustice and misrule, saying they no sooner had a person upon whom they could look as a friend, or one to do them justice, than he was marked for persecution, disgraced, or driven to another parish.*   Lastly, was their appeal to the Queen, whom, I have no hesitation in saying, the whole coloured and black population adore, and the disappointment occasioned by the proclamation of the Governor, was the chief if not the principal cause of dissatisfaction throughout the country.

" You need no additional details of the horrors that were perpetrated on the so-called rebels by the soldiers —Maroon and others of equal savagery — employed in

---

* Mr. Gordon was removed from the magistracy by Governor Eyre, but was reinstated by the Duke of Newcastle, the Colonial Minister at the time, under circumstances of much humiliation to the Governor.

executing summary punishment, or I might tell you of reports still more harrowing than any you have heard,—of men wantonly shot down from the roof of their houses when employed in repairing them ; of women stabbed, in their huts, with children at their breasts, or in other indescribable condition, the children dashed upon the ground and murdered—of men flogged, then hanged—of numbers paraded through the town to execution, with halters round their necks—and of still greater atrocities perpetrated in the woods and open fields. Suffice it to say that the perpetrators of these outrages have fixed a stain upon our country which nothing but their total condemnation by the Government and country will wipe out.

" I perceive that the *Times* and one or two other journals still persist in attributing the outbreak to the Baptists, notwithstanding the decided and palpable evidence that has been brought to bear by Sir Morton Peto and others against their assertions. Men with such proclivities as the editor of the *Times* no argument or amount of evidence would move to recantation. There are, however, others who seem inadvertently to have fallen into the mistake of supposing that, while the Baptist missionaries and their people, in connection with the Baptist Missionary Society, are exonerated from complicity in the riot, the native Baptists, or 'so-called Baptists' in the vocabulary of the Governor, were mostly its originators and agents. This also I consider myself warranted in saying is a mistake. The greater number by far consisted of men connected with no religious society, Africans as ignorant and debased as in their native wilds, supplemented by Church of England men, native Methodists, and others.

" As an evidence of the calumny that seeks to fix the outbreak upon the Baptist body, even including all who bear that name, it is only necessary to contrast the number of that denomination, among the most respectable individuals that have been arrested on suspicion of complicity in the miscalled rebellion, with those belonging directly or indirectly to other communions, and which are as follows :—

  Three Baptists of the Baptist Missionary Society.
  Three native Baptists.
  Three Jews.
  One native Wesleyan.
  One United Methodist.
  One Independent.
  One Scotch Kirk.
  Twenty-six Church of England.
  Thirty and upwards Roman Catholics.

Thus you will see the slender ground upon which our friends were arrested, had their papers rifled, and themselves carried away from their homes and families and cast into a loathsome dungeon for weeks or months. Of the three Baptists first on the list, two have been acquitted, or rather dismissed without charge, leaving one only to take his trial before a commission on the 23rd inst. for imputed seditious expressions at a public meeting held five months anterior to the *émeute.*

"Of the other sixty or seventy, more than two-thirds, after all their losses and sufferings, were told that there were no warrants of detention against them. The residue, about six in number, are out on bail.

"Among other doings which seem to have especially excited the indignation of your journalists and 'humanitarians' at home was the employment of the Maroons in the work of death. And with reason. Fancy them like blood-hounds in full cry upon the track of their victims, or like lions watching for their prey, crouching beneath the thick umbrage of the forest! But what will they think of the policy or humanity of trailing these men through the country, and of extolling and feasting them at festive boards? Past history has surely spoken to our rulers in vain, and the lessons of modern wisdom in statesmanship are equally lost upon them.

" As to the plot that had been so deeply laid for the destruction of all the white inhabitants in Kingston, in which the Haitian refugees were said to be implicated with a view to the transfer of the island to the rule of a new Haitian Republic, it has proved a mere fiction of the imagination. It had not the slightest foundation in fact. It has altogether vanished as a dream, and such as were said to be the principal conspirators were acquitted of the charge. As if to confirm the report of an expected general rising of the people, an individual or two have been arrested on suspicion in several remote parishes, but nothing has been as yet disclosed that would lead to the suspicion that disaffection in an organised form existed beyond the limits of St. Thomas-in-the-East, if even much beyond the precincts of Morant Bay. And what, but to throw dust in the eyes of the British people, is the calling out of the volunteers, special constables, and the police at the present holiday season, including an interval of two or three weeks? All is as peaceful around and everywhere as a stagnant lake, while our rulers, free from fear, have long betaken themselves, alone and unprotected, to their isolated mountain homes, or to the calm quiet of their woods and fields.

" Poor George William Gordon ! my heart bleeds when I think of his untimely death. I cannot for a moment bring my mind to believe that he was in the least privy to the outbreak, or that any man could have a greater horror of such an outbreak. I believe him to be, and ever have done since I first knew him, now many years ago, a sincere, benevolent, and truly godly man. He was called enthusiastic, hypocritical, and many other names which have ever been applied by an ungodly world, and by unreasonable and wicked men in all past times, and as are even now applied, to the greatest of men and the highest ornaments of our country. The men who can stigmatise our Broughams and Gurneys, Buxtons and Petos and Morleys, as *pseudo* - philanthropists and Exeter Hall humanity-mongers, and the noblest and best women in the country as a set of 'idle scandal-mongers,' are capable of any language towards such as condemn their conduct by their Christian zeal and exemplary and consistent lives.

" Among other circumstances of a peculiar character that attended Mr. Gordon's death, and which I have scarcely seen noticed, but which has made a deep impression on the minds of hundreds of people here—which is said, indeed, to have induced the Maroons to desist from their work of blood—was the long-continued shocks of earthquake that occurred on the morning, and about the very hour or moment, of the execution. I was in my room at the time, almost petrified at the severity and length of the vibrations, though not knowing that this was the morning when the martyred spirit of my friend ascended to his blissful inheritance. ' Surely there is a God who judgeth in the earth.' " *

* Lord Chief Justice Cockburn, in his charge to the grand jury in the case of *The Queen v. Nelson and Brand*, thus sums up his review of Gordon's case :—" No doubt a lamentable event has taken place. A man has been condemned, sentenced to death, and executed upon evidence which would not have been admitted before any properly constituted tribunal, and upon evidence which, if admitted, fell altogether short of establishing the crime with which he was charged." In a note he adds, " No one, I think, who has the faintest idea of what the administration of justice involves could deem the proceedings on this trial consistent with justice, or, to use a homely phrase, with that fair play which is the right of the commonest criminal."—"A Charge by the Lord Chief Justice of England, &c." (London: Ridgway, 1867), pp. 153, 165. The same view was taken by the Royal Commissioners. They say, " The evidence, oral and documentary, appears to us to be wholly insufficient to establish the charge upon which the prisoner took his trial."—Report, p. 37.

The English Government lost no time in making arrangements for an exhaustive inquiry into these lamentable events. Sir Henry Storks, G.C.B., Russell Gurney, Esq., Q.C., Recorder of the City of London, and J. B. Maule, Esq., Recorder of Leeds, were appointed Royal Commissioners to investigate the origin, nature, and circumstances of the disturbances, and the means adopted for their suppression. They arrived in Jamaica on the 20th of January, 1866, and the Commission was formally opened on the 23rd, the following Tuesday, and from that time till the 21st of March sat daily, without intermission, except on Sundays. They visited the scene of the disturbances and received the testimony of eye-witnesses and of persons of all classes able to throw any light on the subject of their inquiries. The accusations so freely made by Governor Eyre against Baptist missionaries, as well as one of the Secretaries of the Society, as having been more or less implicated in the outbreak, or at all events contributing to it by their letters and speeches, induced the Committee to engage the services of George Phillippo, Esq., who a few years before had been called to the Bar in England, and was now practising in Jamaica, to appear before the Commissioners on their behalf. No attempt, however, was made by Mr. Eyre to establish the charges he had so recklessly made, or, when challenged, to repeat them. In a letter which Mr. Phillippo addressed to Sir Henry Storks, conveying a memorial from all the Baptist missionaries, then in annual session in Spanish Town, requesting an opportunity of vindicating before the Commissioners both themselves and the Secretary from the charges expressed or implied of being "accessory to the riot at Morant Bay," they received the reply that his Excellency the President " could not accede to the request as no evidence had been given before the Commissioners affecting the character of Dr. Underhill or the Baptist missionaries in relation to the recent disturbances in St. Thomas-in-the-East."

It must not, however, be forgotten that, by the seizure of their letters in the Post Office, and by listening to every foolish rumour in the island, the most active efforts had been made to find "matter of wrong" against them. Mr. Phillippo records that persons were set "as spies to note the principal persons who frequented" his residence, and, "as I was known to be a friend of Gordon's, it was presumed that I might have been in league with him and other promoters of the ' widespread sedition,' or rebellion, conjured up by Mr. Eyre and his half-demented auxiliaries." Happily, every attempt to implicate Mr. Phillippo and his brethren utterly failed, and Mr. Phillippo especially enjoyed frequent opportunities, in his intercourse with Sir Henry Storks and the other Commissioners, of knowing that their conduct was approved, and their character held in the highest estimation, by these gentlemen. As touching these matters, they were blameless. There was not the shadow of excuse for the obnoxious and calumnious charges brought forward by Mr. Eyre in his despatches to the home Government. The ordeal through which the accused missionaries passed left their honour unstained, their integrity untouched, and their Christian character undimmed.

On the general question of the state of feeling among the peasantry, and their condition, several of the missionaries, however, were called to appear. As Mr. Phillippo's evidence is very brief, the substance of it, as recorded by himself, may here be given :—

"I am the oldest Baptist missionary, and, I believe, of any religious denomination in the island. I have been in Jamaica nearly forty-three years. My knowledge extends over the whole island, but I have not been to Morant Bay, in St. Thomas-in-the-East and Portland, until lately.

I have been most acquainted during the last few years with the parishes of St. Catherine, the high lands of St. Thomas-in-the-Vale, St. Dorothy, and St. John. My knowledge of numbers of the people in these parishes has been intimate, having had, I may say, continual intercourse with them as a minister of the Gospel, and in various other ways as a pastor, and in my efforts to improve their social condition. I established the village of Sligoville and several others, and promoted education among the people by the establishment and support of schools during forty years. Sligoville, as a missionary station and village, was begun before the termination of the apprenticeship system. It is a very extensive village; I am not certain as to the number of the population. The people, with scarcely an exception, are sober, peaceable, and industrious. There has never been a grog-shop in the settlement from the time of its first establishment to the present day. Not the slightest indication of disaffection appeared among the people, either at Sligoville or in any other part of the country with which I am familiar, either before the outbreak or during the time of the excitement caused by it, or since. The people were all most peaceable, quiet, loyal. Nothing occurred at any of my stations in the parishes I have named that excited in my mind the least suspicion of discontent with the constituted authorities, or of any intended disobedience to law. There might have been expressions of complaint on account of poverty and distress, but none of disaffection."

On the 1st of March, Mr. Phillippo, accompanied by the Rev. Thomas Lea, started on a visit to the parish of St. Thomas-in-the-East. This journey, which occupied about ten days, was undertaken at the request of the Jamaica Baptist Union, with the object of ascertaining the practicability of commencing a mission in Morant Bay and its vicinity. The subject had been earnestly pressed on Mr.

Phillippo's attention by Sir Henry Storks, who also, on his return to England, had an interview with the Treasurer and Secretaries of the Society to urge upon them the same duty. Mr. Phillippo mentions that they came upon "numerous evidences of the devastation occasioned by the late outbreak and of its repression, and many tales and sights of distress resulting from them exacted our sympathies with the sufferers." The issue of their inquiries was most encouraging, and, before the close of the year, the Committee placed at the disposal of the Jamaica missionaries a sum sufficient to establish stations in and around Morant Bay, and to maintain them in operation for three years. The period of support was afterwards extended to seven years, and, under the energetic action of the Rev. W. Teall, to whose hands the work was committed, efficient churches were established and suitable buildings purchased or erected at Morant Bay and Monklands. The mission in this district now embraces five stations and churches, under the superintendence of two native pastors, with a membership of 1,080 persons.

CHAPTER XXXVII.

HARTLANDS—1866.

WHILE the Commission was sitting, an event occurred which illustrates in a striking manner some of the chief causes of the Disturbances, and, at the same time, the usefulness, activity, and tact of Mr. Phillippo.

It was suddenly announced that a calamity like that at Morant Bay was impending at a settlement called Hartlands, about five miles from Spanish Town, and measures were taken, at the instigation of the partisans of Mr. Eyre, that threatened another " carnival of blood."* The narrative can, happily, be given in Mr. Phillippo's own words :—

" The land on which this settlement was established belonged to a merchant of the name of Hart, and comprised about 2,500 acres. The village was situated about five

---

* Mr. Eyre immediately availed himself of this incident to justify his proceedings at Morant Bay. In a letter he addressed to Sir Henry Storks, on the 6th of April, after referring to the despatch of troops to Hartlands on the 14th of March, he says :—" This incident shows forcibly the state of feeling amongst the Negroes even now in respect to such questions [that is, the occupation of land]; and as there are many cases very similar to that at Hartlands all over the island, but without the advantage of their being near the seat of Government, and within the immediate reach of a large military force, it is almost certain that great difficulty, if not disturbance, will arise wherever attempts are made to ascertain whether the Negro occupants have any legal right to the lands upon which they have located themselves."—Parliamentary Papers on Disturbances in Jamaica, February, 1866, p. 312.

miles from Spanish Town. Almost immediately after the abolition of slavery, portions of this land, in an uncultivated state, were purchased by people principally from the neighbouring estates.

" Some of these, at periods varying with their circumstances, paid for their allotments and had their titles; some paid by instalments, and had receipts given them on that condition. The original proprietor, some years after, died, and his affairs were transferred to his son, or were left in the hands of executors on his behalf. This gentleman neglected his interests at Hartlands for nearly twenty years, hardly considering them, it is supposed, worth the time and attention they demanded. During this long period, trespasses were said to have been committed on the portions of the land unsold. The attention of the proprietor being at length called to the matter, the settlers were required to show the legality of their claims. Some few exhibited their titles, others their receipts, and others again declared that they had paid in full or by instalments for their purchases to an agent appointed by the original proprietor, who had absconded with their money, or, at least, had not accounted for it to his employer, and on various pretences gave them no acknowledgment. Many of the receipts, and some of the titles, were taken to the present owner of the unsold land, and left with him at his request, in order, as he represented, that he might have the opportunity of acquainting himself with the circumstances of the case as they related to each individual settler. Soon after— namely, in 1862—the great fire in Kingston occurred, in which these papers were consumed, together with the premises in which they were deposited. After the lapse of some years, during which the matter was again at rest, the proprietor or claimant sent a surveyor to survey the lands, including that portion of them which comprehended the settlement or homesteads of the people. This was regarded by the latter, many of whom possessed titles and receipts, as an attempt to dispossess them indiscriminately of their holdings, in violation of their rights ; and they quietly, but determinately, resisted by forming themselves in line across the private road, for such it was, leading to the settlement, demanding of the intruders their authority, and signifying their determination to protect their rights by an appeal to law. On this account these people were denounced as squatters, thieves, robbers, factious outlaws, conspirators against lawful authority, &c. With equal untruthfulness also they were said to have possessed themselves of ammunition and firearms—to have thrown up barricades at every entrance to their settlement, &c.— reports which were proved to be utterly without foundation on the authority of the police sent to ascertain the truth ; and their settlement was stigmatised as the asylum or rendezvous of the refuse and scum of the population of the island—in every sense a real modern Alsatia.

"During the suppression of the outbreak at Morant Bay, or rather after the riot there had terminated, threats of exterminating the settlement at Hartlands by the military were common in Spanish Town, and that these threats would be executed as soon as they returned from St. Thomas-in-the-East. About this time I became accidentally acquainted with two or three of the principal persons of the village, and, after referring pleasantly to the notorious character that was given them, I inquired if there would be any opposition by the people generally if I visited and preached to them. Fully assured to the contrary, I fixed the day, and met three or four hundred, who were most orderly, attentive, and courteous. This was before the riot at Morant Bay, and I repeated my visit immediately after the arrival of the Royal Commissioners. In the midst of the sittings of the latter, I casually heard that a body of police, headed by the county inspector and accompanied by a surveyor, had repeated the attempt to survey the lands with a view of ejecting the inhabitants, and that the people, as before, although without any intention of resorting to force, as they declared at the time, besides being without any weapons of offence whatever, quietly, and even pleasantly, yet decidedly, refused permission for them to proceed. These gentlemen, after calling upon witnesses to prove opposition, returned to report to the authorities. The next morning, to my astonishment, I heard that a strong body of police and of the military were on their way to Hartlands, unknown to Sir Henry Storks, or at all events not by his order, and that another Morant Bay tragedy might be apprehended. I immediately hastened to Government House and offered my services to Sir Henry Storks to endeavour to influence the people to obviate such calamity by acquiescing in such an arrangement as would not jeopardise their rights. Sir Henry Storks at once acceded to my request, and, as no time was to be lost, a carriage was at once placed at my disposal by one of the Royal Commissioners. I overtook the police and military when within a mile or two from the settlement, told my object to the inspector of the police, and begged them to halt and not enter the village. I immediately mounted a horse, lent me by the inspector, and proceeded about two or three miles along the settlement, calling the inhabitants, who were standing in groups by their cottages, to meet me in the road on my return. Finding out the principal men, I urged my advice upon them, stating that I had authority to say their claims, if they had any, would be considered, notwithstanding the survey that was to be made; although my object was simply to prevent their ejectment, and the probable destruction of their property, if not of life. They unanimously said,

' Minister is our friend, and we will do what he tells us. The surveyor can go on.' The people followed me in crowds, at my request, to announce this to the police and military, who had by this time advanced near the village, where they halted. I then urged their return. They complied, on condition that I would guarantee the preservation of the peace, or be responsible for any adverse consequences. I agreed, and continued all day on horseback to fulfil my pledge. The soldiers returned, and peace and quietness were preserved. Danger did exist two or three times from provocations by some of the soldiers and others ; but that was ultimately obviated by my promise to those assaulted to present their complaints to his Excellency, which I did the next morning.

" On the following morning I saw the Governor, and communicated to him the occurrences of the day and the results, when I had the honour to receive his thanks. The affairs of Hartlands now shared the particular interest of his Excellency, he having repeated interviews with the deputations from the people. He arranged that the matter between the contending parties should be settled by arbitration. In the meantime the people were advised not to assure themselves too confidently that their hopes in this respect would be realised, but to provide against probable defeat by uniting their contributions to secure the services of a competent and respectable solicitor. The people failed to act on this advice, repeatedly given, partly, as they afterwards said, from inability to meet the expense, from having for years been drained of all their little means without advantage, and partly in the confident hope that the terms proposed by his Excellency the Governor would ultimately be acceded to. The matter, however, was successively postponed by the claimants, until Sir H Storks' functions as Governor ceased. In the interval, as it would seem, between the departure of Sir Henry Storks and that on which a representation could be properly made to the new Governor, Sir J. P. Grant, the claimants, without apprising the defendants of their design, had applied to a court of law, and, there being consequently no representative of the claims of the people present on the occasion, judgment went against them by default, and a writ was issued for the summary ejectment of certain of the inhabitants from their houses and grounds. The deputy-marshal, surveyor, and some police and other attendants lost no time in attempting to enforce the orders of the court. The parties concerned were thus taken by surprise, and the whole settlement thrown into commotion, apprehending that the purposes of their antagonists were now sought to be accomplished by stratagem. The executors of the law, therefore, were again civilly, but decidedly, opposed, those more immediately concerned insisting that the matter was to have been settled by arbitration, and that they had been unfairly dealt with by their opponents ; their feelings, at the same time, were somewhat provoked by the taunt of one of the attendants on the officials, that it ' was not Governor Storks' time now,' thus conveying the impression that an advantage had actually been taken of them, if not an act of injustice perpetrated towards them.

"Representations of this renewed obstruction was at once made to the principal authorities of the parish, and a body of police was ordered to accompany the deputy-marshal and others, to compel obedience by force ; while it was rumoured that a detachment of military was ordered to be in readiness in the event of failure by the police.

"At this stage, his Excellency Sir J. P. Grant signified his desire for an interview with me on the subject. I promised, as the result of his Excellency's representations,

A A

and on a sufficient knowledge of all the circumstances then existing to enable me to act justly towards the opposing parties, to do all in my power to induce the people to yield to the requirements of the authorities. The documents were forwarded to me, and from them, added to some explanations from a party well acquainted with the subject in all its bearings, I resolved to prevent the apprehended disturbance at once. My purpose was to go in person to Hartlands to see the people collectively; but, subject as I had been for some time previously to serious indisposition, I was induced from this cause, and the inclement state of the weather, to send a messenger to request the principal people to come as a deputation to me in town, I purposing, at the same time, to go to them personally if necessary. About forty of them soon after arrived. I explained to them all the circumstances of the case, and urged their compliance with the terms proposed, especially as they included some favourable conditions I had recently secured by conferences with one of the opposing parties.

"To these terms they unanimously acceded; and each individually expressed his acquiescence in my proposal, all pledging themselves to allow the writ of ejectment to be executed without resistance or complaint.

" I immediately represented the promise thus made me to the Governor, and he ordered the detachment to return to Kingston accordingly.

"On the following morning the deputy-marshal, at my request, proceeded to the settlement alone and unarmed. And thus, unattended, he executed the writ, I only sending an intelligent person to see that no cause was given by either party for collision or dispute. On the evening of the day, both the deputy-marshal and the messenger returned and reported that the writ had been duly executed, and that without the slightest interruption.

I announced this fact to his Excellency the Governor, and received his kind acknowledgment as follows :—

"'Sir,—The Provost Marshal General having officially reported the peaceable execution of the writ of ejectment on the settlers at Hartlands, the Governor desires me, on this satisfactory conclusion of the business, to convey to you his cordial thanks for the assistance you have rendered on this occasion to the Government.

"'It is a matter of gratification to his Excellency, and it must be so to yourself, that the people were induced voluntarily to obey the law, and without the exhibition of force on the part of the Government; and he is sensible that your active personal exertions, and the pains you took to advise the people, and to explain to them their legal position, have very materially contributed to this satisfactory result.

"'I have the honour to be, your obedient Servant,
"'HENRY T. IRVING.'

"At the time when the action of the military was obviated, as stated at the commencement of this narrative, Messrs. Harvey and Brewin, the deputation from the Society of Friends, were in Spanish Town, who, hearing of the circumstances, as also of the great destitution of the inhabitants of Hartlands (supposed to amount to upwards of 2,000, all ages) of religious and lettered instruction in regard both to themselves and children, as also their desire for these advantages, very kindly offered to give twenty pounds per annum for three years towards the support of a schoolmaster among them possessing the necessary qualifications as to piety and practical teaching. I almost immediately made arrangements for the establishing of the school, very kindly aided as to some of the minor requirements by two or three proprietors in the neighbourhood. The scholars soon amounted to eighty,

while adults in considerable numbers expressed themselves anxious to avail themselves of the advantages to be
offered by the proposed formation of a night or evening
class. The school was thus commenced under very
favourable circumstances."

Subsequently a suitable school-house was built, and
also a chapel to accommodate two hundred hearers. A
church, however, was not formed till the year 1872, and it
consists, at the present time, of rather more than seventy
members.

CHAPTER XXXVIII.

DURING his brief stay in Jamaica as a Royal Commissioner and the temporary Governor, Sir Henry Storks won golden opinions from all classes. This was fully expressed in an address, prepared by Mr. Phillippo, and signed by upwards of three thousand of the inhabitants of St. Catherine's and the contiguous parishes. The personal and social character of his Excellency had no small share in reconciling differences and in promoting the harmony and good-will which, with few exceptions, prepared the way for the inauguration of the new system of government.

On the recall of Mr. Eyre, which followed immediately on the presentation of the Report of the Royal Commissioners to the Queen, Sir John Peter Grant was appointed Governor, and arrived in the island in the first days of August, 1866. The new Legislative Council met for the first time on the 16th of October. It consisted partly of official personages and partly of prominent civilians nominated by the Crown, and its proceedings speedily displayed a striking contrast to the representative system which it superseded. All departments of the administration underwent the severest scrutiny, and changes of the greatest importance were rapidly introduced. District courts, under stipendiary magistrates sent from England, with improvements of procedure, ensured justice to the people, and not a little stir was made when it became distinctly clear that neither colour nor class could pervert or hinder the due administration of the law. "These judicial changes," says the most recent historian of Jamaica,* "have had a marked effect upon the community at large. Confidence in the rectitude of legal decisions is now general; old abuses have been swept away, and simple, but effectual, remedies are provided for those who are compelled to have recourse to law."

The taxes, at first rendered more burdensome in order to provide for the cost of the " Disturbances " and the heavy deficits of preceding Governments, were modified and more fairly levied, the Governor seeking, through Mr. Phillippo, the aid of the missionaries to reconcile the people to this increase with the promise of ultimate relief. Mr. Phillippo's communication was addressed to the secretary of the Jamaica Baptist Union, the committee of which institution was then in session at Rio Bueno. It was dated March 30, 1867. After stating that it was His Excellency's desire to avoid either dissatisfaction or misrepresentation with respect to the new taxation, and his hope that the ministers of the denomination would, in a quiet and unostentatious manner, endeavour to quiet any discontent that might arise, he says that the increase was owing to the lavish expenditure of former Governments, to the expenses incurred through the recent calamities, and to the formation of new courts of justice which would give ready and cheap redress to the labouring classes. As a compensation the taxes would be more equally levied, and many beneficial reforms be introduced, such as a system of education, which would have in view the welfare of all classes, even the poorest. His Excellency deeply regretted the necessity for these new imposts, but ultimately the people would reap an

---

* Gardner, p. 498.

ample return from the changes that would ensue. " I
need make no apology to my brethren," he concludes,
" for consenting to become the medium of this communication. My residence in Spanish Town naturally led His
Excellency to avail himself of my services for this
purpose."

The promise of alleviation in the burdens of the people
has been amply fulfilled, and in later years the revenue,
partly aided by the improving condition of the country, has
been found more than sufficient to meet the expenditure.
The debt of the colony has been reduced,* and many
useful institutions, such as hospitals and dispensaries, have
been established from the annual surplus. Savings
banks have been placed on a permanent basis, and the
defalcations of former years checked. The post-office
and the roads have undergone great improvement, and
immigration has been brought under more effective
control.

But the greatest and most important of the changes
introduced by Sir John P. Grant were the disestablishment of the English Church and the introduction of a
system of elementary education for the entire body of the
people. The latter was among the first of the many
subjects which engaged the attention of the Governor.
In September, scarcely a month after his arrival, Mr.
Phillippo records that, " having been introduced to Sir
John P. Grant by Sir Henry Storks, I was favoured with
frequent opportunities of intercourse with him. On the
6th of September, after kindly acknowledging the receipt
of my volume on Jamaica, he expressed his desire for my
opinion on the subject of education, when the question
came up before the Council. His Excellency soon after

---

* The public debt in 1867 was a trifle less than £719,000. It was
reduced in 1877 to a little more than £485,000. Since 1868 the
addition to the taxation has been little or nothing.

requested me to call upon him on that and other matters."
A circular addressed to the ministers of all the religious
bodies in the island quickly followed, forty copies of
which were sent to Mr. Phillippo for distribution among
his missionary brethren. To this he replied in a long
and elaborate letter, giving the results of his experience
and practical knowledge during forty years.

The new regulations were placed in the hands of the
Legislative Council in July, 1867, and were adopted, with
a few modifications suggested by Mr. Phillippo and others.
The old House of Assembly had for many years devoted
some £1,400 or £1,500 a year to the purposes of education, but the grants were made to a few favoured institutions only, while nothing was done to promote instruction
among the masses of the population. The principles of
the new system were those with which Sir J. P. Grant was
already familiar as an old East India Governor, and which
were laid down for the promotion of education in India
by the celebrated despatch of Sir Charles Wood in 1854.
It was a system of grants-in-aid, apportioned to the
position of the school as to numbers and the attainments
of the scholars, as tested in an annual examination by
Government Inspectors, judged by certain standards fixed
from time to time by the administration.

Up to this time the schools under missionary superintendence were for the most part independent of Government assistance ; in the case of Baptist schools universally
so, from conscientious objections to any kind of State aid,
which would have carried with it a certain measure of
interference with the religious instruction imparted in
them. Not a few also thought that education, like religion,
was better left to the voluntary efforts of Christian men.
These had been the views of Mr. Phillippo in the early
years of his ministry. But the regulations now adopted
were so comprehensive and liberal in their scope, so

free from attempts or prospect of interference with the religious principles of the managers of the schools, that in a short time the most ardent voluntaries gave way, and the Government school system was accepted throughout the island. It has proved a great success.* At the time of its establishment in 1867 there were 329 elementary schools in the island, for the most part conducted by the ministers of religion. That useful superintendence has not been withdrawn, but the mission-schools are now everywhere merged in the Government system. In 1878 there were 617 schools under inspection, with a registered body of 51,488 children attending them, and the character of the schools has greatly improved.†

The excessive proportion of the revenue appropriated to the support of the Episcopal Church did not escape the attention of the Royal Commissioners, and among Sir John Peter Grant's earliest measures to avert the bankruptcy which threatened the country was one already suggested to Sir H. Storks by the Bishop of Kingston, which threw the miscellaneous charges connected with Church services on the voluntary contributions of the congregations. A saving to the State was thus effected of about £7,000 a year. Some reforms were also introduced in the appointments of the clergy, and several livings in places where their services were not required were left unfilled. Still the entire charge of the Establishment, notwithstanding these reforms, remained at about £40,000

---

* An interesting proof of the growing influence of education is seen in the quantity of books imported. In 1866-67, the value of the importation was £624; in 1876-77, £9,628.

† In 1868, the first year of the new system, only 96 schools could be classed out of the 286 submitted to inspection; in 1878, out of 617 schools, only 44 were left unclassed. The expenditure of the Government on elementary education is now little short of £20,000 a year.

a year. The system was so ill-managed that, in the judgment of the Governor, less than half the money would have afforded a better result than that which was secured by this large outlay. " Practically, the clergy were under no effective control ; for if they avoided gross offences they could not be corrected. Several of them were physically incapacitated, but none could be forced to retire. There was no retiring pension. Whilst the Establishment could boast of many excellent, hard-working, and useful men, there were some upon it whose usefulness was as nothing, or as next to nothing. For such cases there was no remedy. Whilst at some places there were more clergymen than were wanted (an all but empty church being sometimes found close to a fully attended meeting-house), extensive and populous tracts of country were left destitute of all religious instruction of any sort. Such being its condition, that the Established Church was in discredit was not surprising."* Besides all this, the number of adherents claimed as belonging to the Church of England, and which included nearly all the white population, for the most part well able to support their own religious institutions, did not number more than a twelfth part of the entire community.†

The expiration of the Clergy Bill at the end of the year 1869 presented a favourable opportunity for a considera-

---

* *Jamaica Gazette*, December 18, 1869. Despatch from Sir J. P. Grant to Earl Granville, dated July 23, 1869.

† Sir J. P. Grant estimated the population of Jamaica at 460,000 souls. The clergy claimed as their average congregations 31,638 persons; the Nonconformist communities an average attendance of 80,896. According to the Bishop of Kingston, the number of persons under the charge of Nonconformist ministers was 200,000, which the Governor thought was about the correct figure. On the other hand, it was an excessive estimate to take the entire body of adherents to the Establishment at 100,000.—*Jamaica Gazette*, December 18, 1869.

tion of the entire question of State support ; and accordingly the Jamaica Baptist Union, at their meeting in 1866, in anticipation of it, requested Mr. Phillippo and his son-in-law, the Rev. W. Claydon, to open communications with other Nonconformist bodies on the island, and also with the Liberation Society of England, for the purpose of organising an opposition to its renewal. Petitions and memorials to the Queen and to the Governor were presented, in which it was urged that there ought to be no renewal of the Clergy Act, but that on its expiring the churches of the people of Jamaica should be left to the action of the voluntary principle. The petition of Mr. Phillippo and his congregations argued that the connection between the Church and State was hostile to liberty of conscience ; was unjust to all other denominations in the island ; that it was unnecessary as well as inexpedient, impolitic, and inequitable, from the inefficiency of the clergy and their cost ; that it was contrary to the teaching of Holy Scripture ; and that it was opposed to the best interests of Jamaica as much as the disestablished Church of Ireland had been to the inhabitants of that country. Thousands of suitable tracts, furnished by the Liberation Society, were scattered throughout the island ; and at its expense a large edition of a series of letters, published in the first instance in an island newspaper by Mr. Phillippo, was issued. These letters, in their collected form, were entitled, " The Practical Working of the Voluntary Principle in America ; or, Facts for the Episcopalians of Jamaica." It had a wide circulation, and is marked by that fulness and accuracy of information which is a striking feature of all the author's productions. It was from no special hostility towards Episcopalians, he says, that he had taken part in the controversy. " I only object to the connection of their denomination, as I should to any other, with the State—to the support of its ministers and its institutions from the public revenue, and to the injustice and hardship suffered by Nonconformists, who compose three-fourths of the population, and who are mostly of the poorest, in being compelled to contribute towards the church of the wealthy, while they at the same time feel it their duty to support their own establishments."

Writing to a friend on the 8th of October, 1868, Mr. Phillippo gives a very lively account of the agitation in progress. "We Baptists have been inundating the Council Chamber with petitions against the renewal of the Clergy Act, soon to expire, and for the entire separation of Church and State. We possibly have gone too far in creating such a clamour so long before the matter is likely to come before the Council, but it will show our friends at home that we are alive to our condition and rights. We are emphatically the fighting sect. Some others cheer us on, but seem afraid of sharing the obloquy and labour of the first onset with us. Our Presbyterian brethren have shown their sympathy with us in combination, but our Independent brethren are slow in taking the field. From the Wesleyans we have no hope of aid at present. I am not sanguine about the total disestablishment of the Church, but I see that the subject assumes an improved aspect in the minds of the higher classes here, who are mostly Presbyterians and Jews."

The struggle was not confined to Jamaica. In England, in 1868, Mr. Mills obtained from the Conservative Government of the day a measure, which passed without opposition, to withdraw on the deaths of the recipients the grants amounting to £20,300 annually paid out of the Consolidated Fund for the ecclesiastical establishments of the West Indies, of which £7,100 fell to the share of Jamaica. The Bishop of Jamaica was non-resident, and, till his death in 1872, never visited the diocese from which he gained his title and salary of £3,000 a year. In June, 1869, two deputations waited upon the Colonial Secretary, with whom the decision virtually rested, one consisting of Presbyterians from Scotland, the other composed of members of various Dissenting bodies and of persons specially interested in Jamaica. For some time it had been understood that the English Government contemplated a system of "concurrent endowment;" but this idea found no favour either with the Governor of Jamaica or with the Nonconformists. In November Earl Granville definitely informed Sir J. P. Grant that "concurrent endowment" must be regarded as impossible, and that even the mild proposal of the Governor to 'support schoolmasters in outlying districts of the island, who, though not ostensibly ministers of the Gospel, should devote their spare time and their Sundays to the religious instruction of the people, could not probably be adopted, because of the opposition it would excite.'

At length, on the 10th of December, the Governor announced to the Legislative Council a measure for the complete disestablishment of the Church of England in the colony, subject only to the continued payment of the stipends of the clergy during the lives of the existing incumbents. Disestablishment in Jamaica presented no question of difficulty. There were no Church lands or funds belonging to clerical corporations. There were no tithes, nor any funds whereby an income was assured to the holder of any ecclesiastical office. Even the churches, rectory-houses, and glebes were the property of the State; so that the only support of the clergy was derived from salaries paid out of the taxes, under temporary laws, renewable from time to time at the pleasure of the Legislature. There were, therefore, no vested interests to be provided for. It was simply for the Legislature to withhold the customary appropriations, or to continue them on such terms as they pleased.*

In a letter addressed to the Rev. F. Trestrail, one of the Secretaries of the Society, on the 20th of December, Mr. Phillippo reports the decision of the Legislative Council. "I have to inform you, and I do so with a degree of pleasure I cannot express, that the union between Church and State in Jamaica is dissolved. His Excellency the Governor met the Council a few days since, and laid before them a voluminous correspondence between himself and the Secretary of State for the Colonies on the subject.

"It was rumoured, both in England and in this island, that the Governor had recommended 'concurrent endowment' in his despatch to the home Government. This is now ascertained to have had no foundation in truth. The surmise, however, may be in some measure accounted for from the fact that, from the gloomy representations made to his Excellency of the vast numbers of people in the interior parishes relapsing into barbarism, &c., he proposed—in the belief that such people were unable or unwilling to remunerate ministers for their services, and to build the necessary places of worship—that ministers, of whatever denomination, who settled among them should be aided in their support, and in the erection of the churches and chapels required.

"His Excellency seems to have been of opinion that, under such circumstances, little or no objection would be made, even by Nonconformists, to an arrangement of the kind, and so expressed himself to the noble Earl at the head of the Colonial Department. The Earl, although questioning the concurrence of the Dissenters in such a measure, signified his willingness to acquiesce in the scheme, if concurrence on the part of Nonconformists

---

* Sir J. P. Grant's despatch in *Jamaica Gazette*, par. 4.

was general, but that he would await the result with some anxiety.

"After the meeting of the Council a note was forwarded to the mission-house, marked 'Immediate,' expressing his Excellency's wish to see me. It was Saturday, and I had already gone up to Sligoville for the Sabbath. I returned early on Monday morning and waited on the Governor. He informed me of the particulars of the correspondence above referred to, stating that it was still his firm belief that the Nonconformists, under the circumstances, might accept Government grants for destitute localities. I replied unhesitatingly that no Dissenters on the island would accept Government pay for any such purpose, as the acceptance of such pay involved an abandonment of their principles, which they held inviolably, being founded on the Word of God. I added that I was assured not one minister of the three denominations connected with home societies would receive a penny for exclusively religious purposes, and that I thought I could state with equal certainty, from what I had heard, that the Wesleyans were equally firm in their repudiation of such aid for such purposes.

"His Excellency then said that settled the matter, as, if the different denominations were averse to the proposal, he felt he had no alternative than to fall back upon the voluntary principle. At this he expressed his regret, as in that case he could not see how the thousands referred to as being uncared for could be reached."

Considerable discussion then ensued between Mr. Phillippo and the Governor on the practicability of employing schoolmasters as missionaries to meet the wants of destitute districts, and on this point Mr. Phillippo, at the Governor's request, opened a correspondence with some of his brethren. In a few days it became apparent that the assent of the Nonconformist ministers to this suggestion could not be obtained, and that it would be repudiated as involving equally with " concurrent endowment " a violation of their most cherished principles, and be opposed as inimical to the rights of the tax-payers at large. Under these circumstances the Governor felt that he must decide on complete disestablishment and disendowment, for in no other way could the equality insisted upon by the parent Government be secured.

Thus was accomplished an event which, says Mr. Phillippo, in his report to the Jamaica Baptist Union, assembled at Kingston on the 10th of July, 1870, " will be regarded as one of the most important events bearing immediately on the cause of God that has ever occurred in the history of the island—such, indeed, as excites both our astonishment and gratitude. It has been evident that, in this conflict of truth and righteousness against unrighteousness and oppression, Almighty God, whom no stratagems can baffle and against whom no combinations can succeed, has been on our side, and to Him alone be all the glory."

This subject may be dismissed with the gratifying remark of Sir J. P. Grant, in the despatch already quoted, "that it is but justice to all communions to say that nothing could be better than the spirit in which this great question has been agitated here. This acknowledgment is due equally to Conformists and Nonconformists, to ministers of religion and laymen."

CHAPTER XXXIX.

THE public events of the years 1865 to 1869, while they occupied a considerable portion of Mr. Phillippo's time, were not suffered to abstract too much from his more distinctly spiritual and congregational duties. It is matter for surprise that, with many indications of the weakening influence of age, he was yet able to undertake the amount of work that he accomplished. His schools, his Sabbath exercises, his numerous class- and prayer-meetings, were maintained with almost unvarying regularity, nor did he hesitate to enlarge the sphere of his operations when circumstances seemed to require. He was ever ready to labour, even beyond his strength, where the welfare of his fellow-men and the salvation of souls were at stake. At the beginning of 1868 he opened a portion of the buildings of the Metropolitan schools for industrial instruction, and readily assumed the spiritual and educational charge of the new station at Hartlands. He also actively co-operated with the president and committee in the removal of the Calabar Institution to Kingston, which took place in 1868.

On the 14th of October, 1868, he entered on the seventieth year of his age, and a selection from the entries in the diary of the year will best illustrate both the extent and the indefatigable nature of his exertions. "This," he says, "is the commencement of my seventieth year. What a host of long-slumbering recollections does this day awaken! Through mercy, my health is good, but my anxieties and labours are sometimes depressing, and almost overwhelming. May I increasingly feel strength given me from on high equal to my day!"

"November 17th.—A missionary meeting was held this day, when my son Cecil occupied the chair, which was a truly gratifying sight to me and the people who were present. The congregation was overflowing. The brethren engaged were Messrs. East, J. E. Henderson, Clarke, of Jericho; Clark, of Brown's Town; Millard, Claydon, Fray, Roberts, and Edwards. It was an admirable meeting; closed at ten o'clock. On the following morning I attended business connected with the Calabar Institution, as also on the following day, when the site of the college building was decided upon, and other important matters were finally arranged. I had reason to be satisfied that my views respecting the site of the college and other buildings were approved and acted upon."

"December 15th.—After morning exercises and breakfast went to Jones's Penn to marry a couple. Met there several backsliders, and talked to them seriously for a long time, before and after the ceremony—I trust with some effect. The pair were respectable of their class, the man a shoemaker. I found Bunyan's 'Pilgrim's Progress, ' Holy War,' and other religious books on their centre table. They had both been educated in the Metropolitan Schools, and could read and write well. On returning to town called at Government House, but the Governor not in town."

"December 20th.—At Spanish Town. The congregation scant, which grieved me. I thought at first I could not preach I had prepared notes which I hoped would enable me to preach earnestly, faithfully, a sermon which I wished for a larger congregation to hear. If, however, it did good but to a few it will not have been preached in vain. Went to Hartlands after the morning service in the pouring rain. It continued all the way. Found only about a dozen people. Rained on returning. Reached home at dark, and went at once into the pulpit."

"December 22nd.—Suffered much from neuralgia for several days, and am still suffering ; but rose as usual at peep of day, and after an hour's occupation in reading a devotional dissertation of a good old author and attending to some other matters, went again to Kingston to inspect the work done at East Queen Street."

"Christmas Day.—A prayer-meeting at six o'clock as usual. At eleven had prayer-meeting and church-meeting. At the latter, the low financial condition of the church was a subject of serious consideration. Dined to-day at our son's house with our own family only."

"December 26th.—Adjourned church-meeting, ex-amined twenty-one candidates for baptism. Received them, and was glad to find that they had more intelligent knowledge of the great doctrines of the Bible than any others I had previously examined. To be baptized on the morning of New Year's Day."

"December 28th.—Having promised to assist Mr. Claydon at his missionary meetings at Four Paths, I proceeded after service on my journey, hoping to get to Saxony, his residence, that evening. The hired horse refused to draw, and the other, my own, was already fagged from the badness of the road. With this one horse I reached Rosswell. The night was dark, the road dangerous, and my horse was knocked up. I called up a cottager by the side of the road, and requested shelter for the night. He said that he could not offer it, his cottage was so mean ; but putting some chairs together, and rolling myself up in my cloak, I lay till about three o'clock. Then putting my trusty steed into the buggy, he having had a bundle or two of grass for his refreshment, I reached Saxony before the family were up, to their astonishment and gratification. After breakfast went to the meeting at Four Paths and Jubilee. On the following morning was at Porus, and thence to Mandeville. All the meetings were in every respect good."

" "January 1st, 1869, Spanish Town.—At the close of the watch-night service I retired to my chamber, and threw myself on my bed with my clothes on, and after a few intervals of sleep, as the service was being carried on by the deacons and others, I rose, and at four o'clock returned to the chapel, which was crowded with an orderly congregation, and again addressed them. At half-past four we proceeded to the river-side. There the gathering was immense. After an address of twenty minutes, I baptized the twenty-nine candidates. The occasion was deeply interesting and solemn, the vast assembly conducting themselves with the greatest decorum."

"Another new year! How quickly life passes on! Once it seemed to me to walk leisurely onward; then it ran; now to fly swiftly towards eternity, like a ball rolling rapidly down a steep hill. May I reach the goal in safety, trimming my lamp, and continue to give myself to Him who bought me with His blood, until my work is done and my warfare is accomplished."

" "January 9th.—Superintended the voluntary efforts of about twenty members of the church in cleaning the burial-ground. They worked cheerfully and well, several of the female members having subscribed to provide a hearty meal for them. Afterwards, though very tired, went to Orange Grove for the coming Sabbath. [The following day being rainy, had but a small congregation."

"January 31st.—Attended prayer-meeting at six o'clock a.m., and started at nine for Passage Fort Had an excellent congregation and school. Addressed the children, and preached from the parable of the barren fig-tree. The deacons, not liking that the rooms used for the occasional residence of the pastor and his family should be occupied by the school, and the master and his wife, propose erecting a separate residence for them. I was but too glad to express my approbation of the proposal."

" February 17th.—When about to start to Orange Grove, I received a message from a poor young woman from the country to see her as she was dying. She was once in the school and a member of the church. I talked and prayed with her. Addressed myself, also, to several thoughtless, ungodly women who crowded into and around the house. On mounting my horse the stirrup broke and I was obliged to return home. After some delay I reached my destination."

" February 22nd.—Went to the court-house and was welcomed by the judge, who gave me a seat beside himself. He said he wished to see me there sometimes during the sessions, as my presence had a salutary effect on the tongues and tempers of some of the violators of the law and on the loungers at the bar. Crime is evidently much diminished, and I was struck with the fact that hardly ever was a person connected with our mission churches found among the delinquents."

" March 28th.—Started to Old Harbour at a very early hour, accompanied by brother Clark, to assist at the opening of the chapel there after extensive repairs. Brother C. preached in the morning, and self in the evening. The chapel has not only been extensively repaired, but new modelled, and is now one of the neatest and most attractive places of worship in any of the rural districts of the country. It is a real ornament to the village."

" May 14th.—Went over to Kingston to take part in

the recognition services of brother East.   The service took place in the evening.   Representatives of various denominations were present.   Altogether it was a most interesting and impressive service ; the congregation, which was very large, was increased by the novelty of the occasion."

"June 14th.—Rode to Orange Grove by Osborne Bridge and Kensington, a long and fatiguing journey. Met an old black woman near a hamlet named Trial, who asked me to visit her daughter. She was very ill. Talked faithfully to her, as also to several neighbours who had gathered round the house. They had forsaken the house of God, and seemed to regret their present condition. They promised to remember from whence they had fallen and do their first works."

"July 24th.—Brother Hewett, being in Spanish Town for two or three days, drove my dear wife up to Orange Grove. She has not been here for many months, being unable to sit on horseback. They arrived in safety, though the roads were rugged and in some parts dangerous. We spent the afternoon in strolling on the green sward among the orange and other fruit trees, and the evening in talking over occurrences and scenes of early life, and the encouragements and discouragements of recent times. This visit of our friend was very grateful, as it enabled me and my beloved partner to avail ourselves of a respite from constant and oppressive duty, which we so much required. The following day we visited Kensington and other places in the neighbourhood, which pretty much exhausted our physical energies. The evening was spent in the portico looking into the garden, still enjoying the reminiscences of old scenes, old friends, and old times."

"July 5th.—Received a letter from Dr. Underhill in reply to one from me, relating to my relief from a part of my labours, and to which the Committee, with warm expressions of esteem, have at once consented. Next to the approbation of God and my own conscience, I, as most others do, and should do, value the good opinion of good men."

"July 19th —Rose after a restless night in a feverish state of body. My work is evidently too much for me, and begins to affect me sensibly. Made arrangements for opening a school-room at Hartlands, and for an examination of the Metropolitan School."

"August 1st.—Baptized ten persons in the river near Turnbull's Penn. A vast congregation present. Returned to Spanish Town for service at eleven o'clock. The congregation very large, and I preached with more than usual freedom and, I think, earnestness. Afternoon—the Lord's Supper, and received the baptized and seventeen others into the church."

"August 3rd.—The usual thanksgiving meeting. In the evening delivered a lecture on the progress of anti-slavery principles throughout the world."

"August 4th.—The usual annual festival of the children of the Metropolitan School. Went this year also to Cumberland Penn, four of the schools meeting there, viz., Hartlands, Passage Fort, Caymanas, and Spanish Town ; about three hundred children in number and five hundred adults. A very interesting day."

"August 30th.—Received applications for aid from many persons in distress, widows entreating me to petition the Municipal Board on their behalf for relief from taxes ; from persons in gaol ; and from others for compensation for damages sustained in various ways, they having an idea that my advocacy of their claims is sure to secure their success. These and similar demands on my time are so numerous that I had need almost to keep a secretary to enable me to attend to them."

" September 19th.—Preached in town at eleven o'clock and went to Hartlands at one. A terrible journey, amidst rain, mud, and stagnant water. On arrival, but few people present, except children, whom the mud did not seem to inconvenience. Arrived home late and found my congregation waiting for me. Was much fatigued, but preached to a large congregation."

" October 14th.—This is my seventieth birthday. It being rather more than a common occasion among missionaries and a period beyond which the laws of nature and of God seldom suffer human life to be extended, it was regarded with some special interest. My family, brethren, and friends, who were near at hand, spent the day with me. Many things were said, congratulatory of my dear wife, self, and family, much that I felt that I did not deserve. The evening was spent very pleasantly in singing, prayer, and Christian conversation, chiefly in recalling past events of personal history during the seventy years of my pilgrimage and the seventy-sixth of that of my beloved wife. Here one seemed to stand upon the mount, and to review the way in which we have been led. But how little we could penetrate into the future! Shall we all see another decade? or is this the last time we shall all meet on a similar occasion?"

> " Blest is my lot, whate'er befall ;
> What can disturb me, who appal,
> While as my Strength, my Rock, my All,
> Saviour, I cling to Thee?"

CHAPTER XL.

IT will have been seen that towards the middle of the
year 1868 Mr. Phillippo opened communications with the
Mission Committee as to some relief from his arduous
and incessant toil. Nearly two years, however, elapsed
before the subject assumed a practical shape. Early in
January, 1870, he had to mourn over the decease of his
son-in-law, the Rev. W. Claydon. This lamentable
event brought upon him for some months the charge of
the churches in the extensive district covered by the
labours of Mr. Claydon. He soon found it all but impossible to meet the claims of the stations in Clarendon
and Manchester besides his own, and with gladness surrendered his charge at the end of the month of May into
the hands of the Rev. W. H. Porter, M.A., "a good brother
from Halifax, N.S., who had come to Jamaica for health."
Mr. Porter's bad health, however, after fourteen months'
trial, brought about his resignation, and again Mr.
Phillippo was importuned by the people to supply such
services as his manifold occupations would allow. Early
in 1872 he was relieved from this heavy additional burden
to his cares by the arrival of the Revs. Wm. Gummer and
P. Williams, the one from Demerara and the other from
Wales. "I accompanied them," writes Mr. Phillippo,
"on the 12th of March, and some following days, to the
stations and churches under my temporary charge and

care as trustee and pastor in Clarendon and Manchester, and introduced them to these churches, resigning my pastorate over them. The invitation of the churches was cordially accepted by these brethren, and they have entered upon their labours with cheering prospects of happiness and usefulness — brother Gummer at Four Paths, Jubilee, and Porus ; and brother Williams at Mandeville and Cabbage Hall."

But, although thus partially relieved from the weight of care which burdened him, his increasing years constrained him to think of retirement. Mrs. Phillippo's health also began to fail, and he sorely felt the loss of social intercourse which ensued on the removal of the seat of government from Spanish Town to Kingston. Many of his old friends were drawn off to the new capital. His eldest son with his family also was obliged to follow, while the congregation suffered in many ways, both from the diminution of employment and the emigration to more prosperous places which the change necessarily brought about. Towards the close of the year (1871) he therefore prepared for the Mission Committee a full statement of his position, and of the requirements which his pastoral duties laid upon him. It is dated October 14th. He says : "I am now in the seventy-third year of my age, and my dear wife is verging on her eightieth year. I was received by the Society as a missionary student in 1819. I may, therefore, be considered as having been connected with it fifty-two years, and at the close of two more, if spared, I shall have been a missionary in Jamaica, and the pastor of the church at Spanish Town, full half a century. It has long been my hope and determination, if possible, to remain firmly at my post to the end of this latter period at least. I have informed you at times that I felt the infirmities of age creeping upon me, as also that my labours and responsibilities were becoming too heavy a burden for me to bear without progressive diminution of health and strength, physically and mentally. To such a degree have I felt myself worn down by incessant labour and anxiety, during the last few months, that I have been compelled to think seriously about the necessity of circumscribing my efforts within narrower limits, thereby also to diminish my responsibilities and cares, as both my sight and hearing, and even voice as to compass, have begun sensibly to fail. My general health is good and my constitution sound ; with moderate labour and care, therefore, if life is mercifully spared, I may labour on usefully for years to come. But it is evident to others, as well as to myself, that if not relieved of some of my duties soon I may render my future life useless and myself a burden."

" I urge thus my growing infirmities as the principal reason why I think a change necessary, both with respect to myself and the church. But there are two or three other considerations which, while they have no influence in inducing me to seek the change I propose, indicate that it is desirable. I may premise that the contemplated alteration in my position and circumstances is not owing to any cause existing at any of the stations I occupy. The churches are, and have been for years, in uninterrupted peace. Many are being added annually to their number, and the congregations are everywhere increasing. Almost everything, indeed, is more encouraging than in former years, while, so far as I can judge, I believe I have never enjoyed more fully the confidence, respect, and affection of the people at large."

" You may now perhaps ask me how my difficulties may be obviated, and my relief from a portion of my present numerous and arduous labours secured. I reply, by resigning the pastorate in whole or in part at Spanish Town, and of the stations at Passage Fort and Kitson

Town, together with all the minor appendages of such stations respectively, such as class-houses, &c., to a younger brother, I retiring to Sligoville or its neighbourhood, and attending to some dark spots around, giving occasional services at Spanish Town "

It did not require any prolonged consideration or correspondence on the part of the Mission Committee to meet the wishes of their venerable friend and fellow-labourer. On the 4th of January, 1872, he gratefully records that, in reply to his letter, "the Committee had cheerfully and unanimously agreed to give as an annuity all I proposed as necessary to support us comfortably in my retirement. The Committee did this, says the Secretary, in consideration of my long and faithful services in the mission." They warmly recognised the great services Mr. Phillippo had rendered to the cause of Christ in Jamaica, and his invaluable labours in the emancipation and elevation of its Negro population.

At a very large gathering of the church on Good Friday, March 29th, he accordingly announced his intention to resign the pastorate of the above churches and stations on the following 1st of August. The announcement was received with deep and loud expressions of regret, followed by a unanimous vote that "the resignation be not accepted." Many arguments were used by the deacons and others of the more influential members of the church to dissuade their minister from his purpose, and in the result Mr. Phillippo consented to remain the nominal pastor of the church till December, 1873, when he would have completed the fiftieth year of his ministry among them. Not without loud and general expressions of concern was this decision accepted. The crowd of members lingered long in the chapel and its precincts. They were losing, they said, not their minister only, but "their father and their friend ; they had hoped he would never leave them until the Great Master above called him to his rest and his reward," so that they might have buried him among themselves and mourned over his grave.

In the month of May the church invited the Rev. Thomas Lea, of Lucea, to the pastorate, which he accepted, and on the 13th of August Mr. Phillippo, with his family, surrendered the mission-house to his successor, and left for the new home in a cottage that he had hired. "Thus," he records in his diary, "we bade farewell to the old house and premises occupied by us for nearly fifty years, and came to occupy Felstead Cottage in the outskirts of the town. It was not without many reflections that we thus retired to comparative privacy, and not without melancholy musings that we left the old abode, with all its associations of peace and turmoil, joy and sorrow. It is one of the most important events of my life, but one which I trust God has sanctioned."

But if deeply moved on relinquishing so much of his life's work, it was a source of grateful feeling that he could report favourably of the promising state of things around him. In a letter to the Mission House, giving the particulars of the new arrangements, he says, "Our churches are in peace, the congregations increasing, and many, chiefly young persons, are inquiring the way to Zion with their faces thitherward. Hence additions are shortly to be made at Spanish Town, Sligoville, and Old Harbour, while two or three new schools have been established in previously destitute localities. Pious young men, as teachers, are breaking the bread of life on the Sabbath to hundreds hitherto perishing for want of it. Everywhere prospects with respect to religion, education, and morals are encouraging."

His life had indeed been one of great usefulness and honour. What changes he had seen! How many events most important in the history of his adopted country had taken place, in which he had borne no inconsiderable share ! What anxieties he had passed through to secure the harvest now so abundant around him ! He might hopefully anticipate that his few closing years would pass in restful peace, and his joy receive no check.

CHAPTER XLI.

THE interval between his partial retirement from the pastorate in March, 1872, and the jubilee of his ministry at Christmas, 1873, was filled up by Mr. Phillippo with frequent services at the two or three minor stations that he retained under his own care. He also visited with his colleague the churches in Clarendon, taking part in the missionary meetings. His leisure hours were diligently employed on his autobiography, and in completing his lectures on the West Indies, and on two manuscripts that he hoped to pass through the press, one on the " Claims of the World on the increased Benevolence of the Christian Church," and the other on Prayer. This hope, however, was not fulfilled. On his removal from his old habitation he presented his well-selected library to the Calabar Institution. One great trial fell upon him and his beloved wife—the death of their youngest son in the early morning of the 18th of November, 1872. He was the object of their warm affection and of many prayers, and, though there had been much to give them anxiety in the later years of his life, they were comforted by his dying words. He passed away expressing his confidence in God, a firm hope that " his sins were forgiven, and his entire dependence upon Christ for salvation." The funeral was necessarily performed before the close of day. " Brethren East and Lea conducted the service amidst the sighs and tears of a very large assemblage of spectators and friends. The bearers were young men of the church and congregation."

For a few weeks before the day fixed for the observance of the jubilee Mr. Phillippo was seriously ill, the result of being thrown from his horse down a precipice in the mountains. This was not the first accident of the kind he had met with during his numerous journeys among beetling rocks and unfrequented paths. But he was now seriously injured, and for some weeks compelled to keep his room. " I was, however," he says, "much gratified and cheered by notes of sympathy received from my brethren far and near, and among them one from good brother Clarke, who also anticipated the pleasure of being present at the celebration of the jubilee of my pastorate."

This long-looked-for event took place on the 14th of January, 1874. Great preparations were made for its celebration. A large platform was erected on the grounds of his cottage, decorated with flags and cocoa-nut branches. Two tents were provided by the kindness of a friend for the accommodation of the assemblage. Preliminary services were held in the chapel and school-rooms, and there the children assembled to walk in procession, carrying flags and banners, to Mr. Phillippo's residence. A similar display came from Sligoville. At eleven o'clock a very large number of friends arrived, coming from various distances of from five to fifteen miles, all gathered to honour the venerable servant of Christ, and to testify to his usefulness and worth. On the platform might be seen not only his missionary brethren, but many of the higher class of the inhabit-ants of Spanish Town, among whom he had passed so many long years of labour, anxiety, and suffering. After an appropriate opening of the meeting by singing and prayer, conducted by the Rev. D. J. East, who occupied the chair, an address from the church and congregation of

Spanish Town, signed by the deacons, leaders, and members, and adopted at a full church meeting, was read by the Rev. Thomas Lea as the representative of the church on the occasion.   It was as follows :—

" Dear Minister, — We, the undersigned deacons, leaders, and members of the Baptist church of Spanish Town and the adjacent stations, feel it our duty to convey to you our sentiments of gratitude and affection.

" Your long, arduous, and devoted labours amongst us, as churches, in the cause of our blessed Lord ; your untiring efforts for the promotion of the interests and welfare of the masses of the people amongst whom the wise Providence of our Heavenly Father has cast your lot for these fifty years past, and the distinguished and abundant usefulness to our fathers, and to us their children, lay us under greater obligations than any words of ours can express.   We thank God on your behalf that you have been the honoured instrument in His hands to accomplish so much.   Glory be to His great name !

" Reverend Sir,—Your retirement from the pastorate of the church at Spanish Town was keenly felt by us all. We know not how to express our sorrow in parting with you.   You have been, not only a pastor, but a father to us, and we shall always remember you with love and gratitude.   As we have told you before, we had hoped that nothing but death would have severed the tie which bound us to each other ; yet we feel that your advanced age justifies the step you have deemed it necessary to take ; we therefore sympathise with you, and feel obliged to submit.

" And now, on this jubilee of your faithful ministry, we most cordially offer you our congratulations that you, and the beloved companion of your days, have so long been spared to live and labour in the Saviour's service.   This fiftieth anniversary of your ministrations amongst us as

c c

churches and people is a high day to us all, and not only to us, but to the inhabitants of this town and neighbourhood, and not only to this town and neighbourhood, but to a large portion of at least this side of the island over which your evangelistic labours have extended.

"We must also make mention of your zealous service in the cause of education. You have not only laboured for its advancement by the personal superintendence and oversight you have given to it, and by the establishment of schools in numerous places, but you have collected large sums of money in the mother country to aid in carrying on the good work of educating the young and rising race.

"May the Almighty Disposer of all events spare your valuable life and grant you days of greater usefulness; and that your last days be your best is the sincere prayer of your attached friends and people!"

This address was followed by another, also read by Mr. Lea, expressive of similar sentiments from the church at Sligoville, still under Mr. Phillippo's pastoral oversight. Both these addresses were strictly the addresses of the people—prepared by themselves. Their former pastor read to them the reply which follows, under the influence of deep emotion, amid the flowing tears of many who, from earliest infancy, had sat under his ministry, and who were truly his own children in the faith of Christ.

"My Christian Brethren and Friends,—Under the circumstances altogether amidst which I now appear before you, I shall be believed when I say that I am deeply affected by the immense assemblage present, and with the sentiments contained in your address; while I regret that I cannot command language equal to the warm emotions of gratitude I feel in my heart for the distinguished honour you this day confer upon me.

"At the same time, I trust I shall be thought equally

sincere when I assure you that I feel unworthy of the high terms in which you speak of my character and usefulness. I therefore request you to regard my acceptance of your address more as a genuine expression of your kindness towards me personally, and of your sympathy with me in my great work as a Christian minister, than for the extent of usefulness you have attributed to me.

"In my application to the Missionary Society to be employed under their patronage, I expressed my desire to exercise my ministry in any part of the world, and to occupy any sphere to which they might think proper to direct me. My destination was fixed for Jamaica, and Spanish Town was to be my sphere of labour.

"I arrived at my post, accompanied by my beloved wife at the close of the year 1823. Thus, more than half a century ago, I came to this town a stranger, with youth and experience little adapted to the anxious and arduous work I then ventured to undertake. Friends, however, though humble, in the course of time gathered around me, whose esteem it has been my honour and happiness to enjoy. I have had my afflictions, personal and relative, as well as difficulties, in the prosecution of my labours; but, 'having obtained help of God, I continue unto this day,' while I can gratefully testify to the goodness and faithfulness of God that, if my trials have abounded, my consolations have abounded also.

"About the time of my arrival, owing to several causes, more than ordinary hostility was manifested towards missionaries by a certain class throughout the island, of which I had to endure no inconsiderable share, being, among other annoyances, prevented by the authorities from entering upon my ministerial duties for several successive months. These obstacles were at length surmounted, and I at once entered upon my labours, though prosecuting them amidst long-continued obloquy and persecution.   C C 2

" You have been kind enough to say that I have discharged the duties of my office with fidelity and zeal, and that my great work of preaching the Gospel, and gathering sinners into the fold of Christ, has been crowned with success.

" While, I trust, my feeble efforts for the promotion of the glory of God in the salvation and happiness of my fellow-men have not been in vain, I must, at the same time, acknowledge that my success has been, to a considerable degree, owing to the persistent and self-sacrificing co-operation of the deacons and others of my church. Any spiritually beneficial result of my own direct labours I ascribe to the ' Grace of God which was with me,' and can from my heart say, ' Not unto me, O Lord, not unto me, but unto Thy name be all the praise.'

" You have been pleased to refer to my efforts to promote the temporal interests of the inhabitants of the town and other districts of the country by the establishment and support of schools, &c. While this was not a work I was requested to perform by the Society which sent me forth, and although I was informed by them that, if undertaken, it must be on my own responsibility, as they had no funds for appropriation to direct educational objects, yet, seeing the children of the poorer classes, bond and free, abandoned to ignorance and vice, I assumed the responsibility of establishing a day-school for them, providing for its support by the proceeds of a higher department conducted by myself, the former, as you kindly intimate, having continued in operation to the present day.

" Great, however, as have been the anxieties—I may say sacrifices—involved in the maintenance of this and other similar institutions throughout the district, through a long course of years, I have felt myself richly compensated by seeing the blessings that have resulted to the thousands who have participated in their advantages, numbers among whom have been qualified thereby for the duties of estate managers and the engagements of mechanical, commercial, and official life.

"In the great social change occasioned by the abolition of slavery, I did not act so conspicuous a part as some of my brethren, owing to particular circumstances. It is, however, truly gratifying to me to know that I was regarded by many, both in England and Jamaica, as being no indifferent worker in accomplishing the destruction of that monster evil, especially when, to secure its permanent dominion it aimed to interrupt the progress of civilisation, morality, and true religion. And never shall I forget, and I am sure never will you who witnessed it forget, the triumph of that day—the glorious 1st of August, 1838—when, at the head of a procession of upwards of 7,000 of the population, I had the honour to present you before the then King's House in this town to hear the proclamation of full and unconditional freedom from the lips of our veteran Governor, Sir Lionel Smith, by command of our then youthful Sovereign, Queen Victoria, whom may God Almighty long continue to preserve and bless!"

The whole assembly, on the uttering of these words, simultaneously expressed their loyalty by singing "God save the Queen," accompanied by repeated cheers.

"Permit me further to say that it was from the same regard for the temporal as well as for the spiritual interests of the masses of the people that I was induced to do what I could to promote more practically their social condition, by purchasing lands, and otherwise assisting them in the establishment of villages in the districts where my influence extended. But in this also I have been more than rewarded for the time and labour and temporal loss involved, by the knowledge that thereby hundreds of families, otherwise without houses and friends, have been collected and located in their own comfortable freeholds, provided at the same time with all the means and appliances of Christian worship and school instruction in their midst.

"Nor have I been wanting, I flatter myself, in a willing co-operation with my fellow-townsmen in any plan for redressing wrong where it existed; for promoting the elevation of the ignorant; or for advancing the interests, especially of the labouring classes, of the country at large. But for these things I have not asked and deserve no thanks, as I have acted only up to my convictions of right and of Christian duty, endorsing it as a principle 'that everyone capable of doing service to his fellow-men ought to sacrifice his own ease, means, and time to the welfare of those unable to help themselves.'

"In the faithful and conscientious discharge of my official duties I have seen it right to differ from some around me on some social as well as ecclesiastical questions. Whilst, however, I have never shrunk from a candid avowal of my principles, but have ever been ready to defend them, both from the pulpit and the press, yet I persuade myself I have endeavoured to do so with Christian moderation, conceding to others the same freedom of action and purity of motive I have claimed for myself. If, however, I have spoken or acted offensively towards any, I gladly avail myself of this opportunity of expressing my regret.

"Seeing so large an assembly around me, consisting of all classes of my fellow-townsmen, and of all creeds and conditions of life, I cannot but think it due to you, my friends, and to myself to testify to the uniform kindness and courtesy with which I have been favoured, and that not only by the ministers of the different Christian societies in the town and neighbourhood, but by the inhabitants generally.

"I think it impossible, indeed, for any one to have met with greater respect and kindness from any people in any part of the world ; and I have great pleasure in tendering to all the assurance of my high appreciation of their conduct in this respect.

" In all the relations I have sustained to the members and congregation of my late charge, I have met with nothing but confidence and affection. Under the trials and difficulties of my path (and they have been neither few nor insignificant) I have received from you all the comfort and consolation which the tenderest sympathy could dictate. Be assured that the recollection of them, with the deepest gratitude and affection, will be cherished by me and by one equally a sharer in them to the latest moment of our lives.

" Owing to circumstances it is unnecessary to repeat on this occasion, I relinquished the pastorate of the church *de facto* in favour of my friend and brother, the Rev. Thomas Lea, but have remained connected with it in some slight degree, to enable me to fulfil my pledge, long made, of celebrating this jubilee.

" This slender tie was dissolved on the 21st of the past month ; and now on the first public opportunity presented I bid you a FINAL FAREWELL. I do this, I must say, not without feelings of regret, as the ties and association of fifty years' growth are too deeply rooted to be torn asunder in a day without a pang. But the stern behests of duty are not to be disobeyed. My feelings, however, are overborne by the conviction that my successor, by his ability and zeal, will more than compensate for my retirement, and, by the blessing of God, be more successful in our Great Master's work, and in promoting the general good, than my limited qualifications have allowed.

" Having outlived my friends in my native land—having been permitted to see my children and my children's children growing up around me, added to the fact of having formed friendships here which nothing but death can sever—I purpose, should Providence permit, to pass the evening of my days among you, and to find a grave in Spanish Town where my ashes may repose in peace.

"If, in your Address, there is one particular more gratifying to my feelings than another, it is that in which you refer to my beloved partner. She has most nobly and unflinchingly borne with me the heat and burden of the day —has been a 'true fellow-helper in the truth'—and deserves largely to share the approbation you have so kindly expressed to me. I have to request you, therefore, to receive on her account the warmest sentiments of affectionate gratitude.

"And now, Christian brethren and friends, permit me to say in conclusion that it is my earnest prayer that a hundredfold of blessings from on high may be rendered to you and your families, and that the means and opportunities of spiritual enlightenment with which God in His Providence has favoured you may be effective, through Divine grace, to the sanctification of your souls and your preparation for a happy immortality."

By the direction of the Committee of the Baptist Missionary Society, the following letter was addressed to Mr. Phillippo on this auspicious occasion:—

"My dear Brother,—At our quarterly meeting of Committee, held a few days ago, reference was made to the jubilee services about to be held in Spanish Town to commemorate your fifty years of service in the island of Jamaica in the cause of our Lord and Saviour. I was directed to write you and express in the warmest possible manner the hearty congratulations of your brethren on this side the Atlantic. This I do with the greatest pleasure.

"It is a source of gratitude to God that your life has been so long preserved, and that, with few interruptions, you have been able to continue your valuable work during that long period of time with the greatest benefit to the people of Jamaica, and with not a few tokens of the favour of God. You have seen the Gospel take deep root in the island, the number of believers wonderfully multiplied, and the curse of slavery for ever removed. In all this you have had no mean share. You have passed through many painful scenes also. You have seen the people quivering under the lash, disease and death ravaging their homes, and the most savage injustice inflicted upon them. In all this, too, you have sympathised with them, and been their friend and counsellor. Great is the contrast of their present condition with those days of suffering. Peace everywhere prevails, freedom is secured both for body and soul, the sanctuaries of God daily increase in number, and the people cheerfully sustain the cost of their religious institutions; justice is fairly administered in the courts, and a period of prosperity at length rewards their endurance and patient service. Your jubilee might be regarded as their jubilee, even as it is a fitting time for them to display their regard for you and to express the esteem in which you are universally held. It is also a cause of gratitude that your dear wife survives to share with you these blessed memories, and to rejoice with you in the general expressions of esteem and attachment the occasion has called forth.

"You are not unaware that the Committee hold you in high esteem, and have in various ways expressed it. Receive, my dear friend, this one more expression of it, and be assured that we think of you with affection and honour you for your consistent life and your devoted service in the cause of our Lord and Master. May your closing days, and those of your dear wife, be filled with peace and an ever-present sense of the Divine favour; and then at last may the Master welcome you with His words of approval, 'Well done; enter ye into the joy of your Lord'!—Believe me to remain, yours very truly,

"EDWARD B. UNDERHILL."

A few months later a handsome clock and a service of plate, to which contributions were made from persons of every class, were presented to Mr. Phillippo. This generous and appropriate gift did not arrive in time for presentation at the jubilee meeting.

With this touching event, surrounded by those members of his family who were then in Jamaica, and many dear friends with whom he had fought "the good fight" of truth, righteousness, and liberty, the public life of Mr. Phillippo may be said to have closed, though not, as will presently be seen, his services to the churches he had gathered and so long led to the "streams of living waters." The words of the "just and devout" Simeon were on his lips: "Lord, now lettest Thou Thy servant depart in peace, according to Thy word; for mine eyes have seen Thy salvation."

A few more trials, however, awaited this servant of God before that hoary head should receive the crown of an immortal and eternal life.

CHAPTER XLII.

DECEASE OF HIS WIFE—1874.

FOR some weeks before the celebration of the jubilee,
Mr. Phillippo was laid aside by illness, occasioned by a
fall from his horse down a precipice. The injury then
done to one of his legs he never thoroughly recovered,
and, although he endeavoured to supply the wants of the
stations he retained in his charge, and met with great
encouragement in his ministry, he found horse exercise,
by which means only he could reach the stations, increasingly difficult. Growing infirmities led him to resign his
office of " President of the Mutual Relief Society" for the
town and district, which he had held for about eight
years, and he also relinquished other minor engagements
which his energetic nature and active habits had long
enabled him to fulfil. Though with difficulty, he still went
on his journeys of loving ministration to the poor and
needy, and bore the fatigues and peril with a buoyant
spirit.

But a dark day was at hand, the narrative of which
must be given in his own words :—

" June 19th.—On arrival home I was told the sad tidings
of the illness of my beloved wife, whom I had left so
shortly before in her usual health. I left her on Wednesday last to return to Orange Grove to arrange for opening
the new school-room and chapel at Thankful Hill,
receiving from her her usual parting caress with the inquiry

when I should return, accompanied by an admonition to avoid unnecessary exposure to the sun. I returned on the Friday about eleven o'clock. On alighting from my horse, the servant said, with a sadness both of tone and countenance, 'Missus is not well; she got up this morning, but was obliged to return to bed.' I hastened to the room, and found her speechless and insensible. Not a word in reply to my anxious inquiries, nor a single look of recognition! I saw the hand of death was upon her, and immediately sent a messenger to Kingston for our son and daughter. Just then Mrs. Claydon, not knowing what had happened, was driven to the door. Dr. Stamer, who resided in the town, came immediately, and, on seeing the patient, shook his head ominously. My son soon after arrived and pronounced the case hopeless. Everything that a skilful physician and affectionate son could do was done. She lingered, without a sign of consciousness or pain during that and the following day and night."

"June 21st.—At thirty minutes past four o'clock this morning the loved one breathed her spirit into the hands of Him who gave it. I sat by her bedside in deep anguish of mind, and when she drew her last breath it seemed as though my heartstrings burst asunder."

"She passed away without even a sigh. No indication of pain from first to last. This a little sweetened the wormwood and the gall. But hush, my soul! nor dare repine. The circumstances altogether call for gratitude to my heavenly Father. She was ripe for the sickle, and the great Husbandman gathered her into His garner. No; great as is my grief, I must not repine. My loss is her gain; I have lost an earthly friend, she has gained a heavenly Friend. I have, too, other alleviations. My children and my children's children strive to soothe my wounded spirit. Brethren testify their sympathy; while all the tenderness and kindness which long-tried friends can show have been manifested to an extent and in a degree I could not have expected."

Her body was borne to the grave on the following Monday morning amidst an immense number of people, whose lamentations, controlled by deep and sincere feeling, testified more than words can express the high estimate formed of her Christian character and social virtues. Profound indeed must have been the sorrow of the aged husband as, with tottering steps, supported by their eldest son, he accompanied the remains of his life-long companion to the grave. She had been the sharer of his joys and sorrows, his trials, his conflicts, and his successes, for more than fifty years.

Of the numerous letters of sympathy which reached him, there was not one, he remarks, that he valued so much as the following. Its writer was once a slave-girl whose freedom Mrs. Phillippo had purchased by the liberality of some ladies at Reading.

"Spanish Town, June 23, 1874.—My dear and beloved Pastor,—I, as an humble member under your pastorate for so many years, and one who from a child has been with you and your dear departed friend, do sincerely sympathise in your loss. I know you have felt (and will feel) greatly the loss of her; and more so when you think that you were not permitted to hear from her in her last hours what was the state of her mind on the merits of her Saviour. I can assure you, from what I have heard from her at different times, that she was one waiting for her Saviour's coming, and I do believe (according to God's Word) that she is now among the saved. Although we have not been able to hear a word from her this time, yet on a former occasion when she was taken, and after she was a little better, I asked her if she wished me to read for her, and she said ' Yes.' I read to her the 108th Psalm, and when I closed the book she said, ' My heart is fixed ;

my heart is fixed ! Oh, how merciful is God to us, yet we are such unworthy creatures ! Oh, if we could love and praise Him more !' While at her bedside, witnessing her departure, I thought I heard her saying these same words, ' My heart is fixed ! '

"I hope, my dear minister, you will be encouraged by these words, and look to Him who only can save unto the uttermost those that come to Him by faith, ' seeing He ever liveth to make intercession for us.'

"With love and respect to you and your daughter, I am, yours obediently,

"MARY O'MEALLY."

In the memoir prepared by Mr. Phillippo for the pages of the *Baptist Magazine* he begins by quoting the words of Washington Irving :—"No one knows what a ministering angel the wife of his bosom is until he has gone with her through the fiery trials of this world." Such was Mrs. Phillippo to the husband of her choice, through all the long years in which she fully shared the trials, the self-denial, the sufferings and persecutions which befell them. She was possessed of a sound and vigorous constitution, was of an amiable and gentle disposition, in manners unostentatious, of a sound judgment, and endowed with good practical common-sense. Her piety was unobtrusive, but deep and sincere, ever exhibiting its power by deeds of mercy, by her efforts to lead all around her to Christ, by ordering her household in the fear of God, and by a firm persistence in the paths of truth and holiness. Her diffidence led her to withdraw much into the quiet of her own home ; but no one could fail to be struck with her clearness of purpose, the firmness of her resolve, and the blamelessness of her life. Under the painful loss of children, she was resigned to the Divine will, and bore with a chastened calmness the trials through which her path and that of her husband so often

lay. She cheered him in his anxieties, burdened herself
with his cares, and was his surest counsellor and friend.
She made his home a happy one. "It was," says the
bereaved husband, "the dearest spot to him on earth, one
which he preferred to everything else—a shelter from the
ills and anxieties of life. Whenever distant from it, it
was to him always a refuge of pleasant thought. There,
shut in from the outer world of strife and turmoil, he
possessed a peace and happiness he could not find
elsewhere. In thus making home a happy one to her
husband and children, it is hardly necessary to say that
she found it one herself."

Mrs. Phillippo was the mother of nine children. Three
only survived her—two sons and a daughter. They are
still living to testify to the worth and affection of her who
trained their childhood, watched over their later life with
maternal anxiety, and rejoiced in the honourable positions
to which they have attained. That affection they returned.
and now hold in reverence and love the memory of her
virtues, her piety, and example.

She passed away in the eighty-second year of her age
and the fifty-first of her married and missionary life.

> "Night dews fall not more gently to the ground,
> Nor weary worn-out winds expire more soft."

CHAPTER XLIII.

In the year following the decease of his wife, the health
of Mr. Phillippo considerably improved, and with occasional interruptions he was able, for about two years and
a-half, to visit his stations, and to take an interest in
the progress of affairs around him. Soon after the death
of Mr. Dowson he took charge of the station at Old
Harbour, and this church, with Sligoville and Rosswell,
he continued to watch over as his strength allowed. Both
in his visits and in the management of the churches, as
also in his correspondence, he enjoyed the constant and
invaluable aid of his daughter. She accompanied him
in his journeys, kept the accounts of the stations, and
assisted him in his pastoral work. If there were wanting
the vigour, the activity, and the success of former days,
these qualities were more than compensated by the ripe-
ness of his judgment and the mellowness of his piety.
The variety of his labours, and the spirit in which they
were pursued, can best be illustrated by a few selections
from his diary, which, with great assiduity, he continued
daily to keep.

"July 19th, 1874.—Thankful Hill school-house I was
now enabled to open on its completion. A very large
congregation, almost as many outside as within. About
sixty children were present. I preached from 1 Chron.
xxix. 5. All seemed gratified, and gave hope of future

attendance. May God grant the realisation of these anticipations!"

This building, erected for use as a chapel as well as school-house, was on a rising ground in the centre of three or four villages, and in a district that had been described by a late Governor as one of the dark spots which were a disgrace and a danger to Jamaica. There was no other school or place of worship within five or six miles. It was estimated that the villages in its vicinity could very well furnish at least one hundred children in daily attendance.

"August 9th,—At Rosswell. Preached from words, ' If the Lord delight in us He will bring us into that good land,' &c. Things were as encouraging as usual. There really seems to be a good work going on here, which I must place against discouragements elsewhere. This ought to strengthen and stimulate for future action, as well as preserve me from anxious care."

"August 22nd.—Old Harbour day. The congregation was small on account of prevalent sickness. All very cold. Mission-house still untouched. I preached, I trust, in a way calculated to rouse them. They were attentive, but asleep still. I fear this is the result of the apathy of one or two whose worldly speculations absorb all their thoughts and energies. I returned home in the evening, calling, on the way, on a respectable coloured family. The mother had been known to me from a child. I left some periodicals for their perusal, as usual. My horse became lame, and the harness broke, but I arrived safely home, though at a late hour."

"October 14th.—My birthday, terminating my seventy-sixth year. Thoughts crowd upon my mind while I think of all the way in which my heavenly Father has led me.

" How rapidly is my time on earth passing away ! How long my life may be continued, of course, I cannot tell, but in all the circumstances and conditions of it help me, O God, to look for Thy special blessing. I may have many losses and crosses yet to endure; help me to bear them, O my God and Father, as dispensations of Thine intended for my good, and give me wisdom and grace to see Thy designs in them!"

"December 1st.—Final leave was taken this day of Felstead Cottage by Mrs. Claydon, self, servants, and chattels. On taking a last farewell look at this neat and comfortable cottage, associated as it ever will be in my mind with the last hours of my beloved wife, her last earthly home, I became the prey of melancholy reflections, which I found it difficult to restrain within proper bounds. Henceforward, for some days, I was busy in arranging furniture, &c., in the new home at Rivoli, which in some degree diverted my thoughts from the sad retrospect of the past few months."

"December 6th.—At Orange Grove and Sligoville. The morning fine. The hurricane and rain-storm have not proved so destructive as I feared. The congregation was good, and all seemed cheerful. I held a church-meeting before and after service, when several young persons were proposed for baptism, to take place (D.V.) the first Sabbath in January. Preached and administered the Lord's Supper. May the Lord give effect to His Word!"

"December 25th. — Christmas-day. The fifty-first anniversary of it to me in Jamaica. How unlike this to the savage scenes, abominable and wicked customs that prevailed in 1823. The change is wonderful, and all is to be ascribed to the influence of the Gospel faithfully and earnestly preached."

"March 4th, 1875.—According to previous arrangements, a juvenile picnic was held at Orange Grove for the children of Thankful Hill and Sligoville schools; over a hundred and sixty present. It was a very interesting gathering, and managed in a far less troublesome way to all concerned, and also more satisfactory, than on any previous occasion. I trust it will stimulate the parents on behalf of their children's education; their continued interest in it greatly requires incentives."

" March 6th —At Sligoville, accompanied by my daughter. A very large congregation was present. Preached from Matt. xxvi. 56: 'And all His disciples forsook Him and fled.' I tried to produce impression, and looked up anxiously to God for His blessing."

" March 31st.—Unwell; fever hanging about me, and remained in bed the greater part of the day. The immediate cause of this illness was doubtless the exposure to the cold night air after my efforts in speaking at the meetings in Kingston, and driving home after ten o'clock at night."

" May 26th.—I now received the first instalments of the Government grants for my schools: Sligoville, Thankful Hill, Free Town, Spring Garden, and Rosswell. Received £51 8s."

" June 13th, Sunday.—At Rosswell. A very large and attentive congregation was present. I preached on the nature, the necessity, advantages, and means of promoting Scriptural revivals. Several began to exhibit excitement, as at a former time; but I insisted on its discontinuance, requesting such as were really under concern to meet me in the vestry after the service. It is almost dangerous to speak to the people here with very much earnestness, as their feelings are so little under control."

" June 17th.—Particularly requested by brethren East and Roberts, went over to Kingston to the examination of the High School at the Calabar Institution and the distribution of prizes. Colonel Cox, Commander of the Forces, in the chair. I delivered an address. On the following day I returned to Rivoli."

"July 13th.—Morning duties being observed, I held an hour's service with the lame, the halt, and the blind in the poor-house now brought near my residence. Several of these poor people seemed to know the hymns sung, and heartily united in singing them. I addressed them for about half-an-hour on the first Psalm. They paid great attention, and thanked me very heartily at the close. I found it good to be there."

"September 8th.—Called on some of my old friends whose minister I had so long been. Among them was Emily Thomas, a good, devoted woman, who, though ninety years of age, crept by aid of her staff to every public service. She was on her death-bed, and I bade her a last farewell. She said she hoped to be the first to welcome me to her Father's house, where she was going a little before me. In the evening, Mrs. Claydon and myself were favoured with the company of some Wesleyan friends. Had a pleasant and profitable two or three hours in recounting the way in which God had led us the many years past. A tremendous tempest came over the town soon after our friends had left, and continued all night. Awful flashes of lightning and peals of thunder seemed to conspire our destruction. At length, by the force of the wind, which drove the storm before it, it rolled away in the distance. A few thin clouds lingered after the storm and sank slowly to the verge of the horizon. This awe-inspiring scene solemnised my mind, forcing upon my thoughts the mighty thunderings and blinding lightnings of the last great day."

"October 14th.—My birthday. I have this day closed my seventy-seventh year. Although thought by friends to have remarkable health and strength at such an age, I nevertheless feel that my days are fast ebbing away. Age is bringing out the weak points of my constitution slowly, but sensibly. Every year adds to the increasing number of my infirmities. May I, by the inspiration of the Holy Spirit, form such holy resolutions as if I were now about to leave this earthly life to be made a partaker of the Supper of the Lamb! Blessed is that servant whom his Lord, when He cometh, shall find watching."

"November 24th.—Returned to town, and was duly installed as chairman of the missionary meeting in the evening. Many brethren and friends present. I was considerably nervous, finding my memory beginning to fail. My address was about twenty minutes in length. I felt tired and languid after the meeting from the evening air, the excitement, and standing so long. I shall have to discontinue attending and engaging in public, missionary, and other meetings—at all events, such large, exciting ones as at Kingston and Spanish Town."

"January 1st, 1876.—Another year has passed with all its toils and trials, privileges and mercies. The former, I am thankful to say, though numerous and weighty, have yet been mixed with mercy; while the blessings I have received have been such as call for my devout gratitude to God. Oh! for more faith and love, more consecration to Christ, more growth in grace, more and better knowledge of my Lord and Saviour, more likeness to Him, more boldness for Him, more usefulness in His service!"

"January 2nd.—Went up to Sligoville. The congregation was very large, as almost everywhere at the commencement of the year; but, sad to say, the people gradually decline in attendance as the year advances. I preached from John i. 36: 'Behold the Lamb of God!' and I feel I am sincere when I say that I preached 'as though I ne'er should preach again.' In the afternoon the Lord's Supper. The people were cheerful and hearty in their salutations, wishes, and prayers for the best of blessings on their minister and family."

"January 16th.—Preached at the re-opening of East

Queen Street Chapel after repairs. There was a very large congregation of all classes. I felt nervous at the commencement for fear of breaking down physically, but was, as I believe, Divinely assisted, and I hope the blessing of God was largely experienced."

In the month of February, Mr. Phillippo's health was far from good, so as to awaken the anxieties of his friends and to call forth an earnest appeal to him to lessen the frequency of his visits to his distant stations. Their condition weighed upon his spirits and gave him much anxiety, as he was unable to exercise that vigilant watchfulness over their spiritual state so necessary to their well-being.

"April 13th and 14th.—From multiplied and multiplying claims, involving almost incessant labour and no inconsiderable responsibility in relation to churches, repair of chapels, erection of school-houses. and support of schoolmasters, with other things too numerous to detail, I have been depressed for some time past. A dark and impenetrable cloud has seemed to overshadow me. I prayed earnestly for faith to lay hold of the promises of my Lord that He would sustain and bring me through the darksome way. Amidst all, I know that God has not forsaken me, while I sometimes feel that it is really good for me to be thus tried. It draws me closer to God through my adorable Saviour. Take courage, O my soul; endure with patience and fortitude. Let me gird on afresh the armour of hope. faith, and contentment, and press onward to my journey's end."

It was not in Mr. Phillippo's nature to relinquish any post of service till it was impossible for him to hold it; he therefore continued to do his utmost to carry on the work in hand, and amid every difficulty to persevere.

"April 18th.—Unable through indisposition to accompany the inspector to the school at Spring Garden, my daughter kindly undertook my duties, and I was glad to find the result satisfactory both to the teacher and inspector. This Government system is a great blessing to the labouring class of the population and to the country generally, and cannot fail to cheer the hearts of the ministers of the Gospel in particular. But on some of the latter, who are managers, it entails very considerable sacrifices of time, labour, and expense."

"October 14th.—This day seventy-eight years ago I first drew my breath in this world of sin and sorrow. Once again I raise my Ebenezer. The Lord has done great things for me, and for the stations under my charge, whereof I am glad. I would thus record His great goodness and exalt His glorious name. I am not without evidence that my labour has not been in vain, nor has the Lord failed to show me that He has made me useful in the conversion and building up of souls in the hope of the Gospel. To Him be all the glory!"

"December 20th.—Thought it my duty, being in Kingston at the opening of a new wing to the Mico Institution, the Governor (Sir William Grey) being present, and having been introduced to him, to call upon him, when I was invited to luncheon, and was afterwards favoured with a long conversation on the length of time I had been in the country, the climate, the social, moral, and religious state and aspects of the island generally, as also on the condition of the labouring classes."

The active duties of the year closed with a series of missionary meetings at Old Harbour, Sligoville, and Rosswell. At these gatherings Mr. Phillippo presided, and was sustained by various brethren, both of his own and other denominations, in the vicinity. The heavy rains and impassable roads interfered with the attendance at one meeting; but the services were deeply interesting and instructive, while an excellent spirit was manifested by the people. Pledges of deeper interest and increased liberality were given, and the aged Christian's heart was gladdened by the love and esteem that were freely expressed for him. The closing words of his diary for the year are:—" If I am called, O Lord, to continue my action in Thy cause, work in me to will and to do, for my experience proves that without Thee I can do nothing."

CHAPTER XLIV.

THE year did not open without some anxious thoughts. Services that he had long observed at the close of the old and commencement of the new year were not regarded by those around him with the same pleasure and excitement as of yore. He felt painfully, at times, the weight of increasing years throwing him more and more on home employments to fill the yearnings of his active mind. "In my reflections," he says, "I naturally held communion with my own heart, in which I felt much to condemn. Help me, O Lord, to search my heart! Do Thou Thyself examine me and prove me. Oh, let me never be deceived about myself, nor be fatally a stranger to my own spirit, or the principles of action within me! Let these be all simple, pure. May I have no corrupt motives or desires, nothing but what proceeds from Thee, or leads to Thee again! I know not what my future experience may be; be Thou with me, however, and all will be well."

A few days were made bright by the presence of two of his grandchildren and two young Haitian girls of colour, daughters of parents residing in Haiti, and reclaimed from Popery through the instrumentality of the late Mr. Webley, missionary at Jacmel. He was also gladdened by the receipt of a very flattering address which had been presented to his younger son (Mr. Justice Phillippo) by the Bar of Hong Kong, where for some time he had held the office of acting Chief Justice, speaking in the highest terms of the calm, dispassionate manner, acumen, and courtesy with which he had filled that high office. But his mind continually relapsed into a state of dread of the future, as if overshadowed by the event disclosed in the following extract from his diary:—

" March 29th.—I this day received an astounding letter from brother Lea, stating that he had actually applied to the Bishop of Kingston for ordination at his hands, and for admission into the Episcopal Church, he having been of Nonconformist parentage, four years a student at the Baptist College, Bristol, sixteen years a Baptist missionary in Jamaica, and a nephew of William Knibb. It is extraordinary that he never gave me nor the church the slightest intimation of his purpose, until two or three days before his resignation of the pastorate of the church."

This unexpected and surprising resignation was communicated to the church in Spanish Town on the following Sabbath, April 1st. Without a moment's delay or hesitation the members at once turned for counsel and aid to their aged friend, their old and attached minister. Unanimously they pressed him to re-assume the pastorate, and to this request, with deep feeling, he felt it his duty to assent. " I am in health," he said, " and I will never allow, while I retain possession of it, my life-work to be ignored nor to come to an end, nor will I suffer all my sacrifices of labour, and money, and life to be given to the winds. The state of things must of necessity involve me in very great additional anxiety, responsibility, and toil. But while I ask for the wisdom that is from above, I must trust to the God of wisdom to give me strength and grace equal to my day."

The position was indeed a most anxious and painful one. His " life-work " truly seemed in danger of destruction, and the churches he had gathered and watered with his tears and prayers were apparently threatened with dispersion. Earnestly and prayerfully, he pondered the steps to be taken to fill the pastorate in the future, sought the advice of brethren near at hand, and after several sleepless nights, with a bold and marvellous decision, he resolved to leave his people to the care of the Rev. D. J. East; his daughter, ever helpful, and endowed with an energy like his own, could undertake the correspondence necessary to obtain supplies to fill the pulpit during his absence, and he would seek in England the Christian minister who, animated with a truly evangelistic spirit, should henceforth feed the flock in the pastures in which they had so long dwelt. "I did not wish to go home," he writes, "before this crisis came, because I had no special object to accomplish. Now I have. If I am told I might endanger my life by the voyage and excitement, I reply, 'It is necessary for me to go to England; it is not necessary for me to live.'"

Accordingly, gathering up his energies, and strengthened by faith and prayer, he went forth on this toilsome mission. The interval of preparation was short. He left in the packet which sailed from Kingston on the 10th of April. It was thus he hoped to save many months of weary waiting and negotiation, and to bring back with him in a few short weeks a successor in his work. He reached Southampton on the morning of the 29th in health and safety after a moderately pleasant voyage of nineteen days.

During his stay in England, Mr. Phillippo kept his daughter well informed of his movements; but as his letters consist of very little more than a list in some detail of the numerous places he visited and of the many friends he met with, they do not furnish many passages for extract. His first letter is dated from my house, whither he came direct on arriving in London, and he continued to be my guest for several days until arrangements were in progress for obtaining the minister for whom he was in search.   His burden of care was greatly relieved by the deep sympathy which the situation called forth on every side, by the warm affection which greeted him from old friends and new, and by the promptitude with which the Committee proceeded to fulfil his request.   The intervals of his attendance at the Mission House were occupied with visits to former scenes and to the homes of those he had known in earlier years.   Some, like Dr. Steane, even more than himself, were suffering from the infirmities of age; others, like the Rev. S. Green, the friend and companion of his youth, still bore bravely and almost unhurt the assaults of time; while others, as Dr. Brock, had entered in the joy of their Lord.   At a meeting of peculiar interest at Dr. Landels' chapel, at which he was present, he met with a large number of friends who, he says, "expressed their astonishment at my courage in coming home, and at my vigour of body and mind."

After more than one conference with the Mission Committee, and visiting many London friends, he proceeded to his brother's house at Norwich.   There he found a happy home, where he could recruit his strength, and obtain relief from a severe cold that he had taken. Then he proceeded to Leicester and Birmingham.   At Birmingham he was the guest of Mr. and Mrs. William Morgan.   "Here," he reports to his daughter, "I stayed four days, during which my kind friends did everything in their power to render my visit enjoyable, and I may say profitable.   They took me to call upon many friends, some of whom knew my dear wife from a girl, and remembered me a student at Chipping Norton; while we had parlour-gatherings and conferences every night. These meetings were deeply interesting, and said to have been instructive.   All sympathised with me and the

people so suddenly deserted. I have suffered somewhat
from cold and cough, the weather having been unusually
severe; but I am better. I tire in walking, but not in
riding even long distances. I am afraid you will have too
much to do, and too many cares; but you must remember
that overdoing is undoing."

In July he took part in the annual meeting of Regent's
Park College, when he gave the closing address. It took
the form of a brief review of his experience as a missionary in Jamaica for fifty-four years. After recounting the
events of his early years, he thus summed up some of the
results :—

"During these fifty-four years, I have endeavoured,
with my brother missionaries and others, to aid in the
promotion of all the great and important changes that
have taken place in the island—changes civil, social,
educational, religious, and ecclesiastical; in all, indeed,
in which especially the great interests of the masses of the
people were concerned. And while I have assisted in
accomplishing these vast revolutions to the extent of
my ability, I flatter myself that my efforts have in some
humble degree contributed to their accomplishment. In
the abolition of slavery and of the previous system of
apprenticeship, the establishment of free villages, the
erection of school-houses and places of worship, and,
though last not least, the disestablishment and disendowment of the State Church in Jamaica, and the establishment
of a college in Kingston in connection with our mission
for the education of native young men for the work of the
Christian ministry, and as a training institution for
teachers of schools, I have been a sincere, if not a very
efficient, worker. Of the results of my great work of
winning souls to Christ by the preaching of the glorious
Gospel, I thank God, with all humility of mind, that I am
not without witnesses. Some hundreds, I may say thou-

sands, of the once-enslaved and unregenerated sons and daughters of Africans, and their descendants around me who have been turned from darkness to light, have been my joy here, and will, I doubt not, be 'my crown of rejoicing in the day of the Lord Jesus.' Nor have the results of the education of the children of these descendants of Ethiopia been less numerous and satisfactory."

In his closing words he touchingly alludes to his own personal feelings with regard to the past and to the near future :—

" In thus labouring so long in the service of the Master, I have been called to suffer, as may be supposed, much personal and relative affliction—to endure much persecution, with exposure at times to violence and death—to experience much difficulty in my work, and to endure numerous and sore trials arising out of my special employment as a minister of Christ; but I rejoice to say that, though I have been tired *in* the work, I have never been tired *of* it, and that, if 'my trials have abounded, my consolations have abounded also.' I can further say—and I can say it with all sincerity of heart—that had I a thousand lives I would willingly consecrate them all to the same great work, even in prospect of the same great difficulties and trials, and with the same jeopardy of health and life as heretofore endured. It cannot be expected from my advanced age that my life will be long protracted ; but, whenever the hour of my warfare ends, I trust I shall be found with my harness on and my face towards the foe. While thus, I trust, I have been enabled, by strength and grace from on high, to fight the good fight and to keep the faith, I can now look calmly into the grave, waiting till my great Master calls me to my rest. And in this anticipation I can say I would not exchange my present condition and prospects with the greatest monarch that ever swayed a sceptre, looking forward, as I can do, with cheerful hope—I will say with firm confidence—through the alone merits of the Redeemer, to the inheritance, incorruptible, undefiled, and that fadeth not away."

A portion of Mr. Phillippo's time in London was devoted, in company with the Rev. J. Hewett, who was then in England on account of health, in conferring with the Committee on the condition and needs of the churches in Jamaica. In the early months of the year twenty-eight European and native brethren had united to ask the Committee for their aid. They stated that the mission was in a most critical state, and that without a supply of ministers it would sink into decrepitude. For, although in the seventeen years that had elapsed since the visit of the deputation, in 1860, ten pastors had been added to the thirty-six then existing, there had been so large an accession of churches as to render the proportion between the number of churches and pastors less favourable than at that time. The seventy-six churches had grown to ninety-nine, while fifteen more were without any pastoral oversight at all. The members had increased from 19,360 in 1860 to 25,268 in 1877. Thus the lapse of time had made the want of ministers more urgent. The Committee so far yielded to these representations as to promise "to exercise their good offices to assist in the selection of suitable pastors for the churches needing European ministers," and to give grants in aid in cases where the churches were unable to meet the cost of outfit and passage. Some three or four brethren, before the close of the year, were sent out under these conditions. It was gratifying to Mr. Phillippo and Mr. Hewett to recognise the cordiality with which they were received on the part of the Committee and the attention given to the statements they were charged by their brethren to make.

The main object of Mr. Phillippo's visit was accomplished when, in the month of July, the Rev. J. H. Holyoak, pastor of the church at Onslow Chapel, Brompton, accepted the invitation of the Committee to proceed to Jamaica to take the pastorate at Spanish Town.

Previous to departure, Mr. Phillippo paid several farewell visits to friends in various parts of the country. It will be sufficient to record his final visit to his native place.

"Unwilling," he says, "to leave for my adopted home without a last look at, and bidding a final farewell to, my dear old native town, I went over to Dereham, accompanied by my brother. It was Saturday, the market-day, when I might chance to meet old acquaintances from the country, as well as in the town. We went to the Corn Exchange, wandered about the streets, called at some of the old houses, with whose tenants I was once so familiar, and at one or two of the principal inns, but, on my part, without the slightest recognition, except in one instance by a distant relative, though only twenty years had passed since my last visit. That visit, however, was so brief that it may be said I had been absent from Dereham fifty years. Equally disappointed was I in the result of my inquiries after the notabilities of my boyish days. Most of the old families had almost entirely passed away, root and branch. The tenants of the house where I was born looked incredulous when I stated the fact, and requested permission to look around me. The lower story was now occupied as a large ironmongery store, and I should have been at a loss to identify it but for the sign of the ' Black Bull ' opposite. Yes ; there was the ' Black Bull,' unaltered in form and size and noble bearing as eighty years ago. All else seemed changed. The streets looked narrower, distances much shorter, the houses smaller, though externally more attractive ; the old Baptist and Independent chapels superseded by new ones, more conspicuous, larger, and ornamental. Improvements were everywhere considerable, especially in the suburbs, where beautiful villa residences had sprung up, rendering the dear old place still more worthy of the eulogy of the author of 'Lavengro': 'Pretty Dereham! thou model of an English country town!' Fatigued with my perambulations, and straitened for time, I reached the station just previously to the starting of the train, in which my brother and myself took places for Norwich. But I was a stranger at home, and was sad."

His object in coming to England was now accomplished. Farewells to dear friends were said; and on the 3rd of September, in company with Mr. and Mrs. Holyoak and their two children, he set sail from Southampton. It was a cloudy, rainy, and dismal day, but the passage was a pleasant one, the company on board bright and cheerful—of various nationalities, and some of them acquaintances and friends, returning, like himself, to their homes in Jamaica, after a holiday. In one gentleman he found a Norfolk man, and pleasant were the chats over times passed in their native county.

The vessel arrived in Kingston on the 21st, and warm indeed was the welcome, and loud were the congratulations, which greeted the arrival of the old and the new pastors. As they passed along the road and through the streets it seemed as if the whole of the people of Spanish Town had turned out to receive them. "The chapel doors," says Mr. Phillippo, "were immediately thrown open—all were urged on to hold a thanksgiving meeting—thanksgiving to God for His goodness both to those of us who had arrived, and for His goodness to the church in having so graciously answered the prayers presented for what they now beheld."

The bright expectations thus apparently fulfilled were suddenly destroyed, and, to the consternation of Mr.

Phillippo and the church, at the end of six days Mr. Holyoak announced his intention to return to England. Remonstrance was in vain, and by the next packet after his arrival Mr. Holyoak and his family departed for England.

It can be more easily imagined than described with what a weary heart Mr. Phillippo again resumed the pastoral duties to the churches whose hopes were thus shattered at the very moment of their realisation.

CHAPTER XLV.

HIS LAST DAYS—1877 TO 1879.

IF it was with a "weary heart" that Mr. Phillippo again
faced the difficulties so suddenly sprung upon him, he
met them with somewhat of his ancient spirit and energy.
"On Sabbath following," he says, "I entered upon the
onerous duties thrown upon me with all the energy I could
command, stimulated by the sympathies of the vast congregation that had gathered, and by those of all the inhabitants
of the town and district. My text was (purposely to avoid all
details of past occurrences) from 1 Peter i. 10, 11: 'Of which
salvation,' &c. Supported and aided, as I felt sure I was,
by the Divine presence and blessing, I felt unusually at
home, and seemed possessed of more than customary
strength and energy. I felt, moreover, that the Word
would not be like water spilt upon the ground. In the
administration of the Lord's Supper in the afternoon, I
felt equally sensible that God was with me."

The church, on its part, lost no time in assuring their
aged friend that he enjoyed their most entire confidence
and warmest affection. They were grateful for his devotion to their interests and his self-denial; and, though
his arduous visit to England had proved unavailing, they
were only too happy to confide in his judgment for the
future. They were confident that he would be guided by
wisdom from above in his management of the affairs of
the church in this season of great emergency.

Mr. Phillippo immediately made arrangements to meet,

to the best of his ability, the claims now pressing upon him. After three weeks' trial, in a letter to the Secretary of the mission, Mr. Baynes, dated October 25th, he thus describes the nature of the task laid upon him. After referring to Spanish Town, Old Harbour, Rosswell, and Sligoville, he says :—"These places have to be supplied monthly, with half-a-dozen more, and about ten schools to be superintended, and the schoolmasters to be paid and to be kept to their work. Altogether, I have the claims of ten stations, with their schools, upon me, from five to sixteen miles distant, added to almost incessant details of work that these stations involve. They would tax the energies of three or four healthy and energetic men. How am I to get through all this without jeopardy to health and life? It is impossible. After preaching at Spanish Town I was so exhausted as to be hardly able to sit up in the evening. On returning from Sligoville, I felt as though I could hardly venture on horse-back for any distance again. It was much the same after the service and long journey to and from Rosswell yester-day. I fear I shall not be able to undergo the fatigue of these long journeys much longer. Yet the same routine is to be gone through again and again. Old Harbour next Sabbath, then Spanish Town, &c., &c. Of course I have to get supplies for intervals; but these are very expensive, often inefficient, and difficult to obtain."

Under such circumstances, he could not but seek the aid of the Committee. "I will not," he continues, "stir from my post; but my mind as well as my body has lost its elasticity. A mountain of care and difficulty lies before me, and a dark impenetrable cloud overshadows me. I beg that, as soon as a brother of a true missionary spirit offers himself, you will relieve our minds by announcing it to us by telegram."

An accident which he met with in the early days of

January disabled him from going to his more distant stations, and it was not without great suffering that he could take the first service of the year in Spanish Town. Although the condition of his leg improved, it continued throughout the year a source of much anxiety, and, with the sense of his inability to fulfil the duties which were required, there came upon him great depression of mind which it needed all his faith to surmount.

"January 9th.—What am I to do," he writes, "under my complicated trials, for they multiply and almost bear me down? Evidently, to trust, to hope, to wait, that in a short time all will end well and redound to the Saviour's honour and my own comfort. Possibly comfort may come like angels' visits, ministering to me the fruits of righteousness to the glory and praise of God. I will trust, and not be afraid." Again: "January 19th.—I go to Old Harbour to baptize in the sea, but with a heavy heart, not as formerly. Cares, labours, and responsibilities almost overcome me by their number and importance. There are also other causes. I feel myself unequal to bear the load from infirmities of age, additionally so from the sufferings entailed by my late accident."

But brighter moments intervene, and he can say, after recalling the sorrows endured and the fervent prayers which "daily, almost hourly," they led him to pour out before the Father of Mercies, "I can now testify that my prayers are answered, and that I can again, as often before, set to my seal that God is true. May I ever henceforth see the folly of doubts and fears where the promises of my heavenly Father are concerned, nor suffer myself to anticipate evils that may never come!"

Light shone upon his path when he learnt, in March, that a successor had been found in the person of the Rev. Carey B. Berry, the pastor of the church at Cullingworth, Yorkshire. On the 5th of June he had the pleasure of welcoming Mr. Berry to Jamaica, and on the following Sunday of introducing him to his flock. Although many of the country members did not know of Mr. Berry's arrival, he was "enthusiastically" received by a crowded congregation. On the Lord's-day, the 7th of July, Mr. Phillippo finally laid down the office which, so long, and under such changes of circumstances, he had filled, and, amid deep silence and many tears, he bade the people he so loved as their pastor a final farewell. The whole congregation rose up to do him reverence, and in a similar manner, at his request, they bade their new pastor welcome to the honoured post. It was with joy that Mr. Phillippo records : " The welcome was all that could have been desired, while the personal salutations that followed could have left no doubt upon the young pastor's mind, had any existed, that he commenced his work in the full confidence and warm affection of his whole church and congregation." The union was ratified at the table of the Lord, and it is pleasant to conclude with the remark that the issue has fulfilled the hopes and desires of the aged servant of God whom Mr. Berry has succeeded.

For the next few months there is little to record. Mr. Phillippo continued, as his strength would allow, to visit the two or three stations which remained in his charge, and to pay attention to a few matters of public interest. With the cessation of the multiplicity of occupations that had borne him down, the elasticity of his spirit returned ; so that on his eightieth birthday, with "a gladsome mind," he could say: " On looking back I see, indeed, many mistakes, infirmities, shortcomings, and sins ; but I rejoice that the blood of Christ has washed them all away. I know not what may happen to me in the future, but I know that I am in my heavenly Father's hands, and that surely all things will work together for my good. In looking to the future, all is bright, brighter than I can find words to describe. I shall be at length with Christ, and be like Him for ever. Let me, therefore, wait for the Lord, that whenever He comes I may open to Him immediately, and say with joy and triumph to the Lord's promise to come shortly, ' Even so ; come, Lord Jesus.' "

In October Mr. Phillippo was laid aside by a severe attack of ague and fever ; from this seizure he so far recovered as to be able to assist Mr. Berry in the services customarily held at Christmas and on New Year's Day. But from this time forward the indications began to multiply that the shades of life's evening were closing around him. On the 30th of January he records that some threatening symptoms had obliged him to consult his son, and, although on the 2nd of February he was able to ride to Sligoville and to arrange for Mr. Berry's recognition as the pastor of the church there, he was taken worse in the evening, and lay all night in a violent fever. On the next day an attack of aneurism in the femoral artery came on, which paralysed the whole of his left side, accompanied with intense pain. He bore the journey in a litter to Spanish Town, where only medical aid could be procured, with great fortitude. The dangerous symptoms in a few days abated, and, in the months of March and April, he was able to leave his room and renew his intercourse with friends.

The entries in his diary, though necessarily brief, are sufficiently indicative of the state of his mind during this period of retirement. Thus, under February 6 : " The doctor came in again, and signified that recovery was still doubtful. My mind calm and trusting in God, and waiting His will, desiring rather to depart and to be with Christ." February 7 : " Still in great pain night and day. Able to read occasionally, which was a great relief, the subjects most attractive being biographical sketches of the closing days of good men. Oh, that I had that ardour of devotion, that poverty of spirit, which some of them exemplified!"

Several days succeed in which no entries are made, and in which he was confined to his bed. On the 20th they are resumed in pencil: "Continued in bed suffering more or less pain; not out of danger. Mind calm and waiting on God."

"21st.—A night of very great pain. I am still in doubt how it will go with me. But I look to my heavenly Father to soften the pain. 'Not my will, but Thine be done.'"

A few days follow in which much pain was endured; but slow amendment was apparent. On Sunday, March 2nd, he pencils down: "Much better, and was able to concentrate my thoughts on subjects relating to the blessed world to which I feel I am going. I bless God that in prospect of it my faith and hope do not fail."

.. "March 3rd.—Better; got up and sat in the dining-room. Friends and relations congratulate me on my progress thus far; but I can hardly thank them for their wishes for my continuance here. Rather, I say with the Apostle, I desire to depart and to be with Christ, which is far better."

"March 7th.—Not suffering much from pain. It is now probable I may recover. The Lord's will be done. My mind calm, thoughtful, and hopeful. Reflected on all the way He had led me."

On the 13th he was able to take a short drive. "Amidst all," he adds, "I recognise a Father's hand and love. I am especially thankful that I am able to read and thus acquaint myself with the home to which I am going, and my obligations to Him who has loved me and given Himself for me."

From this time a slight but continuous improvement of the ailing limb went on, so that he was able to interest himself in the affairs of the stations, in making arrange-

ments for their future welfare, and in receiving visits from
friends and brethren.   Some were sanguine that he would
sufficiently recover to resume a portion of his old duties;
but he adds, in recording their kind wishes, "I have no
hope of this.   I feel that the time of my departure is at
hand.   I have no desire to know the time; but it is
sufficient to know that my blessed Lord sustains me by
His grace.   May I have the joy this hope inspires when in
the final hour I lie languishing on the bed of death, waiting from moment to moment for Christ and my dismission
to be with Him."

> " Where'er my head must take its long repose,
>   Oh, keep Thy presence nigh, my God, my Friend;
> And tenderly my eyelids close,
>   While to Thy Spirit's care I mine commend."

The final entry in his diary, on the 9th of May, relates
to the departure of his dear friends, the Rev. E. and
Mrs. Hewett, after a brief visit, in which he had greatly
enjoyed their presence.   He also spent part of the day
in dictating to his daughter a letter to Mr. Baynes, in
which he speaks of his expected recovery, and the hope
that he might again visit some of the scenes of his former
labours.   "Why," he says, "I am thus spared I do not
know, but, as God does nothing without design, whatever
He does or permits is right.   It is, therefore, for me
cheerfully to acquiesce in His will, knowing that all that
will is love.   As I am now, however, verging on my
eighty-first year, the time of my departure cannot be far
distant.   My trust is that, whenever the summons comes,
I may be fully prepared to enter into the joy of my Lord."
It was hidden from him that this was the last letter he
would ever write.

Two days wore slowly away, when, after a Scripture
lesson on the Sabbath afternoon to the Negro boy in
attendance upon him, in the evening the Master's voice

was heard. His daughter, Mrs. Claydon, thus describes the event:—" He seemed as well as usual all day Sunday, and retired to rest at his usual hour, but soon after he was in bed he was seized with shortness of breath and violent pains in the chest, and before medical aid could be obtained he had breathed his last. He retained his consciousness until the end, and was perfectly calm and untroubled, saying that his time was come and his work was ended. In an hour all was over." Later she continues: " I do not know that I can add more to what I have said respecting my dear father's death. He knew that his hour for departure had come, and said his work was done. His last words, at intervals, were: ' My Jesus; ' ', my Saviour; ' ' my Friend.' ' Lord, into Thy hands I commend my spirit.' "

Referring to his interview with him on the previous Friday, Mr. Hewett writes:—" I left him on the Friday afternoon, and he passed away quite suddenly and quietly on Sabbath evening. When I left he was cheerful and happy, calmly waiting for the great change. His last words were: ' Father, into Thy hands I commend my spirit.' In his death we have lost the oldest missionary of any denomination in the island. For more than fifty years he has been an earnest worker in the dear Redeemer's cause, abundantly successful in gathering congregations, building of chapels, and in converting sinners from the error of their ways. His life has been a long scene of devotedness, consistency, and usefulness. What more than this can be said to his praise and to the glory of God ? "

From a communication of the Rev. D. J. East to the *Freeman* of the 11th of July the following additional particulars of the closing days of the venerable saint will be welcomed :—

" How beautiful the closing scene ! Except an affection in the circulation of the leading arteries of one leg—

an affection, however, which conveyed to him the last summons—he seemed full of health, and enjoyed cheerful spirits almost to the last. Yet since the removal of his loving wife he had felt that the appointed time of his departure was drawing nigh. He cast up and closed his works and the care of the churches. He arranged his family affairs in an interview by special appointment with the writer. He then bound up the fragments of his life, work, and times for us to read when he was gone, committing the revision and publication of his autobiography to the hands of his valued and beloved friend, Dr. Underhill. He then calmly, placidly waited at eventide the sunset that must rise in the 'morning land' He was to all things here as one who hopefully, instantly expected the coming of the Master. Only nine days before the event, in a farewell letter to the writer of this brief notice of a friend and brother faithful and beloved, he says, 'You must not suppose, from the tone of this epistle, that my mind is disquieted at the apprehension of my departure from this world of sin, and imperfection, and turmoil so near at hand. I am thankful to say it is far otherwise with me, as, my work being to all appearance done, my desire, with the reservation of one family tie, is to be with Christ. My life and times, however, are at the disposal of my great Master and Lord.

> "While here, to do His will be mine,
> And His to fix my time of rest."

It is sufficient for me that He sustains me by His grace, and grants me the assurance that I shall be for ever with Him in the blessed world to which I am going. In relation, however, to your departure hence for a season, how delightful to think that, should we meet no more on earth, we shall meet where there will exist no magnet, no source of attraction, but the Lamb in the midst of the throne.'

" On the Sunday night of his departure, after reading a portion from the Ephesians, he finally closed the blessed Book, to hear in a few minutes the Master indeed calling. He raised his hands, as if to bless his people, in prayer, saying, ' Father, into Thy hands I commend my spirit,' and passed away without a pain or sigh. As an infant on his mother's breast, so he fell asleep on the bosom of his Lord.

" The earthly remains of our departed brother were buried beside those of his sainted wife, while thousands of all ranks from the plains and hills around looked or sobbed their unspoken sorrow. His record is on high !

" In view of such life, what a call his death is for new labourers ! Shall we not pray in his own words in the ' Voice of Jubilee ' ?—' O Lord Jesus ! Lover of souls, Director of spirits, Conqueror of hearts, choose Thine own instruments, select Thine own sacrifices, open to some understandings the glory of this work, touch some hearts with the invisible constraints of Thy dying love. Let him that is feeble be as David—let souls be so bound to this work that they may resolve to engage in it.'

" Whether the monument of our brother be raised or his epitaph be written in marble, or not, may we not quote his own words in his loving portrait of the sainted Burchell and Knibb, and say, ' His requiem will be chanted by thousands who have known him, or who have heard of him, and by millions yet unborn. He occupied the high places of the field—he hazarded his life for the sake of the Lord Jesus. He saw the work of his hand and heart in the freedom of the slave, in the enfranchisement of multitudes of the sons of Ethiopia from the thraldom of the god of this world to a

> " Liberty
> Monarchs cannot grant, and all the powers
> Of earth and hell confederate take away " ' ?

" His actions threw a light around his living steps ; his name was written before his eyes in the temple of immortality. As a servant of the Most High God, faithful unto death, he has now his rest and his reward."*

But few words are required to sum up the life-story of James Mursell Phillippo. He has himself characterised it in the words of the motto with which as a student he began his career. They were, " Energy, Prudence, Economy, Temperance, Perseverance, with ardent love to God and man."† Through weal and woe, with an un-faltering step, he pursued the object to which he had consecrated his life, and whatever powers he possessed, whether of body or mind, were absolutely, and without reserve, given to the service of his Saviour and to the well-being of Africa's children. In person he was of a comely presence, somewhat above the average in height ; in manners, urbane and courteous, and, in his intercourse with men of every sort, considerate of their wants and feelings. Though sensitive to praise or blame, neither to obtain the one nor to avoid the other did he sacrifice his convictions or swerve from the path of rectitude. His principles were firmly grasped and earnestly maintained, and neither smiles nor frowns prevailed to restrain their assertion. In the presence of the direful evils and miseries of slavery, he wrought righteousness, and was the helper and succourer of the oppressed. Every faculty was strained to destroy the curse which darkened the fair land of Jamaica, and to

---

* " Most of the paragraphs between inverted commas, with some slight variations, excepting the extract of the farewell letter which has been interpolated, are from a ' Sermon on the Death of the Rev. Jas. Mursell Phillippo, preached in East Queen Street Baptist Chapel, Kingston, Jamaica, by the Rev. F. Seed Roberts, of the Baptist Missionary Society, London, Tutor of Calabar College.' "

† See p. 16.

remedy the mischiefs, worse than crops of nightshade, it produced. His labours for the education and elevation of the emancipated slave, both morally and socially, were incessant, and often pursued under circumstances of great discouragement. Every undertaking in Spanish Town and its vicinity, for the improvement of men, whether coloured or white, enjoyed his sympathy, and was often benefited by his wise counsel and instructive communications. He was benevolent to the fullest extent of his means, and it was his delight to visit the poor in their homes, to sympathise with their sorrows, and to aid them in their efforts for advancement. Rich and poor, high and low, alike sought his counsel; he was the friend of all. Throughout the stormy scenes of the period in which he lived, he observed a dignified moderation, and won and kept the respect, the good-will, and veneration of two generations of men, often stirred to their depths by the passions and antagonisms of great and momentous events. He preserved to the last the freshness, the buoyancy, and gentleness of his early days; maintained his tastes for literary and elegant pursuits, and was continually adding to his stores of information. His mind was stored with facts, and perhaps no living man possessed such a knowledge of the island of Jamaica, its history and institutions, as he had acquired. His life was more active than contemplative, more addicted to the practical than the speculative. His works abound in knowledge of the facts with which he deals, but seldom touch on the deeper questions which underlie the movements of society, or which occupy modern thought. He was popular as a lecturer on literary, scientific, and historical subjects, wrote with clearness and force, and spoke with fluency and effect.

As a Christian minister, he adorned the doctrine of his God and Saviour in all things. He was simple in his habits, truthful in action and speech, and a faithful preacher of the doctrines he believed. He loved Christ. Christ was the light of his steps and the object of his fervent adoration. The circumstances did not require, nor did his flock expect, disquisitions on the profound mysteries of the Christian faith. The salvation and love of Christ in their regenerating and practical aspects and results were the topics on which he delighted to dwell—

> "For, above all, his luxury supreme,
> And his chief glory, was the Gospel theme."

He lived in constant communion with his Lord, and his strength and purpose were daily fed and sustained by his inner fellowship with things unseen.

As a missionary of the Gospel of Christ, his course cannot better be described than in the resolution passed by the Committee of the Baptist Missionary Society, with which institution he had been so long associated :—

"In recording the decease of the Rev. James Mursell Phillippo, the senior missionary of the Society, the Committee desire to 'glorify the grace of God' manifested in the long and unwearied labours of this excellent servant of Jesus Christ. Born in the year 1798, he entered on mission life in Spanish Town, Jamaica, in January, 1824, and for fifty-five years he consecrated all his powers to the service of the people of that island. Many were slaves when he began to preach to them the unsearchable riches of Christ ; with many other eminent men, he toiled through evil and good report to obtain their freedom. That great boon secured, by well-devised schemes of education, by the planting of villages, by the incessant advocacy of righteous and just legislation, by sheltering the poor and defending the oppressed, and by faithful instruction in Christian truth and duty, he laboured both day and night, in arduous journeys and with unsparing effort, often at the risk of life, to impart the elements of knowledge, and to assure the welfare and civilisation of the emancipated peasantry. He was ever the friend of the distressed, the comfort of the sorrowful, the advocate of the miserable, and the true pastor of his flock. Endowed with both natural and acquired gifts, he was the faithful minister of Christ, the courteous gentleman, and the loving friend. With Christian courage and fortitude he passed through many trials. He was the valued counsellor of his ministerial brethren, and prompt to co-operate with them and to aid in every good design devised for the benefit of the people whom he loved. He lived to see the blessed results of emancipation, the great and successful increase of the mission, and to rejoice in the wide diffusion of the principles of liberty and piety of which he was the manly and conscientious advocate. His long service for Christ has terminated with honour to himself, is crowned with the grateful affection of his brethren and of the Society which he served with so much respect and esteem. His memory will be cherished by thousands of the children of Africa to whom he brought the blessings of salvation, and his name will be enrolled among the noble band of men who struggled for and won freedom for the slave."

> " The exile is at home ;
> O nights and days of tears !
> O longings not to roam !
> O sins and doubts and fears !
> What matters now ? O joyful day !
> The King has wiped all tears away ! "

THE END.

APPENDIX.

I.—LIST OF STATIONS AND SCHOOLS

ESTABLISHED IN WHOLE OR IN PART BY THE
REV. J. M. PHILLIPPO.

1824 TO 1874.

PARISH OF ST. CATHERINE.

Spanish Town ...	... Commenced by Rev. T. Godden. Chapel-house, school-rooms, burial-ground. Built and purchased by Mr. Phillippo.
Passage Fort ...	... Chapel, residence, and out-offices built and purchased.
Hartlands	... Chapel and school-house.
Kent Village	
Taylor's Caymanas ...	
Thankful Hill ...	... School-house, used as chapel and teacher's house.
Kensington ...	... Land bought and two villages established with class-houses.
Clarkson Town...	... Village.
Sturge Town ...	... Village.

ST. DOROTHY.

Old Harbour ...	... Station commenced and chapel erected.
Spring Garden ...	... Chapel or school-house built.
Rosswell	... Chapel restored twice and school established.

ST. THOMAS-IN-THE-VALE.

Sligoville	... Land purchased for village; chapel-house and out-offices and school-house built.
Constant Spring ...	Now Jericho.
Rock River ...	...

St. John's.

Garden River, New Point Hill }	Chapel built.
Kitson Town	Land bought for township. Chapel built and school established.
Beecher Town	

Vere.

Hayes' Savanna ... Station commenced.

St. Andrews.

Rose Hill ... ...

Manchester.

Vale Lionel (Porus)...
Victoria ... ...
Mandeville ... ...
Cabbage Hall ... ...
Four Paths ... ...

DAY SCHOOLS WERE ESTABLISHED IN THE FOLLOWING PLACES :—

St. Catherine's	Metropolitan Schools, Spanish Town.
	Passage Fort.
	Hartlands.
	Taylor's Caymanas.
	Thankful Hill.
	Kensington.
St. Dorothy...	Spring Garden.
	Rosswell.
St. Thomas-in-the-Vale ...	Sligoville.
	Rock River.
St. John's	Kitson Town.
	Beecher Town.
Manchester...	Porus.
	Mandeville.
	Victoria.
	Cabbage Hall.
Clarendon	Free Town.

It is calculated that between five and six thousand persons were baptized by Mr. Phillippo at the various stations, and some five thousand children educated in the schools established and superintended by him.

II.—EFFECTS OF DISESTABLISHMENT.

BY SIR ANTHONY MUSGRAVE, K.C.M.G., GOVERNOR OF JAMAICA.

From a Paper read before the Royal Colonial Institute,
April 20, 1880.

"THE manner in which the people support their religious institutions deserves note and praise. The same writer from whom I have just quoted, himself a minister of long residence and experience in Jamaica, remarks :—

"'This last is a fact specially worthy of remark, as significant not only of the growth of deep-rooted religious sentiment, but of social progress. Religion in this colony has been disestablished and disendowed. Yet I venture to say that the Episcopal Church, which has suffered most from this change, was never, at least to outward observation, so strong and vigorous as at the present moment. As a rule, I believe, the congregations have shown themselves both willing and able to provide for the ministrations of the sanctuary, while, with very few exceptions, we see on almost every side signs of activity and zeal the most gratifying.

"'Other Christian denominations have passed through a similar ordeal consequent upon the missionary societies of the mother country having seen it their duty, either wholly or in part, to withdraw the pecuniary aid which they had been wont to afford. Up to within the last few years these societies were paying the salaries of their agents ; now, for the most part, pastors and missionaries are thrown upon their respective bodies or their individual congregations for support. In general, whatever may have been the difficulties and struggles, this new burden has been cheerfully assumed by the people. Nor do I know of any missionary station which has been abandoned in consequence. On the contrary, there is hardly a parish in which one does not see new and handsome church-buildings erected, or in course of erection, mainly through the voluntary contributions of the congregations, while old ones on all sides are being repaired and beautified.' "
—P. 24.

THE ARCHÆOLOGY OF BAPTISM. By the late
Dr. WOLFRED N. COTE, Missionary in Rome.

" We could wish that a copy of this volume were on the bookshelves of every Baptist minister in England."—*Baptist Magazine.*

" It is of great and permanent value."—*Freeman.*

Demy 8vo., 336 pp., with Sixty-five Illustrations, price 10s. 6d.

WONDERS IN THE WESTERN ISLES. Being
a Narrative of the Commencement and Progress of Mission Work in Western Polynesia. By Rev. A. W. MURRAY, forty years a Missionary in Polynesia and New Guinea in connection with the London Missionary Society.

Crown 8vo, 344 *pp., with Forty Illustrations, price* 3s. 6d.

A SAVIOUR FOR CHILDREN. By Rev. JAMES
DUNCKLEY, Upton-upon-Severn.

" We most heartily commend Mr. Dunckley's book, and wish it a very large sale."—C. H. SPURGEON, in *Sword and Trowel.*

" Mr. Dunckley has a rare aptitude for the work of teaching young children the fundamental truths of Christianity."—*Nonconformist.*

" A copy should be placed in the hands of every child in the kingdom."—OCTAVIUS WINSLOW, D.D., Incumbent of Emmanuel Church, Brighton.

Second Edition, handsomely bound in cloth, with Eight Illustrations, price 3s. 6d.

STUDIES IN PHYSICAL SCIENCE. By W. J.
MILLAR, C.E., Secretary to the Institution of Engineers and Shipbuilders in Scotland ; Author of " Principles of Mechanics," &c.

Contents : The Sun ; Transit of Venus ; Spectrum Analysis ; The Moon ; The Stars and Planets ; Comets and Meteors ; Atmospheric Electricity ; Whirlwinds ; Glaciers ; The Telephone.

" We can confidently recommend Mr. Millar's volume to the attention both of teachers in search of an elementary text-book and to private students, as well as to the general reader. It unites the utmost lucidity with strict scientific accuracy, and deals with ascertained facts rather than with vague theories. The book, we ought to add, is very handsomely got up."—*Greenock Daily Telegraph.*

" Its contents are unquestionably such as may be used in our high schools with advantage, being the results of the latest discoveries."—*Sheffield and Rotherham Independent.*

Crown 8vo, 102 *pp., cloth, price* 2s.

London : YATES & ALEXANDER, 21, Castle Street, Holborn, E.C.

MEMORIALS OF BAPTIST MISSIONARIES IN

JAMAICA. Including Sketch of the Labours of the Moravians, Wesleyans, and early American Teachers in Jamaica, Bahamas, Hayti, and Trinidad, and an account of the Presbyterian and London Missionary Societies' Missions. By JOHN CLARKE, Corresponding Member of the Ethnological Society, and late Missionary in Western Africa.

Large crown 8vo, 234 pp., price 4s.

WESTBOURNE GROVE SERMONS. By WILLIAM

GARRETT LEWIS.

" It is a work abounding in every page with striking thoughts, all more or less manifestly having a practical tendency, and often uttered in language of real eloquence."—*Christian Standard.*

" The clearness of the divisions, the lucidity of the style, and the excellence of the matter will secure for this volume a high place in the homiletic literature of the period."—*Sword and Trowel.*

Crown 8vo, 294 pp., price 5s.

THE BAPTIST MAGAZINE VOLUME FOR 1880.

Edited by Rev. W. G. LEWIS.

Demy 8vo., 552 pp., price 6s. 6d.

THE BAPTIST MAGAZINE VOLUME FOR 1877.

Containing the Popular Series of Papers on the following contemporary Preachers :—

Rev. ALEX. MACLAREN, D.D.
" HUGH STOWELL BROWN.
" C. J. VAUGHAN, D.D.
" J. CAIRD, D.D.
" W. LANDELS, D.D.
" R. W. DALE, M.A.

Rev. F. W. FARRAR, D.D.
" W. M. PUNSHON, LL.D.
" H. ALLON, D.D.
" H. P. LIDDON, D.D.
" C. STANFORD.
" C. H. SPURGEON.

Demy 8vo., 572 pp., price 6s. 6d.

MORNING AND EVENING WALKS WITH THE

PROPHET JEREMIAH. By the Rev. D. PLEDGE.

" A collection of most useful meditations from the writings of the Weeping Prophet."—*Baptist Magazine.*

" The volume abounds in healthy spiritual truths."—*Evangelical Magazine.*

Crown 8vo, 296 pp., price 2s. 6d.

PAUL AND CHRIST: a Portraiture and an Argument.

By J. M. CRAMP, D.D., Nova Scotia.

" It is a fair orthodox presentation of the Apostle's life and chief teachings."—*Christian World.*

" The book is well worth a perusal."—*Sword and Trowel.*

Crown 8vo, 198 pp., cloth bevelled, price 4s.

London : YATES & ALEXANDER, 21, Castle Street, Holborn, E.C.

THE BOOK OF PSALMS (Translated from the Hebrew). By CHARLES CARTER, Missionary to Ceylon.

"The Book of Psalms, Translated from the Hebrew, by Charles Carter, Missionary to Ceylon, is a very different book from Mr. Spurgeon's [Treasury of David], but in its own way it is equally valuable. It is ONLY a translation, but the translation is admirably done. It evinces an amount of delicate scholarship that makes us thankful we have such a missionary, and such a translator of God's Word into the Singhalese. Mr. Carter's work is one that will be 'found after many days.' There are many bigger books in our library that we would rather part with than his little one."—*Review.*

Fcap. 8vo., 156 *pp., price* 2s. 6d.

RAYS FROM THE LIGHT OF TRUTH. Select Sermons by the Rev. F. FIELDER, Baptist Minister.

"The discourses bear throughout the marks of careful preparation, and will stand comparison in point of literary ability with most of the volumes of sermons that are daily issuing from the press. The subjects are suitable to the work of pulpit prelection, and creditable to the character of an earnest and devoted minister."—*Berwick Warder.*

Crown 8vo, 226 *pp., price* 3s. 6d.

JOHN WINZER, THE NORTH DEVON PURITAN. By Rev. SAMUEL NEWNAM, Edinburgh.

"A most suggestive and improving biography."—*Bookseller.*

"We hope that this charming memoir will have a large circulation."—*Baptist Magazine.*

Fcap. 8vo., *cloth gilt, price* 1s. 6d., *with Five Illustrations.*

SEVEN MAY DAYS. Discourses and Lectures to the Young at Stepney on Seven May Days. By Rev. Dr. KENNEDY.

Fcap. 8vo, 180 *pp., price* 2s. 6d.

ENTHUSIAST. By CHARLES STANFORD.

"This eloquent and thoughtful pamphlet has reached yet another edition. It deserves to be printed in letters of gold."—*Freeman.*

Second Edition, price 2d. *paper covers, or* 9d. *in cloth.*

THOUGHTS ABOUT HOME. By Rev. D. BLOOM-FIELD JAMES.

Second Edition, price 9d., *cloth.*

ANY OF THE ABOVE WORKS MAY BE OBTAINED, POST-FREE, FROM THE PUBLISHERS.

London: YATES & ALEXANDER, 21, Castle Street, Holborn, E.C.